Delight
XXX

BY: DOUGLAS L. MAPLES

This story is based on love, drama, mystery and romance dealing with life in the complexity of its own.

Delight, the main character, marriage is on thin ice with her husband of fourteen years. She is a successful lawyer and she suspects her husband of cheating, so she starts having an affair of her own with one of her clients.

Simmion Boyd, a.k.a. "Smack", is a well-known drug dealer from Dayton, Ohio. Delight is searching for affection and attention because her husband hasn't touched her in months. Her husband is back to his old ways... frequently visiting strip clubs to fulfill his fantasies.

Meanwhile, Simmion Boyd runs into a sick individual from Germany by the name of Antwan Klein, who wants to flood the U.S. with a new designer drug and Ohio is his first target.

It's a thriller with morals and values that will keep you guessing and wanting more. Life is full of surprises with infidelity going on every second, every minute across the world we live in.

Sometimes marriage only last for the moment and not a lifetime, so society, must begin focusing more on morals and principle first.

THIS BOOK IS THE WORK OF FICTION BETRAYED BY FICTIONAL CHARACTERS OF MY IMAGINATION. ANYTHING DEALING WITH THIS NOVEL IS NOT ASSOCIATED BY ANOTHER IN ANY TYPE OF WAY. IT IS OF MY OWN IMAGINATION. IT MAY BE COINCIDENTAL TO ANOTHER, BUT THAT'S BY KNOWLEDGE OF SELF.

This book is for my main two guys, Shaun Winn out of Dayton, Ohio and to the memory of "Big Cuzz" Dondi Anderson Sr. and

Mr. Kenny Giles out of Cincinnati, Ohio and to a friend and inspiration, Chantell "Delight" Rice.

ACKNOWLEDGEMENTS

I would like to thank God for giving me inspiration and the opportunity to write these novels and keep me out of harm's way. A special thanks to those in my circle:

Vince E. Turnage Sr., Duane Drain Sr., Wayne Hardy, Jeff Ivory, Mike Bell, Yakuba Lewis, Anthony Pride, Kevin Edwards, Mike Brooks, Terrance Andrews, Arnez Horton, Ernie P., Tillina Whitehead, Ebony, Brandi Holley, Tanya McNear, Annette Drain, Kyma Boyd and Djuna Drain.

To: Don'o Barksdale, Larry Winn, Mike Taylor, Orlando Albright, Lewis (Spider) Carter, Rodney Chambers , Rainell Rice, Robin "Pebbles" Owens, Andre (Crock) Buck, Andre Cole, Michael (Pete) Carter, Angel Rutledge, Wade Jackson (Dayton, Oh), Lonnie Roland, Dionne Frazier, Eva (Lou-Lou) Jordan, Charles (Chuck Nutty) Smith, Lamont Butler, Chris Jones, Karan "Rupp" Ward (Denver), Echelle (Brooklyn NY), Carlos (Boogie Man) Jordan, Camika Swan , Ms. Robin Proctor (Delaware), Dion Freeman, The guys at Cincy Blend, Yep Fitness, Steve Klein, Kev Malone, Jamie Foster, Steve (Weevie) Williams, my lawyer, Shirl Scrubbs, to the Swan family and BCB (Black Chinese Boys). FREE Jatawn Swan. Dickie, T.S., Cheese, K.G., Buffy, Ernie J, T Nelly, Cookie and Family (Charlotte, N.C), Wee-Wee, Lovey, Zero, Fiedale, Dorian, T-Brown, L-Boogie, Lil Pooh, Curt Burt (R.I.P), , Spider, Aristotle Buie, Vince Cook, Chris Tombs, Magoo, Fello (R.I.P), Fat Shit, Shag, Charley Mo, Chrome, Tre Griffin, Scory, Bumps (R.I.P), Dimp, Hog, Darryl Miller, Mel Smith. Christopher Martin Sr. and Lacy and Ryan Gordon. Chantay and Glen, out in Cali. Matt To all the hoods in the Nati, and across the nation. To everyone who's locked up that tried to get some money.

First Edition April 2014 Maples, L. Douglas, Delight-Douglas L.
Maples -1st Edition.
    Love story-Fiction 2. African American - Fiction 3. Sexual –
    orientation - Fiction. 4. Cincinnati (Ohio)- Fiction. Imanii Books.
Edited: By Mrs. Jessica Middleton
Organized; By Mrs. Jessica Middleton
Cover and Graphics by: Jessica Shely, Green Pasture Designs
Imanii Books/ Busy 1 Entertainment
Coming soon by Douglas L. Maples
Stop Wasting Time
Well-Bred
Bonita
Entrance the Trilogy
To: order books go to Amazon.com or contact us at (513) 492-
1084.

CHARACTERS

Delight Scott: A successful lawyer for a major firm in Cincinnati who's married with one child.

Kendall Scott: Delight's husband who works for the same law firm.

Simmion Boyd a.k.a. Smack: A well-known drug dealer throughout the Tri-State.

Stefani Blake: An Australian model and Simmion's girlfriend.

Antwan Klein: A black German with the craftsmanship of guns. He's also a narcotics dealer and terrorist.

Keisha Myles: A pediatrician by day, and a stripper/dancer by night, who goes by the name of Pepsi.

Miesha Jones: A daycare provider by day, and a streetwalker by night.

Heather Heath: Delight's older sister who's a county correctional officer.

Elliot Thrasher: The Mayor of Cincinnati.

Phil Helmet: A well-known judge in Hamilton County.

Jasmine Finch: The head prosecutor in Hamilton County.

Kyle Peterson: A jewelry specialist and thief.

Allen Taylor: A crooked cop for the RENU unit.

Will Edmond: Allen's partner, also with the RENU unit.

Diamond Cut: A group of guys from Dayton known for Hip-Hop music.

The Belvy Boyz: An older group of guys who hustle for a living out of Cincinnati.

CHAPTER ONE
DELIGHT

To live such a life, however, it was necessary to please those beneath and above as well to pay taxes, to offer gifts of money to the minority and of lawyers and decision-making authorities. To feed and flatter principle is something to do making your life delightful and pleasant.

Nothing is more pleasing than the smoky, passionate intimacy of two lovers with the admission of guilt. In a split second, fully aware that the devil's guilt might want to be acknowledged, she made the decision.

"Smack", she said warmly and quietly.

The man interrupted her by placing his fingertips to her mouth.

"Shhh", adding, "Let's go celebrate our victory in court."

She hesitated at first knowing she had obligations with her husband later that evening.

"Okay, but I have to call my husband and cancel our prior engagement," she told him after a long pause. She really wanted to discuss the sex they just had moments ago.

"By the way, what do you have in mind, Smack?" she asked him.

"The Masonnette." He replied.

His eyes darkened like honey roasted nuts over an open fire. She then called her husband to cancel their dinner date. The two got cleaned up and left the Hyatt Regency at around 5:45pm. She didn't ride with him in his vehicle; instead she followed him in her car to the restaurant that relocated from downtown Cincinnati to Mason Ohio. Smack, a well-known drug dealer from Dayton, Ohio, who's government name is Simmion Boyd, was in his late twenties, but his face reminded you of a twelve-year-old boy.

One hour later as they sat across from one another at the table she thought...had she misunderstood something? She hadn't read into his suggestion of dinning close to her home, which was also in Mason, same as the restaurant. She knew she was playing with fire. So, what, she was having an affair with many angles? Then she remembered the sultry look in his eyes when they first met.

Oh, no, she thought, he's just a kid. Now she knew that he was far from being a kid by the blatant desire that skimmed through her body every time he touched her and the way he would satisfy her the way her husband didn't. How could she not remember how his school boy eyes made her moist on contact? He made her feel like she was seventeen again and not two years from forty. How could she explain the way he'd touched her hours ago in the Hyatt Hotel suite?

"Would you like anything else besides the sirloin, Ms., perhaps a side of shrimp?" the waiter asked. She laid her fork on the untouched Caesar salad and came back from drifting off in a daze. "No thank you; that will be all." The waiter grabbed the menus and left the table. While Smack sipped casually on a glass of Moet, he asked, "Is everything okay?"

"Yes, Smack, everything is fine," she replied as her fingers ran up the stem of her glass.

She imagined that the champagne bubbles were laughing at the adolescent awkwardness the two were manifesting. It was the only thing she'd taken in. Their food finally arrived and Smack made no exception by greedily winning the battle of man over cow.

Her plate was hardly touched. "You didn't even touch your steak," he pointed out.

She smiled. "I wasn't that hungry. This day has been really emotional for me."

The comment came to mind, thoughts of the sex and not the trial. Eagerly without thinking he managed to reply. "I know, it's been emotional for me, too."

The waiter returned to check on the party of two. "Is everything okay? Can I get you our dessert menu?" he asked them with a flare. "I'm okay, I'm stuffed," he said, silently adding. "Except for her, oh how bad I need her." Smack could only hear himself as he shifted in his seat trying to accommodate the escalating weight as it is. The thought of his body against hers flooded his mind. His phone rang. He knew who it was looking at the caller I.D. "Is it her Simmion?" she asked. He knew Delight was agitated because she addressed him by his government name. "Yes, it's her. Will you excuse me please?" As he flipped open his Razor cell phone. "Hello, Hello." His voice echoed several times.

"Hey dare darling where are your mate?" The native tongue of the outback Australian spoke through the receiving end of the phone.

"I'm at dinner with a few friends." Simmion said.

"With whom, may I bloody ask." The native tongue asked him on the other end.

"With Delight and the rest of the firm" He looked over at his date. She raised an eyebrow a notch hearing her name.

"Simmion, you are always under those people, especially her. If she wasn't married, I would suspect you are bloody fooling around with her mate." The native tongue reminded him.

"Well I'm not. At least someone was in court with me today." He told her holding the phone.

"Simmion, please don't bloody go there." The sexy native voice told him.

"I guess your photo shoot was more important." Simmion said.

"You know that's my career honey and I couldn't bloody reschedule, but I'll make it up to you when you come and get me from the bloody stinky airport I say." She told him.

"No, I can't do it, not at this moment.   Grab a cab." He told her still looking over at Delight.

"Are you bloody serious, Simmion?" The native tongue cried out through the receiver

"Stefani, don't start, I'm here." Simmion tried not to give in.

"So, you're going to leave me to ride in some bloody stinky cab with a bloody stranger?" She was storming up a fit about to cry.

"Okay, I'll be there in about twenty minutes." He told her.

"Ta-Ta honey, I'll be waiting I say," she said and he closed his phone and closed his eyes.

Stefani Blake is Simmion's girlfriend. She is a gorgeous petite model from Australia. He met her at a Baby Phat fashion show in New York. He opened his eyes and they traveled back across the table to his date. "What do you want from me, Simmion? What could you possibly want?" She asked knowing her body was hot, cold; her body needed his.

"What do you want from me Delight?" he countered.

"That's a cop out and you know it Simmion." Delight said.

"I'm just saying Delight; you know I have a girlfriend like I know Kendall is your husband. I can't have what I really want because of that." He said pointing to her finger. "Besides," he added sipping his champagne, "You know what I want?" He stared deeply into her eyes. "What?" she asked. The word was clear, bold, yet braided with threads of vulnerability. "Say it." She demanded. Delight stalked his eyes for a few seconds. The only sound in the restaurant was the fast beating of two hearts. "Alright," he answered roughly.

He swallowed hard and deep in his throat before answering.

"I won't for you to be my wife. I mean this has been going on for almost six months now." Simmion told her.

"What about that thin Australian bitch?" Delight said with an attitude.

"Delight, I'm not in a situation like you. She is not my wife. I don't have to do any paper work to dismiss her. All I have to say it's over and put her on a plane and say bye-bye." He said.

"Is that so, Mr. Boyd?" Delight sarcastically asked.

"Indeed, it is Mrs. Scott. Boyd should be your last name." He said.

"Okay, seriously Smack, what about your career? Don't you think it's about quitting time?" She asked while holding his hand.

"Yeah, but why quit if I have a lawyer for a wife who can get me off whenever I get busted?" He smiled at her.

"I just did that and I'm not your wife." Delight said.

"I paid you a lot of money to do so, like ten racks for your legal counsel." He told her.

"I only asked for twenty-five hundred." She replied.

"Well think of it as a retainer for other future needs." Simmion said.

She saw that the conversation wasn't going anywhere, so she changed avenues.

"Look at the time. You're going to be late picking up your little white poodle," as she pointing to her watch.

"I'm going to finish my glass of champagne first." Simmion said.

"You know I wanted to make love again before I went in the house. My sex life at home, oh I forgot there is no sex life at home. So, I try to get enough as I possibly can to last me awhile." Delight told him.

"What about a quickie, in your Range Rover?" He asked.

"If that's the case, let's just go into one of the restroom stalls." She looked at him wide eyed knowing she wouldn't dare do anything of that nature.

****

His breath was moist and warm as it fell into her ear. "I'm afraid, Simmion. I don't believe I'm in a restaurant restroom trying to reach an orgasm."

There was a fear in each honest word spoken. "What are you afraid of?" Smack asked her. His breath was penetrating the fabric of her blouse. Her heart was beating with a rhythm against his. "I'm afraid of needing anything this badly, especially in a restaurant restroom." She said.

His hands slid up and down her thighs. "Smack, we don't have any protection." She said. "It will be real quick Delight, I'll pull out." He said.

"I'm not on any birth control, I can still get pregnant you know." She told him.

"I know," as he slipped his hand between her thighs and found his target.

"Oh Delight, baby," as he groaned while his tribal piece entered her passage.   He pumped hard and steady while his body trembled under the weight of her caress.   In this moment, Delight would have given him anything he wanted.

CHAPTER TWO
KENDALL

God had both, the time on the inclination to make things difficult for man by withholding rain, sending too much, making the earth sour, turning male children into female children in the woman's womb, poisoning their blood with sickness and filling the air with bad vapors. The most amusing thing is to see a group of distinguished men together with only each other to make a life of laughter.

They were as suspicious of each other as of themselves. A wild idea came into Kendall's mind. It was a thought of desperation. He called one of his partners.

"Hey Bryant, this is Kendall. Let's go to Sneaky-Peak's."

"Aren't you and the wife out to dinner?" said Bryant.

"She canceled. She had a case that she wanted to tie up, I guess."

"It's Thursday Kendall, I have to work tomorrow."

"Who doesn't? It's Lady's Night, buddy." said Kendall.

"Alright man. Where are you?" Bryant asked.

"I'm leaving my house now." Kendall told him.

"But who's watching Rainell?" Bryant asked him.

"She's over her Aunt Heather's during the week. You know she lives in the Princeton School District. We alternate weeks, and this is her week. Anyhow, school is almost out and Rainell's old enough to watch herself." Kendall explains to his friend.

"Okay, Kendall, I'm waiting." Bryant was excited.

"I'll be there in about twenty minutes, buddy."

On the face of it, it was ridiculous. Kendall Scott hadn't changed since he left college. All sorts of thoughts boiled up inside his mind. Excuses that died before they were formed: self-disgust, remorse and confusion. None of which formed easy words, and perhaps they were better unsaid anyway. He pulled up outside of Bryant's crib in the Water Stone Estates on Lippleman Road, which sat between Tri-County and Sharonville. He could walk to the Tri-County Mall or to Princeton High School.

"Bryant, it's quiet over here in this complex." Kendall said.

"I know, even though it's a lot of Indians, Africans, and Mexicans living over here with hella kids." Bryant sighed.

"It shouldn't matter; you're a bachelor with no kids. I would be trying to fuck one of the funny talking foreigners, if I were you." Kendall joked.

"Man, you buggin. Get us to the strippers and you are buying the first two rounds. Will you stop at the Marathon by the highway exit so I can grab some singles?" said Bryant.

"I got you, Bryant." Kendall told him.

They pulled off in Kendall's dark green Porsche. Sneaky-Peak's was an underground illegal strip club in Lockland. Kendall wanted to see some women of color instead of the same ole blue-eyed blond and brunette white chicks at the Brass Horse in Kentucky. Kendall had his V.I.P. pass to get them in the club with no hassle. He had become a regular in these parts. He had his eyes on one stripper. She was the sexiest woman in this entire place with the most beautiful ass that has ever been born on this earth. They took their usual seats in the V.I.P. section and ordered their first round of drinks. Kendall's eye fixated on the dance floor until he spotted her. Her beauty sent chills up and down his spine; not to mention his manhood. She danced so gracefully, shaking her ass up and down and all around to the sounds of the music beating through the speakers. Her name was Keisha Myles a.k.a. Pepsi. As soon as she spotted Kendall in his usual seat, she slowly and gracefully danced herself over to him. She knew that if she made him the apple of her eye, he would surely put spend lots of cash on her. Bryant slid a few singles in her G-string. Kendall showed him up by slipping in a couple of hundred-dollar bills. She continued to dance around him shaking her ass very close to his face. She slowly turned around to look him in the eyes because she just loved the way his eyes glistened all over her body. She knew she had him mesmerized.

"Can we talk?" Kendall asked.

"I'm working." She said while continuing to sway her hips back and forth.

"What about after work, Pepsi?" He looked deep into her eyes.

"Okay, I get off at eleven." She was still shaking her ass gracefully.

"That's in like twenty minutes," as Kendal pointed to his watch.

"I'm free then, just wait for me." She told him and he winked at her.

He sat patiently waiting on Pepsi to come out of the dressing room and Bryant was getting drunk. The mysterious woman finally joined him at the table they were sitting. She looked him over and he did the same. She batted her eyes and licked her lips.

"So, what's so important that you need to talk to me?"

"I would just like your company. Maybe we could get a cup of coffee or tea and a nice reasonable conversation."

"It wouldn't work." She said pointing at his wedding band.

"That's nothing." He told her.

"If it wasn't anything, then why are you wearing it?"

"Because I like the fit." He smiled at her.

"Bullshit, come again with a more serious answer before I walk away." She scooted back from the table.

"Okay my marriage is on thin ice. There's nothing there anymore with my wife and I." She could see the seriousness in his eyes.

"So, what is it that you want from me, some ass?" she asked him.

"Oh no, I just want to get to know you, that's all." said Kendall.

"I didn't think so, because I'm not like these other bitches who work here. I have an honest job and I don't sleep with the customers." She told him.

"Well, my name is Kendall." He extended his hand to her.

"I'm Pepsi." She replied.

"I know who you are. The fake wig and blue eyes can't fool me." He said.

"Oh, I can't?" She looked at him in shock.

"What black woman you know that was born with blue eyes?" He asked.

"Tyra." She said as she looked at him.

"Stop it I say.   Your eyes are hazel brown and you wear a short haircut, Ms. Keisha Myles." said Kendall.

"How did you recognize me?" Pepsi wanted to know.

"Keisha, I've been attracted to you ever since I met you at the children's clinic.   I kept bringing our daughter to the clinic just to see you.   Why do you think the visits were so frequent?" He was excited.

"So, how did you know that I was a dancer here?" she asked.

"I came in one night and saw you and I've been coming ever since." Kendall told her.

"So how is Rainell doing?" She asked him about his daughter.

"I thought you didn't know me?" Kendall asked.

"I never said I didn't know you, Kendall.   You were the one playing guess my name games." said Pepsi.

"She's doing well.   She's a freshman at Princeton High School."

"It's been a while, plus I know she's going to Children's Hospital now." She said.

"My wife did that, she suspected me of stalking you." He told her.

"That's what this is about Mr. Scott?   You're a sick man, huh?" She gave a fake laugh.

"I like your honesty, that's all." Kendall confessed.

"So just some coffee and a little conversation, huh?" she gave him the look.

"That's all Ms. Myles." He told her.

"What about your boy over there?" She pointed at Bryant.

"I can send him home in a cab." He gave her a wink.

"Well, let me grab the rest of my things and we can leave." She said.

"I'll be waiting right here." He looked at her walk back to the dressing room.

Kendall put Bryant in a cab and Keisha Myles followed him to Perkin's restaurant in Springdale across from the BP gas station.

CHAPTER THREE
DELIGHT

Delight was now at home fingering through a magazine lying under the covers in her bedroom. She had on a silk brown spaghetti strap nightgown. She just finished watching Kobe Bryant and the Lakers lose to K.G. and the Celtics. It was game two of the N.B.A. finals. She loved basketball, being she used to play for Withrow High School in Cincinnati and the University of Stanford while she was going to law school.

She grabbed the remote and turned from ESPN to CNN. They were discussing how the economy was steadily crashing and the price of gas was rising. It was quarter after one when Kendall came in the house. She already knew where he'd been. She just loved to hear him lie. It usually made her feel less guilty about her cheating. He walked in the room unbuttoning his shirt. She looked up at him with her reading glasses at the bridge of her nose. "Hey Delight, you are still awoke? He didn't make any eye contact with her.

"I'm just reading and watching CNN. I couldn't sleep knowing you were still out." said Delight.

"Well, I'm home now. I was at BW#'s with Bryant and the fella's watching the game." Kendall responded.

"The basketball game?" she knew he didn't care for basketball that much.

"Yes, honey, the game." He said sarcastically.

"Who won, honey?" Delight already knew the answer to her questions.

"The Laker's won." Kendall told her.

"Okay then! Go Kobe! That's my boy!" She smirked knowing his pathetic ass was lying.

"I am about to take a shower and it's bedtime for me." said Kendall.

"Okay, Kendall. I am about to call it a night myself."

Kendall put his wallet and watch on the Oakwood dresser and removed the rest of his clothing, throwing them in a chair by the corner. She waited for him to turn the water on and then checked his pants pockets. "Bingo!" she said to herself.

"The Sneaky-Pete's card, like always. The brother couldn't even get his lie together. Just like a man...chasing pussy instead of satisfying some good ole "in house pussy."

Delight thought to herself. She continued, *"He was talking about how the Laker's won while I wanted to scream at the top of my lungs, you lying M.F."*

Her thoughts came to mind and she was boiling hot.

****

Earlier at Perkin's, Kendall and Keisha had a private booth discussing life and principle. The interesting and frustrating thing Kendall came to realize, that no matter how much Keisha Myles he consumed it was never enough. It felt good, really good. Only one thing might feel better would be Keisha making love to him. The thought brought a reaction. His breath came rapidly and his heart raced. He became aroused. Nevertheless, the rush of guilt followed behind those thoughts. Slanting his cup, the dark liquid flowed over the steam to reach his lips. "Ah." He let it be known that the fresh brewed coffee was tasty.

"So, Ms. Myles, why the stripper gig?" Kendall asked her.

"I like to dance and I've always been told I have a body like one of those King magazine models. Plus, it really helps out with my means of living." she gave him a smile.

"What about the clinic?" He asked.

"We are barely getting any business now days with all this stuff going on with health care and so forth." She replied.

"Oh, I see. Well you do have a banging body. Do you work out?"

"Sometimes I hit the gym, but mainly I watch what I eat." she said.

"So, where do you live, Ms. Keisha?" He gazed into her eyes after taking another sip of his coffee.

"I live in West Chester off of Smith Road on Wyndtree Drive. It's a complex with a few small lakes around it." Keisha told him.

"I think I know where that is." He responded.

"I wish I could afford a house like you and your wife." She
told him.
"You never know. Be careful of what you wish for." He looked
down at her with a grin.
"Are you making a pass at me, Kendall?" she asked him.
"I did that the moment I laid eyes on you." He stated.
"Stop it! You're going to make me blush and give in to you. I
can't make it that easy if I choose to break up your happy home."
She smiled seductively at him slapping his hand. She couldn't
help but wonder if she had agreed for reason or another. Perhaps
a feminine reason if that.
"Ha-ha, I see we have jokes. But you wouldn't have to do much,
because my home is already unhappy. I haven't touched my
wife in Lord knows when. Maybe six months now." He told his
business.
"Are you seriously telling me your bedroom secrets so I can feel
sorry for you? I don't believe you, Kendall." she said with
concern.
"I'm serious, Keisha." He confessed.
"She haven't said anything or tried to be intimate with you?" She
asked.
"No, she just keeps quiet and work, work, work." He said.
"I hate to say it, Kendall, but she's sleeping with someone. I
know me and when a bitch gets horny, a bitch gots to have it.
Females are worse than men when they get horny." Keisha told
him.
"If she is, then she's hiding it awfully well." said Kendall.
"You know us girls are smarter that you boys. We plan way ahead
of time and we are strategic planners. We wait until the perfect
time." said Keisha which is Pepsi.
"Oh yeah, well thanks for the heads up, but I'm seriously unable
to get you out of my head. I mean I can't turn it off, Keisha."
"Do you ever jack-off thinking about me, Kendall?" she asked.
"What type of question is that to ask a black man?" He said.
"One I would like an answer to and be honest." she replied.
"Well to be quite honest with you, I've done it a few times."

"Are you serious?" she laughed and smacked his hand. He gave he a shrug and titled his head. "Yeah." She leaned over to whisper in his ear.

"Do you want to taste my nookie or do you want to fuck me?" She said seductively.

"It's a trick question isn't it?" He looked at her.

"Nope," as she continued to whisper. "Are you willing to give that up"? She pointed to his wedding band. Kendall shook his head as if to say "yes". She whispered seductively.

"Are you sure, are you positive?" She asked him. He nodded his head again to say yes.

"How many years were you pretending to be married, Kendall?" He softly said, "Fourteen."

"So, you're willing to throw fourteen years away for a shot of ass?" she asked him.

"Long as it's with you, Keisha." He told her.

She licked her lips and then licked his earlobe giving him a whiff of her breath and said, "Pick me up around six p.m. tomorrow, 2054 Wyndtree and don't be late, Kendall."

Soft he thought smooth and tasting of whip cream and passion. He wondered if it was his imagination or if her breath really stinks. He didn't care the next time he'd offer her a mint or Tic-Tac. He knew that was minor and him getting her was major.

****

The shower stopped in their bedroom and Kendall came out drying off. His tribal piece was semi-hard as Delight glanced sharply at him.

She thought to herself, ***"Oh my God, I wish he would stick that bad boy inside me."***

She watched it swing back and forth from his movement. Her dreams and hopes would soon be shattered knowing he just jacked off in the shower thinking about one of those stripper bitches at the club. She stared momentarily as he put on his pajama bottoms.

He caught her staring at him. "So how is work coming along at the office?" He asked her. The question caught her off guard as she was snug under the covers now naked.

"Okay, I guess I just made some changes to my opening statement, that all."

"Oh, and I heard about your victory in court today."

"It wasn't nothing, just an illegal search and procedure that hot thrown out."

"Delight, why do you won't to represent criminal cases all of a sudden?"

"Kendall, that's why we studied law, that's why we have our own practice in Blue Ash remember?"

"But Slogin and Cummons is where we make our living."

"They don't respect me, being that I'm a woman. You like them, because it's a man thing and I'm the best lawyer in the firm."

He threw back the covers to get in the bed and didn't even notice she was naked. He lay down and turned the lamp off on his side of the bed. He kissed her on the cheek.

"You're right, honey, you are the best lawyer at the firm. Goodnight."

She turned to him. "Kendall, I'm naked. Please touch me. Make love to me."

"Delight, I am tired. I have a seven o'clock in the morning."

"Please," as she went into his pajama bottoms and touched his manhood. She felt the extremities of semen still leaking out from him touching himself in the shower.

"Never mind." She rolled over and tears raced down her face. She was quiet and supple.

Good thing she was a bad girl and got her a quickie in the restaurant restroom. Then she thought about Smack not wearing any protection.

God, please don't let that one time get me pregnant." She closed her eyes and went to sleep.

CHAPTER FOUR
STEFANI BLAKE

She turned from contemplation of her own arousal. Her enemy was light complexion not dark, the light of her own kind; her own people from back home where she'd been cut off from. Looking from the high window, you could see a glimpse of her naked beauty streak across the bedroom floor. Her companion lay in the central air across the bed. She wanted his caress and vivid touch. So stubborn in her own personal use, but beyond him she hesitated and turned away from the bed. Her action caused him to look in her direction. She passed back by him again and quite assures of it he grabbed her arm. He gently pulled her toward him and she knew what he desired. She lay on top of him and then started kissing his neck, his chest all the way down to his stomach. She came eye to eye with his limp tribal piece. She approached it like a cheetah waiting to attack her prey. She gently caressed it with her warm manicured hands. Then like a savage beast she took him in her warm mouth, deep throating his manhood by trying to make it disappear. He easily got rock hard from her swift talent. She was a pro no doubt about it. Her skills were superb. You would think she were a fluffer who gets a guy ready for a sex scene in a porn flick. He tried to pull her away, but she refuses to let go of her prey. He finally managed to pull her away turning her on her backside.
He spread her legs to see the shaved vagina with the cutest pair of lips. Her clitoris was huge and meaty. He tried to enter her passage and she denied him all Hollywood access.
"What are you bloody doing, Smack? You know you're not putting that unprotected flesh in my bloody cunt. Are you trying to ruin my career mate?"
"I'll pull it out in time, I swear, Stefani."
"I can't afford to get pregnant, not at this point in my career mate."
"If you do, we can get an abortion."
"I'm not a bloody murderer, you may be. I've heard stories about you type of guys Simmion."

"Come on Stefani, I won't feel your texture for once. Feel the inside of your vagina walls, you know flesh to flesh."

"It's no Simmion. I've warned you it's either with a bloody Trojan or no sexual penetration at all." She added, "I hate kids anyway, they are so bloody icky, I say."

"Fuck it," as he stood at the foot of the bed pulling her towards him. He put his hard-tribal piece back in her jaws. He couldn't deny that she was a good clean girl and the fact she swallowed made it even better. That's what got him hooked from the beginning. It only took him minutes more to shoot wads of hot semen down her throat. He slapped her lips with manhood getting the remainders out. His cell phone began to ring and he released the back to head to go and answer it. He reached his Razor on the dresser and flipped it open. "Vegas never sleep and neither does me, what's good?"

"Yo, Smack, what's good hood?"

"Kyle, my man, Peterson, what it do?'

"Nothing much, but from your breathing it sound like you are busy."

"I just got finished taking Stefani's temperature."

Oh, you had to put the human thermometer in her mouth?"

"You know it kid. So, what's good with you and those jewels?"
Stefani walked pass him and tried to kiss him with his kids still on her lips. "Don't even play me like that." He told her pushing her away from him. "What you say, Smack?"

"I wasn't talking to you Kyle."

"Smack, I got something hot for you. A ring for her, because I know you are probably going to marry that outback pretty mother-fucka one day. It's a two-karat solid diamond ring set in triple platinum."

"Where did you get it Kyle?"

"You know my line of work. I had to hit up Dodd's Jeweler on Race Street. The shit was easy. The mother-fucka cost like sixteen racks, but to you my man, four racks and she's all yours."

"Okay I'm at you in the morning."

"I see you must have got a continuance today in court, you still breathing."

"Hell naw, my lawyer beat that case today. It's over I'm back to doing what Rick Ross do. Every day I'm hustling, I'm copping me a Lac truck on 22's, birds go for 22, my bitch is 22," as he laughed through the receiver.

*******,

Earlier that day, Kyle was plotting on his lick while Smack was in court. Kyle had already known the original work schedule of the owner and the time he would be in the store. They had acquired a new employee by the name of Adrian. The employee and store manager had never seen Adrian before because he was on vacation when he started. It was Adrian's off day by the master work schedule and Kyle knew it. Kyle was a mixed guy who looked more white than black. He had duplicated the stores ID badge and suit jacket. He walked in the store wearing the employee style uniform.

He had his name badge on and went behind the counter like he worked there. The veteran jeweler questioned himself about Adrian's work schedule. *"He must be the new guy, but he's not scheduled to work today. I don't think so."*

He really didn't know if Adrian was black or white. Kyle knew his jewelry and just about every location in the store. "Excuse me, is it Adrian? I don't think you're scheduled to work today." The small man approached Kyle.

"Excuse me, is it Paul? The boss man asked me yesterday to come in to work. He wanted me to meet you and acquire some hours and experience under you. He probably forgot to pencil me in." Kyle put his hands on his hips.

"I didn't know Mr.," as Kyle cut him off.

"That Mr. D'Amanto cared for blacks. Everyone is not a racist Paul. Every black man is not a criminal. So, should we take this up with Mr. D'Amanto, because you know he doesn't like to be bothered unless it's an emergency?"

"That's not necessary, Adrian." Paul said.

"Well we have customers that we need to attend to." Kyle told him still in character.

"So, you know where everything is as far as the keys to the display cases?" Paul asked him.

"Some I do and some I don't. if I need your help, I'll call you."
Kyle put his hand on his hip and other hand to his ear like he had
a phone. Paul stared at him.
"Oh, now you have a problem with my sexuality. Okay, Paul, I'm
gay...all out gay. Are you prejudice towards gays, Paul?" He
asked him.
"Oh no, not at all Adrian."
"We gays come in all races, shapes and sizes. I hope I don't or
won't have to file my first and last grievance on job
discrimination."
"Adrian, of course not." Paul tapped him on the shoulder. "Adrian,
you attend to this side and I'll attend to that side."
"Well let's get this money Paul, mama has a date tonight." Kyle
snapped his finger and headed back and then switched his hips
walking away from Paul.   *******,
"Smack the shit was like taking candy from a baby. Playing a
gay person can take you a long way. But you know I saw
Kendall Scott soft ass in Sneaky Pete's tonight."
"It was ladies night tonight wasn't it?" He thought to himself, but
out loud where Kyle could hear him.
"Yep, it sure was and he was talking to that bitch, Pepsi." Kyle
told him.
"She was working with her stinky breath ass?" said Smack.
"She had got off about eleven I guess and they left together."
Kyle told the business.
"So, oh Kendall was out being a bad boy tonight. He was
cheating on his wife with dragon breath." Smack laughed.
"Yeah, I guess so, because neither one of them came back into
the club. But as much as you are up under his wife sexy ass, I
would be trying to fuck her ass.
"Now you are tripping Kyle." Smack was serious.
"Look I say the heifer out before in some tight ass jeans, she got
a badooka dook ass on her. I don't know about you, but I would
be trying to fuck."
"Okay Stacey Jr. looking. She's just my lawyer and nothing else.
But I know Pepsi is about to try to trick Kendall.

She's always act like she don't do dicks and we got the little hooker on tape." He laughed.

"I mean Smack we had a ball with her that night at Suave's, but her breath was just fowl as hell, like she ate a shit sandwich." said Kyle.

"We should've called G-Baby and asked him did he want to shoot a movie with her. Goldie would've loved to put her in one of those Nasty Nati DVD." said Smack.

"You would've made her a super star overnight." Kyle laughed.

"She played fair that night Kyle and she took home a lot of dough. Damn I just thought of something I need for you to do." said Smack.

"What's that, Smack?" He asked Smack.

"I need for you to shop around so I can move like fifty of these Jessica Alba's I have left. My cousin and them are on fire in Dayton. I got something for you." Smack told him.

"I think I might have some local cats who might be interested. They own a store downtown on McMicken." Kyle said.

"Kyle you should grab you a few you know switch over. At 16.5 a key you can't lose homeboy."

"I don't fuck around. The most time I can get for my crime is 18 months. But these cats are legit. Do me a favor and give them the same deal at that price and I know they'll move the shit for you. They are well-known and they are thorough about their business."

"What are their names?" Smack asked him.

"They called themselves the Belvy-Boyz." Kyle said.

"What is the store name?" Smack asked him wanting to know.

"It's called the Goodie Bag." Kyle slowly responded.

"They sound familiar. I think I heard this little freak name London mention one of them to me leaving out of Penn Station one day. She saw this guy and she was bitching about him not paying her for her services. I think she said his name was Worm or something." Smack told him.

"Yeah, that's one of their names." Said Kyle.

"So, Kyle, when can I meet them?" said Smack.

"We can go down there tomorrow after I show you the ring." Kyle told him.

"Bet. I'll call you when I leave the rim shop after I cop my Lac truck." Smack said.

"Alright big brah, I'll holla at you." Kyle replied.

"Later, Kyle the heist artist." They hung up and Smack knew he had to meet the guys that Kyle acquired him about, because the people who moved his drugs were on fire.

CHAPTER FIVE
RENU UNIT

The middle-aged man turned his attention to the man asking the questions and obviously felt that his professionalism entitled him to answer.

"The bullet entered the fleshy part of the left chest angled downward and lodging itself in his right side. Fortunately, it managed to miss his lungs, unfortunately it gazed his left ventricle of the heart."

"That sounds serious as hell, Lieutenant," he frowned and added. "I know that's serious."

"Not really. It just caused a lot of bleeding. But if the bullet was an inch higher, Sargent Davis would have died."

"Who in the hell is trying to take out our RENU unit?" the medium built black man had a frustrated look on his face. Trying to silently fill in the missing word the Lieutenant said, "Are you alright, Officer Taylor?"

"Yes, I'm okay. I hope Sargent Davis recovers okay." Taylor answered.

"He'll be just fine. I need for you and Will to get out there and find the perpetrators who assaulted an officer with attempted murder." The Lieutenant told him.

"I'm on it, Lieutenant." Office Taylor told him.

Allen Taylor and Will Edmond were crooked cops who worked for a special unit outside the Cincinnati Police Department, RENU. They were known to go after big time drug dealers using entrapment and any other trickery to bring a suspect to justice. The two men exchanged dry, but firm hand shakes. And yet here to there is an atmosphere of circumstance of unexpected limits having been reached and recognized and quietly sensible settled for. Too late to reduce the scale and crowd everything together, each road, each avenue has an air of being turned inwards.

****

Hours ago, dark tinted black Chevy Impala SS pulled up on Sargent Davis in the parking lot of the building where the Duke Energy main office is located and in the same building is where the RENU headquarters is located.   About twenty rounds of hot bullet spit from an automatic weapon that missed Sargent Davis, but a bullet from a .40 Cal Beretta hit the target.   The car sped off. "Yeah, that's for fucking with the Boss man, you crooked cops in the Nati don't play fair. You fucking with Diamond Cut, we don't play around." said the young man as the car sped off.

CHAPTER SIX
KEISHA'S SEDUCTION

Kendall was at Keisha's door knocking at exactly six on the dot.
She opened the door in a sexy red two-piece covered in a white
see through lingerie nightgown. She batted her eyes and licked
her lips when she saw Kendall standing there in his suit and tie.
"I see you managed to find your way to me. I don't feel like going
out. I thought maybe we could just stay here and entertain each
other." She told him.
Kendall caught his breath and gathered himself from getting a
hard on. "That's fine." She opened the door wider so he could
enter her palace. Her place had flavor. She had a leather pit
living room set with ancient tables and statues. Her colors were
soft like crème. The carpet was crème and fluffy. She had a 52"
flat screen TV. The spacious apartment smelled like a fresh
Sunday morning and air-freshener.
"You can sit anywhere you please, Kendall. Would you like
something to drink?" She asked him.
"A beer, if you have one, please." He relaxed a little sitting on her
sofa.
"I only have Genuine Draft by Miller, because my brother drinks
it. He's shacking up here." She crossed her arms still looking
down at him.
"That's fine," as Kendall watched her walk into the kitchen
nearby.
*"Yeah right, your ex-lover probably drinks that brand and you still
have some left form the last time he spent the night."* Kendall
thought to himself.
She brought him a beer and sat next to him on the sofa. She
then laid a coaster on the table for him to sit his beer on. Keisha
never remembered falling into Kendall's arms. It was just the
right moment; she was alone, while the next moment she was
swallowed up by the incredible warmth of his, massive and
convincing warmth. The warmth that spun itself inside her. She
refuses not to touch him. Kendall had strained to stay away
from her touch. Instead he clung to her side where the fabric
acted like a shield between bare skin. It was a layer of

30

arrangement, but one he could overcome. "You lied," she said, her eyes finding his after a few seconds. "You never asked to fuck me Kendall."

"So, sue me for perjury." He looked at her.

"You know any good lawyers?" They smiled at each other. Genuinely and playfully Keisha thought she might not know a good lawyer, but she knew a lawyer who thought the world of her she could hire. That observation was followed by the thought that, if she wanted to be good to herself, now was the opportunity. She deliberately let her eyes find the hand entwined with hers as his eyes followed...and the wedding band encircled on his third finger from his thumb. It was just going to be sex, a casual sexual encounter they reminded themselves, nothing more they thought. Why did the hand holding hers seem much more than a sexual partner? Why did she want to melt into his body? This time they would avoid each other's eyes as if to remind them they were alone in her place. "Are you sure you want to cross that line, Kendall?"

"I'm positive." He answered even though he got a whiff of her breath.

"You know I might have to acquire you on a regular basis after this encounter, will you be available Kendall?"

The smell of richly scented cologne reached her nose. "Yes, Keisha."

"Well you can leave whenever you like to." He tried to ignore the color of her eyes. He noticed the fresh scented fragrance she was wearing as she stood up to lead him to her bedroom.

****

"Hey Smack, pull over right here." Kyle told him.

"They are some big ass niggas, Kyle."

"That's just Bodean, Kekou a.k.a. Larry and Vino a.k.a. Fat Bastard."

"You mean it's more of them?" Smack asked him.

"Yeah, Kobe, Worm, P-Diddy, Weezy and Dante a.k.a. Packman."

"I see they are clicked up like my cousin Larro and hid Diamond Cut boys."

"I surround myself with thorough niggas who muscle and skills."

"Well let me meet these guys with muscle and skills."

"Okay Smack calm down homie, I forgot to ask you what year was this truck?"

"It's special ordered and it's a 2009 model."

"Here it is June of 2008 and I'm sitting in a 2009 Cadillac truck with my nigga who's balling out of control."

"That's what I do Kyle, stunt like a mother-fucker. You can stunt like yo daddy too just flip a few of these American eagles I got on deck."

"I can't do that type of time, so I don't do the crime. They are giving out football numbers for that shit you dealing."

"Kyle, everyone is getting high off the devil's pie, it's the American way. Doctors, Lawyers, Politicians, Teachers, and the non-working-class people want the rich man high."

"Well Smack good luck with your line of work and let's go meet the Belvy Boyz because they can help you better than I can."

They got out of the light blue Cadillac EXT and me the Belvy Boyz, RENU agent Allen Taylor and Will Edmond were in an unmarked care watching from a distance. They thought the Belvy Boyz were behind their sergeant getting shot.

****

Earlier before Kendall made it to Keisha's house his wife Delight called him from her office at work. Kendall was working out in the field and was making house calls to a few of his clients and Keisha Myles was his last stop since he was in the area.

"Kendall, can you pick Rainell up from Heather's?" Delight asked him.

"I'm on my way to go meet a new client in West Chester." He said.

"At 5:45 in the evening, Kendall?" Delight was frustrated.

"Yes, at 5:46 to be exact, Delight. You go get her."

"I'm still at the office working, cleaning out some of your files too." She told him.

"Well tell Heather to take her home." Kendall demanded her.

"You know she be complaining about gas thinking we live a million miles away from her." said Delight.

"She only live in Lincoln Heights and that's down the road from our house." He replied.

"Forget it Kendall. I don't want to interrupt your business; I'll go get my child myself. Don't worry about it." She slammed the cabinet.

"I won't." Kendall told her and hung up the phone just like that. It took Delight every nerve in her body not to call him back and give him a piece of her mind. She didn't bother to entertain his thoughtless selfish behavior. She knew he was probably going to seek out his own sickening sexual fantasies. She just turned to the man who was giving her pleasure and never told her no or even thought twice about it.

****

Kendall stared at the fair color of her skin, the high structure of her perfectly shaped breast and delta between her legs. He thought if he didn't sex her now, he would go crazy. She threw the bed covers back and laid her feminine figure across the satin sheets. He came to her, instantly bodies tangled in a unison becoming one. His mouth was hot on her breast; his hands roamed the curves of her design.

Kendall was like a man of thirst trying to quench it for the first time. He was desperate, trying to love her slowly, to lover her completely, and to love Keisha until she was satisfied also. She tried to kiss him and he got a good dose of her bad breath. He escaped the kiss by inches. His hands ran the length of her entire body. "So perfect," he whispered.

He fell into the warm Vee. He lay heated, hard and ready to join her juice box. But he didn't not yet. He wanted to please her first, hoping her vagina didn't have a distasteful taste or odor.

"Kendall," she whispered pressing against him. "No wait," she begged him. "Let me handle that." He told her. "No." She shoved him taking charge. She slid her hand downward past his naval, past his hair. He tried to intercept her.

"Keisha wait, oh no...Ah, oh yes."

He moaned as she closed one hand around his manhood and placed her warm mouth over the head of his manhood. His head snapped back as his body tightened. You could hear the slurping from rooms away as she stroked him with her mouth. He thrust hard into her perfectly shaped mouth fitting his tribal piece.

Each muscle and vein were growing inside her grip making him harder and ready. She knew as she released her grip and managed to maneuver beneath him. She eased him forward parting her moist and throbbing pussy lips. She took him into her passage slowly and fully. Panting low moans of exquisite pleasure. She was softer than a new born kitten and wet. He let her grow use to his tribal piece. "Oh, Keisha, it feels so good, so good baby." He whispered in her ear.

"Kendall, we forgot the protection baby." Her words were jittering in a sensual rhythm.

"I know," he said. She felt the pressure of his penetration go deeper and stronger.

"What if I get pregnant, Kendall?" He grinded harder and she let out a fraction of a scream. "Oh yes." She pulled him into her.

"Don't worry, you won't Keisha." He caressed the side of her face.

"Kiss me Kendall and kiss my neck." She begged him. He did momentarily hold his breath. Kendall felt inexorable rush of climax. It was strong like the wind, but was it pre-cum? Frantically increasing the rhythm of his hips, she arched herself against him again and again. Her hands cupped his hips as they moved against hers. She hugged him to her. The other times she made love had been false imitation and she was performing, but she was enjoying the pleasure with Kendall. His warmth and touch made her feel like a new born virgin.

"That's right Kendall, fuck this pussy, fuck this pussy, make me cum, make me cum."

Kendall couldn't take the breath of hers any longer so he faked his own orgasm to withdraw from her clutches. "Oh shit, Keisha, I'm cumming, I'm cumming," as he shook his body slowing down his pace. "No Kendall, keep going I'm almost there, come on," as she kept thrusting against him trying to reach her orgasm. A little ecstasy came through her body as he stopped, but she didn't get the full capacity.

"Damn it, Kendall, it was right there baby," She confessed to him with a disappointed look on her face. He rolled off her still rock hard. Her juices were all on his manhood. He was going to the shower to finish the job himself. He turned to tell her. "I forgot to tell you that I am a lousy lover."

"That's your opinion, Kendall." She gave him a half smile.

Even though her snatch box was fresh, we and pleasing, her breath was a mother-fucker he thought. He didn't want to be offensive or for her to take the suggestion for some Scope the wrong way, so he just pretended everything was okay. She had a bathroom with a shower in her bedroom. When she heard the water running, she finished pleasing herself by masturbating. She rubbed herself hard, but gentle imagining Kendall was still insider her passage. She came hard and strong on her fingers. Her breathing was uncontrollably loud as her heart raced at a high rate. She shook and her lower part vibrated repeatedly. Kendall found himself touching himself in her shower as well. He thought she wouldn't call him again after the weak performance and not satisfying her completely. Keisha was thinking about the ATM, because he said he'd cum insider her. She didn't check, especially after her strong orgasm. When she busted her discharge was thick like please plus she was dripping wet. She would now play him for what he was worth. A married man with benefits, this was her ticket. Boy the evil that men do and the consequences they must endure for their actions.

CHAPTER SEVEN
HEATHER'S HOUSE

Smack's Cadillac truck sat in the drive-way of Heather's house on Wabash in Lincoln Heights. He was listening to Young Joc as he blew his horn for Delight's daughter, Rainell to come out.
Delight had asked him to pick her up after she got off the phone with Kendall. She knew her lover and friend would do anything for her. When Smack looked up, he saw Delight's older sister Heather came out the house in some little shorts and a small tight t-shirt where you could see how big her breasts were. Her shorts rose up in her crouch where you could see her vagina print. Her hair and nails were done as usual. She had a cigarette in her fingertips. She was indeed sexy with a small kangaroo pouch, being she was five years older than Delight, making her forty-three. She was jazzy, sassy and mouthy with much game and attitude.
When she got up on the truck, she rolled her eyes at Smack.
"Turn that shit down nigga, disrespecting my shit. You're not her daddy little boy, so why you out here blowing?" Heather was yelling.
"I know I'm not her daddy. I'm doing your sister a favor."
"I wonder what other favors you're doing for Delight. Kendall gone kick your ass if you are fucking his wife, Smack." She told him.
"You'll love that, but she's just my friend. If it was like that, I would kick his ass." Smack told her.
"Um-huh. We talk and the bitch is lonely looking for some sort of comfort. Don't fuck my sister, Smack, because she's vulnerable

right now." She put her hand on her hips. Smack already knew the damage was done.

"We talk Heather, I know she's going through some personal issues at home, she's my counselor and I guess I'm hers." said Smack.

"That's all it better be. You need to come and get some of this cougar pussy and quit playing; you might grow some hair on your face afterwards." Heather told him.

Smack laughed out loud hitting his steering wheel. "Heather, you need some professional help. You need to go out on Fresno in Forest Park and let my man pray for you."

"And what's out there, Smack?" Heather asked him.

"The Bishop of Word of Deliverance. Girl, you need Jesus."

"No, all I need is for you to put those sexy little lips right down here." As she stood back and pointed at her print in her shorts.

"Now you are tripping. Go on, Heather and tell your niece to come on." Smack told her.

"Nigga, you know the address, my door and legs are open just for you. Oh yeah, you better be careful out in these streets dealing with these snitching ass niggas. They come in the Justice Center, get a special visit, no paper work and back out the door."

"Thanks for the tip, Heather. I'm taking everything in and I mean everything," as he was changing CD's.

"Let me go and get this girl." Heather walked off and put a little twist in her hips hoping Smack would be looking at her strut back into the house. Her ass-cheeks were hanging out a little.

Smack was looking and he was disgusted. ***"Look at her old ass thinking she's a young girl. Her pussy probably all big and blown out where you can throw a Polish sausage in it and it won't touch the side walls."***

He just shook his head thinking to himself. He was now listening to Soldier Boy.

"Hop up out the bed take a look in the mirror and say what's up, I'm getting money."

Smack was humming along with the lyrics. Then Rainell finally came out the house with her bags in shock.

She saw Smack and started in power walk motion towards the truck with an ear to ear smile. Rainell liked Smack a lot, even though she knew he was a grown man he didn't look like it. Plus, he was live in spirit and didn't treat her like a little girl.

"Hey, Mr. Smack, this is hot. Did you just buy this?" Rainell asked him all excited.

"Yes, earlier today." He answered.

"What happened to my daddy? Was he too busy to pick me up as usual?" Rainell asked him.

"I don't know your parent's personal business; I'm just doing Mrs. Scott a favor." He told her.

He got out the truck and grabbed her bags to put them in the back of the truck. She got in and sat on the cool white leather bucket seats. The air conditioning was blowing lightly. He climbed back in the truck and got situated. "Mr. Smack, this is tight," as she looked around. She was shocked from the outside appearance and even more impress from the interior. "Thanks, Rainell."

"Mr. Smack, what you know about some Soldier Boy? You should be listening to some Ice Cube or Scarface."

"I'm not your parent's age. I'm not a 70's baby. I was born in the eighties." Smack told her.

"You ain't got no swag, Mr. Smack." said Rainell.

"Put your seat belt on, Rainell. I'm getting money, aren't I?" he pulled out of Heather's drive-way heading for his house off of Princeton Pike on Tylersville Road. Rainell was ambitious and a split image of her mother and aunt. She was beginning to fill out in all the right places. If a man didn't double look and investigate her, he would mistake her for a grown woman. She had much attitude and was curious. She'd rush into things without thought. Her opinion was all the mattered. She never really listened to her parent's advice only her aunt Heather's and Smack. She was the most willful and arbitrary young person that Smack knew. She was a bit rough when she should be firm and dogmatic where she should be flexible. Rainell started asking questions when they road pass the Tri County Mall.

"This ain't the way to my house." He drove pass the merging ramp of 1-275 that would take them to her house. "I know it's the way to my house." Smack told her.

"Why are we going to your house?" Rainell repositioned herself in her seat.

"Just be quiet and sit back, Rainell." said Smack.

She turned back straight in her seat with an attitude. Now she was hoping maybe he would make possible advancements towards her. She hoped he would be the one picking her up in all of his cars from school. Then she would be the center of attention even though school was now officially out. The new school year would be coming up. Her fantasy came and left just that quick knowing Smack was trustworthy and she seen his girlfriend before. How could she compete with a professional model? She knew even though she now had the body of a grown woman that Smack still looked at her like a little sister.

"Rainell, are you hungry?" Smack asked her because he knew a row of fast food restaurants were coming up ahead.

"Yeah, I guess I'm a little hungry." said Rainell.

"What do you want? You have Micky D's, Taco Bell, Skyline, Penn Station and Papa John's to choose from." He said.

She answered him in a low tone. "I guess Taco Bell." He passed Smith Road and McDonald's, because Taco Bell was on the right of Princeton Pike. He turned in the lot of Taco Bell heading for the drive thru. He ordered her food and pulled up to the next window to pay for the order. When he pulled out a wad of money, Rainell couldn't believe her eyes, "How much is it again?" He asked the employee.

"It's seven dollars and twenty-six cents, sir." The female employee thought Smack was around twelve years old. He handed her a twenty-dollar bill and she closed the window. She couldn't wait to tell her co-workers to come and look at this young boy driving a nice Cadillac truck. "Hey, Diamond, Shayna and Che, come look at this boy in this Cadillac truck. He's a cutie, too."

"How old is he, Teressa?" Shayna asked her.

"Girl, he has to be like twelve or thirteen. He's young...I know that much." Teressa told her.

"You're lying, Teressa." Diamond told her.

"Look for yourself." said Teressa.

When Smack looked up, all four females were standing at the drive thru window. The window opened, "Here's your change and your Mountain Dew. Your food will be up in a minute." She handed him the drink, his money and receipt.

"Thank you. Can I have some mild sauce with my order, please?"

"Sure. I'll put it in the bag with your food." Teressa told Smack. Diamond, Che and Shayna was nudging her to ask him how old he was. "Ask him, Teressa." Shayna told her.

"Excuse me, how old are you?" Teressa asked Smack. He smiled at her and then went up in his visor and grabbed his I.D. and gave it to her. She looked over the I.D. carefully and then looked back at Smack and smiled. "Girl, he's twenty-eight, damn it. I'm sorry sir, we thought you were-," He cut her off.

"Younger than my age. Don't worry; I get that all the time." She handed him back his license and his food. "Thank you, Ms. Lady and ya'll have a nice day." He told her.

"You too, sir, and come again." She smiled at him and he nodded to her and slowly pulled off. He glanced to his left over by the Kroger grocery store to see Kendall and Pepsi getting out of a Porsche. He didn't want Rainell to see her father so he distracted her.

"Rainell, can you look in my CD case and hand me that Bun-B Trill Ville CD?" She did as he asked. By the time she rose back up, he was driving back down Princeton Pike far away from her dad's view. "Her you go, Mr. Smack." She handed him the CD.

****

"Kendall, I just need to grab a few items. The steaks should be almost done by the time we get back to my place." said Keisha.

"Okay, Keisha." He looked around to see if he knew anyone that knew him and his wife. Inclined because of things like heat and humidity; such as conditions react upon the inhabitants to make people strong, active, and sexually active energetic and self-sufficient. Self-satisfaction of people who have had comparatively little to contend with in the struggle of society; made her remember the opening statements clearly, but couldn't understand her motives now that she liked him. She dug in her hormones, it was the moment she loved, but feared. She hesitated toward the propulsive forces at her first leap into the world of unexplored delight which shy could only see a narrow tunnel.   Without experience the mysterious pleasures that existed in those who break, free form their environment.   She broke free veering to the left to participate in the excitement of extraordinary pleasure.   Keisha reminded herself; it was impossible to assure anything when it came to such matters. Unconsciously she held onto him resisting abandonment as they walked around inside Kroger grocery store.   Not aware who may see them, guessing they would be unnoticed. How could they when Keisha had on tight shorts rising up in her goods, in stiletto heels and a pull up blouse.   She was looking very intoxicating as she held on to Kendall's arm for support like they were a happy couple.

CHAPTER EIGHT
SMACK'S HOUSE

Smack pulled up in his drive way that had a two-door garage. His black Q45 Infiniti was sitting in the drive way. He parked right beside it hitting the garage door opener. When the garage rose up you could see a parked hard top convertible LX 430 Mercedes Benz. They got out and walked up under the garage doors.

He pointed to the kitchen. "What channel do you want the TV on?" He asked Rainell.

"Can you put it on BET, 106 & Park is on." she replied.

"Okay, it should be on in a minute." He disappeared and Rainell went into the kitchen. Everything was stainless steel. He had a 32" TV on the wall and when it came on Rainell was in good view. She glanced over her shoulder to see Stefani lying out by the pool in her bikini getting a tan. But the sun wasn't at its highest peak being it was almost seven in the evening. Rainell could see her through the glass sliding doors. She thought that Smack should be on MTV cribs the way his house looked.

While Smack was putting away the ring he bought from Kyle, Rainell was enjoying her food while watching videos. Then Smack reappeared. "Are you okay, Rainell?" He asked her.

"I'm fine, I guess." She shrugged her shoulders.

"The remote is over there to turn up the volume." He pointed to the remote control.

"It's fine. I can hear it. I see Ms. Stefani is here." She said.

"Yeah, and I bet you she didn't do anything I asked her to do." He walked toward the glass doors and opened them. "Yo, Stef, did you feed Shatarah and Cerberus?"

She turned her head in the direction of his voice and said, "Bloody no Simmion. I told you I wasn't bloody handling that meat I say, mate."

"But you fed Bruce's punk ass, didn't you?"

"I bloody sure did. Bruce is my baby, isn't you Bruce darling," as she caressed Bruce while he sat there like a King. Smack stepped back inside the kitchen and went inside a small refrigerator.

She startled the animals in the cage. "It's okay, Cerberus and Shatarah she's not going to scare ya'll anymore, are you Rainell?"

"Scare them, they scare me. What kind of wildcats are they?"

"They are like two months old." He told her.

"Mr. Smack, ya'll have a small zoo going on around here." Said Rainell.

"Na'll I just have two dogs to protect the house in case the security system fails and I always wanted to own an exotic animal." Said Smack.

He opened the cage to pet the lions before sliding slabs of meat to them.   After he put the meat in the cage, he locked the cage back and Rainell watched them attack the meat like they hadn't eaten in days. "Do you ever feed them, Mr. Smack?" Rainell wanted know.

"Twice a day." He said.

"They act like they haven't eaten in weeks." She confessed.

"That's just their instinct to look up while they eat and to devour it." Smack said with a high pitch.

"My friend Daysha wouldn't believe what I seen today." Rainell said still looking around.

"Well since school is out maybe you can invite a few friends over and go swimming or just hang out if you like." He told her.

"For real, Mr. Smack?" said Rainell.

"Yeah, Rainell, if your parents allow you to." Smack told her.

An instant rush rushed through Rainell's body.   What lie would she tell her friends? Is this her boyfriend's house? He uncle's house? Maybe the truth.   He's my mother's client and a friend. Smack's phone rang and it was Delight calling.   He flipped open the cell phone.

"Vegas never sleep and neither do I." Smack answered his phone/

"Alright, Simmion, I know you see my number, quit playing.   I'm not one of your associates you deal with in the streets.   Where's my child?" Delight asked him.

"She's right here." He answered her.

"Well, I'm about to pull up in about ten minutes." Delight told him.

"Are you coming in?" He asked her.

"Is your outback girlfriend there?" Delight replied.

"Yes, she's out by the pool." He answered her.

"No thanks then, I'll just get Rainell and be off." Said Delight.

"Just call me when you pull in the drive way." Smack told her.

"Okay baby, oops, I mean Smack." Delight smiled saying that.

"Whatever, you meant it." He said.

"Bye boy," as she hung up the phone knowing her feelings were growing for him and she couldn't ignore them. How long could she pretend?

****

"Hey big daddy, pull over. You want some of this?" She said.

A Chrysler 300 slowly stopped and the barely clothed autumn complexion female walked towards the car and got in. "Fifty for a blow job and a hundred for both." The female told the trick.

"I just want a blow job, Ms." He responded.

"That will be fifty dollars, grandpa. You can pull over there," as she pointed in the direction of the alley. She got the elderly man off in minutes from her superb mouth action. She had been practicing it over and over to make it perfect.

She was a 5'6" well-built woman with green eyes. Even though she wore a wig, make-up and heels to keep her identity unknown, she was a dime who was trying to hustle sex like everyone else on Dunlap and McMicken. She was working by the Dunlap Park. It was early, but she knew the drag queens would surface and run the real women away after midnight, because that's when they came out to play.

It was 8 o'clock and about to get dark and she had already cleared over five hundred dollars in an hours' time. All the local business men came through Dunlap to fulfill their fantasy before going home to their boring wives and girlfriends. The tricks of the century pay to play with no hassle. No talking on the phone, no stalking, the next meeting is when they pulled up again ready to play.

Being it was Friday, and like always, her money showed up. He pulled up in a 600 Benz. She knew him from the previous meetings. She got in the car.

"Can you go with me?" He looked around as he asked her.

"Do you want me too?" She asked him. Then he held her face. She reached for his hands at her cheeks and threatens her fingers with his. It was a desperate feeling.

"Yes, please, go with me." In some respect, there was something wonderfully comforting, something normal about going with this trick.

Was it the money or just his security? Her eyes went to his, subliminally, she realized he was worried about her. He didn't want her selling her body and she did feel better, at least in some respect. Her eyelashes fluttered and slowly rose. His heart began to beat again. "Miesha." She attempted to smile at him saying her name, but it came across barely. "Well, are we going? Don't just sit there, Judge Helmet."

"Shhh, save your energy." He told her.

"But Judge...the police." She whispered.

"Shhh, be quiet, Miesha. I'm going."

*******,

"Smack, I'm outside and I see you done brought this bitch a new truck." Said Delight.

"Please, that's my new toy. She can't even drive over here remember they drive on the right side and the steering wheel is on the left here. They go right to left not left to right."

"It's cute then since it's yours."

"You are so evil Delight. Leave Kendall and I'll kick her ass out today like Biggie did Faith." He laughed through the receiver.

"You love that funny talking skinny white heifer." She said.

"I love you more, oops, I mean I'm falling for you." He said.

"That's not an oops, you mean it Smack." Said Delight.

"Hey girl, how you doing, my name is Simmion, last name Boyd. I was wondering, can I take you out-." She cut him off. "Quit playing Charlie Wilson and bring Rainell out."

She was laughing through the receiver. Delight had only been to his house once to receive some money for her legal advice. She knew it was probably laid out on the inside from looking at his manicured lawn. He was neat and much welled groomed. She also liked the fact that he wasn't in suits twenty-four seven. She knew if the occasion presented him to dress down, he would be a handsome guy in his attire.   All the top line designers and his shoes were custom hand made from reptiles.

The garage door opened and Delight stepped out of her Range Rover shaking her clinging suit pants from her skin.   She saw the hard-top convertible Benz she was so in love with.   He walked out and Rainell came from behind him. "Hey mommy, you are here."

Rainell hugged her mother. "Where are your bags, Rainell? I know you have some." Delight asked her.

"Mr. Smack is getting them out of his new truck." Smack hit the alarm to open the doors of his SUV. He grabbed Rainell's bags and loaded them into the Range Rover and Delight stared at him the whole time.   Rainell walked up to him and smiled. "Bye, Mr. Smack.   Don't forget what you told me about my friends."

"I won't as long as your parents say that it's okay." He told her and Delight was all ears.

"About her having a few friends over my house to go swimming for the summer."

"Uhn huh, we'll see." As she looked at Rainell hard.

"Mommy, Mr. Smack has African lions and Ms. Stefani has a dragon lizard looking thing." Rainell tried to get a few brownie points.

"Oh, they do? I see you had my baby at a petting zoo." Delight looked at Smack.

"Do you want to see," as she cut him off. "I don't want to see Nevada and Goliath; I already saw them before." She put her hands on her hips.

"Those are the dogs, Delight. Rainell was speaking on Cerberus and Shatarah, real African lions." He told Delight.

"No thanks.   Maybe some other time and plus I don't want to see the white Hillary Banks." Delight said.

"You are jealous of some shit that doesn't even exist." Smack told her and Rainell was now getting in her mother's truck.   Soldier Boys song, "Kiss me through the phone" was playing on the radio.

"Please Smack, it does exist, it's in there," as she pointed in the direction of the house to where Stefani was.

It's not in here though." As he pointed to his heart.

"We'll see, time will tell, Smack. You don't want me for real. I'm just something to do for the moment." Delight told him.

"Whatever! I bought you something special today and I know you'll like it." said Smack.

"Where is it? Is that it?" She pointed to the Cadillac truck.

"When the time is right, Ms. Delight Heath," as he lifted his eyebrow like Hakeem on 'Coming to America'. He said her name using her maiden title.

"You know Smack; you watch too many movies and listen to a lot of music. Quit playing all the time." She looked at him with a look of concern.

"I'm serious, when the time is right, I'll give it to you."

"Well, let me get her home. Will I see you tomorrow? I'm supposed to take her to the movies. If her dad cancels, would you like to go?"

"Sure, just call me, baby."

"Smack, Rainell might hear you." said Delight.

"She's got the music blasting. Can't you hear it?" He said.

"Yeah, I hear it. You know that I miss you. I want to get with you. That's the issue, you know I want to kiss yah, but I can't, so just kiss me thru the phone." She was saying the lyrics from Soldier Boy's song directly to Smack. "I'm a little hip, Smack. Just call me later or I'll call you." She smiled at him and blew him a kiss. He watched her thickness climb into the Range Rover. As she pulled off, he watched them all the while Stefani watched from the front window.

****

Miesha Jones was a Daycare Provider by day and a streetwalker by night. She was now the famous Judge Phil Helmet's playmate. He met her by giving her a break for hustling sex on the streets about nine months ago. In return, he wanted to test her skills. He was attracted to her beauty and her body. She was twenty-seven, single and living in Walnut Hills on St. James across from the Nassau Park. Eden Park, Playhouse in the Park, and Mt. Adams was like five minutes away from her home. Judge Helmet lived in the high-class part of Mt. Adams. He saw her again and again while he was jogging through Eden Park. He reminded her of what he did for her and she told him to pick her up from work.

He picked her up one evening on McMicken and they have been getting together ever since. Judge Helmet was a married man in his early sixties.

They were now over in Erlanger, Kentucky at the Comfort Inn. He stood in his boxer briefs gazing out the window. You could see his gray hairs standing on his chest. She laid naked across the bed waiting for an answer to the question she previously asked. She asked him again. "Judge, why-?" He cut in.

"Miesha, you don't understand. I won't even ask you to understand." He said to her.

"Make me understand." She said in a demanding voice.

"When I..." He stopped as if it were painful to say. "When I stopped loving my wife, I didn't think I would ever love again. Then you came into my life and made me feel alive again. Damn, Miesha, I love you so much." He confessed.

Her eyes tear under the bitter sweet irony of the words he spoke. Unknowingly, Miesha was feeling the same for Judge Helmet. "So, what are you going to do about it Judge?" Being with his wife now, he was more miserable that he'd ever been in his life.

"I have no guarantees or warrantee's concerning us being together, as much as I would like to, I can't promise you anything." His eyes found hers. They were hazy; red stained the ivory in them. Miesha looked deeply into his eyes searching for sincerity. She found it. She thought back to the moment she first saw him in the courtroom, then him jogging. "Yes, I understand that if we do fall in love, you just might not fulfill any obligations because of your job."

"You're having sex with every Tom, Dick and Harry, for crying out loud, Miesha." The Judge told her.

"Judge, get to know me first outside of this world. It's a fucking recession out here. Do you really want to know my real job, for crying out loud?"

"Isn't it being a prostitute?"

"I don't know such a word, Judge, but no! I'm a fucking Daycare Provider. I watch kids for a living. Most of my clients are losing their jobs. The fucking economy is failing, you know. It's a democracy being you only punish the has and the has nots .

These crooked ass cops, like Allen Taylor and Will Edmond need to be dealt with, because they are making my life a living hell."

"Are you willing to stop having sex as a side show for money, Miesha?" He asked her.

"Are you willing to help me out Judge?" She said.

"If you're willing to call McMicken quits, yes, I'm willing to help you." He said.

"Then it's a done deal, but you're still paying me today for this session your Honorable Judge." she told him.

They both gave each other a smile of gratitude. She knew Phil Helmet was open, but how long would that be? DJ Quick couldn't have come out with a better song. 'Sweet Black Pussy.' She knew she wasn't going to stop getting her money, so she decided to make her a few business cards and be on call.

CHAPTER NINE
DELIGHT AND KENDALL

They dined a few times with friends and had been to the movies more than once. There were also events to which Delight had gone alone.

She had imagined it not so and could not. Delight never lived anyone else except her parent's in her childhood. To her, home was a solitary place, a retreat, but also isolation. The house was hers and she had a mistress. The anger was back in her face.

"What you mean Kendall; you don't want to attend the movies with us?" Delight's voice hung in mid-air it was so loud.

"I'm going out with the fellas tonight." said Kendall.

"You're choosing them over your family?" Delight asked him.

"No, we planned this weeks ago, Delight. I just forgot."

"Where Kendall, Sneeky Peaks or Metropolis?" she asked him.

"Metropolis, if you really want to know." He said.

"To see a bunch of drunken bitches, ride a mechanical bull with no shirts on. Have you even bothered to notice your daughter lately?" Delight began to get tears in her eyes.

"Yeah, I saw her this morning watching TV in the living room."

"Kendall, she has titties and ass now. She's probably trying to experience with sex. Don't you think it's time for you to have another talk with her? Oh, I forgot I had the first one."

Delight was steaming mad because she was sweating on the tip of her nose.

"Well, have the second one too." He told her.

"You just don't care, do you?" She had an attitude.

"Delight, I care, but why argue? It's not going anywhere because I'm not changing my mind, I'm going."

"Kendall, I think we should do more things with her since she's the only child to keep her busy. All of her cousins are too old for her to be hanging out with."

"Okay, but not tonight." He walked out of their bedroom leaving Delight standing there in tears. "Kendall, Kendall, I wasn't finished talking to you." Delight yelled down the hall as he kept going, not responding. "Well, fuck him. I know someone who would love to go out with me and my baby." She mumbled to herself.

Rainell was ease dropping on her parent's conversation. She felt that her parent's marriage was going in another direction. She felt like her parent's spent most of their time at work anyway. She heard her mother coming to her room and she ran and jumped on her bed pretending like she was reading a magazine. Her mother knocked on her door with a light tap. "Come in, it's open," as Rainell looked up at the door. Her mom came in and she could see that she'd been crying. "Hey baby girl, what are you doing?" Delight closed the door behind her. "Nothing, just looking through this magazine. Why, what's wrong, mom?"

"It's nothing that your mother can't handle. So, what movie do you want to see tonight?"

"I don't know. I take it that daddy's not going with us?"

"No, he doesn't feel good, Rainell." Delight told her daughter.

"Mom, stop making excuses for him. I heard the whole conversation from the beginning to end. It's okay. We don't have to go. We can just stay here." said Rainell.

"Rainell, are you sure honey?"

Yes, mom, because it's supposed to be family night and we are not much of a family without daddy."

Delight saw the hurt on her daughters face and she came up with her plan B.

"Forget that, Rainell. I have a better idea. You call your friend, Daysha and I'll see if Mr. Smack wants to go with us."

Rainell's frown turned into a smile. "Are you serious, mom?"

"Yes. I'm gonna go and call him now. We can go to Apple Bee's before the movies. If Mr. Smack don't tag along it will be just us ladies."

"I hope he does go. Sometimes I wish he was my dad."

Delight hugged her daughter and shed a tear for the both. "I know baby, I know."

Delight knew that Kendall was losing both important women in his life, his daughter and his wife.

****

Earlier that same day, Kyle and Smack were running around the city conducting Smack's business.

"Kyle, you drive like an old woman. Turn on Grand Avenue and go up the hill." said Smack.

"Damn brah, I come all the way out to Russia to get your ass and then drive all the way back in the city so you can take my cat's some of that bullshit you're dealing. Now I'm going up in hot ass Price Hill. I'm going to jail fucking with you...I know it."

"Quit crying like a little bitch. I gave you two racks, so drive Benson and quit nagging." He told Kyle.

"Fuck you, Smack." said Kyle.

They drove all the way up Grand Avenue across Warsaw. Smack was going to pick up his old school. He had a 1965 drop Chevy Impala with the guts blown out and the engine was getting redone in chrome. "Pull over right here, Kyle." When Kyle puller over he saw racing car parts in the yard, engine crank, a wrecker and tires everywhere.

"Who lives in this dump?" Kyle asked him.

"My mechanic, Nathan and his buddy Randy. They drive stock cars." Smack explained to him.

"It looks like a meth lab is going on over here. Is your truck over here, because I'm not with taking you back to Russia?"

"No, my truck is not over here. Just come on, crying ass nigga. If you were going on a heist, you would be all for it. You petty as thief, but you still my guy hands down." said Smack.

"That's my thang Smack and I'm not G-Money. I don't do the flunky thang." Kyle said.

"You hurt my feelings now tell me you sorry." Smack told him.

"Alright DMX from Belly, fake ass Tommy Buns, I'm sorry my nigga. But you're always quoting a line from a fucking movie Smack." Kyle said with a grin.

They reached the garage and Smack knocked on it. The door slid up manually half way. Kyle and Smack was staring at his toy, a 1965 Chevy Impala. The car matched the color of the Cadillac truck. Light blue, white bucket seats with blue rain drops designed in the seats. A wood grain steering wheel, TV monitors on the doors and on the lower back part of the two front seats. It had 22" white and chrome rims. The top was white. Nathan came from around the front of the car.

"Yo, Nate. What's up, Randy? Are you all finished with my baby, because you said today?" Smack asked his mechanics.

"She's all yours Smack. A two-month job of rebuilding the engine and she runs like a champion. I even washed her for you. I put some lifters on the back extension so the wheels wouldn't rub. I guess the rim shop forgot to. But she's ready to go."

Nathan was standing there with his oily arms crossed.

"Let me see the engine, Nate." Smack told him.

"Come on." Smack and Kyle followed Nathan around to the front of the car.

"See, look at it, brand new isn't she pretty. Everything is working on all cylinders." Nathan told Smack.

"Damn, yo shit is tight Smack; it looks like one of those cars in a car book." Kyle was amazed at the chrome engine.

"Okay Nate, how much do I still owe you?" Smack asked him.

"Like twenty-five hundred more, but I told you to bring me an ounce of that blow and just give me a thousand in cash. That will make us even. You got it?" Nathan asked him.

"Nate, I got you, man." Smack gave him a grin.

////

Delight sat on her daughter's bed trying to call Smack again after trying twice. He was now riding down Vine Street pass Lady Ray's house in Avondale going towards Mitchell Avenue. He had missed her previous calls. Smack blew his horn at Lady Ray, her sister Chandra and her daughter Na-Na, who's softball team he helped sponsor. They waved at him. His music was so loud and clear that you could hear Young Jeezy blocks away.

Good thing he had put his phone on vibrate now and he could catch her call. His phone started vibrating and he answered the phone. Delight thought he was at a concert from the music being so loud. "Hello-hello." He screamed through the receiver.

"Smack, turn the music down and you could hear me." She screamed back through her end. Then she could hear the music slowly dying down. "Hello, who dis?" He asked.

"Smack, it's Delight,"

"Hey, what's up, future wifey." He laughed with the remark.

"Okay, future wifey. Anyway, where are you?" She asked him.

"I'm riding down Vine Street about to get on the highway heading home." He told her.

"Do you still want to attend the movies with Rainell and I?"

"I don't care, Delight." He said.

"It's seven-thirty. Meet me at Heather's house in a half an hour or do you have to go home and change?" said Delight.

"I'm good, but don't have me waiting because you know Heather be tripping." He said.

"I won't baby. We are about to leave out right now." She said.

"Okay, kiss me through the phone." He told her.

"Mmmmm-mm, did you get it baby?" she asked him.

"Yes, Delight, I got it. I'll see you in a minute," as they hung up from each other.

Delight smiled and had a rush of excitement running through her body from hearing his voice. She couldn't wait to see him. She was now moist and wanting his touch. Rainell came back into her room from finishing her hair. "So, what did he say, mom?"

Rainell had her hands on her hips. "He's going with us." Delight smiled at her daughter.

Rainell smiled back and said, "Yes!"

"Where's your dad?" Her mom asked her.

"He's downstairs watching TV." said Rainell.

"Good. Are you ready? Did you call Daysha?" Delight asked her.

"Yes mama, to both of your questions."

"Well call Daysha back when we get in the truck and tell her to walk over your aunt Heather's. Let me grab my purse and we're out." Delight told her.

When they reached downstairs Delight walked past Kendall and didn't say a word.

"You don't have to wait up for me, Delight." Kendall yelled out to her.

"You don't have to wait up for me either." She yelled back at him.

Rainell walked past him. "Bye, daddy."

"See you later, baby. You both have a good time," he didn't look up at his daughter. When they got in the truck Delight put in her Fantasia CD and they hit the road. She did what her heart told her to do and that was to live on the edge. Smack decided to park on Heather's street, but down away from her house. He didn't want Heather to be sweating him. He saw Delight pull her truck into her sister's drive way.

It was five after eight. ***"Where are you, Smack?"*** She thought to herself. She then dialed his cell phone and he answered on the first ring. "Where are you, Smack?"

"I'm right behind you look down the street." He waved his hand, because he still had the top down on the car. "Boy what you done bought now?" Her eyes were glued to the Impala.

"I been had this it was just in the shop getting work done." He said.

"Okay, c'mon you are riding with us." she demanded.

"Na'll ya'll are riding with me. I'm not leaving my car in Lincoln Heights. That's a no-no. So ya'll c'mon." he told her.

"Okay, Rainell go and get Daysha. We are riding with Mr. Smack." Delight had hung up with him. "Where's Mr. Smack, mama? I don't see him?" Rainell was looking around.

"He's sitting down the street in that light blue car." said Delight.

"Oh," as Rainell got out the truck to go get her friend out of her aunt's house. Delight pulled out of her sister's driveway and parked on the street so she wouldn't be blocking her sister in. Smack pulled up so she could get in the car with him. He was watching Beyoncé on DVD when she got in the car. "This is cute, but why the tear drops?" She asked him.

"Those are rain drop Delight, because I can make it rain for months." said Smack.

"Okay, Lil Wayne and Fat Joe. This thing doesn't do like those cars in LA, does it? Delight asked him.

"No. I'm not that type of guy. I prefer to bounce on other shit."

"Smack, this looks like the Cadillac truck." said Delight.

"Exactly. Also, my boat." smack told her.

"Simmion, what boat?" She looked at him like he was lying.

"The one I have in storage in Fairfield." He said.

"Damn, you are the man. Well give me a kiss before the girls get out here." She asked him.

He reached over and gently touched her lips making a connection.

"I've been missing you. We're going to have to find a way for us to be alone. I need you inside me, I'm very emotional right now." Delight explained to him.

He was confused from her statement, **'very emotional and not horny'.**

Rainell and Daysha finally came out to the car and Rainell was telling her about Mr. Smack. They got in and Rainell told him, "Mr. Smack, this looks just like your truck."

"Same thing I said," her mom added.

"What up, Rainell?" Mr. Smack threw his hands up. They saw the two 13-inch monitors that were positioned on the back of the driver's and passenger's seats. Rainell tapped Daysha, while pointing at the monitors that played a Beyoncé video.

"We're going to Applebee's on Springfield Pike and Route 4 in Springdale – whatever they call it across from Perkin's that's ducked off by that little motel," said Delight.

"I know where it is," said Smack.

"I forgot who I was riding with." Delight retorted.

"What that supposed to mean, Delight?" said Smack staring at her intensely.

"Nothing." said Delight waving him off.

Smack pulled off and turned up Beyoncé's "Unplugged." He didn't care if he got the noise pollution ticket, because he was truly with the lady he wanted in his life. His father always told him to find a woman with a career. He knew he wasn't dreaming and she was "rockin' that thang" like right. He saw the ease in her eyes, and glimpsed how fragile she was under a mask of courage. He had never been responsible for other people, for kids who trusted and who were so vulnerable trusted him. At least as far as he knew he had not.

Delight glanced at him then to her daughter in the backseat; she was sage and happy and that's all that really mattered to Delight. She imagined them as a family and how it would be. Would he drastically change like Kendall did? She took in a deep breath. Her neck and shoulder muscles tightened, pulling her *Baby Phat* t-shirt to where you could see each stitch in the seams. She released a sigh out of the car. The wind blew her hair. *Was this what Simmion Boyd wanted? Had he become suffocated by his* own discretions? Had his soul yearned for something mature, more capable-something that challenged the mind and disturbed the heart? Would he be willing to sacrifice safety and his own means of living to protect the lives of three innocent people? Did he grow to loathe being known in different parts of the country and they relied on his movement.

Delight knew Smack wouldn't be the first man to run away from the reality of love and its responsibilities. Instead the illusion and excitement of lust and what might seem like free will only later to realize it was just loneliness.

Smack assumed that Delight thought his only interest in her was lustful, but he knew it was more than that. Delight made him feel unique. She made him feel coveted and that they needed each other with unparalleled passion.

They left Applebee's around 10:10 pm. The Springdale Cinemas was just a few lights north up the road from Applebee's. Smack parked directly in front of the Showcase, flaunting and "raising the roof" on his custom Impala. The alarm chirped twice locking the doors, as he and his companions made their way inside.

"What ya'll want to see?" Delight said to the girls.

"Umm...Roscoe Jenkins," the girls replied.

"That starts at ten-thirty," said Delight eyeing the movie listings on the digital screen. "What you want to see Smack? Cause I don't want to see Roscoe Jenkins. I want to see The Bug myself."

"The Bug? What time does that start?" said Smack.

"It starts at ten-thirty-five," said Delight. She looked at Rainell and Daysha like she didn't trust them being alone in the movie, seeing that they were gawking at some boys their age. "Rainell we are going to see The Bug, and ya'll can go see Roscoe Jenkins by ya'll selves."

"Okay, we'll meet ya'll out here when it's over." Said Rainell and Daysha.

"Let me get ya'll tickets," said Delight. Leaving the girls alone made her feel suspect. She and Smack walked up to the ticket counter.

"I would like to purchase two tickets for the ten-thirty show of Roscoe Jenkins please," said Delight reaching into her pocketbook.

"That will be nineteen dollars, ma'am," said the cashier.
Smack paid the bill unsuspected, "Here my man," and handed the cashier a crisp twenty-dollar bill.
"Here you go, sir," as he gave Smack the tickets and a dollar change.
"Smack, I could've paid for the tickets." Delight told him.
"Chill out Delight." He told her and she looked at him like what?
"Rainell and Daysha, here are your tickets and twenty dollars for snacks." Delight gave them their tickets and was eyeballing Rainell. "Out here in the front when the movie is over. Do you hear me, Rainell?" Delight had a disturbed look on her face.
Rainell looked up at her and said, "Yes, ma'am." Then Rainell and Daysha walked off.
Delight turned and ordered their movie tickets. "Excuse me I would like two more tickets for ten-thirty-five showing of The Bug please."
Smack had other plans that Delight wasn't aware of. "Yo, my man, isn't that same movie showing in the Directory Hall?"
"Yes, but it costs a little more." The employee answered Smack.
"Has anyone bought any tickets for the Directory hall showing of this movie yet?" Smack asked him.
Smack was asking and Delight was listening looking at him.
"No sir, not yet." The employee was confident.
"Well I would like to buy all the tickets for the 10:35 pm showing in the Directory Hall." Delight looked at him wide eyed, "Smack, what are you doing?"
"Just chill Delight, I'm buying us tickets for the movie." He smiled at her.
She looked at the employee serving them and shrugged her shoulders.
"Sir, that would be $2000.00, if you are serious about buying out the show." The cashier told him.
He went in his pocket and counted out the money with ease.
"Here you go my, man." He handed him the bills and the guy recounted the money.
He started pushing up tickets for Smack. "Just give me two and you can trash the rest." He handed Smack two tickets. "So, it's officially sold out right?" Smack asked him.

"Yes sir, no one else can enter the show."

"I just want for the wifey and I to watch the movie where we'll be able to hear it." Smack winked at the employee. The employee looked over at Delight's hand and saw her wedding ring. They started walking towards the concession stand and Delight looked at him and shook her head. "Boy, you are crazy, wasting two grand like that."

"Delight, nothing is a waste for something that's worth more than money can buy. I'll cherish this moment for the rest of my life." Smack told her.

Those words made her feel special.   It was written all over his face that he was up to something and she knew it. After he purchased a super-sized soft drink and two straws, they walked up to the female who was taking tickets so they could enter the theater. Then they had to pass an usher who was patrolling the theater. Smack walked over to him and whispered in his ear handing him a bill with Ben Franklin's face on it. Smack then escorted Delight into the Directory Hall. "What did you tell him?" Delight asked him. "Nothing, but not to bother us." They continued to walk up the ramp into the theater. "Let's sit in the center Delight." Smack suggested and she led the way. They took their seats right in the center of the seating section. The Directory Hall was more relaxing with bigger cushion seats and head rest.

Previews of other coming attractions were playing on the screen when they finally got comfortable in their seats. Smack didn't waste any more time.

"Delight, remember when you got in the car at Heather's and you told me you needed me inside you, because you were very emotional? Well now is the perfect opportunity, we are all alone."

"Smack, in the movies. I was talking about a quiet place like a hotel." She stalked his eyes.

"Hey, it's quiet in here. We did the restaurant and that was courageous."

"Please don't remind me. I knew you were up to something. Boy, you just don't quit, do you?" She was shaking her head touching his hand. She knew she wanted him and no matter what the degree was, she had to have him.

"Live a little, Delight. You only live once in the flesh." She thought to herself. She pretended to consider his suggestion for a moment, desperately searching for a plausible reason not to go through with it. "I'm sure this will not be a strike against me. I'm not that type of girl."

"Quit tripping, Delight and give me a kiss." He reached over and entwined his lips with hers. Without breaking contact of their lips, Delight reached down and unsnapped his shorts. Passion pounded through her as she cupped his tribal piece in her hand. The heat coming from his manhood was intoxicating. Freeing her mouth from his, she went down on him giving him pleasure. He tried to feel her breast as she slurped him repeatedly, over and over. He removed his shirt and became stiff while she came up for air. He started helping her remove her clothes. She was naked and so was he. He then laid her back in the cushion seat and started eating her passage in an awkward position. The feel of her body, taste of her juices was overwhelming to him. She couldn't control her shrieks of spasms as her body weakened. She was soaring in a million pieces as he pushed his tongue deeper inside her. She grabbed his head while she had an orgasm. Her moans and grunts were silent, but powerful not forgetting she was in a public place. The ambiance reminded her of the scene on the movie, 'New Jack City' when G-Money was having sex with the female in front of the movie projector.

Her body slowed down from the panting emotions and Smack wiped his face standing her up backwards so she could ride him in that position. She eased down on his tribal piece and it didn't do in. he pushed and then he pushed again further, only to pull out. He was teasing her, but she wasn't going to allow him to do that. "Put it in me now." She demanded him. He pushed it insider her and was up in her.

It was an act of raw possession. She held the sides of the seat for balance as she bounced herself up and down on his manhood.

Her juices began to flow. Her insides were warm with passion. He gripped her hips for steadiness as he thrust every pump upward inside her passage. A lot of heavy breathing was being conducted by the both.

"Get it baby, hit this ass Smack, it's yours baby, get this pussy."

Delight demanded him in a rough, but sexy voice and this was the first time she'd talked dirty to him while they were having sex. He joined in. "Is it mine, baby, is it?" He asked.

"Oh yes, baby, this pussy is all yours," she whispered to him.

"Oh shit, Delight, I'm about to cum." He told her as his body tightened.

Beads of sweat trickled down his face to his chest.

"Me too baby, make sure you pull it out, Smack. Oh shit, I'm cumming, I'm cumming, I'm cumming." She screamed out loud. She vibrated on his tribal piece. Her excitement made him bust also. "Oh, my shit is – damn, I'm cumming, oh shit," as he grabbed her tighter by the waist. She turned her head around and looked at him with a frantic look on her face. He didn't pull out and she knew eventually it would happen, she would get pregnant. How would she explain her conceiving to her husband and he hadn't touched her in months?

"Smack, you know you should've pulled out. You're going to be satisfied until you knock me up."

He just pulled her closer to his damp skin from the sweat he managed to break while they were having sex. She lied back against his chest while he held her cozy and snug. They watched the rest of the movie of what they didn't miss. The sex was in the air, fresh intimacy. Her juices were clammed between his thighs and ran between his ass crack getting the seat wet. Her own juices had traveled down her leg leaving a stain. Towards the end of the movie they started getting dressed. Smack smelled like her sex, but he didn't care. He knew Stefani didn't check him like his last girlfriend did after being out all day. It was fifteen after twelve when they walked out the Directory Hall. The both went to the restroom and returned to one another. They were hugged up like true lovers. Delight had her head leaned against his arm holding it for security.

She saw Rainell and Daysha talking to a couple of boys their age. She instantly became insecure. "I know she done lost her damn mind. I know them little boys only want one thing." She lifted her head from Smack's arm to see her daughter better.

"Chill out, Delight, don't embarrass her, I got dis okay."

She calmed down and continued to rest her head on his arm. "Okay, Simmion, you da man, you da man." She let him know calmly.

They were approaching them and Rainell looked up to see her mom on Smack's arm and she smiled. "Don't be smiling little heifer." Delight mumble to herself.

"Hey, Rainell, who is this young fella trying to talk to my daughter?" Rainell smiled even harder from hearing Smack acknowledging her as his daughter. Even though she was probably being mannish, little girls love that sense of protection and security from their dad.

"Oh, not me, sir. I'm not trying to talk to your daughter. We were just keeping them company until her parent's came, that all I swear." One of the boys told Smack.

Smack looked as young as they did, but his swag presented him to be bigger than life.

"Okay, my guy, but if you were trying to get to know my daughter, she's not allowed to have phone calls after eleven and I will check you out thoroughly. What school do you attend?" Smack was curious.

"I go to Colerain, sir." The little boy answered and was terrified. Rainell and Daysha were giggling while Smack drilled him.

"You play any sports?" Smack went further.

"I play football and run track for the school, sir." The same boy answered him.

"What about you over there?" Smack asked the other boy. The boy pointed to himself wanting to know if Smack was talking to him. "Yeah you. You look sneaky."

"Umm, I play ball too, sir," said the other boy.

"What grade are ya'll in?" Smack asked them.

"I'll be a sophomore this coming school year." The first boy answered him.

"Me too." The other boy quickly answered.

"What are ya'll names?" Smack asked them.

"My name is Tyree Terry, sir." That was the first boy answer.

"And my name is Kris Bowen."

"Tyree, what are your grades like in school? Because my daughter can't be going out with a dummy." Smack smiled at him.

"Oh sir, I'm a 'B' student with a 3.0 grade average."

"Okay, Mr. Tyree and Kris, ya'll finish talking to them so we can go, you know exchange digits or whatever ya'll do."

"Yes, sir," as the both answered together.

Smack and Delight walked towards the entrance of the Showcase. Smack turned around and winked at Rainell and she smiled at him. She knew her real dad would've just told her to separate herself so they could leave. Her mom wouldn't have allowed her to be talking to the boy. "Since you are taking over the job as daddy, you need to have the sex talk with her, since her real daddy doesn't want that responsibility and challenge."

Delight rubbed his arm gently. "No problem, I can do that. As a matter of fact, when Stefani leaves for her trip to Cape Cod, I'll let Rainell and a few of her friends come over to the house. You know have a little cook out and maybe let them sleep over and then we can have that father and daughter talk."

"Smack, you know she told me earlier she wished that you were her dad. I cried because I kind of wished it too. Kendall's going to lose her and it won't fall back on me."

"He'll come around, I guess, but if he doesn't, I'll step in and do what I can Delight to be a father figure, okay?"

She looked up into his eyes and replied, "Thank you, Smack, but if you keep cumming inside of me you'll have to be that father figure for your own child." She gave him a pleasant and warm smile.

Rainell and Daysha walked up all cheesy looking with bright smiles.

"Hey mom and Mr. Smack, we are ready to go." said Rainell.

"Let's go then." Said Smack and he led the way.

Smack didn't let the top back down because it was a bit chilly out. He started the car up and put 'Guys' CD in the CD player. It sounded like a live performance. Rainell burst out and said, "It smells funny in here.   What's that smell, Mr. Smack?"

Delight and Smack looked at each other, because they knew it was them smelling like sex. "Here spray this coconut nut air-freshener." Smack gave it to Rainell.
Daysha knew what the smell was because she was sexually active.

CHAPTER TEN
ANTWAN KLEIN

"Tell me just one more thing. How do you manage to outsmart the authorities, Mr. Antwan Klein?" the frail looking man asked him.

"I just do Mr. Elliot Thrasher. Think of it as me against the world." Antwan told him.

"And you find that most sufficient, Mr. Klein?"

"For the ordinary wear and tear of daily life. It's all the same to me. I'm bound to admit there have been various occasions in my work, occasions which I blink to think of, where all was almost lost." said Antwan.

After a stiff drink and brunch, Antwan Klein showed Elliot Thrasher to his study. It sat behind the doors on the other side of the restaurant. Lenhardt's was the restaurant they were in which Antwan Klein owned in Cincinnati. It was located by the University campus in Clifton on McMillan Street.

"I have some very valuable guns here," he told Elliot Thrasher, adding, "Some very powerful and some amusing too."

"I see, Mr. Klein. You also have a very tasteful library." Elliot glanced at a few books he had on the shelf. 'A Girls Torture Chamber, Imprisoned at A Girls School and The Girls with The Golden Whip'.

"Indeed, one takes pleasure in reading, Mr. Thrasher. There's no principle if one is an absolute idiot."

"Well, you have a good sexual taste, I'd say, for women."

"Mr. Thrasher, did you ever watch Benny Hill when you were younger?" Antwan asked him.

"Yes, I must say I did. Why do you ask, Mr. Klein?"

"My grandmother was one of the beautiful women who appeared on every episode. So, I appreciate a good sense of quality in everything I do."

"Likewise, Mr. Klein. Can I see the weapons now?" He asked.

"Indeed Elliot, you don't mind me calling you Elliot?"

"I don't mind at all." Elliot told him.

Antwan opened a secret cabinet exposing a fine arsenal of artillery. Elliot Thrasher saw an Ak-47 7.62 Russian assault rifles that held a 75 round drum, G-3 7.62 German assault rifles that took 30 round box magazines,   a Heckler & Koch German MP-5 that took 30 round .9mm shells, a German Walther .9mm pistols, Swiss Sig Sauer .40   cal. German Heckler & Koch USP .45 and Italian Beretta .40 cal.

"You have quite an impressive stock, Mr. Klein. How many can I have delivered to me?"

"However, many you desire, Elliott."

"Let me get this again, Mr. Klein. Your mother is from Nigeria and your father is full blooded German?"

"Yes, Elliott, why are you uncertain?"

"No, it's just your dialect is simple.   It is like an American, Mr. Klein." said Elliot.

"Oh, I see. I can change it when needed. I speak four languages besides German. But I would like to bring this drug to the U.S. soil, first stop, Ohio. Like Cincinnati, Cleveland, Columbus, Youngstown, Dayton, Toledo, Lima, Springfield, Xenia etc...." said Antwan.

"Why, Ohio first, Mr. Klein?" Elliot asked him.

"Because most drugs hit places that have ports first, cities like LA, Miami and New York. I want to start small and then expand to bigger cities. I don't want America to get burned out so quickly." Antwan explained.

"What is this new drug called?" He asked him.

"Black Ice! It is made up of heroin, cocaine, hash and speed in a tiny pink capsule. They are using the drug heavy in the clubs overseas. They pay a lot of cash for its use. I say one capsule cost a hundred and fifty American dollars. I can manufacture the drug overseas and be a billionaire in no time." said Antwan.

"So, what's stopping you, Mr. Klein?" Elliot asked him.

"I need your diplomatic hand, for me to shallow behind a political figure here so I'll be out of the picture. With inquisitiveness, I'd say you're the man who can make it happen," as Antwan gazed beyond his soul reaching out to his fear. "Then I'll be able to place any type of weapon in your hands, Mayor Elliot Thrasher." Antwan told him.

"What about the other drugs that surround this area?" Elliot was curious.

"I mean, you have your normal crack and cocaine pushers, your heroin pushers and pill pushers. I'll attack the hustlers or should I say dealers who are controlling most of the distribution around here." Antwan paused afterwards, but didn't say anything.

"Why he's Simmion Boyd, also known as, Smack. My girlfriend Jasmine Finch is the head prosecutor in this region who's been trying to take him down. He relocated from Dayton down here and she's been following him." Elliot told him.

"I don't wish to take him down or out the picture at least not yet, I would like to introduce him to the wild side of this new drug first. I would like to make him a business partner."

"He has two strong alliances with the Diamond Cut and he just linked with the Belvy Boyz." Elliot told him.

"Are they like terrorist groups?" Antwan rubbed his hands asking him the question.

"Indeed, by the way of the streets. I don't know about professional hit men, but they get the job done. He has a girlfriend, Stefani Blake, the Australian super model who's hot now." Elliot said with convincing words.

"Why yes Stef-Stef. I thought I saw her in the State and all of the places she's in Cincinnati." He paused and added.

"She's a tropical type of female, I would've pictured in LA or Miami. So, the Herr has him a model for a girlfriend. He must be powerful like Russell Simmons?" Antwan knew.

"I must say Mr. Klein the blacks are taking over, but in no offense to you sir."

"Indeed, we are getting back what was rightfully ours in some sort of way. Like my mother's culture when the women dance freely butt naked for the men in the tribe, for a spiritual warfare or to ward off evil. The white man steals their art and shows it to the white woman who doesn't have any idea about what the dance is all about naked, so they say pay them for showing their naked bodies. Now we have exotic dancers and strippers as career all from the African culture. So now it's our turn to steal back what's ours."

"I will run this across Jasmine and try to get Stefani Blake to reach you so you can meet Simmion." Said Elliot.

"That would be the correct thing to do Mr. Thrasher. *Sprechen Sie Deutsch?*" Antwan asked him.

"*Nein!*" Elliot replied quickly speaking the language saying he didn't speak German.

"See Elliot, that lie was entirely pointless, because if you didn't speak German, why answer me "no" in German? I don't expect for you to confine in me, but need not to treat me like an imbecile."

****

Smack entered the kitchen and saw his beautiful girlfriend eating a bagel and grapefruit. She was long in length much taller than him. She stood at 5'8" even with long beautiful legs. It was ten thirty in the morning and she had on a short sleeve silk pajama top that was open exposing her cleavage, her stomach and the "V" shape of her vagina.

"You could put something on Stefani."

"Why cover up this body with a heap of clothes? I'm about to bloody go out and bathe in the sun, I say."

"Naked in the kitchen thought? That's unsanitary don't you think?" Smack looked at her.

"Where I'm from, we done a lot around the house in the nude. I'm not out doors I say huh mate?" She sucked on her grapefruit.

"Did you feed them since you are up bright and early this morning?" Smack asked her.

"I fed Bruce his veggies and I gave the dogs their, bloody Bill Jack, but those savage beasts out back, no I haven't gone near them. You feed them the bloody meat I say." Stefani answered.

"I will do that. Stefani you need to bond with them, because you probably haven't touched them since they were cubs." Smack told her.

"Simmion, you're probably bloody right," as she continued to eat her grapefruit with her hands.

"Isn't your trip to Cape Cod coming up soon?" he brought it up.

"Yes, the following week, why? Do you plan on cheating again Simmion? You know I smelled them other bitches scent a mile away when you came in last night, bloody early this morning. It was strong fresh like flowers. I hope you used a bloody condom." Stefani was furious.

"What are you talking about, Stefani?" Smack knew she smelled Delight's scent.

"You bloody well know what I'm talking about. You brought another woman's bloody scent into our home. Simmion, my people are trackers, we can track like bloody hound dogs I say. We can smell the finest odors and I smelled another woman's sex when you came in the bedroom this morning. You can't fool me mate, I say just wear a bloody condom." Said Stefani.

"If you say so Stefani." Smack brushed her off.

"Look honey, I can't bloody help it. I know men and women cheat and I'm just looking at it from my angle. So about high noon I'll need for you to come out and fuck me like animals do in the wild. There's nothing like hot sweaty sex at high noon in the sun. I have two condoms with me so just bring your bloody sex Simmion and I'll be waiting I say." She opened the glass doors and went out to her personal handmade Armani lounger, removing her pajama top to bathe in the sun.

Smack grabbed the raw meat to feed his lions. When Smack walked pass Stefani naked body he jumped at Bruce and Bruce ran under the lounger. "You little punk," said Smack.

Stefani shades covered her face and the sun lit her skin making it seem much darker than her normal pale look. He fed his lions and walked back towards the house and she lifted her shades.

"Smack, darling, don't keep me bloody waiting, the sun is making me horny I'd say." Stefani told him.

****

He held his glass of Patron firmly in his hand, while looking at the perfectly rolled blunt of Cush he had in the ivory ashtray. He noticed the day was pleasant to his likings. It appeared someone were in the shadows watching him. He was of much arrogance savoring every challenge.

"You've made quite an adversary, so why become a mere thought?" Antwan blurted out.

"How did you know I was in the room?" The voice spoke back to him.

His eyes narrowed as he took in the disfigurement. "Maybe ten or twelve minutes you've been watching me. I've been waiting on your arrival." Antwan told the voice.

"When did your flight come in?" the voice asked him.
"Two days ago, while you were probably dancing in someone's bedroom." He laughed.
"So now you don't trust me anymore?" The voice said.
"You're correct, but you're not one who will dirty her hands." He said.
"I follow orders though." The voice said.
"How many times have you slept with him since I've been away?" Antwan asked her.
"Maybe five times in the eight months you've been away. He's not strong like you; he's of a weaker breed. He's not only, he's very small if you know what I mean." The voice said.
He was still standing with his back to the female who was approaching him slowly.
He put his drink down on the end of the Oakwood desk.
"Did you miss me, darling?" He asked her.
"Of course, you know I did. I lone for you now, I need your touch, your lips, your cock inside me, I need you." The voice said.
"Well come and show me, don't just stand there," as he turned around to face the beautiful brunette with green eyes who looked like a movie star.
She jumped into his strong masculine arms feeling his powerful embrace. She kissed him passionately. "Oh Antwan, what took you so long?" she said.
"The Europeans Jasmine, they just don't get enough of killing."
"So, did you speak with Elliott yet?" She asked him.

"He left the restaurant about two hours ago, going to call his girlfriend which is you." He sighed.
"He hasn't called me yet. Antwan, by him being the Mayor do you think your plan is going to work?" she asked him.
"Have you ever doubted me?" He lifted an eyebrow.
"No, honey, no not ever." She looked up into his brown eyes.
"Alright Jasmine, who is this Simmion Boyd that I haven't met yet?" He asked her.
"He's a local drug dealer with a lot of avenues. I've tried to build cases on him to see if he'll negotiate on others terms, but he finds the best lawyers who are not on the take." She said.

"I heard Stefani Blake is his girlfriend?" He looked at her.

"Yes, that is true, but she's just a side show for him. She doesn't know his business and he's very smart like you, but you're smarter." She smiled at him.

"I'll have to get to know him personally. Try to get Stefani and him to visit the restaurant so I can introduce him to my world."

"Okay, I will, but first can we right now, in your office make a difference? I need you inside me now." Her eyes fluttered and had a glossy look.

"So, you miss the Chocolate Dream?" He asked her.

"They say once you go black, you won't go back. White men don't do the trick for me Antwan, and I'm tired of my toys. I need to feel real veins rub my vagina walls." she told him.

"Would you like a drink first?" He offered a drink.

"Yes, from your fountain of love," as she went down and unzipped his pants getting on her knees.

All this was in Jasmine Finch face, his dark lengthy tribal piece. She had a face of kind, but well-proportioned nose that stood at guard. A firm chin, a mouth whose lips were by no means thin, but were a firm set. She was shaped like an hour glass and her hands were well manicured, she was a beautiful woman. For many nights and days, she waited on his return to the States. Her lover, her associate, her means of separating herself from the rest above was now back in her life. One hand held to her breast and the other one clutching his manhood. Impulse went into her throat and she could feel his veins begin to grow and pulsate. Uneasy Jasmine looked behind her, but saw no one and then turned back to him.

****

Presently in Lincoln Heights, Delight and her sister, Heather, was in the middle of a discussion.

"I beg your pardon; I've put everything in place. The point I intended to make was that, friendly and physically Smack is on the surface. It's important as well to treat him cautiously as well as considerately, because he may go elsewhere Delight."

"Heather, I don't have time to let that worry me. All I know is of right now, the effect he has on me is filling this void I have."

"Bitch, you mean the holes he's filling. Because I know he's fucking you Delight and he's probably fucking you good too. That nigga hot that little boy, but he doesn't fool me one bit. You haven't been touched by Kendall in how long? That nigga got you on cloud twenty-nine not nine." Heather crossed her arms.

"Exactly, that's my point. I mean it's something necessary for me to remember dealing with someone ten years younger than me. He's young, attractive, well-educated and speaks with manners. He's not one who thinks he's above everything and everyone and believe me I've had some experience with those types." Delight pointed to her wedding ring.

"Well you be careful with what you are doing. I think you should know, because you're a grown woman and a Heath." Heather smiled at her.

"I'm tired of Kendall's pathetic ass. I bring up Rainell and how she's filling out as a young lady and he ignores it like she's not capable of fucking at her age." Delight told her.

"Girl that's sad, because she gets it honest. I had ass like that at her age and Lord knows what I was doing while mama and daddy were at work." Heather laughed.

"I use to hear you and Todd Bo, Lord knows, rest his soul. You were hot Heather; you had all those boys coming around looking for you trying to buy you some candy and shit."

"Delight, I was the one giving out the candy back then." She smiled at her little sister.

"That's why you had my nieces at an early age, fifteen, seventeen and twenty."

"Guess what Delight, ain't none of them bitches living with me, all them hoes are grown and on their own." said Heather.

"They need to come home." Delight told her.

"They are good right where they are. Paulette's in Cleveland, Tonya's in Texas and Mya's in Detroit. All of them have good jobs following in their aunt's footsteps." said Heather.

"Look who helped raise them before I left for college."

"Bitch, that's why I'm returning the favor with Rainell," Heather looked at her.

The road was now shaded by thoughts lived by the wall of inexorable leaving her behind to think if Smack had a hidden agenda. She knew she was well-bred. She certainly had no intentions of casually accepting and becoming thoughtlessly implicated in it, which is what she thought Smack had done. She thought about when she was younger and when young boys talk to her, danced and played basketball with her, invited her to go bike riding or to the movies, became amorous or fumbled with her unromantically in the dark. She had the impression they did it on purpose until now.

Yet another situation was in process. It fascinated disturbed her to have suddenly an insight into it. Kendall doesn't want to be married to her any longer

What and I? She questioned herself.

Just like I was before, just as I've always been, just as if I'd never tried, but I did try, I did try. She answered herself.

What did I try?

I tried to make a life with him, I tried to build. I tried to love him completely! Did he love me back? Hell no. How could he when he was too busy loving someone else, himself.

Delight sat quite still on her sister's sofa while Heather was on the phone now gossiping. It was Delight rocking back and forth, held by it and by the revelation, what seemed to be the revelation of what had laid behind the game that seemed to have ended today.

The game of *Delight playing Delight, Delight nothing? Delight alone?*

She pondered the meaning of, whatever you do and wherever you go you'll always be yourself and recognize the truth.

She was back to herself, because her sense of self-consciousness and individuality was tenacious resistance to surrender in exchange for an illusion any longer. The perfect solution for her problem an inner voice of truth spoke out.

"Leave his ass girl, tell him it's over and end your marriage today. You can do bad all by yourself, Delight."

She stopped rocking back and forth and came out of her thought.

"That's right leave his ass girl, you don't need him. You built that law firm not him. You're the stronger vessel Delight not him." She paused and then yelled out.

"Rainell, c'mon we are leaving right now." Delight yelled out.

Heather saw her sister snap while she was on the phone. Heather was looking at her like she was a mad woman, like the living dead just came alive. She saw much anger and attitude in Delight's face.

"Hey Tasha, let me call you back, this bitch done went crazy or something. Na'll let me call you back Tasha." Heather screamed at the person on the receiving end.

Heather hung up the phone trying to catch up with Delight. Delight had got up and was heading out the door with Rainell. They were getting in the Range Rover when Heather came out the house. "Hey lil sis, hold up, where are you going?" Heather was walking towards the truck. The air conditioning was blowing hard, but Delight had beads of sweat on her nose. Heather knew her sister was very angry.

"Delight, where are ya'll going? The food is almost done."

"I'm going home to tell Kendall it's over. He won't tell me, so I'll do it for him. He scared to tell me, but I'm not scared to tell him." Delight said.

"Are you sure Delight? I mean ya'll have a lot to discuss."

"No, the fuck we don't, either he's leaving or me; and my baby is going with me. He can have that mother-fucker all to himself."

"Well Rainell need not to hear the break up Delight." Heather looked concerned.

"Heather, she's a part of this marriage and she's not a baby anymore, that's her house too and she might have a few issues to address to his sorry ass. Hell, we might jump his ass."

Rainell looked over at her mom and smiled.

"See that's your daddy Big Larry Heath coming out of you Delight. Okay girl, but don't be a dumb bitch like that heifer on 'Waiting to Exhale' and burn your truck up. Call me later."

"Bye," as she backed out of her sister's drive-way like a bat out of hell.

Heather yelled out. "Bitch, don't have a wreck before you get there."

****

"You were fantastic Antwan, I'm full." Jasmine told him licking her lips.

She sucked all her fingers making sure of it. He sat back in his chair and grabbed the blunt out the ashtray. He lit it taking in a collective of drags, exhaling slowly. He tapped the desk a few times with another thought coming to mind.

"Jasmine, I thought you said your brother was going to assist you in this matter?"

"My step-brother Will, yes he is. Him and his partner Allen Taylor works for RENU. They are taking the proper steps to approach Simmion with a proposition." said Jasmine.

"Well it's like the second week in June. I would like the designer drug to be on US soil before September. I can't bring it, if I can't get rid of it Jasmine." said Antwan.

"Do you have any samples of the drug Antwan?" she asked.

"What kind of idiot question is that Jas? I see Elliott Thrasher pathetic nature is rubbing off on you. You know I have the drug here." He said.

"I meant to say, how much darling?" she cleared it up.

"Around fifty bottles containing three hundred pills in each bottle." He told her.

"Do you still have Stefani's number? I know she used to be your lover." she asked him.

"No," as he rubbed his hands together. "Can you manage to get it for me?"

She gave a nod of her head to say yes.

✳✳✳✳✳✳✳

"That's it Simmion, fuck my bloody cunt, I say. Pull my hair, pull my bloody hair."

Smack had Stefani on her knees in the lounger ramming her from the back. He was gripping her sides for leverage and you could see all her vagina from this position. She was petite and fresh. The sweat from Smack's forehead was dripping on her back mixing with her dampness. Bruce watched his master getting sexed like in the Animal Kingdom. Good thing he had a fourteen-foot privacy fence, because her screams and utters could be heard by his neighbors if they were home.

The strength, assurance and stamina were being displayed by Smack. While they successfully represented aspiration and mastered the art of excitement, Smack didn't realize the friction caused the condom to break.

"Oh, Simmion, I bloody say, you're growing inside me. It feels so bloody good mate." said Stefani.

Smack felt a sudden change in the warm passion he was feeling. It went from warm to hot. "Shit Stef, this outback pussy is good as hell." He whispered to her. He knew he was now flesh to flesh insider her wet pink hole.

"I know ooh weesh there goes another one, back to back bloody orgasms. Oh, that feels so bloody good." She released a sigh.

"Damn Stef, I'm cumming," as he grabbed her sides tightly.

She felt the hot semen rushing insider her. "Simmion, what are you bloody doing?"

She pulled away realizing the condom had broken. "Are you pathetic or what? You're putting that bloody junk inside me. Did you not realize the bloody condom broke Simmion?" She was now looking him in the eyes.

"Uh-uh no." He stuttered while he was still holding his manhood jerking off trying to get the remainder out.

"Look at this bloody junk running down my leg Simmion. Wads of it, I bloody swear you better hope I don't get pregnant or catch a disease Simmion."

He ignored her and grabbed his shorts going towards the house. He went through the sliding doors and his phone was vibrating on the kitchen counter. It was vibrating like crazy. He had six missed calls. He answered it knowing who it was from the missed calls.

"Hello, what's wrong?" He asked.

"I'm on my way home to tell Kendall that it's over." It was Delight.

"How on earth did you manage to come up with this idea?" Even though he liked the sound of it.

"Because I want to show him, I'm not scared to leave his ass. This is what he wants, plus I'm in love with you Simmion. This is what I want whether you be with me or not. I'm strong enough to move on with my life without him."

"Why can't this wait until a day in the week?" Smack asked her.

"Sunday is the day; it's doing down today. I was just calling you to let you know me and Rainell might need a shelter until I find us somewhere to live. Smack, I'm making moves towards us being together." she told him.

He could hear the sincerity in her voice.

"You know ya'll are more

 than welcome her Delight. So, you are serious?" He asked her.

"Yes, I am and I'm coming to you, baby." Delight was confident.

Rainell looked over at her mom and smiled.

"Okay, let me know how everything works out." said Smack.

"I will Simmion, I love you." Her voice echoed in his ear from hearing those words.

Rainell looked at her mother wide-eyed. Even Smack was caught off guard.

"Smack, did you hear me? I said I love you." Delight said.

"I heard you and the same here." His voice was dry and low.

"You don't feel the same way I feel now or is Ms. Outback in front of you?" Delight asked him.

"No, it's just that I do love you, but it's rather odd that you are telling me what I've been wanting to tell you for a while now."

"Well tell me, Smack." Her voice lit up.

"I love you, too." The words froze him in a time zone.

"I love you, bye," as she hung up the phone. Rainell smiled because she never suspected her mother to be messing with Smack on that level. She was happy for her mother. Stefani on the other hand caught the end of his phone conversation with Delight.

"Why didn't you tell Mama Boyd I said bloody hello, Simmion?" Stefani was standing there naked holding her pajama top.

"I did, Stef. I told her you were out getting a tan." Smack was confused. Now he was hoping Stefani wasn't there and that the sex they just had wouldn't result in her getting pregnant, but wishing and hoping Delight was pregnant.

CHAPTER ELEVEN
DELIGHT'S SHOWDOWN WITH KENDALL

Delight and Rainell entered the house to find Kendall in the living room watching a Sunday matinee. She stood looking at him and Rainell stood in her shadow. The anger, anxiety and attitude were still fluttering inside Delight. Her emotions were raving touching every nerve in her nervous system. He didn't bother to look in her direction, because if looks could kill, Kendall would be a dead man. She made a windy husk to let some of her pressure out and her presence be known, "Smm-Smm." She stared even harder.

"Oh, Delight, you're home. How long have you been standing there?" He asked her.

"Not long, but we need to talk." She had her hands on her hips.

"About what? Can it wait; I'm watching 'Sleepless in Seattle'.

"No, it can't wait, now is the perfect time, Kendall." she said.

"Only if you insist." He turned the TV off.

"Kendall, you know and I know that something is wrong with our marriage, so why keep pretending to be married to me?"

"Pretending what, Delight?" said Kendall.

"That you still love me and want to be married to me." Delight responded.

"I do, I'm still, here aren't I?" He said with anger.

"Right, you're here, but we don't do shit together anymore. You don't even have sex with me anymore, so why fake it. Be a man and just say it's over, because you spend all your time in Sneaky-Peaks and I know you are sleeping with someone else."

He caught a glimpse of Rainell standing behind her and said, "Don't you think we should be having this conversation without our daughter being here?"

"Fuck that she's a part of this marriage and she might have a few words for your black ass too." Delight had an attitude.

"Delight, you're going crazy." Kendall said.

"You're right. I am going crazy for fooling myself into believing this was happiness and you loved me. You never did, but don't worry somebody does. I'm here to do what you were apparently afraid to do. It's over. I want a divorce. Either you can leave or I will, but it's over, today." She stood strong not shedding a tear.

"I'm not leaving and you'll come to your senses shortly." Kendall told her.

"I just did, come on Rainell and pack you some clothes." They both left from his sight.

He responded. "Where ya'll going to Lincoln Heights with your sister?"

"Don't worry about that; but wherever it may be, it won't be here with you," as her voice faded.

Delight packed her two suitcases of clothes and removed her wedding ring leaving it on the dresser. She went to make sure Rainell was finished packing.

"Get a good look at this room Rainell, because this will be your last time in it."

Delight told her.

"Where are we going to live mommy, over Aunt Heather's?"

"Hopefully with Mr. Smack until I find us somewhere else to live."

"Are you serious mom?" Rainell got excited.

"Yes, I am serious, Rainell. Would you like that?"

"I would love that mommy and no matter what happens I won't choose his side." Rainell hugged her mother.

****

Smack was getting dressed and Stefani had come out of the shower wrapped in a towel and one around her dampened hair. He was still in disbelief from Delight's phone call. No threat of any kind would regard his way of thinking now. He knew Stefani would have to be dismissed, to the Sharks of the entertainment world she must go. But how? When would he cancel her like Nino did his girl in 'New Jack City'? He hoped at that very moment that Delight would wait before she terminated her marriage. His phone had rung bringing him out of thought. Stefani was now on the bed moisturizing her skin with Latoire Crème. Smack looked at the caller ID knowing it was Delight. He sighed before answering the call.

"Hey, what's up?" he answered dry.

"It's over. I did it Smack. Rainell and I are on our way to your house, if that's not a problem?" Delight was excited.

"That's cool; I'm here waiting on you." Smack was looking at Stefani.

"You don't sound too happy. Maybe we should go to Heather's." said Delight.

"No, you both are welcome here. Come on over."

"Alright baby, we are on our way." Delight was having second thoughts.

"Okay, bye." Smack responded and closed his phone.

Delight had forgotten completely about Stefani being there, but she stayed on course to West Chester.

"Simmion, who was that, may I ask?" said Stefani.

"It was Delight. She and Rainell will be staying here with us for a little while."

"Why, doesn't she have a bloody home, Simmion?"

"It has been told to me that she and the husband are calling it quits. She asked me if they could come here until she finds a place." said Smack.

"Now you are the bloody drop-in center for the homeless?" Stefani was getting an attitude.

"Stef, this is my house remember, not yours. You don't pay for anything the last time I checked. You don't even cook or clean, so don't question me about what the fuck I do for a friend."

"I'm just saying, I bloody like it quiet around here and enjoying myself in the nude. I hope it's not for bloody long, I say."

"No matter how long it is, we will show them respect and the utmost of hospitality around here. That means no snarling and funny little attitudes, Stefani." said Smack.

She looked at him and turned her nose up at him. He got up from the edge of the bed.

"Do you hear me, Stef?" He stood over her.

"Yes, Simmion, I bloody hear you, I bloody fucking hear you mate."

He left out the bedroom going to prepare for his guest when they arrived.

CHAPTER TWELVE
ANTWAN CONTACTS STEFANI

"Of all the days my truck doesn't want to freakin start." Delight hit her steering wheel. You could hear her Range Rover trying to crank and turn over in the drive-way. Smack heard her vehicle wouldn't start and came outside to assist her in his gym shorts. "Hey Delight, you're flooding it. Stop!" He yelled, but she couldn't hear him from the windows being up. She looked up to see him and was still upset with him, because she separated herself from Kendall and he was still with Stefani.

What does he want? It's been three days; I'm in the same house as my lover and can't even touch him. I totally forgot that Australian bitch was here, how stupid of me. I'm in love with this guy." As she still tried to start her truck. She mumbled more words to herself as he approached the truck. He pointed for her to let down the window and she did. "Stop trying to start it, you're just flooding it. Just take the Benz to work and I'll have my mechanic come and look at it."

"Smack, I'm not okay with this situation. I'm close, but I want to be closer. I need you inside me." She pleaded with him.

"I know, Delight; I know it's an awkward situation for me too. After her trip to Cape Cod, I'm putting her and that damn Komodo dragon out." He smiled at her.

"What about now? I want you now. Shit I need some dick, my hormones are raging." Delight told him.

"She leaves this Friday, Delight. Can you wait one more day?"

"That's two more days, Smack." Delight pleaded...

"She leaves that Thursday night, Friday morning around three."

"I'll try Smack, I'll try." She let up her window and got out the truck. They walked up the drive way. Her stylish skirt and crème colored blouse by Vera Wang fitted her perfect. Smack stared at the curves on her and got aroused watching her walk towards the garage. He went and got her the spare key to the Benz. He came back out and handed her the set.

"Delight, be careful and I'll see you later. I'm taking Rainell over to Daysha's before I go into the city."

"Okay, honey, give me a kiss." They magically kissed in the garage. Smack wanted her just as bad, but he respected the enemy on enemy lines. He opened the door for her and then quickly showed her a few major buttons and other gadgets to operate the vehicle. She put her Coach purse and briefcase in the passenger seat and then let the top down. He leaned over in the Benz and kissed her again before she pulled off. Her thoughts of Stefani quickly faded as she drove off down the driveway to the street. She knew by her being in the Benz, she was the best woman. His woman and the best were yet to come. Oh, how material things can change a person's attitude.

****

Around twelve noon that same day Antwan Klein called Stefani's phone for the first time in a long time. He managed to get it from one of Jasmine's sources. She was wearing a pair of red Capri pants and a white t-shirt with cotton balls in between her toes from polishing her toenails. She was sitting in the mini theater watching 'Lady in the Lake' on DVD.

Smack had his basement decked out with a full bar, pool tables, a 62" flat screen and other small flat screens set up like a sports bar.

She answered her phone with a delicate voice. "This is Stefani Blake, I say."

"Why hello darling, how is life treating a beautiful woman like you?" Antwan asked her.

"Is this bloody Antwan, Antwan Klein, I say?" She was overwhelmed.

"Why yes, it is, Stefani and how are you doing?" He was quite charming.

"I'm bloody terrific mate. Where are you, in the bloody States?"

"I am, by the way. I'm in Cincinnati, Ohio at my relative's restaurant in the Clifton area." He told her.

"Antwan, I haven't seen you in quite a while, I say. You bloody animal you." Stefani giggled.

She laughed in a naughty way.

"Well, where are you? I'll fly to you so I can have a drink with a long-lost friend." He told her in excitement.

"Antwan, I'm in Cincinnati also mate. I'm at my bloody boyfriend's house. Maybe we can get together later and have dinner at the restaurant."

"Stefani, that would be wonderful and I could meet your Herr that you're madly in love with."

"Stop it Antwan. Bloody in love hardly. After you no one can get my heart that way ever again. But I like him a lot, he reminds me of you in so many ways, I say."

"Well come to the restaurant later and dinners on me. It's called Lenhardt's on McMillan Street in Clifton up by the University of Cincinnati's campus."

"What type of delicacy is served there Antwan?" She asked him.

"It is European cuisine of my father's background, German."

"We'll bloody be there, seven-thirty sharp, mate." She told him.

"I'll be waiting darling." He said.

"TaTa Antwan." She hung up with a smile on her face.

****

Smack was with two of the Belvy Boyz going to meet another Belvy Boy, Worm because he had some of the money, they owed Smack on him. Worm was in Avondale fighting one of his dogs. He bred and fought pit bulls. He was behind uncle Milts bar fighting his red nose pit bull, Maniac against Rap Dog killer pit bull Cocaine. Cocaine was all white with blue eyes. No dog from coast to coast had beat Cocaine. Big Sube from English Woods had helped Worm train his dog. Smack wanted to bet on the dog fight. He pulled up in his Q45 Infiniti and they all got out meeting Worm. Every known dealer or player was at this event, even females. It was Like Las Vegas with all the locals out.

A host of others were in the crowd. The bets were heavy and if the jack boys showed up, they would most likely walk away with close to four hundred thousand dollars. The local police who patrol this area was paid off this day. At one pm in the afternoon Cocaine and Maniac engaged in a fight to the death. You could hear the growling, the ripping and blood spitting as the two dogs were in combat.

Smack knew dogs and waged a ten thousand dollar bet on Maniac even though he heard stories about Cocaine. He was showing his loyalty to the Belvy Boyz. Maniac defeated Cocaine this day convincingly.   Cocaine had a record of twenty-six and zero. Now she was twenty-six and one. Worm stopped Maniac from killing her. Rap Dog was mad, but he knew she had a good run. He told Worm if he could nurse her back to stable conditions, he could have her to breed with Maniac, because he never mated her before. All he wanted was one of the puppies.

Smack had placed his bet with Fat Shaun and he told Smack, "You got me for ten racks, come down to Duke's later and gamble with us. We are having a fifty thousand dollar freeze out, if your dough is long like they say it is lil nigga."

"I'm there Fat Shaun, you act like I don't have any dough," said Smack.

"Just show me by showing up and that will say it all. Oh, and yeah bring that model chick with you, because you gone need a shoulder to cry on." Fat Shaun laughed.

"She's for sale if you got the dough to pay for her." They laughed and shook hands.

Smack's phone started ringing and he flipped it open to answer it. "Vegas never sleep and neither do I. What's up?"

"Simmion, where are you, mate?" It was Stefani calling.

"I'm at a dog fight, why?"

"I just bloody asked. Don't get your bloody balls in a jam. We are having dinner at Lenhardt's in Clifton tonight seven-thirty sharp. My friend Antwan is in town and he's treating us to dinner at his family's restaurant." She told him.

"What about our guest at the house, Stefani?" Smack asked her.

"Who Delight? She can bloody come, I don't care."

"Alright, I'll call her to see if she would like to join us. I'll be there later." He said.

"Simmion, seven-thirty sharp, not bloody ten o'clock, I say. I want you to meet Antwan."

"Alright, I hear you, Stef." He hung up the phone.

****

"Hey Kendall, what are you doing for dinner tonight, since there's no wifey around?"

Keisha asked him being sarcastic a little.

"Nothing, I'm free for whatever." said Kendall.

"Well, I made reservations for us at Lenhardt's in Clifton."

"That's fine, Keisha," said Kendall.

"After getting that rotten tooth pulled two days ago, I've been starving. The dentist said the tooth probably made me have bad breath. Was my breath tart Kendall, and don't lie?" said Keisha.

"Uhn-uhn Keisha, if it was, I didn't notice it." He knew he was lying, because her breath smelled like shit.

"Well meet me over my house at six; our reservation is at seven-forty tonight." Keisha said.

"Okay, Keisha, bye."

"Bye baby," Keisha sounded sexy in his ear.

Delight walked pass his office mugging him and rolling her eyes. Kendall just looked at her. He mumbled to himself. *"She's just evil."*

Delight's cell phone rung and she answered it while standing at the fax machine.

"Hello, Slogin & Cummons, Delight Scott speaking attorney at law. How can I help you?"

"Delight, it's me, Smack." He called her cell phone.

"Oops, I'm sorry baby; I thought I was at my desk. Plus, I just saw Kendall's punk ass and it threw me off. I realize I can't stand that man., what's going on? Did you get my truck fixed?" She asked him.

"No, I called to see if you would like to join Stefani and me for dinner tonight?" He asked her.

"You and outback?" Delight said out loud.

"Yes, me and outback, Delight." He replied.

"Sure, I don't care." Delight wanted to go just to piss Stefani off.

"The reservations are for seven-thirty." He explained.

"Who's going to watch Rainell, Smack?" She asked.

"I told her that she could stay all night at Daysha's." said Smack.

"Okay, daddy. I'm glad you are taking that role to make decisions with my child." Said Delight.

"Correction, our child, Ms. Heath." Smack replied.

"Oh, yeah," said Delight.

"Yeah and some. I told you that you are my future." He looked into his phone.

"Well if I'm so much of the future, let the future get some of that dick." Delight was serious.

"Delight, be patient. It's coming up shortly." He'd insistent.
"We'll see. You talk a good game," as they continued to have
small talk while she was at work.

****

Later, that evening, Smack, Stefani and Delight were getting in
his 750 BMW. Stefani had on an elegant fitting silk Baby Phat
evening gown with the back out. It was turquoise. She wore her
diamond necklace and bracelet and some Stiletto heels to match
her gown. Delight had on a dark purple Sarong with a pair of
wine color Stiletto heels. Her Sarong showed every possible curve
she possessed. Smack wore a Versace silk multi-colored shirt
with a pair of Versace casual slacks and some suede Ostrich slip
on loafers to match his shirt. His diamond earring stuck out and
the Rolex watch he possessed.

They reached the restaurant in no time. He parked in the
restaurant parking lot. Smack got out and let both ladies out the
car like a perfect gentleman. He held out both his arms to escort
them to the entrance door. Stefani held him tightly and Delight
did the same looking like a movie star. The two women snarled,
but glanced at each other courageously.

Delight wasn't going to let Stefani outdo her, she was now
competing for her man, she thought. The hostess greeted them
as they entered the restaurant.

"Good evening, what's the name please?" She gave them a bright
smile.

Stefani spoke for the group. "Stefani Blake and company."

The hostess looked over the list she had and couldn't fine her
name.

"I'm sorry miss, but there's no reservation for a Stefani Blake."

"Are you bloody sure, I say? Can you please check again?"
Stefani asked her.

Delight chuckled a little before blurting out. "What is this
madness, she can't make a simple reservation, a dinner
engagement, yeah right?"

"Delight, my bloody friend made the reservation, I bloody didn't.
I'm bigger than life, it's just bloody sad that the hostess doesn't
recognize me." Stefani said rolling her eyes.

The hostess was still checking the list. "Save it, Stefani, for how a model went wrong." Delight told her.

"Ladies, stop it. That's not the problem at hand. It must be a mix up
. Let me handle this and get us a table." Smack told them.

Antwan saw the dinner party standing at the front entrance and headed in their direction, before Smack could offer the hostess money for a table.

"Awe, Stefani, Ms. Stefani Blake. You made it." As you could hear Antwan's voice approaching them.

"See Simmion, that's my bloody friend, Antwan Klein. I knew he wouldn't forsake me and leave me out to bloody dry like lawyers do in the courtroom." She looked over at Delight.

"What's the problem, Peggy? Why haven't you seated these lovely people?" Anywan asked the hostess.

"Sir, they weren't on the reservation list Mr. Klein." Peggy looked up at him.

"Oh, I'm so sorry, I must have forgotten to pencil you in Stefani," as he grabbed her shoulders and gave her fake kisses on each side of her face.

"Cherry roses to you too Antwan. You're looking quite handsome I must bloody say." Stefani told him.

"You're quite astonishing yourself Stefani, now who are these lovely people you have with you?" He asked looking over Delight and Smack with a grin.

"This is my mate Simmion and his bloody lawyer friend Delight Scott." She gave a frown saying her name.

"Hello Simmion," he shook his hand firmly. "And Ms. Delight, what a beautiful name, how are you?" He kissed the back of her hand sending an emotional wave up her spine causing her to get moist.

"I'm fine, Antwan." Delight gave him a smile.

"Well follow me, I have a perfect table for us." Antwan led the way.

It was a table for five and he pulled out Stefani's chair for her and Smack pulled out Delight's seat. "Why so many bloody seats Antwan?" Stefani asked him.

"My lady friend, Jas, will be joining us in a few," said Antwan.

The restaurant was semi-packed with familiar faces when Delight surveyed the room. She saw Judge Phil Helmet with a young black woman and not his wife sharing a candle light dinner. Antwan called for the waitress. "Fraulien Hannah, Kommen sie bitte."

He told Hannah to please come here in German and Smack recognized the language off hand. She came to the table and gave everyone a wave of her hand.

"Vier mochten etwas zu drinken. Wasser for the table and something easy, but delicate." He ordered water and champagne for the table.

"Jah Herr Klein." She answered yes sir to him.

"Abe ich mochte ein club soda bitte." Smack asked for a club soda in German.

"Ah Herr Simmion, sie sprechen Deutsch?" Antwan asked him did he speak German.

"Jah ich sprechen Deutsch, warum?" Smack told Antwan he spoke German and why.

"I just asked. I see we have something in common." Delight and Stefani just stared at the two. The conversation went on and on. They ordered dinner when Jasmine arrived and Delight was surprised that Antwan knew her.

Jasmine Finch was a dreadful prosecutor. Delight saw her all up under Mayor Elliot Thrasher before.

Delight Heath Scott, took a deep breath from the conversation to sit back and silently look over the two couples in her presence. Jasmine's quick spirit complimented Antwan's more studied approach

to life. Glancing from one face to another as the conversation flowed around her, Delight congratulated herself for being around them. She didn't feel out of place being the fifth wheel. Feeling momentarily superfluous, she let her gaze meander among the elegantly dressed people in the restaurant. She spotted more familiar faces on the far side of the restaurant and when her attention returned to her dinner party, she met Jasmine's eyes. Jasmine's brow lifted toward Delight.

"Flash?" Jasmine thought looking at Delight. "Delight Scott, the powerful female attorney from Slogin & Cummons law firm who is *now dealing with criminal cases. Simmion Boyd's friend and lawyer, he's witty and brilliant for retaining a civil lawyer to fight criminal who's not on the take to be a sellout."* Jasmine gave her a smile. Delight smiled back and took her glance over the room once more to see her husband having dinner with Keisha Myles, their daughter's old pediatrician.

Her blood pressure shot to the roof. "Why that sleazy slut." She mumbled, adding, "I knew all along he's been chasing her trifling ass. That's why I took Rainell out of that clinic."

Her frequency was now on. She was boiling as the others were in laughter about a corny joke that Stefani said. She tapped Smack's arm leaning over to him to whisper in his ear. He leaned forward as the others watched. "Smack, Kendall is in the restaurant to our left in the far corner with our daughter's old pediatrician." Delight told him.

She rubbed his arm as he leaned back over glancing to his left. Then he took a sip of his club soda looking again to see Kendall and Pepsi sitting at a table. He leaned back over to whisper in Delight's ear. "That's Pepsi, she works at Sneaky-Peaks, and she's a stripper and not a pediatrician, Delight."

Delight whispered back to Smack. "Her name is Keisha Myles and she's a pediatrician and her breath stinks like crazy."

Smack knew then that Delight knew what she was talking about, because her breath did stink. ", her government name Is Keisha Myles and she's also fronting like she's a pediatrician when her real profession is a stripper." Smack thought to himself.

"do you want to leave, Delight?" Smack asked her.

"No, I'll be fine, but I knew that mother-fucker was fooling around with her. Probably since Rainell was seven or eight years old." Delight was upset and Antwan saw it in her face. Antwan interrupted them by saying, "I see we are getting restless, perhaps you all would like to join me at my club across the river in Covington, Jillian's nightclub?" Antwan said.

"Sure, Antwan, we will bloody join you I say." Stefani answered for them. Smack looked at her with a grudge, because he really didn't do the club scene.

He never been to Jillian's, he only heard about it. He knew it was a mix crowd with many levels of activities from a word of mouth.

Delight didn't decline from joining them at Jillian's, but before they left the restaurant, she would let Kendal know that she busted him cheating with her own eyes. She excused herself and walked over to their cozy table and Kendall just so happened to look up to see his wife of fourteen years coming in their direction. He was caressing Keisha's hand smoothly and gently making romantic seduction to her hand. He eased his hand away.

"What's the matter, Kendall, you look puzzled?" Keisha asked him.

Kendall could see the husky wind building up in Delight's windpipe. His eyes grew looking beyond Keisha making her turn around to see Delight.

"Kendall, this is what's going on? You're fucking this bitch slut of a pediatrician?" Delight said standing strong.

"Now wait a minute, Mrs. Scott," as Keisha stood up in her own defense.

"Sit your tired ass back down before I put you through the floor." Delight started to sweat at the nose. Keisha sat back down and Delight stared her down.

"Kendall, how long have you all been fucking around?" Delight asked him.

"We just ran into each other the day after you left me. It shouldn't matter because you left. I didn't leave you." Kendall told her.

"You damn right, I left your sorry ass. Well if this is what you want, you got it buddy. Its official, I'll start the paper work tomorrow. Fourteen years, a child and a career wife who looks damn good than any stripper bitch and the bitch breath stink. Pepsi, huh? You had a Coke bottle. Be happy with her and I'll be to get the rest of our things, move that bitch in with you, because I'm never coming back. All for a cheap thrill have a nice life." Delight turned around and put up her middle finger and walked away.

"But Delight, it's not my fault," as Kendall tried to plead his case. He saw her join Smack, Stefani, Jasmine and Antwan. Her sarong made her look like a different woman, more stacked, more appealing, but now another man's treasure.

"Delight, who was that you were, bloody arguing with?" Stefani asked her.

"It's my husband." Delight answered and walked off ahead of them. Smack caught up with her and asked her, "Is everything alright, Delight? You look troubled."

"I'm fine, let's go party. I feel like dancing," as she looked Smack up and down.

Stefani road with Antwan and Jasmine in his 1969 Shelby GT 500 Mustang which was a classic with everything original. Delight was now alone with Smack and she was massaging his manhood as they road across the Purple People Bridge into Covington, Kentucky.

"Smack, I'm fucking you tonight, some way somehow, if I have to fuck you in the car." Delight told him.

She shouted over the music. He didn't respond with words; he just nodded his head.

They reached the club parking lot where Antwan pulled his car into the valet and Smack was right behind him. They stepped out the cars and saw the long line to get in the club. On a Wednesday night the line was out to the curve. Smack handed the valet guy a twenty-dollar bill and he gave Smack a ticket.

They didn't enter the main entrance, because Antwan took them through a private entrance. Big security guards spoke to Antwan. "How are you doing, Mr. Klein?" One of the four guys spoke to him. "I'm fine, Tony. Chris, Paul and Stevin?" Antwan nodded to them. "Mr. Klein, Chantell is waiting on you, she's on four." Chris told him.

Antwan just nodded again to him and they got on an elevator to the first floor of the club. It was a bar that went from wall to wall with TV's. people were eating while watching Boston and the L.A Lakers play one of their Finals games, Boxing was on a few other monitors. It was a Sports bar in this area of the club. You could hear music coming from down the hall. Antwan led them down that same hall and they passed a bowling alley, pool tables and video games. Hip Hop music was playing.

Antwan grabbed Smack and whispered to him. "I want you to help me run and operate this spot, one day. I know you are the man in that city. My type of guy. You haven't seen nothing yet my friend, you like this?" He asked Smack.

"This is hot, no doubt, my guy. I didn't know all this was going on over here." Smack replied.

"Well, let me take you to the next three floors." Antwan looked at him.

"The next three floors?" Smack asked him.

Smack thought he'd seen more than enough already.

"Yes, this is just for the family or the non-partying crowd in this area. The real club is upstairs on the next three levels." Antwan gave him a grin.

"I hope it's not like butt naked Tuesday's in Dayton." Smack blurted out.

"It's probably way better my friend, follow me," said Antwan.

Everybody followed Antwan to an elevator with steps on the side and four security guards checking for ID and weapons. Two patrolled the steps and the other two checked people getting on the elevator. Antwan and his guest walked straight pass security getting on the elevator. They went to the second floor and got off the elevator and they heard club music like "Techno" playing. It was so packed it was unbelievable. The crowd was mixed and the women were dancing half naked. The lights were flashing and smoke was everywhere.

"Simmion, this is how the Europeans party. You've seen 'Triple X' before? That's how it really goes down over there. They got high and loose off the drug called Black Ice. It's way better than Ecstasy-Ex." Antwan told Smack.

"What's Black Ice, Antwan?" Smack was curious.

"I'll tell you all about it when we get upstairs." He smiled at Smack.

"Upstairs? It's another floor in this place?" Smack asked him.

"Two more floors, Simmion, let's go." They followed Antwan back to the elevator. The women were right behind them. When they reached the third floor, Reggae music was playing and once again it was packed. Marijuana smoke filled the room and you could hear Steel Pulse "Body Guard" playing in the background.

A strange female pulled up on Antwan and passed him a blunt and kissed him in the mouth blowing smoke in his mouth. He inhaled and exhaled her smoke and then puffed on the blunt. He passed it back to her and winked at her. She turned around to walk away and Antwan slapped her on her butt. They looked around briefly and headed back towards the elevator. "Simmion, do you smoke marijuana?" Antwan asked him.

"I only smoke Kush, Antwan." Smack answered.

"See Jas, this is my type of guy, he smokes what I smoke and he speaks German." Antwan told Jasmine.

Antwan smiled at Jasmine and shook his head.

"Simmion, I didn't know you smoked weed." Delight looked at him confused when she made that comment. "Just some expensive stuff every now and then," said Smack.

"Delight, that's my bloody man and it's none of your business what he does. Your mate is still back at the restaurant." Stefani told her.

"Stefani, that's my friend and I can ask Simmion whatever I please too, he answers for himself. He's a grown ass man out here and plus there's no ring on your bloody lonely pale ass finger." Delight had an attitude.

"Ladies, we're trying to enjoy the evening. Let's not cat fight," as Antwan eased the situation. They stepped off the elevator to hear, Kanye West "Good Life" and then Keysha Cole and Monica "Trust" came on. It was also a mixed crowd on this floor with much flavor. Smack saw females he would normally see In Vito's or Annie's nightclub. The females were taking shots of liquor at the bar and then he thought about what day it was, a Wednesday, it goes down like this over here?

There were cages up on another level in this area on the dance floor which had females dancing in them half naked. They were dancing on one of the bars the same way. Smack's eyes had to adjust to the wild mixture that was taking place. Yeah, this was way better then Butt Naked Tuesday's in Dayton.

"What are ya'll drinking?" Antwan asked them.

"I'll have a bloody Yeager bomb mate," said Stefani.

"Can I have a strawberry daiquiri with Patron, please?" asked Delight.

"I'll be drinking Apple Sauer with lime, honey," said Jasmine while rubbing Antwan's arm.

"And what about you, Simmion?" He asked Smack.

"I'm drinking a man's drink, Remy on the rocks for me, Antwan." Smack had that glare in his eyes. They all stood behind Antwan while he ordered their drinks.

A caramel complexioned female came to the section of the bar where Antwan was standing to take his order. "Ah, Chantell darling, can you make me an Apple Sauer with lime, a Yeager Bomb, a Strawberry Daiquiri with Patron and two Remy's on the rocks, please?"

"Is that all Chocolate Dream?" She asked him calling him by his nickname.

She looked like Meagan Goode, but much thicker. She was his favorite barmaid, because she'd slept with him several times.

"Yes, that's all darling." He said.

She reached over the bar and gave him a kiss on his lips for a long moment.

"I miss you, Antwan. We all do." Chantell told him.

"Did you get the package from Buddha Monday?" Antwan asked her.

"Yes, Antwan, I even sampled the pill and it was marvelous. I've been passing it out all night since I got to work, like you asked me to." Chantell told him.

"That's a good girl." He smiled at her.

"Antwan, when am I going to see you? I need my Chocolate Dream." Chantell begged.

"Probably tonight. Look over my shoulder. You see Stefani Blake? Would you like to go to bed with us?" Antwan asked.

"You know I would and especially Jasmine, I miss her too." Chantell told him.

"Well after the club shuts down, we will make love. Now get me my guest's drinks and don't keep us waiting. That's rude."
Antwan gave her the look of important.

She walked away from him to fix their drinks.

"Antwan, I see you're very fond with the women." Smack told him.

"Simmion, you are quite a specimen yourself having two women fight over you. But this is what we do Simmion get money and the women follow. Look I'm connected in six different countries around the world. Have you ever been to China?" Antwan asked him.

"No, I've only been to Hawaii and the Virgin Islands outside the country." Said Smack.

"That's not outside the country. It's still US territory. Then where did you learn how to speak German?" Antwan asked him.

"I studied German from K-12 at a Bilingual Academy." Smack told him.

"Oh, I see. Well I have two extra V.I.P. passes to the Olympic Games in China in July. Maybe you and Stefani would like to join me and Jasmine." Antwan proposed to him.

"I would love to go to China, but excuse me Antwan, this is my song." Said Smack.

T.I. and Rihanna, "Live Your Life" came on and Smack wanted to dance. He tried to grab Stefani, but she declined by snatching away from him, he took Delight to the dance floor. "Stefani, why didn't you go out there with Simmion?" Antwan asked her.

"I have a headache. I think it came from the food at the restaurant. I don't think the Sauerbraten was soybean." Said Stefani.

"Well take this pill with your drink and it will take your headache away." Antwan handed her a pink capsule which was the Black Ice.

"What is this pink pill, Antwan?" Stefani asked him.

"You'll like it Stefani, trust me." Antwan smiled at her and then Chantell came with their drinks. Antwan handed Chantell some more pills and they took a table close to the bar. He also gave Jasmine a pill to take. Delight was dancing all seductively on Smack and then she got close and personal up on him. "Yeah, I'm fucking you tonight, even if I have to get in the bed with you and outback." She told him in his left ear, because the music was loud. He didn't respond to her comment. Then her song came on, Soldier Boy "Kiss Me Thru the Phone". They remained on the dance floor. You could hear them both reciting the lyrics.

"You're my future wifey, I miss you, I miss you," as her booty was pressing up against the print in his slacks.

Back at the table, the pill was now beginning to take its effect on Stefani and Jasmine. They both were feeling good. The adrenaline started to flow within them. Stefani's hormones were now in an uproar and her headache was gone.

Stefani leaned over to Antwan and stuck her tongue in his mouth. After pulling away she said, "I want to fuck you and Jasmine tonight." Antwan gave her a grin, but Jasmine was calm as ever enjoying her high. Antwan told her. "Before we do that Stef, go and play with Vamps out on the dance floor."

She got up and made her way to the cages. Then T-Pain "I'm in Love with a Stripper" came on as Stefani entered one of the cages.

Delight and Smack made their exit from the dance floor. They reached the table and Stefani wasn't there. "Yo, where's Stefani?" Smack asked Antwan.

Antwan pointed to the cages. Smack saw a different side of Stefani in the cages. She was getting loose. She was dancing and pulling her gown up showing her thong. She started rubbing herself in her private area repeatedly.

"Delight, here's your drink, darling." As Antwan passed her the glass.

"Thank you." She replied with courtesy. Delight wasted no time drinking half way down.

"Here you go, Simmion, my friend." He gave Smack his drink.

"Excuse me, where's the restroom? Delight asked Antwan.

"Right over there along the wall in the back." He pointed in the direction where the restrooms were located.

"Smack, I'll be right back, baby." As Delight excused herself to the lady's room.

It gave Antwan a chance to explain the Black Ice to Smack. They watched Delight leave. When she was far away Antwan showed Smack the pill.

"Simmion, this is Black Ice." Antwan handed him the capsule.

"What type of pill is this and why is it pink?" Smack questioned him.

"It's a drug to relax the brain cells as well as get you high. It's cocaine, heroin, speed and hash. This is what the Europeans use over there. We could make a fortune over here on American soil, Simmion." Antwan was massaging his goatee.

"How does it work?" Smack asked him.

"It stimulates the mind like marijuana and then it's a downer and roller coaster giving you a rush. A high that last for hours and it makes the females horny. Look up there at Stefani and then over at Jasmine they both taken a pill."

He looked up at Stefani and she was fingering herself in the cage still dancing naughty like a zombie. The Eurhythmics "Sweet Dreams" was playing. Then he turned and looked at Jasmine and saw her yearning to be touched making sexual gestures.

She was rubbing herself between her legs and her breast. "Touch one of her breasts, Simmion. She won't say anything, she wants you to." Antwan told him.

Smack looked at Antwan and he nodded for him to do so. Smack reached over the table and massaged one of Jasmine's breast through her silk blouse. It was firm and the nipple was rock hard.

"See Simmion, I told you she's perfectly fine with it. You could fuck her right there on the spot." Antwan gave him a smirk.

"it's like Ex, pretty much?" Smack asked him.

"No, Simmion, it's better than that junk. It doesn't make you do foolish things, like accidentally kill someone or black out. The drug does have that one type of illusive in it."

"How much does it cost, Antwan?" Smack asked him.

Antwan knew he had Smacks interests when he asked how much it cost.

"One capsule cost one hundred and fifty American dollars in Europe. I say we get it over here and market it for fifty to one hundred dollars a pill. Three hundred pills come in a bottle. What if we go seventy-five dollars a pill time three hundred? Now that good money. Yeah, twenty-two thousand and five hundred dollars, now that's good money."

Antwan told him and Smack zeroed in on the numbers.

"That is good money off of one bottle of pills in a gel capsule. Twenty-two bands and it's easy to move. Even if we charge twenty-five dollars a pill those are still good numbers, because everyone is not going to be able to afford the pill between fifty and one hundred and fifty a pop. Especially if we are trying to take over from the cocaine users, heroin users, and other pill poppers." Smack broke it down to Antwan not knowing he was getting sucked in.

"See Simmion, that's why I want you to help me, because you are a thinker, a business man. I need your street smarts on this one." Antwan told him.

"Where do we sell the pill, Antwan?" Smack asked him.

"That's where you come in at. You already said it. Your witty mind and the people you know, we can spread the drug easily. First, we give samples to make people want it and talk about it and then we market it. I have fifty bottles here in the US, a new drug that everyone's waiting for. I've given out hundreds of pills already in the club and people are asking for it. You see the barmaid, Chantell, over there?" Antwan turned to show Smack.

"Yeah, I see her."

"She's not just serving drinks; she is passing the drug out." As they saw transactions go down. "Simmion, my friend, it's just a matter of time before the break out, but honestly I need you on the team. We can make it up in foreign land and distribute it on American soil. what do you say, Simmion?" Antwan reached out his hand to him.

"Let me sleep on it, Antwan, like a few hours and I'll call you," said Smack.

"That's fine with me, Herr. Here's my card and bout two hundred pills in this bottle."

"Okay and this is the number?" Smack wanted to make sure because of the area code.

"Yeah, it's 216-683-4242. I always keep a different code from the city I'm in." said Antwan.

"I got you. I'll let you know my decision tomorrow." Smack assured him with a smile.

Delight returned to the table and Jasmine was still feeling good not saying a word. She was horny as hell and Delight knew she seemed a little different.

"What's wrong with Jasmine? did I miss anything while I was away? Delight asked.

"No, you didn't miss anything and Jasmine is fine." Smack looked at her.

"Well I'm ready to leave Smack," as she looked at him licking her lips fanning her lower area.

"Okay, Stefani's on her way to the table now." Smack looked up to see Stefani coming. Stefani was high, horny and hot. You could see it on her face. She snapped when Smack told her they were ready to go. "I'm not fucking bloody ready to leave. I need another drink. Get me a bloody drink, I say." She stumbled and pointed her finger at him.

"C'mon Stef, you're wasted," as he tried to grab her arm.

"Get your bloody paws off me," as she snatched away from him.

"Simmion, you two go ahead and I'll make sure Stefani gets home safe." Antwan told him.

"Yeah, Simmion, you and that bloody heifer go ahead," said Stefani almost falling over.

Delight looked at her crazy but didn't respond and then looked at Smack. He shrugged his shoulders. "Antwan, are you sure man?" Smack asked him.

"Simmion, I'm positive," as he tilted his head to Smack. Smack looked over at Stefani and gave her a disgusted look. He grabbed Delight's arm and they headed for the elevator. Antwan watched them get on the elevator.

"My beautiful butterflies, the both of you have done wonderful. Are you two ready to have sex with the Chocolate Dream?" Antwan asked Jasmine and Stefani.

"I'm ready baby," said Jasmine looking like a zombie.

****

"Smack, you are driving into Newport," said Delight.

"I know Delight, I know," as he drove down Green Up Street from 12th Street heading for the Catwalk in Newport on the river. Smack wanted to clear his mind from what he just witnessed after leaving Jillian's. It was 1:30 am and he took in Antwan's proposal, but was really wondering what was wrong with Stefani. She was acting all weird. What is this Black Ice?

Delight saw something was worrying him and was concerned. "What's bothering you?" Delight asked him.

"Nothing. I just wanted to walk along the river to see how calm it is at night. Also, I have never done this before with a female, so I'm taking the opportunity with you." Smack told her while putting the car in park.

"I've never done this before either." Delight confessed to him.

"I guess we will both cherish this moment. Did it seem like Stefani was acting strange to you?" Smack asked her.

"Fuck that Australian bitch or do you really care for her? You're with the future, but you're thinking about that bitch." Delight caught an attitude.

"It's not that. It was just odd because she doesn't like for me to be alone with you. That night when we had sex in the Showcase, she smelled your scent on me. She even questioned me of cheating and the only thing she told me to do was wear a condom the next time." He put his head down.

"That's what white bitches do, Smack. They'll give you some head before some pussy. Don't worry about it, she'll be out of the picture soon, right?" said Delight.

They got out the car and walked over to the Catwalk. It was a slight breeze on this June night. Summer was coming up in a few days. They sat on a park bench and looked around to see not a soul. It was quiet and romantic and the ambiance was perfect. They studied each other horizontal and parallel coming back to the surface of being eye to eye, nose to nose, and lip to lip. Somehow their tongues came together in a tongue fight with pleasure.

He wanted Delight and she wanted him more. She stood up and removed her wet panties and then bodily tugged at his belt and zipper. She managed to get the slacks open exposing his boxers where she could reach inside the slit and stroked his manhood to a perfection attention. She then mounted him while he sat on the bench underneath her and her Sarong hid their nakedness as she gradually began to ride him aggressively. She grabbed the back of his head for support. Her juices were warm and her texture was smooth getting Smack's thighs and boxers wet. Her moans were unadulterated with soothing rhythm. She nibbled on his ear as she had multiple orgasms. "I needed this Smack, I wanted you bad and I'm still horny for you, but I can wait until we get to West Chester." She was shaking in spasms saying those words.

"You drained me, Delight. You might have to drive us home." He looked at her.

"Smack, you already bust?" She asked him.

"A long time ago, I guess I wanted you just as bad." He said.

"At least that tells me you don't be fucking Stefani like I thought you were, especially if you came so quickly," as she climbed off him.

She looked down at him and said, "Fix your pants, baby, before someone comes walking along here."

He didn't even try to wipe any of her fluids from his Tribal piece. He just slid his manhood back into his boxers and fixed his pants. He was thinking about Antwan and decided that he wanted in on the designer drug. He also knew he would surely have to quit the game shortly with Delight on a serious note.

He loved her and was falling in love with her. He knew to get in and make a mill ticket and get out. His life was becoming more complex and more real. He had a friend in Cleveland named Mucho that he wanted to introduce the drug to. He would tell the Belvy Boyz and his cousin Larro and the Diamond Cut, also. He did the figures in his head for six months dealing over a thousand bottles of the new drug. He knew that him and Antwan would have to bring whole sale price down to $25.00 a capsule. He wanted to attack the dealers selling them a bottle for seventy-five hundred a bottle and let them sell it for profit. They would make their profit selling at $50 to $100 a pill if needed and it would keep them out of the lime light with the product. But how could he keep this from Delight? How could he present his ring to her when she knows he's still in the game?

Many thoughts came and went on their way home going up I-75 to Tylersville road. When they reached the house, they ended up in the basement getting it on and ended up in Smacks master bedroom where him and Stefani slept

****

Meanwhile in a private office at Jillian's Antwan had it set up like a mini apartment with a king-sized bed and entertainment center. Antwan had his hands full with Jasmine, Stefani and Chantell. He was about to have a foursome, but his mind was wondering what Smack was thinking, hoping he would consider his proposal to promote the Black Ice.

He stared for a moment watching the three women touch and taste one another's juices. Then he finally joined in like a King of the jungle taming these females. All three women had taken a pill and was firing hot on the inside. Their wild side had come to life and Antwan loved it. The aroma in the room was lit up with three different scents that made Antwan sexual drive go to the roof. He had all three women before, but not at the same time. He smiled to himself because he was in heaven. Stefani ended up spending the night with Antwan, Jasmine and Chantell

CHAPTER THIRTEEN
THE MEETING

Daylight came quickly and Smack woke up in an empty bed. No Delight and no Stefani. He knew he had sex with Delight in his bed and realized he had to get up and clean up. It was nine in the morning when his cell phone rang and he answered it. "Vegas never sleeps and neither do I."

"What up cuss, dis Larro, what's good your way?" His little cousin Larro asked him.

"I got something good in the makings. You've must have read my mind, because I was about to call you," said Smack.

"what's good hood, the natives are restless?" Larro asked him.

"Get your boys together and be in the Nati by twelve noon." Smack told him.

"I got you big cuss." Larro responded.

"I'll see you when you all get down here and put you up on game." Said Smack.

"I'm out my guy, one," as Larro hung up with Smack.

Then he called the Belvy Boyz to let them know to meet him at the same time to.

He was meeting them at one of his stash spots in the Westwood area the Four Towers apartment complex. It was at a chic's named Fox apartment that he dealt with and she also knew the Belvy Boyz and was creeping with one of them on the low.

Smack got up and removed the bed linen and made it up with fresh linen. He thought he had touched up the evidence pretty good from him and Delight's sexual encounter. He washed the dirty linen and sprayed his bedroom and the theater hoping her scent wouldn't be detected by Stefani. He fed all the pets and was dressed leaving out the house at about twenty-five after eleven with the pills in his possession.

He got in the BMW and hit the garage door opener to see Stefani getting out of a cab. She looked like she was fucking all night. He pulled down by her and let down the window.

"I'll be back later. I have some business in the city with Antwan. I fed all the children in the house and even Bruce's punk ass." He didn't even question her about where she'd been all night. "Okay,

Simmion. I'll see you bloody later." Her voice was dry and sluggish. He didn't even bother to hear her last words as he pulled off.

Out at Slogin & Cummons that same morning, Delight got morning sickness. She threw up at least three times at work. The last time she felt this way was fourteen years ago when she found out that she was pregnant with Rainell.

She knew it; she knew it would eventually happen. How would Smack act now about her when she tells him? *Should I tell him now or wait? Should I find out for sure first, because I did eat that German food last night and was drinking? Maybe it's coming from that?*

She thought to herself. She came out the restroom fixing her clothes and when she reached her office, she had roses on her desk with a note. She smiled thinking the roses were from Smack and she started feeling a little better. The note read:

I'M SORRY DELIGHT. WE NEED TO TALK. KEISHA AND I AREN'T FOOLING AROUND. I LOVE YOU. I WOULDN'T DO YOU LIKE THAT. PLEASE HAVE LUNCH WITH ME SO WE CAN TALK ABOUT IT.

LOVE KENDALL

She balled the note up and threw it and the roses in the trash can. Then she stormed out of her office to Kendall's to let him know face to face that it was over. When she left out of his office you could hear her say, "It's my new man's convertible hard top Benz." She slammed his door behind her and all the attorneys were watching. "What are you all looking at?" said Delight. Everyone looking acted like they were doing something in front of them. She went back to her office.

****

Back at home in West Chester, Stefani was going through Delight's dirty laundry smelling her panties that she had on last night that were wrapped up in her Sarong. Her scent was so familiar to Stefani and she knew it was the same scent Smack had on him when he came in that night smelling like another woman. She was positive about the scents being alike. She took her investigation further while smelling the dirty clothing Smack had on last night. His boxers and slacks had the same exact smell and they were stained. Stefani now really suspected them of messing around as she felt that she had proof of it now. She now understood why he had just changed the sheets this morning when she had just changed them yesterday.

"I knew they were bloody fooling around; this is the same fresh vagina smell I bloody smelled that night Simmion came in late when he was cheating. You're bloody busted Simmion."

Even though he was cheating with Delight, she liked her scent and it even turned her on where she took Delight's panties into the shower with her. She smelled her panties and then masturbated while in the shower.

She would confront them when they both came home. She would be going to Boston in the morning and then catching a ferry to Cape Cod. The beautiful Cape Cod is where vacationers and retired people escape to. This is where she was shooting her next project.

****

Over at Fox's apartment in Westwood, Smack was holding his meeting with the Belvy Boyz and Diamond Cut. They weren't smoking or drinking, it was straight up business.

"Look, I'm positioned to land a new major drug, a new designer drug better than Ex. But I can't market this new narcotic without the help of you all. It's so much room for everyone to make a real good profit. Forget the coke and heroin, this here capsule is the way to retire everyone from the game." as he showed them the pink pill.

"What is that, Smack?" P-Diddy asked him.

"It's called Black Ice, consisting of cocaine, heroin, hash and speed. It's not like Ex, it's way better. I have seen it in action." Smack explained to one of the Belvy Boyz.

"How much does it go for, cuss?" Larro asked him.

"On the streets from fifty to seventy-five or even a hundred dollars, but we will be marketing it for twenty-five dollars. Over in Europe they are paying a hundred and fifty American dollars for one pill."

"Wow, for one pill, huh?" asked Worm.

"Yeah, for one pill. Three hundred pills come in a bottle. I have samples so we can put it on the streets and in the major clubs in Cincinnati and Dayton first. Then we put it in the geek's hands.

We are trying to get rid of the cocaine, crack and heroin users all together. We will even try to push if off on the marijuana users. Karmen, Tricee, Bob and Fox are willing to sample the pill to show you guys the effects it has and what it does." Smack told them hoping it would do the same to them as it did to Stefani and Jasmine last night. He gave each one of them a pill and they took it. Everyone waited patiently to see the results. After about five minutes their eyes began to lower and get glossy.

"I feel warm on the inside, but calm. A rush just came through my body and my pussy is getting wet." Karmen confessed to everyone.

"I'm floating on air right now and my pussy is leaking. Damn, this is better than snorting pow-wow," said Tricee.

"Fuck smoking some crack and shooting heroin, I like this high. It's rather mellow and I'm not geeking." Bob told them.

"Fuck this shit, I'm ready to fuck and suck something. I'm horny as hell. What's up with some dick? D$Boy, Dante, Smack, Worm, P-Diddy, somebody come and handle this," said Fox while she was rubbing herself between her legs. "Damn, I'm high as hell." Fox added. She started taking her clothes off in front of them and was rubbing herself harder and harder. "I told you this is the truth, it's what it does. No dummy effects, we won't have any worries about people killing someone or flipping out. No cooking, no sifting, no clean up job or scales. Who's in?" Smack asked them.

"Shit Smack, we all in," as Dante was groping Fox and fingering her in the corner.

"Yo, Dante, you and Fox can take that shit to her bedroom," said Smack to one of the Belvy Boyz who was engaging in sexual pleasures with Fox.

"Yeah, Packman, take that shit to the back," said Kekou one of the Belvy Boyz and Dante's cousin. He called Dante by his street name, "Packman".

"I'm going with ya'll, I want some dick too," said Tricee. She followed the two towards the bedroom in the back.

"Listen P-Diddy, Worm and Kekou, ya'll take my cousin and his click over to Good Fella's and I'll meet up with ya'll in about an hour. Make sure that nigga Dante is with ya'll and not here when I meet back up with ya'll." Smack was calling the shots.

"We got you," said P-Diddy.

"I'll see ya'll in a few." Smack got up and left. While he was riding in his Beemer, he called Antwan. Antwan told Smack to meet him at the restaurant in Clifton. Smack wanted to make a few million from this new drug before quitting the game. His calculations and time frame would allow him to do so. Life successors build on a lack of foundation with less, but with more to offer. He didn't know Antwan Klein was a master mind and a killer. When everything would begin to go in motion, Antwan would get rid of Elliott Thrasher. It was about to be another epidemic on American soil, a takeover like New Jack City.

Judge Phil Helmet didn't make it home this night nor did he make it to the courtroom that morning, he was still in Miesha's bed. After dinner they spent the rest of the evening on St. James. Judge Helmet was still asleep when Miesha was piling in her Daycare kids. She was so scandalous and protecting herself that she was now video recording her and the Judge's sexual encounters by hiding a video cam inside her Dumbo stuffed elephant. She was now protecting her best interests with him if he tried to dismiss her with a broken heart and empty purse. Blackmail was in the back of her mind ready to surface. She was now a gutsy female with much ambition. That morning she received a phone call from her cousin. He wanted to invite her to a cook out.

"Hello Miesha, dis is your big cuss." She held the phone for a long moment before answering. "Hey Kyle, what do you want, because I don't have any bail money."

It was Kyle Peterson, Miesha's big cousin on the receiving end.

"Miesha, do I ever call you when I get into trouble?" He asked her.

"Umm, yes you do, all the time to be exact. What's up?" She asked him.

"Nothing, I was just wondering if you would like to attend a cook-out with me in West Chester this Saturday." Kyle asked her.

"Whose house Kyle, or do you really want for me to help you case out someone's shit? You know you are always up to something." said Miesha.

"My dude, Smack, is having a cook-out at his place. You and I haven't kicked it in a while and I was wondering, would you like to go?" Kyle was being naïve.

"You got my money nigga?" She asked him.

"I got it and it's going to be some major cats at the cook-out." Said Kyle.

"what, I'm doing me." She was being sarcastic.

"Please, Miesha." He begged her.

"What time, Kyle?" She asked him.

"It's at two in the afternoon." He pleaded.

"Alright, call me before you come and have my money." She told him with aggression.

"I will, little cuss, love you," said Kyle.

"Bye nigga." Miesha hung up the phone.

She knew her cousin was up to something and she thought about what he said, "Major cats' will be there."

Judge Helmet came to the entrance of the living room in his Mickey Mouse boxers.

"Miesha, do you have any coffee available sweetie?" Judge Helmet asked her. He stood there showing his hairy chest and pale legs. She looked at him and said. "Go put some clothes on; these kids don't want to see you like that. I'll make you some coffee."

She rolled her eyes at him. "Oh, I completely forgot about your day job. I'm sorry," as he tried to cover up. All six of her Daycare children were asleep.

****

"Tyree, my dad wanted me to invite you and your parents to our cook-out on Saturday." Rainell told Tyree, the young fella she met at the movies.

Smack had called her earlier after meeting the Belvy Boyz and Diamond Cut at Good Fella's letting her know he was throwing a cook-out Saturday and she could invite her friends. Smack wanted to celebrate the upcoming events surrounding the new drug and his organization.

"Hold on Rainell," as he took the phone away from his ear. You could hear him scream. "Mama, my friend Rainell is inviting me to their family cook-out. Can we go, Ma, please?" Tyree asked his mother.

"When is it, Tyree?" His mother asked him. Tyree got back on the phone. "Rainell, when is it again? He asked her.

"Tyree, it's this Saturday afternoon at two o'clock," said Rainell.

"Hold on Rainell," as he put the receiver away from his ear again, covering it up with his hand.

"Ma, it's this Saturday at two o'clock."

"Where does your friend live, Tyree?" His mother asked him.

"She lives in West Chester." He answered his mom.

"Well get the address and I'll see if Mr. Doug wants to go with us." His mom told him.

"Okay, Ma. Rainell says hi." Tyree smiled at his mother.

"Tell her I said hello." His mom replied.

"Yes, ma'am," he said as he got back on the phone and his mother went back into her room.

"Rainell, what's the address? We are coming." Tyree said.

"See if you can bring your cousin Kris with you, because Daysha is going to be there."

Rainell suggested because Daysha was nudging her to do so.

"I'll make sure he comes too." said Tyree.

"Well the address is...," as Rainell gave him the information and she finished talking on the phone.

****

Earlier Smack was being greeted by Antwan in the restaurant. "Guten Tag Herr Simmion," as Smack walked into the restaurant which was empty at this time of day. Antwan greeted him with a German passage telling him 'Good day'. He shook his hand and took him into his private study. They discussed their business over a blunt of Cush and a glass of Remy. Antwan agreed to Smack's idea and made him an equal partner. He told Smack he had guns if things needed to be handled in the streets. When Smack left from Lenhardt's, he had twenty-five bottles of the Black Ice. Antwan made a call to some foreign people over in Europe and he told Smack they would be letting off their own fireworks come the Fourth of July.

Smack left the restaurant going down McMillian to Vine Street. He made a left on Vine Street and went over to short Vine Street by the University Plaza to get to Good Fella's.

****

Smacked walked into Good Fella's and everyone accounted for shook his hand and Larro handed him a drink, which was Remy. They were eating hot wings and waiting on the next move which Smack had it. They had the whole back area occupied in the establishment. They were in a low whisper as customers came into the restaurant to pick up orders and who were dining in.

"Listen, we have to work quickly because the order is in and by the end of June, I want for us to be rocking and rolling," said Smack.

"How are we going to do that, big cuss?" Larro asked him.

"I have twenty-five bottles. Each party gets ten bottles and ya'll divide it up as needed," said Smack.

"Yo, Vino, you can hit Biff's Trotters, the Golden Nugget and ya'll end of McMicken with Worm. Umm, Kobe and Kekou, ya'll can stay down at the store, Queen Ann, Parktown, the Phoenix, and Shakers in Town and ya'll end of McMicken." P-Diddy paused and continued, "umm, Bodean you can hit Sonny's on Reading Road and California, Vito's, Brandy's, Phat Daddy's and Shakers in College Hill. Dante, you can go out to Jelly's, Debbie Destiny, Cruise Inn, Double D's, The Garage, Metropolis and Rhino's out your way. Weezy you can hit up Annie's, the No Name, the Living Room, Bella, The Blue Rock, Club Seven, Club Dream, the Mixx, Red Cheetah and the 12th Street Bar in Covington. I'll go to the VIP, Omar's, Perkins, The Tropicana, Coconut Joe's, The Legacy and Evolution." P-Diddy was calling the shots for his click, the Belvy Boyz.

"Oh, I almost forgot, we all can hit the Ritz, Motor Cycle Club, Suave's and the Candy Shop." P-Diddy added.

"And up our way in the Gem City, Bo-Gotti you can hit the K9 in Jefferson Township and OHO's on Adelite. D$Boy, you can hit up Evolutions on Dixie and Yellow Rose out in West Carrolton. Fila, you can hit up Foundry, Fusions and Fat Cats.

Me, Chill and Freaky-D will go downtown to Cream Rain, Hammer Jack's, Santana's and Sloppy's in the Oregon District. Oh, I forgot about Club 22 over by the Coast on James H. McGee. We can all hit those spots," Larro was calling the shots for the Diamond Cut. Those were the main clubs in Cincinnati and Dayton they were targeting to expose the Black Ice.

It sounded good to Smack and he knew the loyalty and hard work would pay off.

"Dante, we'll let you politic with the main hustlers around the city because you know damn near everybody." P-Diddy was still calling the shots.

"Okay, I'll holla at Dickey, Spivey, Daren, Fat Shaun, Tone, Chrome, Ronnie B., Deaf Chris, Lil Shaun, Boogie, Da-Da, Lockie, Quincy, Dooly, T.D., Fiedale, Hot Rod and his brother Kenny, Big Cheese and Poochie in Avondale. Then I'll go on the Westside of town and holla at Fello, Day-Day, Keith, Big Sube, Ed-Lover, and Ronny," said Dante.

"What about Walnut Hill, Evanston, OTR, Bond Hill, College Hill and Madisonville?" Bodean asked him.

"I can go to Walnut and holla at LB and his brother Lamar, T-Brown, Fat Shit, Lil Pooh, Renzo, Catfish, Red & Rod, Willy-D, K-Mersh, June, Melvin, Ted, Lil E, Edmond, Lovey, Jody, Dondi, Sam, Sonny Red, Stank and Big Don. Then I'll go to E-Town and chat with Big Andre, Todd-Bo, Ethy, Jerry, Fred, Boozer, K-Stone, Squirrel, E-Links, JB, Vick, Opie, Germaine, Tim, Frank Nitty, Lil Chris, Sick, Erk, Reese Skeeter, Al Ford, Roni, and Millio." Dante knew a lot of people.

"Then I'll go out to Mad-Ville and Kennedy Heights and holla at Psych, Big Dominique, Big Head Duane, Keith, Deek Jr., Ears, Charlie, Chris, D-Blue, Mike J., Tony, Star, Shag, T-Kelly, Cuff, Bumps, Lil Joe, Ernie, Wayne, Ryan, Rob, G, Boo-Dock and Serge. After I stop over there I'll head out to Bond Hill and put those cats up on game. Like Jell-O, Dirty, The Baker Boy, Montez, Jazz, Butchie, Trey, Zero, Lomax and Lil Brian.

"Then I'll hit downtown and holla at Ike, Tank, Nic-Boady, Big L, Scory, Moe, Jacque, Ford, Rex, Zay-Bo, Reesy, Dimp, Veal, Hog, Jazzy, Ralph, Squally, Lucky, Venom, and Many Train," said Dante.

"What about College Hill?" Kobe asked him.

"Oh yeah. I'll go holla at CHP, Yo, Black Ralph, Germ, Spider, Rah-Rah, Kenny, Ron Mack, Skeet and my dude Rashad." Dante was counting on his fingers.

"Dante, if we bring those cats in it will be no problem getting the new drug all throughout the city that sounded like an All-Star team." Said Smack.

"I told you that nigga knows every fucking body." P-Diddy added.

"Then everything is set. I'll holla at my cat Mucho in Cleveland, my guy K.G. in Akron and Big Aaron in Springfield," as Smack took a sip of his Remy and continued.

"Everyone knows the game plan? I have about fifteen bricks of blow left at fourteen-five and after I pay off these Columbian cats, I'm not getting any more work. Whoever wants it, it's available to you. I'm having a cook-out this Saturday and I would like everyone to attend and bring your girl's and kids. The food and drinks will be provided by me and I have a pool so bring your swim gear. This shit is going to be bigger than BMF, let's toast to a new beginning of getting rich," as Smack lifted his glass in the air and everyone did the same.

****

Later, that day, Delight reached the house in West Chester at around 5:45 that evening. She pulled the Benz in the garage and the 750 BMW was missing. Her Range Rover was still in Price Hill getting worked on. Smack wasn't home yet when she entered the house to see Stefani sitting in the kitchen eating some yogurt. It was complete silent and hard stares when Delight went into the stainless-steel refrigerator for bottle water. She felt Stefani's eyes burning the back of her neck. When she turned around their eyes locked and a bomb went off. "Damn, Stefani, what the fuck are you staring at?" asked Delight. Stefani placed her spoon in the almost finished yogurt with her legs crossed and she folded her arms. "Delight, you bloody think I'm stupid. I know you and Simmion are bloody fucking. You are pathetic, I say," said Stefani.

"Girl, you are tripping," as Delight placed her water on the counter.

Delight wanted to tell her the truth, but respected Smack as just being her mistress with a secret. "I'm bloody not tripping; I'm bloody on to you two. I found out because Simmion is bloody careless, I say. But in our home, that's going to bloody far, don't you think?" Stefani looked at her.

Delight didn't say anything while Stefani continued.

"He changed the linen and I couldn't bloody figure it out at first, because I just changed them yesterday. Then I found your bloody scent on his boxers and pants he had on last night and your bloody Sarong and panties had the exact same scent, your bloody cunt smell. He's came home several times with your bloody scent on him. You have a man, a bloody husband, why don't you take yourself and your kid home to him, I say."

"Bitch, are you serious? I know you weren't snooping through my clothes and shit. What type of bitch are you sniffing my panties like some sick individual with a fetish? Bitch, you are nasty. So, what, we're fucking and we've been fucking for several months now and that's the truth. What are you going to do about it?" Delight was more than angry; she was pissed off. She exploded and couldn't take it anymore.

"I'm bloody here, this is my house and Simmion is going to have to bloody choose either me or you. That's what I'm going to do, leave it up to him," as Stefani unfolded her arms and Smack was coming in on the end of Stefani's last words. Delight looked at him as well as Stefani. "Hey ladies! What's going on? What do you want for dinner?" asked Smack. He wasn't aware that he had just walked into a battle field.

"Fuck some bloody dinner, she has to leave our bloody home now, Simmion," said Stefani.

"Wait a minute. What's going on here?" asked Smack.

"You are bloody fucking Delight, in my face Simmion, in our home. Are you bloody stupid, mate?" said Stefani. Delight looked at him and said, "She knows Smack. She's been sniffing my panties and your boxers. She called herself checking me, so I let the outback bitch know the truth. I'm sorry. I know it wasn't my place to tell her, but she provoked me."

"You either bloody choose between me and her right now, Simmion," as tears began to flow down Stefani's cheeks. Delight just looked at her wondering how she would feel if this blew up in her face like this. Even though she saw Kendall out with Keisha, she didn't catch them in their house. "Smack, you don't have to choose, I'll leave," said Delight. Stefani and Smacked looked up at her. She started for the entrance way and Smack grabbed her arm. "Wait Delight, I'm not choosing shit right now, it is what it is. I mean you are my girlfriend Stefani, but I'm in love with Delight and when you get back from Cape Cod, I'll have things sorted out."

His response made Delight feel warm on the inside and Stefani's shallow smile turned back into a frown. "You're in love with her? Are you bloody serious, Simmion? You're making my bloody head hurt," as she got up. "I'm going to bloody lie down and maybe this nightmare will go away and this bloody man stealing heifer will be gone. She's over the bloody hill. What, she's forty plus? She'll be nothing but a bloody fat cow in a year or two," said Stefani. She walked out the kitchen leaving Smack and Delight standing there.

"Why that little bitch. I should beat her ass. Bitch, by the way, I'm thirty-eight," Delight said. It was loud enough for Stefani to hear. Then Delight received a sharp pain in her stomach. "Awe shit," as Delight grabbed her stomach.

"What's wrong, Delight?" said Smack.

"I don't know, but I think I'm pregnant, Smack. I've been throwing up all day at work and the last time I felt this way was when I found out I was pregnant with Rainell." Delight looked up at him. Smack helped her over to a chair. "Sit down right here. What you want me to do? Did you take a pregnancy test? Have you made a doctor's appointment?" Smack was nervous and happy at the same time.

****

When Stefani awoke around twelve midnight, she let Smack have his way with her. She allowed him to put his tribal piece down her throat, in her anal and her pussy without any protection. Her last words were, "Simmion, I bloody love you and I want for us to have a bloody family one day. But I want Delight to be bloody gone when I return from my trip darling." She kissed him and then she kissed his manhood looking up at him. That early Friday morning around two a.m. Stefani was leaving in a cab for the airport. She had taken like fifteen pills of the Black Ice that

Smack had in their room. She had taken one earlier for her headache. She recognized the pill from when Antwan gave it to her at the club. Smack didn't know she had confiscated the pills. Smack went into the guest room and got in the bed with Delight. "Hold me, Smack," said Delight in a low whisper and they fell asleep.

CHAPTER FOURTEEN
THE COOK-OUT

That Friday morning Delight called in sick and instead of going to work she went and retrieved a pregnancy kit from Walgreen's. Smack was out feeding the pets when Delight was taking her own urine sample on the strip. When the results came back it showed that it was a strong possibility that she was pregnant. She was in a state of confusion, mainly because she was thirty-eight, still married to a man she no longer loved and the child wasn't going to be his plus she had a teenaged daughter.

Even though she was happy with Smack, and somewhat in love with him, she really didn't believe in the wrong she was doing. No matter the degree of happiness one would like to have, pleasure principle is still a sense of responsibility and security. Delight knew she didn't have Smack's full attention because Stefani was still around. But she knew he wanted to be with her and she needed his mind all to herself now that she might be pregnant by him.

How could she get him? She knew a baby couldn't keep a man and wasn't going to play in to that. Her style and character were of a Goddess so why did she feel like she was competing for his time and mind? Because she was!

He entered the guest room to find Delight sitting on the bed lost in many thoughts. He sat right beside her rubbing a portion of her thigh gently. Then their eyes locked with much respect and the both had on poker faces.

"What's going on, Delight?" Smack asked her a soft question of concern.

"I did the pregnancy test and it came back positive showing I'm most likely pregnant. I have a doctor's appointment in two weeks," as she started crying.

"Delight, baby, why are you crying? You should be happy as I am," said Smack grabbing her face and wiping her tears with the heel of his palm.

"Smack, are you really happy? Will you just leave me for someone who's younger and prettier? I'm thirty-eight not twenty-eight, like you," said Delight.

"Delight, I'm here for you and only you. I want you and only you. You're pretty enough for me. You are the complete package. You have brains, beauty and a wonderful personality. A woman like you are one in a million and I told you I want to marry you."

"Simmion, you don't have to do this because of the new news, I'm okay. I'm going to have this baby regardless if you are with me or not. But whenever you don't feel like being with me anymore just let me know ahead of time, okay," said Delight.

"That will never happen. Stefani is out when she gets back from her trip. I want for you and Rainell to be here with me as a family. We are having a cook-out tomorrow, I promised Rainell." Smacked looked at her.

"Oh, we are huh?" asked Delight. This news was new to her.

"Yeah, a few friends are coming over to eat, swim, drink and you know, have a little fun. I told Rainell to invite her little friend that she met at the movies and his parents. Also, we had the father and daughter talk. Boy can she ask a lot of questions. I think it would be best for you to start her on birth control now, Delight."

"Why Smack, do you think she's...you know...?" Delight looked at him.

"I don't think so, Delight, but I know Daysha is a hot one and that's her friend and I know they talk. We can't keep our eyes on her 24-7 so let's be safe and not sorry," said Smack.

"Yes sir, super dad. I will do that. Anything else, baby?" Delight asked him.

"I'm about to go and get Rainell and then go to the grocery store. When I get back, we are going up on Route 4 to get your new truck."

"What new truck? I like my Range Rover, Smack," Delight looked at him confused.

"A 2008 Infiniti QX56 fully loaded. I already priced it and we are trading in your Range Rover. The QX56 is $42,900 and the dealership is going to knock off fifteen grand for your Range Rover. I will pay the difference after that." He told her.

"Is my truck fixed, Smack?" She asked him.

"Yes, it's fixed and Nathan is bringing it out here now."

"Can I go to the grocery store with ya'll, Smack?" Delight asked him.

"I don't care, that's if you feel up to it, Delight."

"I'm going, we are a family, right? We should do family things together," as she reached up and kissed him.

Smack didn't tell her that the cook-out was to let his new organized crime family get more acquainted. He also would ask Heather to cook on the grill.

****

That Saturday morning Heather was on the three-rack gas grill cooking. Smack bought enough food to feed a homeless shelter. He had liquor and champagne to add to the festivities. He cleaned the pool and had extra loungers with tables and tents set up. D.J. Rob G was setting up his equipment in the backyard. Goliath and Nevada were in their kindles by the lions and Bruce was chained to a tree. Heather was looking like a young girl with her tight Apple Bottom shorts and tight t-shirt showing off her pretty feet in her thong sandals. Rainell was helping her cook. Delight wasn't feeling good at this time and she was lying down in the master bedroom, because she moved her belongings into the master bedroom. It was one-thirty in the afternoon when Smack was pulling the all-white Infiniti truck closer to the garage doors next to the Cadillac truck. He also had to move Heather's all red Lexus GS400 in the driveway. D.J. Rob G was already playing music in the backyard.

Dante and Worm were the first ones to arrive to Smack's house. They were in Dante's white drop top 650ci BMW with two females, Breyon and Joan. Breyon was with Worm, she was gorgeous a sure dime with two golds on the side of her top arrangement. Joan was with Dante; she was a young female who owned her own Escort service with her cousin. Joan had on a two-piece white bikini set with a wraparound mini-skirt and some slip-on heels. She was a dime with much body, style and attitude. She also had a logo tattooed on her back real big of Dante's nickname. *"Packman's Property"*. Larro pulled up next with Freaky D, Auni and Shia in a 2006 silver Chevrolet Z-28 convertible nap on 22" chrome rims.

D$Boy followed in his 2004 yellow Ford Mustang Mach I sitting on 22" chrome rims. He was with a beautiful chocolate stallion by the name of Secret.

Bo-Gotti and Chill was right behind D$Boy in a black on black 05 convertible GT Mustang with two red bones, Zabrina from Arlington Heights and Nikki from Fairborn. Fila showed up on a 07 Suzuki Hayabusa GSX 1300 with a thick white girl who could be Co-Co's twin sister. She looked like her from the hair, boobs, height, face, nails and booty, her name was Precious. She was sitting on back of the Suzuki in a green thong bikini set and some green stiletto heels. The way she was positioned on the bike you could see her vagina lips poking out the side.

P-Diddy pulled up with his girl Asia and their two kids in a 08 Dodge Charger SE on 22" chrome and black rims. Bodean followed him in a 05 Cadillac Deville on 22" rims with his girl Lula. Kobe and his brother Kekou pulled up in a dark blue 07 Chrysler 300 with their baby mama's Qui and LaDonda. Vino a.k.a Fatbastard pulled up in a white 07 750 series BMW on 24" rims with his wife Chandra and two of his kids. Weezy came through in his 05 convertible Corvette with his girl Stania and their son.

More and more people were showing up to the cook-out. Worm's sisters, Puff and Yvette, came with their friends Nez, China, Adina, May-May, Fox and Ruthy. Dante's baby mama, Eva and their daughter Khalani were present. Even Karmen, Sonja and Tasha were there representing the Satin Dolls.

D.J. Rob G was playing Bird Man's 'Fast Money' when Delight came to the pool in a two-piece orange bikini and a white wrap around in some Gucci heels. You could see all her curves and some.

Besides all the other beautiful women at the pool, Delight was holding her own. Secret, Breyon, Joan and Precious were probably the baddest females on sight at the cook-out. They had no stretch marks or cellulites with flat stomachs. Rainell's friend Tyree showed up with his mom, Denise and her boyfriend, Doug. He brought his cousin Kris and his parent's Lacey and Howe. Daysha was there and no one could believe that Smack had lions in his backyard, Rainell was the happiest teenage girl on the planet.

Then Smack associates from Akron and Cleveland showed up. Mucho was from Cleveland and K.G. was from Akron. Heather was eyeing K.G. and besides her kangaroo pouch she was looking good in her tight shorts. It was like a Luke party in Ohio. Delight was having a conversation with Tyree's mom Denise and her cousins Lacey when Miesha and Kyle walked in. Miesha was shitting on everything at the cook-out in a bikini or in regular clothes.

She was light complexion with green eyes, naturally curly hair. She had on some white tight Capri pants and a tight pink Polo shirt. Her nails and feet were done. You could see her pretty feet from her flat Cole Haan with the toes out. Her ass was like 42" and perfectly round. The white Capri's showed that she was wearing a thong. She turned a lot of heads even a few females and Mucho and Worm were eyeing her.

"Who are all these people, Kyle?" said Miesha in a whisper.

"That's the man whose house you are in, Smack he's from Dayton. I don't know the other two guys he's talking to." Kyle told her.

"Kyle, he looks like he is twelve," said Miesha.

"He's grown Miesha, he's older than me. The Cadillac truck you were lusting over is his and he has a hard-top convertible Benz, a 750 BMW, a 65 Chevy Impala identical to the truck and an Infiniti Q45." Kyle told all of Smack's business to his cousin.

"He's balling like that? I might have to give him some pussy and get close to him cuss. I can see myself riding in the Benz with his young-looking ass." Miesha was plotting.

"He has a girlfriend, Miesha. The Australian model Stefani Blake, but she's out of town right now."

"So what Kyle, niggas be wanting new pussy every day, just introduce me and I'll do the rest nigga. Who are those big nigga's over there?" Miesha asked Kyle pointing in the direction of the Belvy Boyz.

"That's Worm, P-Diddy, Dante, Bodean, and Fatbastard, some of the Belvy Boyz," said Kyle. Miesha could see that they were passing two blunts around between them.

"That's Weezy, Kobe and his brother Kekou a.k.a. Larry the rest of the Belvy Boyz," as he pointed them out.

"I see they are rolling too. I like this crowd and I can smell money. This is a fucking goldmine for a bitch like me. I knew it was something big going on seeing all those nice cars parked

outside. I have to be a part of one of these nigga's bankroll."
Miesha knew she had to catch a fish in a pond.

"Chill out Miesha, just chill, okay." Kyle told his little cousin.

"Who are those nigga's over there with their little female friends?" Miesha asked.

"That's Smacks' cousin Larro and his click the Diamond Cut, they are from Dayton," said Kyle.

"They're rocking all that ice; I know them niggas are rolling. Braids and blunts, yeah them nigga's rolling." Miesha smacked her lips.

"Miesha, quit being so thirsty, these cats are probably with their main girls so don't go starting any trouble, flirting and shit. I got a lick for us if you need some extra cash."

"I knew it, Kyle; I knew you had something up your sleeves. What is it, Kyle?" as she looked at him in the eyes not blinking once.

"I'll holla at you later about it, but in the meantime just keep your eyes open and mind your own business." Kyle told her and they walked over to where they could make their own drink.

"Miesha, what do you want to drink?" Kyle asked her.

"I'll just have a Jack Daniels wine cooler if they have any." She looked over her nails.

"He has Bartle's & James." He told her.

"That's cool, Kyle," as she took a quick glance over the backyard again, seeing a lot of females in bikinis. She thought, damn it I should've wore my swimsuit. But she did have on a matching thong and bra set. "C'mon Meisha, let's go and meet Smack and them," as he gave her the wine cooler and a straw. Everyone was wondering who Kyle was with. Bodean had seen Miesha before down on McMicken by Dunlap Park. They approached Smack, Tyree's mother's boyfriend and his cousin Howe. Doug was finished talking to Smack and they were walking away, but Doug couldn't help but to turn and see Miesha's ass walk pass them. Smack was now looking at a bad bitch in front of him.

"What up Kyle, who is this fine last of the dying breed you have with you?" said Smack.

"Hi," as she waved at Smack giving him a half smile.

Smack connected with her green eyes and she followed his eyes down below her neck, to her navel as he gazed at her womanly possessions. She just put her head down as if she was shy and not naughty, but afraid of what a man could do to her goods. She had much game with a soft, but ruthless side. She was what a guy would call a woman whose killing them softly.

"This is where you've been hiding the real diamond, Kyle. You are beautiful, Ms. Lady; I know your man has a tracking device on you." Smack told her.

"I don't have a man, so I guess I'll roam around wherever I please," said Miesha.

"You're lying, I know someone is keeping all of that warm, someway somehow, I know I would. I most definitely would," said Smack.

"what's stopping you?" Miesha asked him. Smack could now see Delight making her way towards them. "Um-um I'm in a relationship, but if I wasn't...," as Smack was cut off by Delight.

"If you wasn't what...? Did I miss something honey?" Delight asked Smack kissing him on the lips and looking Miesha up and down. Miesha looked at her not backing down. Kyle was in shock because Delight had kissed him on the mouth.

"You didn't miss anything. I was just talking to Kyle and his cousin, Miesha. It is Miesha, isn't it?" Smack assured that was her name.

"Yes, it's Miesha Jones to be exact, Smack." Miesha told him looking at Delight.

"Oh, I'm sorry, Miesha and Kyle...this is Delight, my fiancée. Delight, you remember Kyle, don't you?" Smack asked her.

"Yes, I do. Hi, Kyle," said Delight with a big smile.

"How are you doing Mrs. Scott?" Kyle asked her. Smack looked at him and Kyle just shrugged his shoulders.

"It's Heath Kyle. I'm no longer married so I'm back to my maiden name until your boy marries me." She gave another huge smile. Delight stared at Smack, because this was new news to her as well as Kyle.

"Oh, I'm sorry Ms. Delight, I didn't know, I apologize," said Kyle.

"It's okay Kyle. Smack when you're finished out here, I need to see you in the house." Delight reached up and kissed him on the lips. "Okay," Then she walked away throwing her hips making sure she had his attentions as well as Miesha letting her know she was the new bitch in town. She was letting Miesha know if she was after her man, she would be in a fight with a stallion.

Miesha was stuck on stupid, but her mind rewind Delight's face into her memory bank before Delight reached the cool interior of the house. It came to her.

"Right...Miesha, you saw her at the restaurant when you were out with the Judge having dinner. She was arguing with some man who was having dinner with another woman. Okay, I remember Smack now...he was with her and two white women and a dark-complexioned bald guy with a goatee. Delight is a slut. Oh, and Smack's whore he'll go, I know I can fuck him and get in his pockets easy, the right place and time. I'll have his nose open."

Miesha just looked at him and watched Delight go into the house. At the same time, Delight was trying to figure out where she saw Miesha before. Then it came to her.

"Delight, that's the chick Judge Helmet was at dinner with at Lenhardt's the same night I busted Kendall with Keisha Myles. She must be a call girl or an escort."

She kept going into the house to her destination.

Kyle turned to Smack and said, "You're crazy! All this time you've been fucking Delight? Damn, you're sleeping with your lawyer. You are the man, lil brah; hands down you are the man." Kyle was smiling at him clapping his hands. Smack was lost for words.

Miesha nudged Kyle and said, "I thought he was with the model chick?"

Kyle shrugged his shoulders. "Smack, how long have you been bashing Kendall's wife?" Kyle asked him.

"Kyle, she's just staying here until she fines a place for her and her daughter, that's all."

"But she kissed you like ya'll been fucking and that wasn't no granny kiss. Plus, you introduced her as your fiancée, remember?" said Kyle.

"Kyle, we'll talk, but ya'll enjoy yourselves at my Casa. You know where everything is at. If you get bored Miesha, I have a recreation place in the basement, but excuse me I'll catch back up with ya'll later," said Smack.

"Smack, what if I get bored and need some special attention from a man?" Miesha asked him.

"I mean it's plenty to choose from and I have guest rooms, but Kyle knows where everything is at." She made Smack kind of uncomfortable.

"What if it's you I desire and want Smack?" Miesha asked him.

"Miesha, it was a pleasure meeting you...maybe some other time." He walked off.

"Yeah, Smack, maybe some other time." She responded, but he couldn't hear her.

You could hear laughter and splashing from the pool.

"Kyle, I'm going to fuck your boy and I'll be living out here with him. You'll be invited to my functions and please don't steal anything," as she laughed.

"Miesha, he's not your average sucker, he'll break your heart. He's been with some of the baddest bitches known to man. He's even been with Super Head way before Ray J had her and Kim." Kyle told her.

"Cuss, if you weren't my peeps and we can't fuck around I'll give one of these chumps a sample of this drug between my legs."

"Miesha, you are crazy for real."

"Na'll I'm dead serious. You see the real big knocked knee one over there with the braids?" as Miesha pointed to one of the Belvy Boyz.

"Who Bodean?" Kyle asked her.

"Yeah him big boy." She replied.

"What about him?" Kyle asked her.

"He's my target, he'll get some of this bomb ass pussy for free, because he looks like the gossiping type that will run tell everything," said Meisha.

"Well let's go and meet them too." Kyle suggested and they walked in their direction.

****

Cape Cod was a beautiful place for anyone vacationing at this time of year. The photo shoot was a success for Stefani and day one. Stefani and a formal male friend were in her hotel room relaxing and drinking cocktails. She shared a few of the pills with the guy and took three of them herself. Not knowing the effects of what three pills would do, she didn't bother to question it, because she really didn't know what she was really taking. They started getting warm and sexually aroused. She wanted to entertain him with her personal fleshy tissue, so she did. They were getting it on strong when he caught chest pains and had cardiac arrest. She was so out of it, she also experienced cardiac arrest and died, because her heart exploded.

It was breaking news on CNN and World News. Antwan saw it first and Smack wasn't aware of it, because he was entertaining his guest. They really didn't know her cause of death, but it was from an overdose. Smack didn't even know that any of the pills were missing. Antwan would make the call to inform him of his dead girlfriend.

****

"Smack, what's wrong with you? Who was that on the phone?" Delight asked him.

He looked at his cell phone. "It was Antwan." Smack turned on the TV in the bedroom. When he changed the channel to CNN, they were airing the news about the super model Stefani Blake and her tragic death.

"We are live in Cape Cod where super model Stefani Blake and an unknown male friend were found dead in her hotel room. Apparently, they died from a drug overdose. Medical examiners found traces of heroin and cocaine in her blood stream. They also recovered a small pink pill that is getting test ran to see if there's any connection to her death. This is still developing news and we will keep you updated. Okay, back to you Bob, at headquarters."

"Alright Phil, we will keep this story updated at the bottom of the screen and will have a full report this evening."

Smack turned the TV off and was in shock.

"Oh my God, I'm sorry baby, I didn't know she was on drugs like that Smack," said Delight.

"Me neither." He answered her in a low tone. Then he looked over at the pill bottle sitting on the dresser. "Well baby, I'm about to go and finish entertaining our guest and I understand if you want to be alone." Delight held his hand.

"I'm cool; I'll be down in a minute." Delight kissed him hard and long before making her exit.

He was numb, but humble. He secured the door and grabbed the bottle and dumped the pills on the dresser. He counted two hundred and ninety pills so that meant ten were missing. *"Damn it Stef, you didn't even know what the fuck you were taking."* He stumbled back onto the bed and shed a few tears. He didn't want her to leave this way. He killed her. He wished she was gone.

"Bodean, how do you lock this door?" Miesha asked him, because they were in the mini-theater all alone. Bodean had snuck away from his girl, Lula. He and Miesha managed to secure the doors not allowing anyone to enter. It was dark, but a small light came through a back window. They could hear the music playing from the backyard. Bodean couldn't believe the mounds of woman Miesha was. She took off her capri's and her thong and didn't waste any more time by undoing Bodean's shorts and taking him in her mouth making him melt. When he got hard, she slid a condom on him with her mouth. She bent over on one of the lazy boy theater seats and let him enter her passage from the rear. Her 42" booty was in the air and she was so wet it was like a running river coming down her leg. Her juices even got on his boxer shorts. When she felt his manhood begin to swell, she pulled the condom off and sucked him until he exploded in her mouth. His toes curled in his shoes and he was weak almost falling over.

"Damn, Miesha, you are cold with your mouth action and you swallow. My niggas aren't going to believe this shit," said Bodean. Miesha's plan was already beginning to work.

"They can play to big fella, if the price is right. It ain't no fun if the homies can't have none. You have the number, turn them niggas on to a good thing, a group thing, especially your boy, Smack." Miesha told him taking a pause. "Maybe one day ya'll can close down that store you was telling me about and it can be a fuck fest 2008 featuring me and the Belvy Boyz. Let me get dressed and you can think about it," said Miesha.

I'll tell them niggas and we will hook that up ASAP. Here you go, baby girl," as Bodean tried to hand her a fifty-dollar bill.

Miesha looked at him and smiled. "That's on me this time, the next time it's on you."

******

You could hear Jim Jones 'Ballin' as Miesha and Bodean surfaced back to the backyard. When they separated Bodean gave the rest of the Belvy Boyz a thumb up on Miesha. Kyle, Mucho, K.G. and Smack were standing around having a conversation of their own. Miesha pulled up and winked at her cousin Kyle and Bodean was running his mouth to his boys. Kyle knew right then that Miesha did something naughty and devious from her wink and then he saw how the Belvy Boyz was staring at her.

"Kyle, are you ready to go? Because I am, I'm full and tired." Miesha told him and Mucho was eyeing her. She caught him during Kyle's reply. "In about a minute, I'll be ready to go, Miesha," said Kyle.

Miesha let Mucho know he didn't have a chance at her in any form or fashion.

"Sorry boo-boo, I don't fuck with nigga's who think they look better than me. You might be fine, but I like soldiers in Timbo's, braids and tattoos." Miesha looked at him.

"Oh, you look like a pimp, smell like a pimp so pimp on pimping, because pimpin' ain't easy," as Miesha walked off shaking her 42" ass in his face. She went over by the food to fix her a plate and K.G. was laughing hard, "I told you that Super Fly shit doesn't work all the time. Nigga, casual don't fly 24-7," said K.G.

"Nigga, fuck you, I have enough bad bitches in my stable," said Mucho, because he was heated. He always said if a bitch didn't like him, they didn't like men.

"Mucho, you know she's bad and you want her, she shitted on you and you can't accept it. She is shitting on everything in your stable nigga, especially up in the Land." K.G. told him.

"Nigga, I have bad bitches in L.A., the Chi, Vegas, and NYC. Pimps up and Ho's down she wants me," said Mucho.

"Ya'll niggas are silly as hell, but on a more serious note, I got this Black Ice jumping off and it's room for everyone to eat. This will get rid of all those sherm smoking mother-fucker's," as Smack took a sip of his Remy.

"Do you think your girl, Stefani really overdosed off the drug, Smack?" Mucho asked him.

"She had to. She didn't know what the pill was. Tell your people not to take more than one pill at a time. I think she took more than one pill." Smack just shook his head.

"It's all good, I'll even swing by Youngstown and holla at the Big Face Gangster King Tut on my way home, but I'm in, what about you, Mucho?" K.G. asked him.

"Shit, I'm in. You can't make all the money K.G.," said Mucho.

"Good, I'll give you all a bottle a piece. Three hundred pills come in a bottle," as Smack received the blunt from Kyle while taking all this in. Kyle was choking off the weed, but Smack wanted him to hear the conversation hoping he would be interested.

"What's that Purple Haze, Smack?" Kyle asked him and continued to cough.

"Na'll you know I smoke nothing but Cush," said Smack.

You could see a lot of commotion going on at one of the tables. Two females were arguing and it was Miesha and Lula. They were pointing fingers and kicking off shoes.

Bodean had to separate them.

"Well Smack, I think it's time for us to go, it's like 5:45. Everyone's talking about Sneaky-peaks, later right?" Kyle asked him.

"What's that? I heard about Sneaky something down this way." Mucho asked Smack.

"It's our strip club. Tell Smack to bring you all through there later," as Kyle was still walking away talking at the same time watching Miesha. He could hear her cursing.

"Let that bitch go and I'll paint her ass right here." Miesha was loud.

"Kyle, I'll bring them to Sneaky-Peak, make sure you bring little cuss," said Smack pointing towards Miesha. He smiled at Smack and turned back around to get Miesha. He grabbed her and they left.

****

Around nine p.m., it was getting dark and the cook-out was just about over. Denise, Doug, Howe, Lacey, Kris and Tyree were leaving. They said their goodbyes to one another.

Delight went and snuggled herself up under Smack. K.G. and Heather were all cozy kissing like they knew each other for years.

Young Money was playing while D.J. Rob G. was gathering up his equipment. They Belvy Boyz were already gone and the Diamond Cut was still hanging around waiting to go to Sneaky-Peaks. They were inside the house in the basement with their female companions shooting pool.

Delight and Smack were sharing a slow dance out by the pool. Mucho was on his cell phone sitting on a lounger. Rainell and Daysha were just looking at Delight and Smack dance the night away. "Rainell, I thought they were just friends. Your mom is doing Mr. Smack," as she giggled at her own comment.

"I know that's crazy. Who would ever think that?" said Rainell. She felt her mother's happiness and smiled.

"Rainell, did you kiss Tyree?" Daysha asked her.

"No, that's nasty. What were you and Kris doing in the mini-theater?" Rainell asked her.

"We were grinding and kissing until we had to hide because this big guy with the braids came in with the chick who had on the white capris with the big booty and green eyes."

"Are you for real? Did they see ya'll, Daysha?" Rainell was excited.

"No, but we saw them doing the nasty and the big guy told her she was cold with it and tried to pay her." Daysha explained.

"What all did you see, Daysha?" Rainell asked her.

"They did the nasty and then he put his thing in her mouth and she sucked it like a lollipop. He tensed up and almost fell over from whatever she did to him. All I know is that she is too nasty." Daysha told her.

"I wish I would've seen it too," said Rainell.

"Rainell, you haven't done it before?" Daysha asked her.

"Did what, Daysha?"

"Let a boy stick his thing inside you," said Daysha.

"No, my stuff is sacred. I'm saving myself for marriage not for a carriage. That's what Mr. Smack told me. He said that's all that young boys want anyway at our age." Rainell told her.

"Girl, you tripping, it feels good. At first it hurts...I'm not going to lie, but after that it feels so good," said Daysha.

"I don't know Daysha, that's where babies come from and diseases; I don't want neither one. I have goals for myself, I want to be a doctor one day," said Rainell.

"That's why they sell condoms to prevent all that. Have you seen a nasty movie before?" Daysha asked her.

"No and I'm not allowed."

"Well I have one in my overnight bag. We'll watch it when everyone is asleep." Daysha told her. They walked towards the house talking so no one could hear them.

****

Later, that same night Smack, Delight and their guest who were still at the house went to Sneaky Peaks. At one a.m. they walked into the club to hear Plies and T-Pain 'My Shorty' and the strippers were dancing on stage. Worm, P-Diddy, Bodean and Weezy of the Belvy Boyz were already there along with Kyle and Miesha.

Miesha's was now wearing a tight black Baby Phat mini dress with two splits up the sides and gold emblems. They had a section of the club just for them. The Belvy Boyz had two bottles of Belvy and four champagne bottles on the table. Everyone got re-acquaintance again, speaking, giving out dap and the women waved, saying hello. Kyle already seen Kendall ducked off in a corner watching Keisha Myles a.k.a. Pepsi. Kyle immediately got in Smack's ear. "Yo Smack, her husband is over in the corner watching stinky breath dance," said Kyle. Smack located Kendall and leaned over to Delight. "You know Kendall is in here." Smack told her.

She shrugged her shoulders and replied. "So, fuck him. I'm with my man." She gave him a kiss and Smack shrugged his shoulders as if to say fuck him too.

Delight whispered back in Smack's ear. "So baby, this is what the men do when they are out playing in the streets; putting hard earned dollars in these bitches' panties?" asked Delight.

"Not all the time, but look around you, Delight; the women outnumber the men by a long shot. Look at all those females with bills in their hands trying to give it to the girls stripping; I would say they are very supportive." Smack smiled at her.

Delight looked around being more observant and couldn't believe her eyes.

"Oh my God, is this a gay club?" Delight asked him.

"No, not really Delight. The women are just supportive or are on some swinger type stuff trying to bring another woman into their bedroom to satisfy their man fantasy so he won't just go out and cheat. I would say some are out here shopping around." Said Smack.

"Are you serious, Smack?" Delight asked.

"Yes, I'm serious." He answered.

"Well don't ever think I'm going to spice up our thing with another woman mister, because I don't do the coochie to coochie thing. I'm strictly phallus." Delight gave him that look.

Mucho was in his other ear. "Yo Smack, I'm digging this club. I'm about to go see what a player can come up on," said Mucho.

"Go ahead Mucho," said Smack.

Mucho went to mingle in the crowd of women trying to catch a trick of their own. Delight looked over on the stage and saw Keisha shaking her nakedness on the stage.

"That is Keisha," as she pointed to her in shock.

Smack saw her pointing to Pepsi and said, "I told you that was Pepsi and that she worked here, Delight."

Keisha just so happened to turn in their direction showing her perky nipples and cute cut pubic hair. She locked in with Delight and almost fell on the stage. Keisha ran off stage without finishing the song she was dancing to, Fat Joe 'Lean Back'. She was embarrassed and the Diamond Cut click laughed at Pepsi.

"Hey D$Boy, tell Secret to go and turn shit out." Larro whispered to him.

D$Boy looked over at his girl and said, "Secret, go show them amateurs how we do it in the Gem City at Evolutions."

Secret got up on stage and Precious followed. They started getting the club crunk when they were stripping. Nelly 'It's getting hot in here' came on and they were getting loose. Miesha couldn't let them show her up and she joined in takin off her Baby Phat dress. Miesha had on a white ruffled G-string thong.

A crowd of women rushed to their side of the club going crazy throwing bills at Miesha, Precious and Secret. The bouncers and security didn't even try to stop them. Miesha and Secret use to be entertainers and Precious just knew how to shake her ass making it look hella good.

Miesha was stacked at every angle and Smack saw it all. Now he wanted her and he knew that she wanted him, because she was looking at him the whole time while she was dancing and licking her lips seductively with her tongue being as nasty as possible.

Delight got up and went to the restroom with Heather, because Heather knew where it was. They ran into Kendall and Keisha making an exit out the club. Keisha didn't want to be in the club after seeing Delight and it was like a stare down; Heather was looking at Kendall, Delight looking at Keisha and Kendall looking at Delight.

"Look at here, Heather, your ex-brother-in-law with his new woman. This is what he left me for girl," as Delight pointed at Keisha indirectly, but in her direction.

"Is it that bad Kendall; that you're picking up strippers?" Heather asked him.

"No, Heather, she's a pediatrician Keisha Myles, you know the one I was telling you about," said Delight. They didn't give Kendall a chance to respond and it wasn't like he really wanted to anyway. "Delight, I thought her name was Pepsi, that's what they call her in here when she's prostituting her body?" said Delight. Kendall couldn't take it anymore. "Excuse us Delight, we are leaving, just like you left me. But I see you are out with Simmion Boyd. So that's who Benz you were driving a known drug dealer? Kendall had a little aggression in his voice.

"Yep, my new man and baby daddy. We've been fucking like wild animals," said Delight. You could see the fury in Kendall's eyes grow with hatred. He balled his fist.

"What did you say, Delight?" He asked her.

"You heard me, my new man and baby daddy. That's right, I'm pregnant by him, a real man who's been taking care of your daughter and this pussy," said Delight with an attitude. Delight was feeling herself. Heather was in shock from the news because she didn't know her sister was pregnant by Smack, but she knew they were messing around. He lifted his hand as if he was going to smack Delight's lips off her face.

"I wish you would nigga, and she'll be the last woman you'll ever slap," said Heather.

"Fuck you, Delight, I'll see you later," as Kendall bumped into Heather pulling Keisha's arm and they left out the club.

Heather gave her little sister a high five and they laughed heading to the restroom.

"Girl, did you see his face when I told him Smack had me pregnant and he was taking good care of this pussy?" Delight asked Heather.

"Did I, girl he gone kill you," as Heather laughed making choke gestures with her hands. Heather stopped laughing and gathered herself. "Delight, are you pregnant for real?"

Delight looked at her sister and gave her the look and Heather knew she was.

"Oh Delight, congratulations," said Heather and she hugged Delight.

The DJ in the club was mixing T-Pain & Lil Kim 'Down Load' with 50 Cent '21 Questions' and Miesha, Precious and Secret continued to dance on stage.

After partying at Sneaky Peaks, the Belvy Boyz took them down to the Motor Cycle club on Central Avenue and they ended up at Dukes after hour spot on Oliver and Linn Street. Delight stood behind Smack in Dukes watching him gamble. He was playing against the famous Rip Cord and the invincible Skinner. Skinner and Rip Cord were partners and the most feared flat foot hustlers known to man. They ran a con from the pigeon drop, three card molly and the bottle top. They have trick over millions across the U.S. Rip cord and Skinner had just won twenty racks from Fat Shaun and Hog. Smack had to check the dice several times making sure they weren't loaded or they were dropping tees. Usually when someone is dropping tee's the only numbers would show on the dice were 1, 3 and 5.

Heather was like a celebrity in Dukes. Anyone who ever got processed in the Hamilton County Justice Center knew Heather Heath. A lot of guys were still trying to get with her because she was looking good, but she also had a reputation.

They gave her respect and just spoke because she was with K.G. and they didn't know if he was her husband or not. She was on his arm and her goal was to sleep with the young man from Akron, Ohio.

After Smack won like ten racks, they left Dukes at around a quarter till seven that morning. It was daylight out and Larro and the Diamond Cut jumped on I-75 north heading home to Dayton. K.G. road with Heather in her Lexus and they got on I-75 north but they would get off on the Lincoln Heights exit. Mucho had departed from them at Sneaky Peaks with some strange female he met named Candy out of English Woods.

Smack and Delight hot on I-75 also from downtown, but they merged on I-74 Indianapolis that would take them to I-275 east that would get them to West Chester quicker. Delight hadn't had this much activity in her life at one time before, even when she was in college.

She was now wrapped up in a life that didn't love anyone if things hot out of hand. Looking pass the money and material things he had to offer her, she knew he really had a placement for her in his heart. He loved her unconditionally and would most likely marry her. She sat back and took it all in riding down in

CHAPETER FIFTEEN
THE MOVEMENT

Things took off as planned and the Black Ice was **being marketed at a fast pace. It started in Cincinnati** and adventured to Cleveland, Akron, Columbus, Dayton, Springfield, Toledo and Youngstown. They couldn't believe the rate that the drug was moving and the people wanting it as bad.

Delight found out she was officially pregnant at her doctor's appointment. She was excited and more than ready to have Smack's child.

On the other hand, Rainell was planning on experiencing with sex. Peer pressure from her friend Daysha after they watched the porno that night of the cook-out. Rainell was now curious, a little scared, but still curious.

Smack had cleaned his bedroom of Stefani's belongings as well as anything else she had around the house. He kept Bruce and the issue of People Magazine that had Stefani on the cover in Miami with her mystery man which was him.

He purchased a new bedroom set for him and Delight and she went to gather the rest of their things from the house in Mason. Delight decided to leave Slogin & Cummons and just dealt with criminal cases and traffic court in Hamilton County making a name for her.

It was now at the end of June and the streets were calm with less criminal activity. The police were shook wondering where the major drug dealers or the users were. The only two spots that didn't catch the Black Ice wave were Lincoln Heights and Mt. Auburn on Glencoe. On Glencoe was the drive thru for marijuana and they did have some of the loyalist customers. Guys like Meechie, Jay-Bo, Fat Jeff, Clever, Droopy, Tiger, Monty, Tommy, Dre, Tink and Lil Harold wasn't budging with the movement of the Black Ice.

****

"What's going on in the streets? Why haven't we found the hoodlums who assaulted one of ours?" the senior officer asked.

"Lieutenant, we've been looking in crack everywhere. It is less movement out there and it's hardly any dealers or users out, sir.

Something is wrong; we haven't won the war on drug this easy. The crime rate has dropped in a week," said Officer Taylor.

"What do you suggest then Officer Taylor?" the lieutenant asked him.

"We will find those who are responsible, sir. I promise you that," said Officer Taylor.

****

Jasmine Finch and Elliot Thrasher were having brunch at the Country Club out in Indian Hills. Antwan was in Asia making sure he had enough pills for a six-month run coming to the U.S. Jasmine was ready to dismiss Elliot and be faithfully in her lover's arms for good. They had already gained Elliot Thrasher's best interests at hand and he was on their team. She looked at him and noticed how pale he really was. She realized that her time with this pathetic fool was up and he would soon perish by the hands of her lover. What a sad sight he was to her eyes.

"Jasmine, I hear Antwan and Simmion are making good progress with the drug. I wonder why Antwan hasn't given me five percent yet. The police are not in his way," said Elliot Thrasher.

"It's not because of your input Elliot, the police are clueless to what's going on in this area. Please don't flatter yourself," said Jasmine.

"Antwan doesn't know that he's an arrogant man and quite an asshole. God the man thinks he is untouchable," said Elliot.

"I'm a woman who knows things and hear things and you'll be surprised what I hear. Like you have this thing for young women, I mean underage girls. I take no one, no man, not anything for granted," said Jasmine.

"Well I won't be careless and I'll let them exploit the drug for six months before making a resolution to get rid of the both. Hell, I'm running for office again and I'm sure with their downfall I will have the people's vote." You could see the greed in his eyes. Jasmine looked at him thinking to herself. "You're already careless you damn fool, because you have a mole in your business, me."

"That's clever, Elliot but what about your life being at risk, my life?" Jasmine asked.

"Jasmine darling, I'm the Mayor of this city," said Elliot with confidence.

"Exactly Elliot, the mayor like Jerry was, not the President. You're not guarded 24-7," said Jasmine stopping in between pauses.

"Don't just think about yourself, I'm a prosecutor and I've sent a lot of innocent men and women to prison versus those who should really be behind bars. It's a lot of people who wouldn't mind getting revenge on me especially for a nice sum of money. Don't think about yourself, Elliot." She had a full face of concern.

"No one would dare harm my princess girlfriend."

"Elliott, you are a damn fool," as she sipped her fresh brewed tea.

"I'm just modest my dear, are we playing doubles against Judge Helmet and his wife today, Jasmine?" He asked her.

"No, his wife is in the hospital battling cancer, he's bringing a lady friend with him today to replace his wife," said Jasmine.

****

"Will, who is that pulling up in the Infiniti QX56 sitting on 26" rims? Call the plates in and see who the vehicle belongs to." Officer Allen asked him and Will Edmond called the plates in on the vehicles.

Smack was getting out the vehicle in some blue polo shorts and a white and blue stripe polo shirt, a visor and some Ari Force Ones.

"Will, never mind, it's our boy Simmion Boyd," said Officer Taylor.

"Al, the plates came back to a Delight Heath-Scott," said Will.

"Isn't she a lawyer, Will? Allen asked him.

"Yeah, but why is he trying to go in the store and they are closed, Al?"

"Will, I don't think they are closed, something is going down in there," said Allen.

"Should we call for back-up, Al?"

"No. Let's wait and see who comes out after he goes in...if he gets in."

They watched Smack enter the Goodie Bag and they both nodded their heads.

****

Smack came in the store to see all the Belvy Boyz having an orgy with one female. You could smell the sex in the air. It wasn't an awful fishy smell, but a pleasant fresh smell of a perfumed aroma. The female was getting rammed from the back by P-Diddy while she was sucking Worm's tribal piece.

There were Magnum condoms everywhere opened and in reach. Vino, Weezy, Kobe, Dante, Bodean and Kekou was standing in their boxers waiting on their turn with the female. It was three other unfamiliar guys Smack was introduced to by Kobe.

"Yo Smack, this is Gutter, Ron Don, and their little dude from Atlanta, 'G'. They want in on the Black Ice so they can take it to Atlanta."

Smack looked them over and then spoke. "What up," as he threw his head up.

"What up yo, we just want in on the new," said Gutter.

"It's all good, just hollas at my man Kobe," said Smack.

"That's what's up," said Ron Don.

Smack eyes traveled around the store and plus the females moans and grunts caught his attention. He saw a white tennis skirt with a matching shirt, a black bra and black French cut panties sitting on the counter. Then he saw some pink and white Lisa Leslie shoes. He knew these items had to belong to the female they were having sex with. P-Diddy yelled that he was about to cum and pulled out taking his condom off going to the front pushing Worm out the way. He put his manhood in her mouth and cum down her throat. You could tell he was weak from the expression on his face. The female's ass was huge, pretty and smooth from Smack's view. Then Bodean made a comment.

"I told ya'll she swallow and had that work."

Smack nudged Kobe. "Yo Kobe, who is that? He pointed at the female.

"That's the girl from your cook-out, your boy's cousin," said Kobe. Then she got up to turn around for a towel that was close by her and she locked eyes with Smack's. Her body was perfect, flat stomach, perky nipples, hips and as cute as the way she was that night at Sneaky Peaks. She smiled at him and then pointed her index finger to him telling him to come here. Smack was surprised to see the green-eyed female in this position. The sexiest woman he'd ever seen was having an orgy with a gang of nigga's who were 'bout it, 'bout it. It was Miesha in the flesh of her flesh.

****

"Tyree, make sure you call your mother after the movie is over, because she is picking you all up, okay sweetie?" said Delight. Rainell, Daysha, Tyree and Kris got out of the Cadillac truck.

"Yes, ma'am, Mrs. Scott," said Tyree.

"Tyree, just call me Ms. Delight, honey." Delight told him and he nodded his head.

"You kids have a nice time. Daysha, do you have any money?" Delight asked her.

"Yes ma'am, I have some money and I'm staying overnight at your house," said Daysha.

"Okay, bye." Delight looked at her daughter and tried not to think about her times at the movie with a boy.

"Bye mom," as Rainell walked off.

"Tyree make sure you call your mom as soon as the movie let out," said Delight. "I will. Come on Kris." Tyree told his cousin and they waved to Delight. She looked at them wondering what the boy's angle was with her daughter and her friend. They were out at the Cincinnati Mills Mall in Forest Park.

****

"Smack, can you drop me off in Walnut Hills? I'm drained and my pussy is sore as hell. Those niggas can go, especially that Worm nigga, he kept wanting some head," said Miesha.

"Yeah, I can give you a ride Miesha," as he watched her get dressed showing her beautiful curves. She had a change of clothes in a black gym bag.

"Miesha, we appreciate your services. You got that work and our little brother, Turkey and Vino cousin Candy will love these pictures of you up in Lebanon," said Kekou.

Miesha looked over at him and smiled. She thought to herself, *"Boy, I stopped counting my orgasms after the tenth one. I'm good on the Belvy Boyz and I'll never do all of them again, a bitch paid for it and they got their money's worth and more. Those fat niggas know how to fuck and that Worm nigga is sick with it."*

"Ooh my pussy is sore," said Miesha out loud.

"It's all good Miesha, we famo up here and now you are part of the team, just take one of those one things I gave you and you'll be good." Bodean told her.

"I will thank you very much, I have to go and stuff my pussy with some ice after I get home. My shit is on fire from the friction and not letting my shit get wet before going hard again," said Miesha. She was exhausted.

Miesha was dressed and she left with Smack. Kobe turned the closed sign around to open for business. Officer Allen Taylor saw them leaving out the store and woke his partner up. "Yo Will get up, Simmion is leaving and he's with Miesha Jones the trick who works Dunlap, yo girl," said Officer Taylor.

Will Edmond was rubbing his eyes trying to focus. "That's her and she has a bag."

"I wonder what she has in that gym bag. Do you think it's what I think, Will?" as Officer Allen looked at his partner. They both were curious.

"No, Al, it couldn't be. Only way to find out is to pull them over," said Officer Edmond.

Officer Allen Taylor started up the car with tinted windows and rims to fit in. Miesha was now dressed in some tight khaki shorts, a tight t-shirt and some dark blue Gucci slip on heels with the toes out. She climbed in the truck and Smack started the truck up and the air conditioning was blowing hard and cold, "Smack is this yours too?" She asked.

She was controlling the vent in her direction making it blow between her legs, while she opened her legs wide.

No, this is Delight's truck. She has my Cadillac truck," he said and they pulled off.

Smack didn't notice that the police were following him.

"This is nice, Smack," as Miesha was admiring the truck. "Smack, I wish you would've fucked me back in the store," as she grabbed his hand placing it in her crouch area.

He gently pulled his had away looking at her. "You cool, Miesha, and if things were different, I would probably take you up on that offer. I'm involved with someone that I care deeply about. I hope you understand," said Smack.

"Smack, it's only a little pussy; I know you're not scared of a little pussy. I'm not asking you to marry me and I know you liked what you saw," said Miesha batting her eyes at him.

"I'm in a relationship Miesha and I've played on that side of the fence long enough. I've had my share of events dealing with women. I'm about to settle down and get married. I know it's good, but it's not for me Miesha, not at this stage in my life."

"It is for you Smack, but I respect that. I heard you fucked Superhead before, is it true?"

She asked him He looked over at her for a long moment for her asking him that question. He knew Kyle told her that. "Yeah, I fucked her. She's not all what she claims to be like them other cats said. Her under arms must be musty and shit," Smack told her.

Miesha burst into laughter. "Smack, are you serious, her under arms though?"

"Yeah, hell yeah, musty as fuck and she can't suck a dick all that good. Miesha you'll have to show me," as he looked at her and she licked her lips. "Show me where you live in Walnut Hills." He knew she probably thought he was going to ask for a lube job, but he cleared it up quickly.

"I will and Smack, you are cool people. I see why my cousin likes you so much.

Make sure you invite me to your wedding or convince your girl to let me be in it okay, Smack," said Miesha.

"You got that coming, Miesha; I can do that for you." Smack smiled at her.

He was turning up off Ravine onto W. McMillian which would take him across Vine Street pass Euclid and Auburn Avenue to Walnut Hills.

****

"Tyree, are you comfortable?" Rainell whispered to him while they sat in the far corner of the movie theater at Cincinnati Mills Mall. Daysha and Kris were sitting closer to the front on the other side. They were already doing the unknown being mannish.

"I'm fine, Rainell," he answered in a low tone.

Rainell took his hand placed it on her thigh caressing his hand gently. She looked at him and smiled and he smiled back at her and then turned back to watch the movie. Rainell had on a B.B. blue jean skirt and a white and red t-shirt with the logo. Her hair was in a tight pony-tail.

Rainell gently moved his hand on the inner part of her thigh not looking at him and then easing his hand towards her warm bushy immature snatch box. Her panties were moist from her sweating and being nervous, but he could feel the heat coming from down there and he yanked his hand away.

"Rainell, what are you doing?" Tyree asked her.

"Tyree, don't you want me? Don't you want to do it?" asked Rainell.

"Rainell, I like you a lot, but I'm too young to be caught up in peer pressure involving sex. If you're loose like that, I'm good. I don't want to be involved with you," said Tyree.

"I thought you were like all the other boys, that's what Daysha said. I'm not that type of girl, Tyree, and I really do like you. I've never done it before. Myself, I would like to be with you when I'm older, Tyree, and I apologize for being judgmental."

"Rainell, Daysha doesn't know me like that. Just because Kris is doing the grown-up thing, that doesn't mean I am. He is trying to get me to swag like him especially with them older chicks at school who think I'm a star athlete. All the upper classmen be at me, but I'm not on it," said Tyree.

"Well like I said Tyree, I truly apologize. Do you forgive me?" said Rainell.

"It's cool and I forgive you," said Tyree showing her his pearly whites.

"Can I at least have a kiss Tyree?" she asked him.

"Rainell, I don't know how to kiss." he replied.

"Me neither," as she giggled. "But I have seen it done before," said Rainell.

"Me too." Tyree smiled at her again.

They gradually connected their lips bumping noses before pressing up against one another. Tyree had bubble gum lip gloss on his lips from Rainell when they separated. She had her first kiss and so did he.

****

"Smack, you can turn on Windsor Street at the light," as Miesha directed him down Gilbert Avenue.

Soon as Smack turned onto Windsor Street going pass Fulton Street, the police came from everywhere flashing their lights.

142

They were in unmarked cars and cruisers. Some of the unmarked cars had tint and rims on them. One was a white Lexus sedan with rims and tint.

"What's going on Smack?" Miesha asked him and was about to panic.

****

Earlier while RENU officers Taylor and Edmond were following Smack and Miesha, Will Edmond received a call from Elliot Thrasher. When he hung up, Allen Taylor asked him.

"Will, what did the Mayor of Cincinnati want with you?"

"He said that Simmion Boyd is a part of a new drug ring with some European cat named Antwan Klein. They are moving this exotic drug called Black Ice into this region."

"Oh yeah, well we are about to see if he has any on him, or bust Ms. Jones for soliciting if she doesn't cooperate and comply," said Allen Taylor.

"Al, Elliot said the pill is in a pink capsule."

****

"Be calm Miesha, you don't have anything illegal on you, do you?" Smack asked her.

"I have a few of these exotic pills Bodean gave me. Kyle had already introduced them to me and they help me relax when I'm taking care of my business," she paused. "I took one before fucking all of them at the store earlier, the pill makes me super horny, like I can fuck a whole football team or King Kong," said Miesha.

"Damn it. They gave you the Black Ice?" as he was watching two undercover police come toward them after getting out of a white Lexus.

"They gave me what?" Miesha asked him, because she wasn't familiar with the name.

"Don't worry about it, Miesha." Smack told her.

Miesha caught a glimpse of the undercover police and knew who they were.

"Oh shit, Smack, that's Taylor and Edmonds. They work for RENU."

"You know them Miesha?" Smack asked her.

"Yeah, the white one be busting me soliciting sex on Dunlap and he always want a personal favor from me in exchange for my freedom of not going to jail. They both are some dirty mother-fuckers," said Miesha.

"Well stuff those pills down your panties or something," said Smack.

"I'm not wearing any panties Smack."

"Well put them inside your pussy or bra." Smack told her as he watched the police get closer to the truck. Miesha resorted to putting the pills in her bra. Smack eased the driver's window down. "Good afternoon officers, how may I help you?" Smack asked them.

"First, you can step out of the vehicle, sir. Do you know you picked up a known prostitute on McMicken," said Taylor?

Miesha heard him and responded. "Yo mama's a fucking prostitute, you son of a bitch."

"Watch yourself, Ms. Jones," said Edmond. Smack looked over at her and gave her a look. "No, sir, you must have the wrong guy and person. She's my friend's cousin and I was giving her a ride home. I don't think she's a prostitute, sir." Smack told officer Taylor.

"Tell us anything, pal," said officer Edmonds.

Smack got out of the truck not giving them a reason to commit police brutality.

"I'm telling you officer, I'm just giving her a ride home, nothing more." as Smack tried to plead his case. "Do you have an ID sir?" Officer Taylor asked him.

"Yeah, it's in my wallet in my back pocket." Smack told him looking in the sky.

"Do you have any weapons or foreign objects that can harm me?" Taylor asked him.

"No, sir." said Smack.

"Can you turn around for me and place your hands on your head, sir?" Taylor asked him. Smack turned around and did what he asked him. "Spread your legs, sir." Taylor commanded Smack and he did so. Officer Taylor searched Smack thoroughly.

Edmonds was getting Miesha out of the truck. "Come on Ms. Jones, you know the drill and bring that black bag with you."

"You all are on some bullshit. A bitch leaves the block and you all still sweat this pussy, with your faggot ass," said Miesha.

"Shut up and open the bag, Ms. Jones." as Will looked at her. She opened it and Will snatched the bag and dumped all her belongings on the curve of the street. "Where are the drugs, Ms. Jones?" Officer Edmond asked her.

"You tell me, you're the law white faggot. I don't deal drugs just this sweet black pussy that your shitty wife doesn't have. you fantasize about me when you go home."

Miesha laughed at him.

"Ms. Jones, you are pushing it. you don't know where the drugs are and you are riding with the man?" Officer Edmond questioned her again.

"I told you this is what I deal in," as she lifted her skirt to show him her private part in her pelvic area. "This is all I deal in, sweet black pussy. Go ahead and taste it, show your partner how you be eating a bitch out, go ahead Officer Edmond," said Miesha. It struck a nerve, because Officer Edmond didn't even search her, just the bag.

"Al, she's clean. What about him?" Officer Edmond asked his partner.

"Same thing here. Should we call for a K-9 unit?" Taylor asked him.

"I don't think Mr. Boyd is that stupid to be moving narcotics in his lawyer's vehicle," said Officer Edmond.

"I'll see if they threw anything on the floor, Will. Mr. Boyd, can you go stand over there by Ms. Jones, please," said Officer Taylor.

Allen Taylor went to search the inside of the Infiniti truck. He came back and said, "Mr. Boyd, we are on to you and Antwan Klein. This new drug you're trying to bring to this area we won't tolerate it. watch yourself and find you some new friends, because I know Mrs. Scott wouldn't want a known streetwalker to be riding in her vehicle." Taylor told him.

He caught Miesha's attention. "Fuck you, Uncle Tom ass nigga. Yo mama is a fucking streetwalker, you crooked ass cop, ya'll gone get yours one day," said Miesha.

"Keep it up, Ms. Jones and you'll go downtown for threatening an Officer, disorderly conduct and soliciting," said Office Taylor. She folded her arms and just stared at him.

"Here you go, Ms. Jones," as Officer Edmond handed her the empty black bag leaving her belongings on the curb. She was steaming hot and if looks could kill, the two cops would be dead mother-fuckers.

"We'll be in touch with you, Mr. Boyd," said Officer Taylor walking back towards the Lexus sedan. "Yeah, Ms. Jones, especially you keep that nookie warm for daddy," said Officer Edmond giving her a grin.

"Ooh, I hate those mother-fuckers. I can't wait until those bitches get theirs," said Miesha.

She started gathering up her belongings and Smack helped her.

"Come on, Miesha, so I can get you home," said Smack.

Smack was now puzzled more than ever. He was wondering how these two cops knew about the business and they tied him to Antwan Klein. He didn't discuss Antwan to the Belvy Boyz or to Diamond Cut.

There was a mole amongst them and he knew that was dangerous because now he was under the radar. He had to inform Antwan and let him know that the cops were aware of their plans.

CHAPTER FIFTEEN
KEISHA MOVES IN

Keisha was sitting in the driveway in her gold 07 Saturn Aura XR with factory rims, she was blowing her horn for Kendall. She had on a scarf with a tank top and some boy shorts. It was hot outside on the second day of July at 11 a.m. on a Saturday. Kendall came out to meet her in some long shorts with no shirt and slippers. She smiled at him coming closer to her car. When he reached her, he leaned in and gave her a kiss. "Hey baby, I'm all pack as you can see," said Keisha.

Kendall quickly looked over the front and back seat to see a lot of boxes and clothes.

"Do you have everything from your place, Keisha?" he asked her. Yes, I have all my things and I sold the furniture and other appliances to my brother and his girlfriend. You told me I wouldn't need anything but my personal items and clothes," said Keisha looking at him.

"Well let's grab your stuff and get you settle into the house," said Kendall.

"Are you sure, Kendall? This is what you want, right?" said Keisha with sad eyes.

"I'm positive, Keisha. I told you Delight and I are over. We go to court soon to finalize the divorce. Her and my daughter are living with Simmion and she's pregnant with his child," as he stood back away from her car so she could get out.

She got out looking sexy with her tight attire. Kendall couldn't wait to get his new live in girlfriend in the bed of his old home, but their new arrangements.

This was the house that Keisha had always dreamt of. Her breath wasn't stinky anymore and now she was perfect for him. The woman he always pretended Delight to be. She stood perfectly in front of him touching his manly structure, every muscle in his stomach and chest. She looked up at him and then back down towards the pavement of the driveway and said, "Kendall, I'm pregnant too. We are going to have a baby," she said.

He grabbed the bottom of her chin lifting her head up and looking deeply into her eyes. "That's the best news I've had in a long time, Keisha." He kissed her.

She hugged him tight and hard not wanting to ever let go. She felt safe and secure being in his arms. Kendall was moving in his lover and new baby mother into the house that he and his ex-wife once built and shared together.

Kendall knew that it was a possibility that Keisha could be pregnant by him, because he'd been having unprotected sex with her on a regular basis. Kendall was cumming inside her. They both grabbed a few items and went inside the house. When Keisha stepped in the house, she inhaled a large sum of oxygen and exhaled it slowly. They were supposed to have been unloading the car, but ended up going to town in the living room. It was a beautiful beginning for her and recreation for him.

"Hey Simmion, Guten Tag Herr." Antwan told him good day.

"Guten Tag. Was ist los?" Smack replied asking Antwan what was up.

"Ich mochten du sehen etwas. Ich habe die polizie, diese persona das spreechen zu veil."

Antwan told him he had something for him to see, the police the person who was talking too much.

"Wo ist sie?" Smack asked where they were.

"Hier mit ich, komme sie zu Das Restaurant bitte." Antwan told him that the person was there with him and for him to come to the restaurant, please.

"I'm on my way," said Smack and he hung up the phone.
****
"So, Mr. Frank Toggle and Donnie Black, I hear ya'll have some information for us?"

Will Edmond of RENU questioned him.

"Yeah, we know where this new drug, Black Ice, is. as long as we get cut a deal." Said Frank Toggle.

Will knew this is what they were looking for and maybe it would link back to Simmion Boyd and this Antwan Klein guy. Will looked him square in the eyes.

"Ya'll got caught with three kilos of cocaine so this better be some good information. No bullshit or I'll make sure ya'll receive ten years a piece," said Will.

"Well we know this guy named Larro who's down with the Diamond Cut out of Dayton who be having the drug," said Donnie.

"Where is he getting it from?" Will asked.

"I don't know exactly, but I know he be having it. My girlfriend's sister messes with him and he be stashing it over their house sometimes," said Frank Toggle.

"Can you get him to sell you the drug, set up a buy?" Will asked him.

"That shouldn't be a problem," said Frank Toggle.

"Okay, you two stay in touch with me and after the 4th of July we will make arrangements to set up a bust," said Will Edmond.

"Okay, we got you," said Donnie Black.

Just like that they walked out the detective's office at the Duke Energy building.

****

Smack walked into the restaurant which was empty and Antwan greeted him and they walked back to his study. He saw a big Russian guy slapping a frail looking white man in the face while he was tied to a chair naked. The man was being tortured.

"Wally, that's enough," said Antwan and the big Russian guy stepped away. The frail man was bleeding from the mouth.

"Simmion, do you recognize Herr?" Antwan asked him.

"No, I can't quite tell who he is. I know it's not one of the cops that pulled me over. They were much bigger and it was a black and white cop," said Smack.

"I know, it's the man who told our business to the cops that pulled you over. He's the one who is supposed to keep us out of harm's way. He doubled crossed me, us. Do you know what beats the double cross, Simmion?" Antwan asked him.

"No, Antwan, what beats the double cross?" Smack asked him.

"It's quite simple Simmion, the triple cross...and the triple cross for this pathetic fool is death by dishonor. He's a dead man," said Antwan.

"No Simmion, don't listen to him. He's a mad man," as the man yelled out spitting blood.

"Who is that? How does he know my name?" Smack asked Antwan.

"That's the mayor of this conservative city. He's rather a racist or should I say prejudice toward poor people and he doesn't like our kind...Afro-Americans nor Black Germans," said Antwan.

"The mayor, Elliot Thrasher?" Smack asked him.

"Yes, it's him. He has a wicked tongue. He told my good friend, Jasmine Finch, that he was going to sick the police on our operation instead of helping us as agreed. He was going to take his five percent cut, get rich and feed us to the wolves, Simmion," said Antwan. His look was devious and concrete.

"He knew about the drug, Antwan? Smack asked him.

"Why, of course. I told this weak politician first. He was going to be the outlet. He's been fucking my girlfriend, Jasmine, while I was away visiting the Scandinavian countries." Antwan looked over at Elliot Thrasher.

"Jasmine's your girlfriend?" Elliot asked, because it was a surprise to him as well as Smack.

"Yes, she's my weapon under disability. She's very impatient and she doesn't like for anyone to fuck over the Chocolate Dream. I gave you my bitch and the weapons and you double cross me, you damn fool," said Antwan in a high-pitched voice of anger.

"Why, that double crossing little bitch of a prosecutor," said Elliot. Wally slapped him for disrespecting Antwan's girlfriend and he almost turned over in the chair. The slap was loud.

"So, Simmion, you can rest now and I'll get rid of this problem. Just watch the eleven o'clock news tonight," said Antwan.

"What about..." Smack was cut off by Antwan.

"Don't worry, just get ready for our trip to China after the 4th; I told you we would have our own fireworks." Antwan lifted an eyebrow at him.

"Help me, Simmion, you're not like him, you're not a killer. Your hands will be just as bloody as his," said Elliot Thrasher.

Smack looked over at Elliot and turned to Antwan. Smack nodded his head to Antwan and Wally looked at Antwan to receive the nod from him. Wally grabbed Elliot's arm and snapped it. You could hear him scream in pain. Antwan led Smack out of the study still hearing Elliot's screams. Antwan reassured Smack by telling him. "Don't worry buddy, I've got this. go home to your future wife and unborn child."

Smack looked at him long and hard, how did Antwan know that Delight was pregnant?

Antwan put a finger to his mouth, "Shhh." said Antwan as he put his finger to his temple to let Smack know that he knows everything.

Smack was puzzled, but he didn't question him and went to his car. When he pulled off, he was listening to Jay-Z, 'Say Hello'. Was he really the bad guy? Was he caught up in a world he knew nothing about?

****

Later, that night, Smack and Delight was lying in the bed watching TV. He was rubbing her stomach while they cuddled. She knew this was the life beyond anything petty, a unique representation of the good life. The empty pint of butter pecan sat on the nightstand where Delight put it. She was already craving even though she was in her early stages of pregnancy. It was five minutes until eleven when Smack grabbed the remote and turned to Channel 12 to watch the news.

Breaking news came on at the beginning of the news cast. As promised, it was true. Antwan had delivered. The mayor was found dead in a hotel room along with a seventeen-year-old blonde girl. Both were dead, she from an overdose and the mayor was brutally beaten. The homicide detective found several pink pills on the scene. Smack knew that the pills were purposely left behind for the police to find. Delight couldn't believe it. "Damn, that's crazy. Who would ever think that the mayor was having an affair with a minor and they were doing drugs? But they want to make harsh laws for drug dealers and not pedophiles," said Delight.

Smack didn't say anything, he knew he just help killed the mayor and an innocent girl even though he wasn't there.

****

Smack had another cook-out for the 4th of July. This time Antwan and Jasmine showed up briefly. His cousin Larro invited Frank Toggle and Donnie Black.

Smack and Delight would be flying to China on the 7th with Antwan and Jasmine. The four stood out by the African lions holding a conversation.

"Simmion, you have much taste in the finer things in life. A man who likes wild beast, who knows nothing but survival," said Antwan puffing on his blunt.

"I'm just a normal man, who shoots for the stars. You only live once," said Smack.

Jasmine looked at Smack with lustful eyes. "Simmion, they are beautiful. Will you mate them?" Jasmine asked.

"No, I'll probably have to get rid of them in due time, because I think Delight is scared of them," said Smack.

"No, I'm not. I just don't believe in taking a wild animal out of its natural habitat...that's all," said Delight.

"What about me? You're trying to take me out of the streets," said Smack.

"That's different, because you are mine and the streets don't love you like I do. They never will. Additionally, the streets are not your natural habitat," said Delight.

"She made a good point, Simmion. You need to think about owning your own business, you are getting older...not younger," said Antwan still puffing his blunt.

"I'll have to do something real soon because I'll be out the game shortly," said Smack.

Antwan didn't want to hear those words, not yet anyway.

"Did you two get your passports?" Antwan asked them.

"First thing tomorrow morning we have to pick them up," said Delight.

"Good, we are leaving Thursday morning. We have to fly to Chicago and then to LA. The flight from LA will land us in China," said Antwan.

"We'll be ready, Antwan." Smack told him.

"Be sure that your business here is squared away, Herr," said Antwan.

"I will, Antwan, don't worry everything is under control," said Smack.
Smack didn't introduce Antwan to the Belvy Boyz or Diamond Cut, because he and Jasmine made an early exit from the cook-out.

CHAPTER SIXTEEN
CHINA (INSIDE THE DRAGON)

Thursday had come and Smack was driving himself and Delight to the Greater Cincinnati Airport. They were in the convertible hard top Benz. He put her Infiniti truck in the garage and his Cadillac truck was in storage along with the Impala. Heather and K.G. were house sitting and keeping an eye on Rainell for them. He made sure that the Belvy Boyz and Diamond Cut had enough Black Ice to last until he returned to the States.

They were all sitting comfortable in first class on Delta Airlines. They would be in China for two weeks and Delight had two digital cameras with her. After changing flights twice and sitting sixteen hours, they finally landed inside the Dragon in Shanghai China. In Shanghai they left the airport in a black Toyota Camry SE.

Antwan had the car waiting for them. They checked into a fancy high-rise hotel in the Presidential Suites on the 32nd floor.

They showered and got dressed for a night out on the town. Shanghai was lit up like Las Vegas at night. It was early around ten o'clock pacific time. One of the famous boutique spas was still open for business and Jasmine was explaining to Delight the 13 types of facials that they offered and a chocolate pedicure for $48.

Jasmine and Delight agreed to return for a little girly session in the spa tomorrow. They left their ended up in the Guangzhou Yumin Seafood restaurant. They had live crocodiles with their jaws taped shut roaming the cavernous lobby of the restaurant before ending up on some customer's plate.

Delight took pictures of the restaurant and everything in it. Even though she was in pure shock she still managed to take a few pictures of the live crocodiles roaming inside the restaurant. "Oh my God, why aren't those crocodiles in a cage or something?" Delight asked Antwan. "They are being served on the menu. You know how you can pick out your lobster live in a tank, well you can do the same with the croc's," said Antwan.

"They eat crocodile? I heard of turtle and snake before, but not crocodile," said Delight.

"Yes, stewed or steamed the meat is believed to cure coughs and prevent cancer," said Antwan. They were being seated when Antwan was explaining it to her.

"How much is it Antwan?" Delight asked him.

"It's rather pricey, but it's good. I'll order some for us so you can try it and you can pick the little fella out if you like," said Antwan.

"I'll pass on the crocodile. I'll just keep it simple maybe lobster or shrimp and plain rice." Delight told him looking around. Even Smack was taking in the new surroundings.

"Simmion, you have a very cautious lady who doesn't take chances. She's probably very easy to please," said Antwan with a grin. Delight gave him a half smile.

They ate in the dazzling restaurant and Antwan ordered just about everything that was exotic. The crocodile meat, sushi, monkey brains, lobster tails with spicy rice and vegetables was exquisite. Smack tricked Delight into tasting the crocodile meat and the monkey brains. She liked it and the rice wine had her buzzing a little. It was something new and she realized she needed to practice being culturally diverse. She was off balance from being pregnant and her taste buds were not telling her what an awful taste to her was. Delight ate like she was a three-hundred-pound man. After dinner they took a buggy carriage through some parts of Shanghai with a frail man pulling them. Delight thought the tiny Chinese man was so powerful and strong to be hauling four people around in the buggy. They returned to their suite on the 32nd floor. Smack and Delight retired to their room after Antwan and Smack smoked a blunt. Jasmine took a Black Ice pill.

When Delight and Smack entered the room, it was lit up from the fireplace. You could hear the crackling of the logs burning in the fireplace. The ambiance was cozy and romantic. Delight knew this night would be so promising, so pure and unique. They entwined in the cool bed with silk linen. He lay between her thickness, her Vee pressing up against her smooth skin. He touched her breast, her hair, her shoulders caressing up against her smooth skin. He touched her breast, her hair, her shoulders caressing her arms repeatedly. She returned the touches by caressing the side of his face and portions of his back.

She wrapped her legs around him as he eased inside her wetness, slowly grinding into her natural juices. Neither one could remember how the other got out of their clothes. She felt every vein he'd ever possessed in his Tribal piece as he made passive strokes inside her vaginal walls. It was the stroke of an elderly woman stirring a fresh cup of coffee. The sweet sounds of Mariah Carey. 'We Belong Together' quietly whispered thru a sound system that was in a wall unit in the bedroom.

Beads of sweat formed on her nose and forehead as their passion heated the bed. The crease in the middle of his back became moist as she dug her French manicured nails in his back. She was gripping, digging holding him tightly as he thrust all his manhood inside her. Her moans increased; her juices flowed rapidly from the crevices of her vagina. She became weak and limber as her climax released from her body.

"Oh, my goodness, I'm cumming Smack, I'm cumming and it won't stop baby. Oh shit, I love you," as she screamed her last words to the top of her lungs.

She reached up to embrace his lips with a passionate kiss still trying to catch her breath. After his explosion insider her, they sat in front of the fireplace cuddling each other staring into the fireplace. They were wrapped in one of the silk sheets.

"Smack, this is what I dreamt of when I was coming up as a young girl. A romance, a true romance, a prince, a man with ambitions and principles. You complete me. I spent fourteen years of doing absolutely nothing of this magnitude," said Delight.

"Don't say that, Delight. You didn't tap out and good things came with those fourteen years, like Rainell and your career," said Smack taking a pause. "I mean life doesn't come sweet like candy. If life was so perfect, they would sell it in a jar. We must endure a little pain and defeat before we obtain happiness. It's not my rule, it is His," as Smack's eyes went upward to the ceiling.

"You are too much for me to handle. Your age doesn't speak on your wisdom. You're like twenty-eight going on fifty. You are very wise, far from a street hustler, more like a Prophet. What does the future really hold for us, Simmion?" Delight asked him.

156

"Something very fruitful having no doubts and no worries. Our eyes see the same picture being painted into a master piece," said Smack.

"What's that picture, Smack?" she asked him.

"Family oriented, you know, marriage and kids. You and I raising Rainell from a hamburger to a steak and the child you are carrying to be honorable as well."

"Come here, baby," as she kissed him and they lit another round of fireworks on the rug that they were relaxing on.

****

Jasmine and Antwan had two Chinese women in the bed with them. Antwan was a man who had an appetite for more than one woman when it came to sex. He loved to watch two women go at it. He thought it was a work of art, pure beauty when two women engaged in sexual intercourse.

The two Chinese women had Jasmine in a series of twists and turns. One was eating between Jasmine's thighs at her rouge clitoris and the other one was sucking her pale breast giving her much pleasure. Antwan just watched while stroking himself to attention. You could hear the Chinese woman slurping Jasmine's juices as she ate her vagina deeply. It was turning Antwan on arousing him. Jasmine moaned in pleasure gripping the silk sheets tightly feeling her stomach become hollow as her body heated in passion. Her orgasm was strong as he screamed in ecstasy, "Awe, I'm cumming, I'm cumming. That feels so good. Antwan, I need you inside me now, come and fill my hole up baby with your sex," said Jasmine.

He went over to the bed and lied down avoiding the small puddle Jasmine made beneath her. Jasmine straddled him and the two Chinese women went and sat on Antwan's face. Both women rode him on both ends producing natural juices. The room was filled with the fresh catch of the day.

****

Back in Cincinnati, RENU was booking Larro for the possession and sell of an unknown narcotic drug. Frank Toggle and Donnie Black set him up for the sell. Larro didn't talk when they tried to get him to snitch on the people from whom he received the drug. After hours of interrogation, RENU Officers Taylor and Edmond took him down to the Hamilton County Justice Center for processing.

Heather was working and saw him come in. After he was thoroughly shaken down and processed, he was placed in a holding tank. Heather decided to go and talk to him hoping he would recognize her as Delight's sister, being that Smack was his cousin. He had his head down when the door was being unlocked and she stood half way in.

"Hey fella, what's going on with you?" Heather asked him.

"Not a damn thing, just waiting to get a bond," said Larro and he didn't even bother to look up and see who was talking to him.

"Damn Boo, you don't have to be nasty. I'm not the enemy. It's Delight's sister, Heather, from the cook-out. Aren't you Smack's cousin?" asked Heather and Larro looked up to see her standing there in a correction uniform.

"My bad, I didn't' know you worked down here. These nigga's done set me up and now the police asking me questions about Smack and some Antwan cat...man shit is fucked up," said Larro.

"I saw a report, what type of drug are you dealing? They called it Black Ice on the report. I have never heard of it," said Heather.

"It's a new drug, like Ex, but I need to bond out of here ASAP. I have to tell my cousin about this and warn him," said Larro.

"He's out of the country with that Antwan guy and my sister," said Heather.

"He's what?" Larro raised his voice in shock.

"He's over in China attending the Summer Olympic. He didn't tell you?" Heather asked him.

"He didn't exactly tell me that, he just said he would be taking care of some business for a week or two," said Larro.

"You don't have a bond honey they stated no bond on your paper work and most likely the Judge will honor their request. Is there anything you need for me to do?" Heather asked him.

"Yeah, I need for you to give Smack a message for me if you can." Larro told her.

"They are supposed to call me around eight tonight when it is daylight over there. I'll be sure to tell him what's going and I'll give him a time to call my cell phone so you can talk to him personally. Are you hungry?" asked Heather.

"Yes, Ms. Heather, I'm starving," said Larro.

"I got you, Boo, don't worry and everything is going to be okay and just call me Heather," said Heather licking her lips seductively batting her eyes at him. She had a hidden agenda for Larro.

****

The next morning Smack and Delight awoke to the smell of a continental breakfast. They showered together and joined Jasmine and Antwan in the living area of the suite. Everyone was wearing the designer hotel bathrobes that were offered. Antwan and Jasmine was sipping freshly brewed tea.

When they sat down to join Antwan and Jasmine, Delight remembered that they forgot to call Heather. "Simmion, we were supposed to call Heather at 8 over there," said Delight.

"What time is it here?" Smack asked Antwan.

"It is exactly 9 a.m., which means it is 10 p.m. in the US." Antwan told him.

"Let me go get my cell phone so I can call her," said Smack going into their room to get his phone. When he dialed his house number Heather picked up on the first ring.

"Hello Delight, hello," as Heather's voice echoed.

"Heather, it's me, Smack," he said.

"I've been waiting on you to call. Boy it is trouble back here, I tell you," said Heather.

"What did you say, the phone is breaking up?" Smack asked her.

"I said its trouble back here. Your cousin, Larro in the Justice Center, with no bond. He was set up by somebody he was dealing with. They busted him with some drug called Black Ice. I have never heard of it. He also said they, being the cops RENU, mentioned your name and Antwan, the guy you are with. He really didn't give me all the details."

Heather told him and was speed talking.

"Is he alright, Heather?" Smack asked her.

"He's fine. I fed him some Popeye's Chicken and I'm taking him some BW3's tomorrow. I told him that I'll have you call my cell so he can talk to you even if it risks me losing my job, because I hate snitches. I see them mother-fuckers leave in and out all day," said Heather with an attitude.

"I'll try to call your cell phone tomorrow at around nine or ten here so it will be in the morning there. What's your number?" said Smack.

****

"Miesha, what's wrong darling, you seem up tight?" Judge Helmet asked her.

"Nothing Judge, nothing is wrong. I'm just thinking about the loneliness I adore when I'm not waking up with you," said Miesha letting the white side of her take over being she was mixed.

"Well it may be soon that you'll be able to wake with me every morning. My wife's cancer had spread all over and they can't save her. Your wish may come true like the wind that blows upward and out," said Judge Phil Helmet.

"Judge, I'm sorry to hear that. My heart goes out to you and your family," said Miesha. He looked at her like, *"Yeah right, how can your heart go out to a woman whose husband you are fucking?"* The Judge was up on game and knew when someone was blowing smoke up his ass from all the cases he handled in the past.

Allen Taylor and Will Edmond put out the word about the new drug to the Judges and Prosecutor's in Hamilton County and who was probably behind it.

"Thanks for the concern, Miesha. Have you heard about this new drug in streets call Black Ice?" He asked her.

"No, Judge, I'm not a street person and I don't do drugs," said Miesha.

"The drug was found when the super model Stefani Blake was found dead and now it has been found when the Mayor and that young girl were found dead in the hotel room. This pill I have in my hand that I found on your dresser by my things is the same pill the police described as Black Ice, Miesha," as he had the pink pill in his fingertips visible to her.

"That's a sinus pill, Judge, give it to me," as she had her hand out to receive with her other hand on her hip.

"Well, let me take it because my sinuses are bothering me," said Judge Helmet.

"Not that one, I have some Tylenol sines gel pills in the medicine cabinet that you can take. That pill is prescribed by my doctor, so give it to me," said Miesha.

"It won't hurt. Can you hand me my bottled water, please?" He looked at her.

She gave him the water, but she knew by him taking the pill it could harm him, because of his age. He unscrewed the top and Miesha's conscious wouldn't allow her to let him take the pill.

"Stop, Judge! Don't take that pill, please don't do it. I'm sorry, it's the Black Ice," She confessed.

"Where did you get it, Miesha?" He asked her.

"I was introduced to it by my cousin and I think he got it from the guys who call themselves the Belvy Boyz." She told him all that she knew in tears.

"We have to rid this new drug from this region and out of our communities before it takes over. It's said to be worse than meth, cocaine, crack, marijuana and heroin. There have already been three deaths from this drug. Why is it here and not in LA, Miami or New York?" said Judge Helmet with anger in his voice.

****

Back in Shanghai, Delight and Antwan were curious about Smack's phone call back in the States with Heather. Smack was puzzled, but he knew he couldn't discuss the business in front of Delight. She wasn't aware of the new drug they were promoting. All she knew was that Antwan invited him and Stefani to China who was no longer available so she stood in for her absence. Smack acted like nothing was wrong and grabbed him a plate. He piled food on his plate and sat next to Delight who was still starting at him, with a concerned and worried look.

"what's going on back home, Smack?" Delight asked him.

"Nothing, my little cousin Larro, is in the Justice Center," said Smack.

"If that's the case then why did you program my sister's phone number in your cell?" Delight questioned him.

"I can call her at work so I can deliver Larro a message myself." He looked at her then over to Antwan.

"Something else is going on you are acting all weird and shit. I can see it in your body language and face, Negro," said Delight.

"Delight, everything is okay, I promise. Trust me baby, I'm good. I'm just hungry, that's all." Deep down on the inside he was stressing.

"I hope so. Jasmine and I are going to that Boutique and Spa that we saw last night. I guess we will see you all later on this evening," said Delight.

"Okay." Smack replied.

"I'm about to go get dressed...give me some," as she poked out her lips for him to kiss her.

He kissed her and she walked off to their room.

Antwan looked over at him and said, "Simmion...," Smack cut him off. "We'll talk later, Antwan."

He didn't try to question Smack anymore and threw up his hands. An hour passed by and the women were dressed. Delight had on a short V-neck white blouse that showed her cleavage along with some red capris and some Coach slip on heels. Jasmine had on a yellow and orange ruffle Vera Wang dress with no panties or bra. Her school girl leather flats had the same colors of her dress.

When they arrived at the boutique, Delight received the chocolate pedicure while Jasmine sat underneath a nanometer wave machine that the therapist in China used to treat addictions.

After the spa, they went to a fitness club. It was in a big building. It was a total fitness club with 11 branches in Shanghai that offered six kinds of yoga, classes in salsa and pole dancing. They changed into some workout attire provided by the fitness club. They attended the yoga class first and then did a little salsa. Jasmine took Delight to the 20th floor to get on a 180-degree treadmill with monitors to look at our, the glass window while they exercised. After they finished playing with the treadmill they went and sat in the sauna. Delight was unbelievably relaxed sitting there still wondering what was going on with Smack.

Delight and Jasmine took showers at the fitness club and then received the ultimate massage. The technique the masseuse used on Delight's feet hurt like hell, but Jasmine was used to it being she had been here several times before.

"Don't worry Delight the pain will go away," said Jasmine.

"Ouch, now that hurts," said Delight while the masseuse tried to massage her legs gently.

"You'll feel better later and it will let your orgasms flow quickly through your body," said Jasmine giving out a sigh of relief.

"If you say so, Jasmine," Delight said.

After the massages they got dressed and went to Hefei's Anhui New East Cuisine Institute. Delight saw mixed intense of heat with oil and woks as students who were trying to become the next big Chef in Beijing and Shanghai as well as going to New York to cook. Delight guessed they would eat for free after Jasmine paid close to five hundred dollars to play in the spa and fitness club.

After they ate lunch, Jasmine took her to the Three on the Bund retail complex for designer labels. Jasmine bought a white frock dress that cost two thousand and two hundred dollars.

****

Antwan and Smack were visiting the Five Dong Clan village on the country side of the Guizhou Mountains. The Mang, Mo, Mu, Wei and Yin have grown together to form the Dimen, a community of over a thousand. In the Guizhou Providence, the villagers were still recovering from a fire in 2006 that destroyed or damaged about a hundred homes. They road along the Dimen River passing rice fields and then Antwan drove across the Double Dragon Bridge out of the Mang village into the Mu village. Antwan drove towards the Drum Towers and Smack couldn't believe his eyes.

"Simmion, you are about to enter the Mu village, the Underworld. This is the world of the old so whatever you see and hear, it is not an illusion," said Antwan.

Smack just nodded his head and surveyed the village as they drove into it. It was nothing of the modern-day society like the big buildings and lights in Yumin and Shanghai. Smack saw women in their traditional dresses and thought they were warriors. He saw the children playing in the road next to the Rice fields.

"This is like other rural communities where many members of China 55 ethnic minorities live, they remain largely untouched by the economic and social changes now transforming the East," said Antwan.

"I see, so this is worse than the projects where I grew up." Said Smack.

"They are extremely poor not enriched by the government because they don't want to change. These people still believe in traditional healings with plants making their own potions. There's no medicine or technology, look around you," said Antwan. Smack looked around him carefully. "So, why are we here, Antwan?" Smack asked him still looking around.

"This is where we are going solo to make the pills. At twenty Kwai's we'll be making a very good profit to have the pill put together. Twenty Kwai's is like two dollars in American money. We will be paying about two dollars to a hundred villagers a week to put the drugs in the capsules," said Antwan.

"That's a rip off Antwan, way below minimum wage what a person gets for an eight-hour job," said Smack.

"I know. I'm like a prophet over here, Simmion. I'm saving a nation of people who denies their own government. They don't want anything more but a few dollars to buy things of the New World of entertainment. The man power will produce like two thousand bottles a week. We are about to plant a virus in the U.S. with the Black Ice. We only pay out two grand a week for two thousand bottles to be produced, now you do the numbers," said Antwan. Smack quickly did the numbers in his head and he knew they were great numbers he could never see in a short period of time dealing cocaine or heroin.

"Come on, Simmion, let's go and meet the villagers," said Antwan and they got out of the car. The women and kids ran up to Antwan and he had a small bag in his hands.

He threw the bag in the air making it rain with Kwai's and Yens. The villagers scattered with the money and then they entered the Flower Bridge with a pleasing design. It was a typical span that offered shelter from the winds and rain. Smack had only seen these types of structure in old Marital Arts movies. They crossed the bridge to go into a complete structure where the operations were set up. Smack couldn't believe his eyes. He knew then Antwan was a man of business and not only a man of color, but a black man thinking like one of them rich white guys who try to take over the world. Then an elderly woman came out to greet them with an antique style vase and cups with ancient scriptures written on them. She handed Antwan a cup and then Smack bowing her head. Antwan bowed his head to the woman and

Smack did too. Antwan drunk what was in the cup and Smack followed suit. "Sppp...spp, yuck! What is that stuff, it's awful?" Smack said trying to get the taste out his mouth. Antwan was laughing at him.

"That's rice wine and Anyu, don't worry the taste will go away. It makes you see and hear things of this world," said Antwan.

"That was nasty as fuck," said Smack.

"Malign Tai, we are okay...you may leave now," said Antwan and the elderly woman made her departure. "Do you like the setup, Simmion?" Antwan asked him.

"Yeah, this is like a real lab in a warehouse. Why are the women working with no shirts on?" Smack asked him.

"It is general policy, so no one will get any ideas of cuffing the pills under their breasts. No one is too fond of this way of living and is trying to escape to the new world. They are very smart and know this pill can get them there," said Antwan.

"You're like a mad scientist for real, Antwan. You're worse than those cats who were in New Jack City, the movie," said Smack giving a fake laugh.

"I'm just being careful and putting everything under the radar, Simmion."

"That's real, Antwan, but I think we might have a problem back in the States. My little cousin just got busted with the drug and they mentioned our names to him. I think it might be the same cops that pulled me over," said Smack.

"Do you think he'll talk, Simmion?" Antwan asked him.

"No, he's pretty solid. I'm going to talk to him later when I call Delight's sister. He's in the county with no bond. Delight's sister is a Deputy Sheriff in the county, so she's looking out for him," said Smack.

"Good. Find out everything and we'll go from there, Simmion. Jasmine's step-brother is a cop and I will touch base with him when we return to the States," said Antwan.

He looked at Smack and continued, "If I have to go to war with the Cincinnati Police, I will.   Our plans will follow through someway, somehow, Simmion."

Antwan had the look of the devil in his eyes.

****

"Miesha, I will take care of Allen Taylor and Will Edmond. I know they're crooked cops. I have a federal agent that I am very close with who's about justice. I'll introduce you to Steve O'Hara, but I'll need for you to tell him everything you know. Elliot Thrasher was my first cousin and I must bring his killer to justice," said Judge Phil Helmet.

"Judge, I'm not talking to any police and that include the Feds, DEA, ATF, nor the Vortex...none," said Miesha as she started to cry.

"If you are willing to have a life with me, that's comfortable with no hassle or having to want for anything you'll be a wise woman and do as I ask of you, Miesha," said the Judge.

Miesha could see the redness in his eyes and the veins pop in his forehead. She didn't know which way to go, but she knew she wanted a life of luxury having to pay no bills or taxes. A life she tried to get by selling her body, a priceless idea, but an idea that would make her pay consequences in the end. Her life flashes before her and she didn't really know Bodean, but her cousin, Kyle, was like the brother she never had.

****

The rhapsody of cultures opened a side for both Delight and Smack. Massive structures of reality hit home on their relationship and possible future together. Episodes played in Delight's head as she laid across the bed watching him talk to her sister before they went to bed. They were flying to Beijing in the morning on Antwan's private helicopter. The flight would take three hours. Smack swayed back and forth across the fluffy carpet that covered the bedroom floor, it was much different from the living area carpet. He tried to keep it at a low tone, but his voice carried throughout the bedroom.

****

"Good morning, baby, I got you some BW3's last night. Its twelve spicy garlic, twelve mild and twelve hot chicken wings. I didn't know whether you'd like ranch or blue cheese, so I got you both, okay," said Heather.

"That's cool, Ms. Heather," said Larro.

"When you get out of this mess you know that you owe me one or two. I want it from the back, doggy style...that's the way Ms. Heather likes it," said Heather with a smile.

"You're silly, Ms. Heather, you are old enough to be my mother," said Larro with a laugh.

"Guess what, Larro, I'm not her. A bitch just wants to taste that young dick. I want to eat you up real good and fuck you real good. You do me real good and I'll do you. Young protein is good for a bitch like me," said Heather.

Larro saw that she was serious so he asked about K.G. "What about your dude?" He asked.

"Who, K.G.? I just met that nigga at the cook-out. This is my pussy, ass and mouth. I pay my own bills at 2055 Wabash Street," said Heather and then her cell phone was vibrating in her pocket. She took it out and saw Smack's number on the caller ID.

"Hold on, I see your cousin is on time. We'll finish this conversation later this is Smack calling," as she flipped open her phone to answer it. "Hello," as she stared in Larro's eyes whispering, "I want that." She said to Larro pointing to the print in his pants.

"Heather, it's me, Smack." Smack's voice came through her receiver where she and Larro could hear him. "I know it's you...hold on, he's right here. Look don't be long, because these hating ass nigga's and police are nosey in here. I've been in his cell for a while now," said Heather.

"Alright," said Smack. She handed Larro the cell phone.

"Hello, Smack," said Larro with excitement in his voice.

"What's going on?" Smack asked him.

"These mother-fuckers set me up with RENU, this nigga Frank Toggle and this white boy, Donnie Black. The nigga, Frank, messes with my girl Jenny's sister Emily and both of them were at your house on the 4th of July," said Larro.

"What girl, the one in Cincinnati who's pregnant by you? And what two were at my house?" Smack asked him.

"Yeah, my girl who's pregnant by me in the Nati. I only fucked with the nigga Frank because of Emily. You probably didn't notice them at your crib on the 4th, but anyway they wanted to buy three bottles of the pills. They usually cop like half of bricks or whole ones," said Larro.

"And what else?" Smack asked him.

"They tricked me cuss, they put these RENU cats on me. I didn't bring them any work through and they are holding me for conspiracy with intent to sell. They mentioned you and some guy named Antwan Klein, who that maybe I don't know, but Heather said it was the guy you were with out of the country," said Larro.

"Did you tell them anything, Larro? Be honest with me, I need to know what was said up front. No bullshit, lil cuss," said Smack

"Big cuss, I'm still sitting down here with no bond, no fucking bond. I'm thorough brah, I'm not telling them ho's shit. I'll bite my own bullet you just make sure my seeds and Jenny are well taken care of," said Larro.

"Just be patient, cuss, I should be back real soon. Sit tight and Delight will represent you. She'll get you a bond at your disposition hearing. Make sure you fire any public defender they appoint you," said Smack.

Delight was really staring at Smack as she sat up on the bed now from hearing her name and him recommending her without asking.

"Okay, big cuss, I will do so. I'll sit and wait on you," said Larro.

"Do you have any money down there?" Smack asked him.

"No, they took eight racks from me. I haven't called Jenny yet and I know she's bugging out. She's due in about three weeks," said Larro.

"Call her from Heather's cell phone and tell her to come and see you with one of her friends. Don't have her leave you anything. I'll have Heather drop you four or five hundred for right now on your books. Let me talk to her and keep your head up. Love you lil cuss, one," said Smack. He was puzzled but he had to think for everybody.

"One," Larro responded and gave Heather the phone back.

****

Smack hung up his cell phone after telling Heather to go in one of his stash spots at the house and put it on Larro's books. Delight didn't waste any time drilling him about offering her services without asking her first. "Simmion, you didn't bother to ask me if

168

I would be willing to represent your cousin," said Delight with an attitude and arms folded. He knew she was upset because she called him by his government name.

"I'm sorry baby; with no disrespect will you represent my cousin on this case, please?"

Delight tilted her head a little. "What type of case is it, Smack?" she asked him.

"It's a drug case, Delight," said Smack.

"What? Cocaine, heroin, crack or marijuana?" she asked him.

"Neither of the above," said Smack in a low tone.

"What do you mean neither of the above? Is it ecstasy?" she asked him.

"No, it's that new drug called Black Ice," said Smack.

"Are you telling me it's the drug that supposedly killed Stefani and the young girl who was found with the Mayor?" Delight looked at him with a long stare.

"Yep," as he said it in a low tone. She was now curious and she got up off the bed walking towards him. She was now in front of him looking him into his eyes.

"Simmion, I'm not understanding this, so be totally honest with me or I'm walking out that door going home without you," said Delight getting even closer to him still looking in his eyes. "Are you mixed up in this new drug and tell me the truth?" she asked him. He didn't budge or blink. He was still focused on her stare and he came right out with it.

"Yes, Delight, Antwan and I are dealing the drug. I will be out the game after this run, I promise you. The year 2009, the New Year my life will be changed. I never knew the drug would harm anyone and that's the hones truth," said Smack.

"What about Stefani, Smack? I know I wanted her gone, but I didn't want you to kill her. Would you take me out the game too if you wanted me gone?" she asked him.

"Delight, I never wanted anyone to get hurt behind this drug. I didn't kill Stefani...she killed herself. She didn't know I was dealing the drug. My drug life is my life." He told her.

He paused and his eyes got glossy. "Apparently, she already knew about it, because she took ten pills from my bottle. I think Antwan introduced her to the pill. I put it all together from the club when she was acting weird and her death in Cape Cod. I blamed myself for her death and it hurt like hell," he said shedding a small tear. He continued with, "But, I can't allow it to damage my life because of her own carelessness that she brought upon herself and that's the truth," said Smack catching another tear.

"So that's why you and Antwan are getting so close, acting like the best of friends. He probably gave Stefani the drug. You know they used to be lovers. I hope he's not rubbing off on you," said Delight.

"What do you mean by that, Delight?" he asked her.

"I mean, you sleeping with different women, Smack. Last night when I got up to go get me a drink of water, I heard them having sex, but I also heard two other voices that sounded different. You know me, nosey as fuck, so I went to their room and peaked in the cracked door and saw they had two Chinese women in the bed with them," said Delight catching her breath. "So, I'm saying, are you interested in having threesomes and shit like that? Because I'm not on it. I know that night when Stefani stayed behind at the club with Antwan and Jasmine, they fucked her," said Delight.

"How do you know that, Delight, because you left with me that night?" he asked her.

"I overheard her phone conversation talking about it with Antwan," said Delight.

"Why didn't you tell me about it?" Smack asked her.

"Bitches gossip and I don't do that Smack. It was none of my business and everything that's done in the dark will come to the light," said Delight lifting an eyebrow.

"I hear you, but will you take the case?" he asked her.

"Yes, I'll take the case, but you need to dismiss yourself from being involved with anymore drug activity. I don't want our child to be raised by a dad behind bars," said Delight.

Smack knew this day would arrive before he would officially quit the game. He didn't say anything, because he felt her wants and knew she would need him to be a parent as well as herself. The road to redemption would be a huge step for him, but he would have to take that road. The 48 Laws of Power was his mentor his rock like Christians use the Bible and Muslims use the Quran as their stepping stone. It made him confident to fight the principles of law. Murphy's Law, Newton's Law and the law of physics couldn't determine his faith, only the 48 Laws of Power.

****

That morning around three, Smack just so happen to see two Chinese women leaving the suite in traditional robes. Jasmine was letting them out the door standing in a short silk traditional robe of her own. Her back was to him as she let the women out the door. They were bowing to Jasmine as they made their exit. Jasmine turned around and Smack startled her. "Simmion, you scared me darling," said Jasmine with her robe open so Smack could see her rouge nipples and bushy vagina.

Her eyes locked in on him as she took her left hand to pull more for the robe to open so her full breast could be seen by his eyes. Then she took her right hand placing her index finger on her bottom lip. "Jasmine, I can see you. Don't you think you should cover up?"

Smack told her still looking at one of her perky twins. Jasmine was in her own thoughts, thoughts about him touching her, "Jasmine?" Smack said.

"Oh, I'm sorry, Simmion, I don't know what came over me," as she pulled her robe together. She started to walk pass him and stopped. She whispered to him, "I was just thinking about you putting this inside my mouth," as she gently grabbed his manhood through his boxer shorts. "I know you taste good, because Stefani told me all about you, Simmion," said Jasmine releasing her hold and walking off back to her room. He was standing there now with a hard on and his heart was pounding fast. Many thoughts raced through his mind. He knew he had to stay clear out of her path. It was tempting, but what road will that lead to? He wasn't going to find out, because he was in love and his heart was set in place and anything else really didn't matter to him. He retrieved a bottle of water and went back to his room and cuddled with Delight after calming down a bit.

Later, that morning at around 11am, the four of them were putting their luggage in a helicopter at the airport. Smack was now feeling a little uncomfortable around Jasmine, because she was giving him seductive looks and he knew she wanted his human thermometer in her mouth.

Antwan had his pilot's license and it was just the four of them flying in the air. Smack knew this guy was smart, but dangerous like Lex Lugar. His mind was troublesome as he listened to Tupac's song "Troublesome" on his I-pod. Delight was steady taking pictures of them, Antwan, Jasmine and Smack, she was also taking photos of the beautiful land below them.

They flew over Wuhan, Henan, Yukou, the Mu Us desert and through the sandblasted ruins of the Ming Dynasty Great Wall that traced the boundary between the Ningxia and Inner Mongolia regions.

They saw the 180-foot-tall turbines of the Helan Mountains that captured energy to drive China's future. Delight couldn't believe her eyes as she continued to snap photos from her digital camera. Then they flew over Hebie and then landed nearby in the beautiful city of Beijing. It was more fitting to the people of New York Smack thought. Billboards of models displayed perfume and lipstick ads. A jumbo Tron screen was in the middle of Tiananmen Square, the Xidan district in downtown Beijing like Time Squares in New York.

As they rode around Beijing in the blue 05 Audi A6 3.2 Quattro, Antwan took them to the National Center of the Performing Arts which was complete in 2007. Antwan told them, "A famous architect by the name of Paul Andreu from France designed this beautiful facility and it was done in 2007."

The art center sat right next to the Great Hallo of the people of Tiananmen Square. Then Antwan took them by the National Stadium that was completed in early 2008.

The steel twig cradles Beijing Olympic Stadium with 91,000 seats. Its nickname was the Birds Nest named by the locals of Beijing. Antwan showed them how the high-rise trumped the history in Beijing where traditional courtyard homes awaited demolition. He showed them that they were the same homes that were once in the places where the new high-rises stood now. After the small tour they went and checked in a towering high-rise hotel which was very expensive. Many tourists were staying in this hotel for the Olympic Games. Their room was already booked under some name that Antwan gave the receptionist. "Shaback Limio-Ra" Smack nor Delight couldn't pronounce it.

"Mr. Shaback Limio-Ra, here are your key cards to your suite, sir. If you need anything else please let us know and we will accommodate you. Please enjoy your stay," said the Asian receptionist at the desk.

"That will be all, Yin Len, thank you," as Antwan read her name tag and gave her a smile.

"You're welcome, we are glad you came back to visit us in Beijing," as the young clerk bowed her head to Antwan and he returned the gesture.

They made their way to the elevators and to another Presidential Suite. This suite had a chandelier hanging from the living room ceiling, a full kitchen, marble floors, a huge flat screen, a bar and expensive exercise equipment, it also had a balcony looking over Beijing.

It was now six p.m. in the city they were in. Delight and Jasmine went to take showers and change clothes while the men stood on the balcony looking out at Beijing sipping the finest Exo-Remy known to man.

"Simmion, you see those buildings standing over there?" Antwan asked him pointing.

"Yeah, aren't they being built?" Smack asked him.

"They sure are, that will be China's Central television headquarters. It is expected to be completed in 2009, and over there next to it is China's World Trade Center, its crown's Beijing central business district," said Antwan.

"What about the welfare of those in the area's where the lights don't light up at night?"
Smack asked him.

"They are the forbidden fruit. History untouched grounds that are sacred, Simmion. Unlike Americans who destroyed a lot of their history with developmental projects," said Antwan taking a sip of his Remy, "Simmion, do you think 9/11 was a fluke when the World Trade Center was attacked and it was undetected?" Antwan asked him.

"Antwan, all I know is that airplanes flew into the World Trade Center killing innocent people," said Smack.

173

"Simmion, think about the technology we have today, they have tracking devices that can pin point an ant in a small crack thousand miles away. They can even listen to a conversation clearly a hundred miles away. 9/11 was designed to force the economy into a situation like 3rd world countries it was a plan by the American government to make this country go into a recession. Everything is done by design," said Antwan taking another sip of his drink and adding, "Soon it will no longer be middle-class people in the U.S. just the rich and the poor." Antwan pointed around Beijing, "Look around you, Simmion." Antwan paused and continued. "See how things look? You saw the underworld in Dimen all the poor people and the U.S. is heading in that direction. what you have a black president now, the damage was done from the previous president who served the two terms. He destroyed a lot for the American people in eight years. The U.S. let one man hold too much power, a man that bleeds like you and I Simmion, a man who is not perfect and will die like us. what do we owe the people in the U.S.?" Antwan greedily asked Simmion.

"I don't know Antwan and I never looked at it that way," said Smack.

"We owe the American people a chance at the riches of the world and with this drug, we can take them there. Other countries are waking up to the lies and betrayal of the United States. They destroy other countries and don't rebuild them fully. It's ugly and it's going to get even worse," said Antwan. He pulled out a perfectly rolled blunt. He looked at Smack and nodded his head. Smack gave him a nod for him to light it up.

"The riches of the world, Simmion," as Antwan put heat to the blunt and puffed it slowly and then exhaling "being oil is going to start another world war in the future. Whoever controls the oil will run the world. That's why they killed Sudamm. He never owned any weapons of mass destruction; he only made a man-made canal to control the water in that region. I ate dinner with the man and some U.S. officials who were dealing arms to him that I'm currently dealing with. The man sons were messing with the previous president drunken daughter's and had naked pictures of them."

He paused to pass the blunt to Smack. "It was very personal between the two."
Antwan told him.
"So, do you think they'll know about our import of the Black Ice?" Smack asked him.
"Hell yeah, they'll know about it. They want it to come to the States. The Middle East produces the majority of the heroin in the world, Cuba and Mexico produces cocaine and what American brings the majority of these drugs through custom besides the government? Exactly none, they are waiting for a new epidemic to break out it takes the attention off of them," said Antwan with confident.
"I think I'm going to move my family out the country before things get ugly and a revolution occurs," said Smack.
"That would be brilliant Simmion; any third world country will welcome you and your American dollars. You would be a filthy rich man in a third world country. Just imagine being in a country like West Africa with five thousand or more with you, you'll be a God," said Antwan giving him a grin.
"Are you serious, Antwan?" Smack asked him.
"Am I serious? Yes, I'm fucking serious, look how other foreigners migrate to the U.S. to work and accumulate American dollars to send back home to their poor families," said Antwan.
"You're right they are flooding the U.S." Smack told him.
"They are smart, Simmion. They come over with three or more family members and live in a one-bedroom apartment and they send all their money back home," said Antwan.

****

She stepped into the Federal building not knowing her destiny. Her mind was in a blithe from the drug she was on, her palms were sweaty, her eyes were stained red from crying. She was high and her adrenaline pumped at a steady rate. Based on turmoil unlikely circumstances holding nothing in life, but the truth, Miesha stumbled into Steve O'Hara's office. Miesha's Prada shades hid her sorrow and pain that set deeply in her eyes. Her heart pounded drowning out the sound that was around her and what Steve O'Hara said to her. "Hello, Ms. Miesha Jones. How are you doing today?" He asked her. She stood at the entrance of the office like a zombie in a trance.

"Ms. Jones, you may sit down," said Steve O'Hara and she snapped out of her trance.

"Oh, I'm sorry, I didn't hear you, sir," said Miesha.

****

The walls were in a dark prism of colors. It was a small room where lawyers could meet with their clients in the Justice Center for privacy. Heather managed to get Larro out of his cell for a work detail that required the work of him being at her personal use. She was on her knees engulfing him in her precious mouth. Larro was cramming her head between his legs grabbing the back of her head. She wasn't having him touch her hair at all. She removed his tribal piece from her mouth still having a grip with one of her hands.

"Hold up nigga, this hair due has to last four more days. Don't be trying to pull my tracks out and shit. I know this head is off the chain so just calm down and enjoy it," said Heather. She put his hard manhood back in the clutches of her strong wet jaws. Larro looked down at her saying, "My bad, ma, I thought it was your real hair. Your shit has been fly ever since I first saw you," said Larro. She released him again. "Na'll nigga it's a built-on wig with glue tracks. My natural hair in underneath this bullshit. But my shit is still long and tight," said Heather.

"Okay, I feel you, but 'em c'mon don't start anything you can't finish, ma," said Larro.

"Shut up nigga," Heather said aggressively looking up at him. She slapped his manhood on her own lips and then started back taking him whole in her jaws. Her performance was of an extreme pro. She pulled at him with every suck making it sound like she was sucking a lollipop. He held onto the sides of the walls trying not to grab her head. She went up and down the sides of his shaft making her own rhythm. Her tongue laid flat up against his manhood and Larro could see the thickness of her tongue as she licked him motionlessly to the beat of a drum which was his racing heart. She then took and sucked his testicles making him sigh in pleasure and pain. Her procreation prevention would probably end up on her face or down her throat as she stayed steady with her head clinic. His toes began to curl in his county shower shoes and he couldn't hold back any longer, he bust in her mouth and got weak at the knees.

"Oh shit, Heather, you're good. You are real good, you got me. You got me, Heather," Larro said as he tried to catch his breath. He tried to push Heather away, but she refused to let him go trying to suck him dry. Butterflies formed inside his stomach as he melted in her jaws. He was now wide open and that's where Heather wanted the young fella gone off her water mouth action. Super Head, who? It was Ms. Heather Heath who had the Super Head clinic. She finally released him from her jaws and told him. "I want to cum, nigga. So put this condom on and you better know how to fuck. I need for you to fuck me like you be fucking those young bitches you be dealing with, because I know you probably don't know how to eat pussy," said Heather looking at him with her sexy eye lashes batting a way.

They captured the nightlife by flying back down towards Shanghai to Guangzhou. They took a taxi from the air landing strip after landing the helicopter safely. They went to the Baby Face club on the Pearl River and it was packed. Delight saw Kobe Bryant, Carmelo Anthony, Dwight Howard, Lebron James, Dwayne Wade and Michael Redd in the club. Antwan knew the owner of the club and got them in VIP with the U.S. men's basketball team. Delight managed to get pictures with the players and her favorite player, Kobe Bryant. This trip was becoming the best vacation she'd ever had. She met Kobe Bryant in the flesh and she did get to talk to him for a while in the club. Even though the pictures would say enough, she finally met her favorite basketball player.

The club was jumping like a club back in the States. Smack thought he was in Roxy, The Mix or Club 112 in Atlanta. Antwan ordered champagne, Tequila 1800 silver and convinced Delight and Smack to try a Flaming Lamborghini. It was one of club's famous drinks. It cost $12 a drink, even though Smack was more of a dark liquor guy and Delight wasn't much of a drinker they tried it and liked it. Delight couldn't really drink the alcohol because of her condition so she took a few sips and let Smack finish it. Delight had a mixture of orange juice and cranberry in slush form. Sean Paul's 'So Fine' came on and the club went crazy. The Chinese crowd was jamming doing all the latest American pop dances. Delight couldn't believe her eyes as her and Smack was on the dance floor. She didn't know that Smack would take their relationship to another level this night in China. As of right now, on the spot, he was the man, her man for the job, her man for any job her everything and some.

They left out the club to get some fresh air, so they took a stroll along the Pearl River. It was lit up like South Beach, but the river was lit from the romantic lighting of the moonlight. Delight removed her Louis Vuitton sandals and shook her clinging Louis Vuitton slacks from her dampen skin. They walked down to the back and stood there watching the calm water flow and Smack stood behind her holding her. Her shirt managed to rise a little from his hold and it was moist from her perspiration, but the apple perfume still had its lingering smell of its sweet scent. His wine color summer Polo shirt blew amid a slight breeze that roared over the river sending the smell of his 9IX cologne in the air. Delight closed her eyes praying to God in this very moment, that this would never end. She prayed that God wouldn't deliver a fatal blow by removing Smack from her life with a long prison term for his participation in the streets; or some thirsty individual ending his life trying to rob him.

Her eyes re-opened and she was still standing on foreign soil staring at the Pearl River she'd only read about in a tour guide. She was still in Simmion Boyd's arms and she knew she wasn't dreaming. She leaned her head up against his chest and took in a deep, deep breath exhaling it real slow. "Simmion, promise me that you'll never leave me deliberately, can you promise me that much?" said Delight.

"I can promise you just about anything, but promises are meant to be broken. I can guarantee you that Simmion Le'Andre Boyd will never leave you, Ms. Delight Heath," said Smack and then he spun her around from his arms and kissed her passionately. He released her lips from his and stood back holding her left hand breaking down to one knee. Delight grabbed her mouth with her free hand in shock, knowing his next move would prove his love for her in concrete stone; his loyalty and wanting to be with her forever. Her eyes instantly began to water. He spoke strong and deep within the deepest part of his voice. "Delight Heath, my debt to society is unlikely not paid and may not ever be paid, but my debt to you and unborn child is a given. I know I love you and my time is now to act on my true feelings," as he gazed into her eyes searching for another breath. A tear began to run down her cheek as he continued. "With all due respect, I'm not being forced in any form or fashion to make this decision nor was I made any promises, it is a decision to my likings and desire. I want to spend eternity with you, because you complete me in more ways than one. Only other person who knows of me doing this is our daughter, Rainell. Since your parents are no longer with us, I asked Rainell for your hand in marriage and she gave me permission," as he paused briefly.

"Now as God as my witness and the many angels that roam this earth, Delight Trice Heath, will you marry me?" as he showed her the ring he got from Kyle. The beautiful two karat diamond glared in the moonlight.

Delight was shaking and trembling in emotions as she tried to answer him. "Yes, yes, oh yes, Simmion, I will marry you!" said Delight still trembling.

He slid the ring on her finger that he had re-sized to fit her. She stuck her left hand out for him to place the ring on her finger.

The diamond was very large and made her previous ring look like costume jewelry. She kissed him holding him tight. Then a small audience from the club started clapping, congratulating them both. The small audience was watching Smack propose to her the whole time, because Antwan knew he would, he saw the ring at the hotel room back in Shanghai.

Antwan was coming to get them and saw Smack on his knee and he knew he was about to ask her to marry him. He went back into the club and got Jasmine bringing the small crowd with him. Delight felt special, so intact with her life, so in control with her own destiny. She cried tears of joy holding her man.

That night they flew back to Beijing and Antwan had the hotel restaurant make them a cake to celebrate their engagement. After cake and champagne Smack and Delight retired to their bedroom. Delight lit a few candles that were scented. They made love on the oriental style bed that silk veils surrounded it.

They seduced each other like never with endless counts of oral seduction. Over a long period of time the candles burned down tremendously. They didn't notice at some part of their sexual encounter that a pair of mysterious eyes watched them through the crack of the door that they managed to open without being noticed. It was the eyes of Jasmine Finch. Jasmine wanted Smack for her own personal use, the mere images of creativity swarmed her eyes and she started to masturbate watching them. At high stages black and white, we live for excitement no matter the costs. The global ethnic couldn't take away Delight's happiness at this point.

****

The next day, Jasmine, Delight, Antwan and Smack paid a visit to the Great Wall of China. Jasmine had on a pair of Dereon dark colored jeans, a red V-neck Dereon shirt to match and some black Cole Haan sandals. Delight was wearing a tight fitting mini-dress by Patricia Field that showed her thick stallion like legs that were so beautiful. She had on some pearl bangles, some ankle strap platinum and black sandals by Giuseppe Zanotti. Her engagement ring set the tone for her black dress with platinum stripes. Smack had on a pair of Roc-A-Wear jeans and a long sleeve shirt and some Rockport shoes. His Rolex stood out and he had on a Cincinnati Reds fitted ball cap. Antwan had on an asymmetrical hooded sweatshirt by YSL, a white t-shirt underneath, a pair of limited edition jeans by Roc-A-Wear Premium Collection that were light blue, a monogram Louis Vuitton scarf an interlock Gucci belt and some Superstar 2BSC shoes.

They filtered on the Great Wall of China spending priceless time together. Incredible icons couldn't imagine the status Delight and Smack mind state. Delight emotional side was in tuned with her mental state. All nine levels that could possibly trigger an orgasm were on point. Her emotional wave was under control. She didn't have a stressful bone in her body. She wasn't worried about getting the divorce from Kendall any longer or the fact she wasn't with the firm anymore. Her relationship with God, her daughter and Smack was all that matter to her.

Smack was feeling like he was above anything petty being out the country seeing things he was long over- due to see. He had money and now his money meant something worth value. He was ready to move forward with his life with Delight. They toured the rest of Beijing and attended the Olympic ceremony. They saw the torch being carried to the stadium and Delight snapped pictures of the world around them with each one of them in it for her photo album. The love so honestly pure no matter how it came about, but it happened and the price for it was an equal opportunity.

CHAPTER SEVENTEEN
SHIT HITS THE FAN

"Your Honor, I wish not to obtain any assets from Kendall Scott. No spousal support of anything of that nature," said Delight.

"Mrs. Scott, what about child support?" The Judge asked her who was handling their divorce case.

"Your Honor, I don't think that will be necessary. We can handle those issues outside of the courtroom. I would like for this divorce to be final as of today with no complications. Mr. Scott can have the house in Mason leaving me with no obligations to help out with any mortgage or taxes on the property. I would like to remove my name off any bills or contracts dealing with the property or that we have together under my married name in exchange that Mr. Kendall Scott going his way not giving me a dime or any hassle," said Delight.

"Mr. Scott, do you agree to these terms that Mrs. Scott is suggesting?" the Judge asked him.

"Yes sir, your Honor, I don't have a problem with it. I would just like visitation rights with my daughter," said Kendall.

"Your Honor, he can visit his daughter whenever he wishes," said Delight.

"Well Mr. Scott, you will be entitled to that. This case is over. The divorce is final. I wish you two the best of luck in the future, this court is adjourned," said the Judge hitting his mallet.

Delight and Kendall left the courtroom after each other and neither one of their current lovers attended court with them. Kendall stopped Delight in the hallway.

"Hey, Delight, hold up a second," he shouted. She stopped throwing one hand on her hip and her head in the air blowing out a head of steam. "What now, Kendall?" she stood.

Kendall caught up with her and asked her. "I'm just curious because I see you have on an engagement ring and it looks very expensive...did he ask you to marry him?"

"Yes, he did, last week when we were in China. Why?" Delight had an attitude.

"Because our divorce wasn't final and it's obvious that you accepted and didn't care about us," said Kendall.

"I sure did accept and you're right, I don't care about us. Hell, you didn't give a fuck about me. Look Kendall, our thing is over; it was probably over before it even started. You should've been a man; long ago and just said you wanted some ass; it would have been just that simple. So is that all you wanted, because I have to be at the Justice Center in twenty minutes." Delight told him.

"I think you are making a big mistake, Delight," said Kendall.

"What do you know about mistakes? Right, because you made one by marrying a good woman," as she walked off, so bold but so calm. She had her head high to the sky smiling a mile long with her back towards him giving a good view of the tight skirt she was wearing.

Miesha Jones and Judge Phil Helmet sat in the Olive Garden restaurant on Colerain Avenue. Things were safely sound between them but she still felt somewhat guilty about the information she gave Steve O'Hara.

"Judge, what are those things again?" Miesha asked him.

"They are Mussels, try one they are good, Miesha," said Judge Helmet.

"No, thanks," as she turned her nose up.

"So how did things go with you and Steve O'Hara last week?" He asked her.

"It went okay, I guess. I told him about my cousin's friend and where they hang out. He wanted for me to wear a wire on the guy and I'm still thinking about it," said Miesha.

"So, what are you going to do?" He asked her.

"I told you that I'm still thinking about it. I gave him enough of what I knew. Now to ask me to participate in a bust sending a black man to jail is way out of the question. I'm not the police, I don't get paid for that shit, I could get killed behind this," Miesha told him.

"I'm paying you swell, Miesha now that my wife has passed away. I think it's time for us to have some guarantees and warrantees in our relationship." The Judge told her.

"Oh, so now I'm eligible for the good life or will I forever be your puppet?" said Miesha.

"What do you mean, Miesha?" He asked her.

"Come on Judge, I'm a young black woman who's barley educated, I will never be your equal you will always try to run my life. Your career makes you that type of person always calling the shots. Well I think it's time for Ms. Miesha Jones to start calling the shots. Fuck you and Steve O'Hara, I'm not setting anyone up for ya'll. Get out there and do your own dirty work, because a bitch like me ain't even on it. You don't care about me, only your cousin, Elliot Thrasher," said Miesha. She stood up from the table and walked off not bothering to look back. She caused a scene in the restaurant, because she was indeed loud. She dialed Kyle's number to see if he could come and get her because she had a lot of explaining to do to him about what she did.

****

"Hello, I'm here to see my client Larro Boyd, please," said Delight to a woman working behind a control center in the Justice Center.
"Who are you, may I ask?" the woman asked Delight.
"I'm his lawyer." Delight answered her.
"Does Ms. Lawyer have identification?" the woman asked her.
"Yes, I do," as Delight handed the woman her ID and a business card.
"Okay, let me call up to his floor, Ms. Scott, attorney at law," as the woman cut and rolled her eyes at Delight being sarcastic. She turned around and called up to the floor that Larro was on.
Delight mumbled to herself. *I know this little heifer didn't roll her eyes at me with her trailer park ass."*
"Here you go, Ms. Scott," as the female CO handed Delight back her ID and business card along with a visiting pass sticker. "Put the visiting sticker on and take the elevators on the right up to the fourth floor of the South building," said the female CO.
"Thank you very much and I'll be sure to tell Heather Heath about you, L. Moore," said Delight giving her a look of her own.
"What did you say?" The female CO asked her but Delight kept walking showing a little cleavage and her diamond necklace. "Old trifling ass bitch, mad because a sister is an important bitch with a career, she's watching dicks for a living," Delight said getting on the elevator. When she got off the elevator you could hear Larro Boyd being called for a professional visit.

She had waited for the metal sliding doors to open. Then she entered a small sally port that circled around a patrol booth where two CO's sat watching the inmates. She could see the other inmates beyond the glass windows. The inmates saw the beautiful top flight lawyer and were stalking the glass. Larro came out to meet her from one of the pods; she smiled at him and then shook his hand to greet him.

"Hello Larro, sit down please," Delight said and she joined him. She opened the folder containing his paper work. Larro stared at her, because his cousin had a dime. He couldn't help it, but to notice the huge rock on her finger. He never saw a ring on her, 'I'm taken' finger before. He knew then that his cousin did it, he proposed to her.

"Okay then congratulations, I see Smack did it, huh?" Larro put his hand to his mouth, smiling. Delight didn't know what he was talking about, so she asked him.

"I'm lost Larro, what did he do? What are you talking about?"

"That," as he pointed to her engagement ring.

"Oh, this! Yes, your cousin proposed to me while we were in China! Let's get down to business. Let's discuss your case and get you out of here. Do you know these police?" She asked him showing many pictures of police officers.

****

Kendall was sitting at home frustrated and mad. He couldn't believe Delight agreed to settle back down so quickly, especially with a made-man, a known drug dealer. He couldn't let it go; he wasn't going to let it go.

He was drinking a fifth of Hennessy straight from the bottle while sitting in the living room. He had his white Steve Harvey collection dress shirt open showing his masculine chest and six pack, as he lounged on the couch.

Keisha came in the house using her key with grocery bags. He had startled her, because she didn't know if he was home or not, because his car was in the garage. She jumped when she saw him sitting there. "Oh shoot, Kendall, you scared me baby," as she dropped the bags and her keys. She saw a troubled man, a very out of sync man; she knew something was bothering him. She didn't want to ask him, but she did anyway.

"Kendall, what's wrong? What happened in court today?" She asked him.

"I don't believe this woman, she's about to marry Simmion. You should've seen the ring he bought her. This drug dealing, low life mother-fucker. I feel like killing this guy," said Kendall slumping in the couch.

"Why is that any of your concern, Kendall? You have a new family to worry about. You must be still in love with her and just wanted a piece of ass from me, huh?" said Keisha with an attitude.

"It's not that, Keisha, I just don't want her to do something she'll regret and get caught up in some bullshit and my daughter...," as Keisha cut him off. "Fuck that Kendall, Delight is a grown ass woman and she takes good care of Rainell. You can't dictate her life and take care of this pussy too; it's not going to happen. It's over between ya'll. I asked you did you want to cross that line," as she paused trying not to get emotional. "You looked me dead in my eyes and told me, yes. You can try to play me and this baby if you want to, Mister. You're sitting up here drinking your sorrows away over some bitch who don't give two flying fucks about your sorry ass. Look at you, pathetic as hell, you stupid, Kendall," as she picked up her keys and went upstairs leaving the groceries on the floor. He picked up the bottle and took another gulp of the business he was drinking and threw the bottle against the wall making it shatter. He was angry, knowing Keisha was right. He was having a sucker attack about Delight being with Simmion.

"Come here Keisha, baby. I'm sorry...I love you," as he stumbled trying to go after her barely able to walk.

****

Kekou, Bodean, Kyle, Vino, Dante and his cousins Ike and Tevin, who just got out of prison were sitting in Good Fella's with Smack. They were sipping on Jacques Cardin Cognac VSOP imported from France. They were having a conference about the new shipment coming in.

"This apple flavored cognac is almost better than my Remy. Who found this? I thought you all only fuck with Belvy?" Smack asked them.

"I found it and we might switch our Belvy to this," said Kekou.

"You can switch to this Kekou, but I'm sticking to my Belvy," said Bodean.

"Yo, Smack, I want you to meet our cousins Ike and Tevin, they fresh out the pen today," said Dante introducing them to Smack. They shook hands and Smack continued to tell them how much Black Ice was coming in. Then he received a phone call from Delight.

"Hold on fella's this is wifey calling me, she might have some good news about my cousin, Larro," said Smack. He flipped open his Razor cell phone and answered her call.

"Hey baby, what's up?" Smack asked her.

"Where are you, baby?" she sounded a little nervous.

"I'm at Good Fella's in Corryville with the fella's," said Smack.

"What fella's? Are any of Larro's boys around you?" she asked him.

"No, I'm with the Belvy Boyz. Why, is something wrong, Delight?" He asked her.

"You bet it is. The white chick who was with Fila, Precious at the cook-out, she's with RENU down here. She's been going undercover as a stripper and they have been investigating the Diamond Cut, baby she's the police." said Delight.

"How do you know this, Delight?" Smack asked her.

"I just left your cousin and I went to see Jasmine first and she gave me a folder containing all this information on the RENU staff. She told me the contents in the folder would help us figure things out. Larro noticed her picture and he wanted to call D$Boy, but I told him not to because they be recording conversation. Oh, her real name is Patricia Simms," said Delight.

"I'll call D$Boy to let him know what's up. What else is going on?" He asked her.

"The guys on his case are Allen Taylor and Will Edmonds. The C.I.'s are Frank Toggle and Donnie Black. This Donnie Black guy has taken down Magoo and his brother, Perm; he's one of their top informants out here. Here's the catch, Larro never said anything about drugs over the phone or gave them anything when they met. He'll most likely be out tomorrow when we go to court, but you all need to be careful because they are after the Diamond Cut. They also want the people behind this Black Ice

junk, but Jasmine gave me her word that she wouldn't try to prosecute this case knowing that he is on of ours. That's what she told me, being she is on our side...whatever that is supposed to mean," said Delight.

"Okay, baby, where are you now? He asked her.

"I'm on my way to the house," said Delight.

"I'll call you later. Let me wrap things up here and I'll be home shortly. I'll call D$Boy and let him know what's going on," said Smack.

"Okay, baby. I love you," said Delight.

"I love you too, bye," Smack and her hung up the phone.

Smack shook his head in disbelief. "What's up, Smack?" Kyle asked him.

"Larro is good but we have a problem and we are definitely under the radar. The bad white bitch that look like Co-Co Fila's girl, she's Five-0. And this white guy named Donnie Black is RENU's top informant so be on the lookout," said Smack.

You're lying about the white girl, Smack, she's too loose to be the boys," said Bodean.

"Yeah, cuss, she let me hit that twice on the DL," said Dante.

"Wifey got her information and picture. Her real name is Patricia Simms, she's working for RENU and they are after Diamond Cut, me and whoever else is dealing the Black Ice. I have to call D$Boy to let them know," said Smack.

"Damn, that's fucked up," said Bodean while holding himself.

"What's fucked up, Bodean?" Dante asked him.

"That the freaky ass white bitch is the police. She slid me her number at Sneaky Peak," said Bodean shaking his head and adding, "Miesha is blowing up my phone, I wonder what she wants. I'm not going there with her and these fucking pills," said Bodean.

"Kyle's cousin gonna kick your fat ass, nigga and you better answer her call," said Dante giving him a fake laugh after making that remark.

"You need to worry about Eva kicking your ass for still messing with that white girl, Beth and Joan's young ass," said Bodean. Dante just waved him off and Bodean continued to ignore Miesha's phone call. Kyle had left his phone in Smack's Cadillac truck. Miesha figured she would give Bodean the heads up since Kyle wasn't answering his phone. Also, she was hoping he would come and get her from Colerain. Smack called D$Boy while Bodean and the rest of the guys continued to drink. D$Boy picked up on the second ring. *"What up, cuss? Hold on a second,"* D$Boy told him and the phone went silent.

"Okay, who dis?" D$Boy asked Smack.

"D$Boy, who's all-around you?" Smack asked him.

"Who is calling my phone asking questions?" D$Boy asked him.

"This is Smack, nigga," said Smack.

"Oh shit, what up cuss, is Larro out?" D$Boy got excited asking Smack.

"No, probably tomorrow, but like I asked...who's all around you?" Smack asked him again.

"Auni, Secret, Precious and Fila. We are in Trotwood at 8-Ball & Wings shooting pool and kicking the Bo Bo," said D$Boy.

"Don't say shit, just listen and listen carefully. That bitch, Precious is the police. Her real name is Patricia Simms. My girl, Delight, just found out. Let Fila know he's been fucking Karen Cisco all this time, telling that bitch all his business. She's undercover for RENU." Smack told him and the phone got quiet.

"I wonder if Larro know, and why he didn't call me. I got money on the phone?" D$Boy asked him.

"He already knows about her from my girl and the reason he hasn't called you because they are recording his phone conversations being that he's a member of D-Cut," said Smack.

"So, what are we going to do about the police slash stripper in our circle?" D$Boy asked.

"The Heineken Red Star Soul Festival next week up in Cleveland, the mistake by the lake, you all are performing, right?" Smack asked him.

"We got a slot after Alicia," said D$Boy.

"Then she'll disappear in Cleveland, bitch will be at the bottom of Lake Erie," said Smack.

"That's what's up. I'll holla back big brah, I'll put the word in Fila's left ear," said D$Boy.

*"Alright, D$Boy,"* said Smack and they hung up, but D$Boy had plans of his own to get rid of her if she got out of line.

****

"Answer the phone, Bodean, I know your fat ass see my number. You're probably up under some bitch tricking. I'm trying to make things right, damn it," said Miesha walking down Colerain Avenue pass the Northgate Mall. She hung up out of frustration. It was now four-thirty in the afternoon and hot out, but not humid. Even though it was the beginning of August, it wasn't that bad out. She had on some Miss Me jeans and a multi colored t-shirt to match caring her Prada purse over her shoulder. Her 42" ass could be seen a mile away. Many horns blew at her as she walked down the street.

Then a familiar car was blowing at her as she continued to dial Kyle's and Bodean's numbers. The all black 08 Dodge Charger SE sitting on 22" chrome rims pulled over in the Speedway gas station as Miesha stood in front of the gas station. Then the Dodge Charger pulled closer to her and one of the tinted windows came down on the passenger side.

"Hey, Ms. Lady, do you need a ride?" the guy asked her.

She ignored the guy trying not to be a real damsel in distress. She was still trying to call her cousin and Bodean. "Ms. Lady, Bodean is probably out with the family and is not going to answer your call," said the guy. Her eyes lit up when she heard Bodean's name, because she knew whoever said his name knew she knew him. It didn't spook her that the guy knew Bodean; she closed her cell phone and slowly turned around to Worm and P-Diddy. She smiled at the person on the passenger side and started walking towards the car. *"Worm," she said to herself.*

How could she forget the big nigga who put the smash down on her pussy when she had sex with them down at the store? She felt warm and safe seeing them and she knew they could deliver the message to Kyle and Bodean before she could.

Men always know where other men are...when they don't want a bitch to find them. It's just the code of the streets.

****

"Yo, we are going to the Red Star Soul Festival next week in Cleveland, no females tagging along, just us from down here. Those nigga's in Dayton are bringing their female friends and we have a surprise for Ms. Precious. I'm out, come on Kyle, if you're riding with me," said Smack as he shook everyone's hand. He and Kyle left out of Good Fella's while the Belvy Boyz continued to drink and eat. Smack didn't even see Steve O'Hara and another federal agent sitting at the bar as he walked pass the bar. They were watching Bodean.

Kyle's phone was dead when they got in the truck and he couldn't even see that Miesha had called him several times.

Bodean got up and went to the restroom and Steve O'Hara followed him. He pretended to use the urinal waiting on Bodean to finish. When Bodean was finished they both stood at the sink washing their hands and then O'Hara spoke to him.

"What up, Bodean, or should I say Jamal Irvin?" said O'Hara. Bodean stepped back and looked at the husky white man and was wondering was it the Jacques Cardin talking to him, because he didn't know this white man from Adam.

"Damn, my nigga, Bodean, it's cool I'm not the ghost from Christmas past or the future, I'm the present. It's not you that I want," said O'Hara.

"My man, you don't know me," said Bodean.

"Jamal, I'm a federal agent. My name is Steve O'Hara and I know everything about you. I just want to ask you a few questions concerning the Black Ice," said O'Hara with a smile.

"Fuck you, cop, whoever you may be. I don't talk to the police," said Bodean.

"Mr., Irvin, don't be stupid and save yourself, your girl Lula is pregnant. Look, you didn't even know that and I did. She's scared to tell you because she doesn't know if it's your baby or some guy named Lomax," said O'Hara and Bodean took a swing at the federal agent and missed. O'Hara grabbed him and cuffed him all in one motion.

"See, Mr. Irvin, that's an assault on a federal agent. Come on, I'm taking you down to the Federal building to talk to you and don't end up over in Boone County, because that's your next move," said O'Hara.

"Fuck you cop, suck my dick," said Bodean with aggression.

"Keep it up big boy, just keep it up," said O'Hara as he led him out of the restroom in handcuffs. He was pushing Bodean through the aisle way of the Sports Bar.

"Take these cuffs off and I'll kick your ass," said Bodean.
"Yeah, yeah, yeah," said O'Hara still guiding him towards the front door.
Dante, Kekou, Ike, Vino and the other customers were looking in shock. Dante approached them, "What's going on, sir? As a matter of fact, who are you?" Dante asked.
"My name is Steve O'Hara, I'm a federal agent and I need to borrow Mr. Irvin for a little while, so excuse me, sir," said O'Hara moving Dante out of his way.
Bodean was still fusing as the other agent was helping O'Hara take Bodean into custody. Now everyone was wondering if they were in Good Fella's the whole time, they were having their meeting.
"Yo, Kekou, did you notice them at the bar?" Dante asked him.
"No, they came in after your dude, Smack, left out. I saw them come in," said Ike.
"Hold up, this is P-Diddy calling my phone," said Kekou as he slipped open his phone.

****

"Damn it, Bodean, pick up your phone," as P-Diddy mumbled to himself.
Miesha had told Worm and P-Diddy everything and they were heading down to the store on McMicken. She was scared and now fearing for her life, but she knew she had to inform them on what she told O'Hara.
"Yo, P-Diddy, Bodean isn't answering?" Worm asked him.
"No, for some reason he is not picking up," said P-Diddy.
"I told you all he wouldn't answer my calls either, my cousin also. I hope they are okay and nothing has happened to them on my account, I wouldn't be able to live with myself," said Miesha getting emotional.
"Don't worry, Miesha, everything is going to be okay. Let me call Kekou to see if they are still together," said P-Diddy. He dialed Kekou's number and he picked up.

****

"Yo, Larry, have you seen Jamal? Is he still with you?" P-Diddy asked Kekou addressing him by his nickname.

"Man, the Feds just took him out of Good Fella's in cuffs. I don't know what the fuck is going on," said Kekou.
"I do. Meet me down at the store in about ten minutes...I'm almost there," said P-Diddy.
"Okay, we are out of here," as Kekou hung with P-Diddy.
Things were getting really shabby all around the board it was a bubble waiting to burst. Everyone was spooked, so spooked they didn't even call Smack to let him know what was going on. Kekou, Dante, Ike and Vino left Good Fella's heading down Vine Street to the store.

BACK UP IN DAYTON D$Boy, Secret, Precious and Fila were at Fila's Condo on Philadelphia and Needmore. They were relaxing just sitting around talking and D$Boy hadn't told Fila that Precious was the police yet. He couldn't at 8-Ball & Wings. D$Boy was mean mugging Precious the whole time after he found out the news. Then D$Boy sparked up a conversation with Fila that he wouldn't had never done around any females. He stated the business about the new shipment of Black Ice that they were getting.
"Yo Fila, Boss man said Larro should be free tomorrow and about two thousand bottles of the pills should arrive in a few days," said D$Boy and Fila was looking at him crazy like what the fuck are you doing. Precious was all ears and D$Boy knew it.
"Yo, D$Boy, holla at me later about that business, nigga," said Fila.
She was acting like she was so tired with her hand over her forehead. Secret had nodded off. D$Boy watched Precious's movement and then she suddenly had to use the bathroom.
"Excuse me, I have to use the bathroom," said Precious getting up in her tight jeans and t-shirt.
D$Boy had noticed that she took her purse with her and that made him curious.
"Yo, Fila, is your girl on the rag?" D$Boy asked him.
"No, nigga, she can't bleed, because she wears the birth control ring inside her. It stops her from having her menstrual cycle.

Why, are you trying to get down tonight and swap out?" asked Fila.

"Yea right, you tripping, I'm not trying to swing with you all, that bitch is the police, nigga," said D$Boy.

"Where is all of this coming from, D$Boy, you know my bitch is legit? calm down with all that, nigga," said Fila.

"Nigga, Smack called earlier when we were playing pool. The lawyer his girl is on Larro's case and she has Precious's information. Precious works for RENU in Cincinnati," said D$Boy.

"You lying dog, I don't believe you. She has done too much to be the jakes. She smokes hella weed and have served mad dope for me," said Fila.

"Yeah, she's just building one of those ooh-wee cases against you and us, stupid. She got your nose so wide open I can drive a Semi-truck up the mother-fucker. Why did she take her big purse to the bathroom with her then if she's not on her period?" D$Boy asked him.

"I don't know, that's what women do, I suppose," said Fila.

"Yeah, if they are bleeding or are going to freshen up. She's at home with her man. Secret don't do shit like that at my place, once she comes in, she throws her shit in a corner until she's ready to leave. She's going to make that call to her contact, I bet you," said D$Boy.

"You have got to be kidding me, D$Boy," said Fila.

"I'm serious, let's go listen at the door," said D$Boy.

Fila looked at him and D$Boy gave him that look. "Come on," said Fila and they went to the main bathroom and she wasn't there meaning she was in the bathroom in the master bedroom. When they got to the master bedroom, they heard the water running in the shower. Her purse wasn't nowhere in sight and her clothes she had on wasn't visible. Then they put their ears to the door and heard a conversation going on, but they couldn't make any sense of it. Fila was now leery and knew something wasn't right. She'd always strip down in the bedroom before getting in the shower. she would lay out her underwear and nightgown across the bed. Fila couldn't hold back any longer.

"Yo, Precious, Precious, what are you doing in there?" as Fila was banging on the door.

"Umm-umm, I'm taking a shower, baby," Precious yelled back to him.

"Who are you talking to on the phone then?" Fila asked her.

"Umm, no one honey, no one," as you could hear her words fumble.

It got quiet suddenly, but the shower water was still running. She continued her conversation on her cell phone with another RENU officer.

"Hey Tom, I have to go, he's getting suspicious, but give my message to Allen or Will for me. In two days, I'll call and let them know where the Black Ice is going to be," said Precious.

"Be careful Patricia they are some dangerous guys. And what about the shooting, didn't you find out if they were behind it?" Tom asked her.

"They were definitely behind the shooting on the sergeant, we'll be ready to take them down on everything in about two weeks, Tom," said Precious.

"Okay, but like I said Patricia, you need to be careful," said Tom.

"Tom, I'm a big girl, I got this okay, but I have to go bye," said Precious hanging up her cell phone.

Fila and D$Boy stood outside the door and the water finally stopped running. Precious wrapped herself in a towel. She put her purse over her shoulder after taking her Beretta out and placing it under her dirty clothes she had in her hand.

She got prepared for any case scenario, because Fila never questioned her like this before. The door opened and she saw Fila and D$Boy standing there with curious looks on their face. "Damn a bitch can't have any privacy, there's another bathroom in the house. I'm not fucking your friend tonight that's out of the question, sorry," said Precious.

She walked pass them going over to the bed sitting down still holding her clothes and the gun out of their sight.

"Don't nobody want to fuck you. I'm just trying to see what going on with all this secretive shit suddenly. On the phone in the bathroom with the door locked. If it was me you would swear that I was cheating," said Fila.

"It was only Carla and she didn't want anything important. Now can you all excuse me so I can get dressed, please," said Precious.

D$Boy had noticed something about her that was very odd and looked at her carefully and said, "Damn, Precious, I know you're not that nasty, your hair isn't even wet so don't you think you should wash your ass before putting on clean clothes?"

He noticed that she wasn't wet at all not even her towel was damp.

"What are you talking about? Fila, you need to get your boy. I'm not his bitch, he's worried about the wrong female all up in my business and shit," said Precious.

"Yeah, Precious, you're not even wet, so what were you really doing in the bathroom?"

Fila asked her with his arms folded.

"Yeah, Patricia Simms, what were you really doing?" D$Boy asked her and her eyes lit up. She looked at him with a disfiguration.

"We know you are the police, Ms. Simms," said D$Boy. They slowly began to move towards her and she jumped up off the bed pointing her Beretta. "Don't move or I'll shoot so back the fuck up now," said Precious. Fila threw his hands in the air. "No, oh no, Precious say it's not so, you're not one of them. I love you baby," as Fila dropped his head in disbelief.

"I told you, Fila," said D$Boy shaking his head.

"I'm sorry Fila, it wouldn't have never worked baby. I'm the law and you're the bad guy. It was fun while it lasted and if things were different...well I liked you a lot, but I can't let my feeling get involved with my job," said Precious with a tear lingering in the corner of her eye.

"Fuck that, Precious, I know you love some Fila, somewhere inside you. You got love for Fila and I know it," he said with much pain in his voice and the ivory began to stain in his eyes.

"No, I don't love you so quit saying that," as tears began to creep down Precious's cheeks. "All I want is the people who are behind the Black Ice and D$Boy for shooting a police officer in Cincinnati. I'll put in a good word for you, Fila, if you're willing to testify against them," said Patricia still holding her aim.

"Bitch, I'm not going down for shooting a cop, you'll have to kill me first," said D$Boy.
D$Boy was trying to locate in his waist for his Heckler & Koch.
"Don't do it, D$Boy, show me your hands now," said Patricia in a demanding voice.
Fila looked at her and had tears storming down his face. He was mad in love.
"Precious, baby, why?" Fila asked her.
"I'm sorry Tuffy, but it's my job and I must uphold the law. You've been in this situation before when you told on Benzino," Precious told him still holding her aim at D$Boy's chest. Fila balled his fist and he couldn't take anymore. "Fuck this, Precious," as Fila rushed her and she dumped two shots in his chest. This gave D$Boy time to pull his gun. Precious teared up watching Fila fall to the floor and she came back around to D$Boy with her gun pointed at him and his weapon was pointed at her.
"See what he made me do? I'm sorry Fila fight baby and I'll call 911. D$Boy drop your weapon," Precious told him.
"I can't do that. You drop your gun," said D$Boy still pointing his weapon at her.
The shots startled Secret and she grabbed her chrome 3-80 out of her purse. Secret was D$Boy's side-kick a real Robin Hood in the streets. She was unknown to man for her witty ghetto traits, because all they ever saw was a pretty face and a fat ass.
"I can't do that either, you're a fugitive a wanted man that I must bring to justice. I know Smack is giving you all this new drug, but where is he getting it from?" They both briefly looked down at Fila because he was speaking his last words, "Precious, I love you," said Fila before he took his last breath. Precious began to cry and both of their eyes met back up with one another.
Out of nowhere darkness came to Precious, a silent dream stormed her mind, she didn't know what or where she was. All she knew was that she was now trapped in another world, because Secret shot her in the back of the head. Her body just melted to the floor. Her eyes closed and her body was motionless. Secret saw the standoff and Fila's body on the floor. Precious's body fell on top of Fila's, a true Romeo and Juliet hood

love tragedy that went sour. D$Boy looked at his right hand and lover that came to his rescue.

"Boo, are you alright? I heard the gun shots and it woke me up, I thought I was dreaming, but I guess I wasn't. So why did you shoot Fila, baby?" Secret asked him.

"I didn't, Precious shot him," said D$Boy with a concern look on his face. He knew they had to get out of there and out of town fast and hurry.

"Why, baby?" She asked him.

"We confronted her about being the police and Fila couldn't, didn't want to believe it and I guess he got emotional and tried to rush her and she shot him," said D$Boy.

"I thought she was a stripper, baby," Secret told him.

"Yeah, an undercover stripper, she was the mother-fucking police. She had us fooled and this mother-fucker was in love with her. I don't know what she did to him, but he was gone off on her," said D$Boy.

"So how did you all find out she was the police?" Secret asked him.

"Earlier from Smack when we were at 8-Ball & Wings. You were knocked out on the couch when I told Fila. He didn't believe me, so we confronted her and Ms. Patricia Simms was indeed the jakes," as D$Boy was now going through her purse to verify it. He found her badge and ID showing it to Secret.

"Damn, Patricia A. Simms, a RENU agent. I killed a cop, a white bitch and a cop. You've got to be kidding me, right?" Secret was confused and in disbelief.

"No, ma, you see it for yourself, let's get the fuck out of here. I know his neighbors heard the shots. Help me find the shell casings and I'll grab her purse and the glasses we used. Don't touch anything else without pulling your sleeve over your hand," said D$Boy.

"What about prints, baby?" Secret asked him.

"I'm going to wipe everything down, just find the casings," said D$Boy.

Secret found the shell casings and they fled, but before doing so and wiping everything down D$Boy and Secret looked at Fila for the last time and the pretty undercover cop. They heard sirens coming in their direction and he knew someone called the police.

****

Smack and Delight were at home romancing the stone just lounging around in their bedroom. They were doing nothing of the ordinary, real simple and plain. She was out of her work clothes in some sweat pants and a tank top and he had on his basketball shorts and a t-shirt. They were just acting like normal couples after a hard day at work. He was changing the channel and she was fingering through a magazine.

"Hey baby, turn that back to American Idol," said Delight looking up briefly at him and Smack just looked at her. "Delight, you're reading a magazine," said Smack.

"No, I'm not. I'm just looking through it," said Delight.

"It's either Lifetime or American something with you or that black ass nigga Flavor Flava and the Flavor of Love," said Smack.

"Just turn it back, please," said Delight and he did. Smack started playing with her stomach and breast trying to get her aroused.

"Okay, Simmion, that's how you got me in this situation I'm in now," said Delight grabbing his hand pulling it away from her swollen nipples. Then his cell phone rang, she looked at him and grabbed his hand.

"No, baby don't answer it, finish touching me, come on let's do it," said Delight.

"Make up your mind...you just told me no," said Smack.

"Well I just changed my mind, you know my hormones have me acting all funny and stuff, baby," as she guided his hand back across the course of her breast and then down to her warm spot between her legs. He could feel the warmth coming through her sweat pants. His phone kept ringing and ringing repeatedly back to back.

****

All the Belvy Boyz was at the store with Miesha except Bodean. They were smoking Cush trying to figure out why Miesha did what she did. They closed the store to get an understanding on the situation and what they were going to do.

"So, Miesha, you told who about the Black Ice?" Dante asked her.

"I told Judge Phil Helmet and his friend a federal agent by the name of Steve O'Hara. I know I fucked up and it's been on my conscious. I only mentioned Bodean and Kyle and no one else," said Miesha.

"Why would you tell the Judge and what is his connection in all of this?" P-Diddy asked her.

"He's my lover, my Sugar daddy. We're supposed to be living together in the big house with the white picket fence if I helped him get rid of the drug," said Miesha.

"But I'm saying why would he care? He's just a fucking judge. His seat is not in jeopardy," said P-Diddy.

"His cousin, Elliot Thrasher, was the mayor and he died behind this drug," Miesha told them.

"Miesha, I understand Bodean, but your own cousin though. He thinks the world of you no matter what your personal life consists of. You must find a way to get this Judge out of the way and get Bodean back, "said Kobe.

"I know Kyle loves me and I'm sorry. That's why I didn't go on with it. They wanted me to set up Bodean, but I couldn't do it. I can probably help, I have me and the Judge on DVD having sex several times," said Miesha.

P-Diddy looked at the rest of his click and said, "Are you all thinking what I'm thinking?"

"Blackmail!" They responded at the same time.

"Yeah, we might have to use that, Miesha. In the meantime, I'll take you home to grab the DVD's and some clothes. You'll have to hide out because they'll be looking for you, especially what I have in mind they might even try to kill you," said P-Diddy.

"She can stay at my crib until things die down," said Worm looking over at her giving her a smile. Miesha liked the suggestion, not only because of her safety, but she knew she could have sex with him again. Her eyes lit up and a twinkle came in them.

"Well, Worm, you can take her home and then out to your crib. Weezy, Vino and Ike will follow you all in case they need to make an escape route for you all. I'm going to call Smack and Kyle to let them what's going on," said P-Diddy.

******

Smack reached his phone to find he had missed calls from D$Boy and P-Diddy. Then his phone rang again and it was P-Diddy. Delight just looked at him while he answered the call, "Vegas never sleeps and neither do I," said Smack.

Delight was now looking through the pictures from their trip to China. Smack was carefully listening to P-Diddy and every so often Delight would look up at him when he responded with a lot of, "Yeah, okay, umm hmm, she did what? Okay, call me and let me know and don't wait until the last minute, P-Diddy," said Smack. He hung up the phone. He shook his head and said, "Boy oh boy, when it rains it pours."

"What's wrong baby is everything alright?" Delight asked him.

"The Feds picked up one of the Belvy Boyz today, Bodean. Miesha, Kyle's cousin, the one he brought to the cook-out," said Smack.

"Yeah, what about her?" Delight asked.

"She told Judge Phil Helmet which is her lover that she received the Black Ice from Bodean and Kyle. He supposed to be Elliot Thrasher's cousin. He convinced her to help him and a federal agent to find the people dealing the drug. She gave up Bodean and Kyle," said Smack.

"I knew it, I knew it. I knew I had seen her somewhere before; she was with the Judge that night at Lenhardt's when we went to meet Antwan with Stefani," said Delight.

"Guess what though, she has the Judge on DVD, so they are going to try to blackmail the him and call off his federal friends," said Smack.

"Does Kyle know what's going on, Simmion?" Delight asked him.

"I don't think so, Delight," said Smack.

Delight just so happened to look up at the TV to see Precious's picture being flashed on breaking news. She really couldn't hear it, but she knew it was her.

They showed Fila's picture too and Delight told Smack, "Look baby," as she pointed to the television. "Turn it up, Delight," said Smack and she grabbed the remote and turned the volume up.

"Tonight, in Montgomery County, Dayton, Ohio, we are live on the scene of a double homicide. Patricia A. Simms, an undercover RENU agent was found dead in a condo on Philadelphia and

Needmore. Tuffy Holiday a.k.a. Fila to the streets of Dayton and a member of Diamond Cut was found dead. The police are suspecting foul play. Patricia Simms was working undercover on a sting to bring down the members of Diamond Cut.
Apparently, her gun was discharged at the scene, but the police haven't recovered another weapon so they are ruling out that Tuffy shot her. Whoever killed them fled from the scene and the police need your help in finding the suspect who committed this crime. We will have a full report from the police chief at 11:00 here on Channel 7, back to you, Paula," said the news reporter on the scene.
"Thank you, Tom. Tom Harris is live on the scene at Philadelphia and Needmore in the Northwest part of Dayton, where the bodies of Patricia Simms, an undercover cop and Tuffy Holiday were found….," Smack now had the remote and he turned the TV off.
"Simmion, what's going on baby? I'm getting scared. I hope you didn't have anything to do with that," said Delight holding herself by folding her arms tightly rocking herself.
"Delight, what are you talking about?" Smack asked her.
"Smack, I tell you that she was the police and now she's dead. Something is not right Smack, and to tell you the truth some other shit is going on and you're not being totally honest with me," said Delight.
"Delight, I only delivered the message I didn't order a hit I don't do that, I'm not a murderer a Mafia type of guy. Yeah, I get money illegally true enough, but I don't go around bagging people, I'm not a killer you should know that," said Smack.
"Please, Smack, I'm not all in your business like that, so I don't know what you be doing in them streets," said Delight looking up at him.
"Delight, I didn't have anything to do with her getting killed," he told her.
"I hope not, because if you have blood on your hands, I'm just as guilty," said Delight.
"I don't know what's going on, but I think D$Boy has some answers, because he's been blowing up my cell," said Smack.

"Well you need to be finding out what happened if he does know what's going on," said Delight still rubbing herself rocking back and forth.

****

The sweat came down heavy from his forehead and his whole body was wet from the adrenaline as he perspired heavily. Shambles rambled through his veins straining while he tried to explain the trouble, but not saying a word. How could he when he was trying to concentrate? He was humble well in the mix of things, but confused because his mind wasn't sober. His voice was husky as the world he was in was turned upside down. He couldn't figure out why him? Why should his life go down the drain and hers be so perfect? He challenged the fact and only to deal with the situation at hand. His face had a grimaced look as he wiped sweat from it. His facial expression changed several times before becoming calm. His body was stiff, but his heart was racing rapidly. "Oh, Keisha, I love you," as Kendall released energy inside of her vagina walls. She was griping his buttocks as he laid on her gently. Both of their sweat mixed and the sheets beneath Keisha were soaking wet.

"Kendall, I love you too and I'm sorry baby. It will never happen again. I'm yours and I'll support you any way I can," said Keisha.

"I believe you baby, let's take a shower and I'll cook for you," said Kendall looking into her eyes. She released her grip from his ass cheeks and her nail print was in his buttocks.

Kendall added, "I got to clean up the bottle I threw against the wall baby."

"Whatever you were drinking, we have to buy you some more of that real quick, because you put it on me. And you're always talking about you're a lousy lover you could've fooled me," said Keisha.

"It was Hennessy 1800 and I hope I didn't hurt the baby." Kendall said.

"You didn't, but mommy had three strong orgasms back to back and speaking of the baby, I have a doctor's appointment at Mercy Hospital in Fairfield on Friday. Can you go with me?" Keisha asked him.

"What time is the appointment, Keisha?"

"The appointment is at 11:00am," said Keisha.

"I have a water scandal case from Dublin, Ohio that I must handle and it might just run over to the afternoon. Maybe I can get David to sit in for me so I can be there for you and the baby, okay?" said Kendall giving her a kiss.

"Okay, but if you can't make it, don't worry about it." She looked up at him.

They rose up off the bed together and looked at the bed and then at each other laughing. Then together they stripped the bed linens before heading to the shower.

****

"D$Boy, where are you?" Smack asked him.

"I am on the highway headed to the Nati. I can't talk on the phone, but we need to talk ASAP," said D$Boy.

"I think I already know, because it's all over the news. Call me when you get to the Tylersville exit and I will come to meet with you," said Smack.

"I got you, big brah," D$Boy responded.

"Stay focused D$Boy," said Smack and they hung up.

****

D$Boy pulled into the BP gas station off the exit and Secret was calm, but wondering how could she be in this situation protecting her boo. She couldn't believe that she killed a police officer and her nerves were raging, but she didn't let it show. They sat in the dark blue 08 Mazda which was spooked with limo tint. D$Boy had a fifth of Patron drinking it out of the bottle to calm his nerves. They waited patiently on Smack to arrive and it was almost twelve midnight.

D$Boy was listening to Jada Kiss 'Kiss of Death' on CD.

"K.I.S.S. me and I just wanna make love, love" came through the 10 speaker Bose system that surrounded the inside of the car. Secret puffed on a Di'Jorum cigarette wondering how exclusive her life really was. Now she was public enemy number one and the moment of reality would set in later, even though she wasn't the type of woman who would panic. She was probably more thorough then most men who set out to be grimy. She was solid and knew her place as a woman being in the streets where the code was holding court in them. She cared, but she didn't give a fuck when it came to her own survival. She knew now that it was a matter of life and death and she knew if D$Boy showed any signs of weakness she would have to end his life and be a loner. She glanced over at him after taking another drag of her cigarette and didn't say a word. She watched him sip the Patron as she continued to puff her cigarette.

She finally asked him, "D$Boy, what are we going to do?"
"Let me holla at Smack first and then I'll know, Secret," said D$Boy.
"Fuck Smack, you be your own man, nigga. Why the fuck you have to answer to this nigga, he's getting all the money and ya'll are getting all the heat," said Secret.
"Secret, it's not like that; he might have a better solution for our problem at hand. But I don't have to follow his lead, so don't say shit," said D$Boy.
"Okay then, so let's be out of her and fuck him. I know you have enough money for us to live comfortable in St. Thomas or Belize or something out of the country," said Secret.
"Let me think, Secret," he told her.
"Let you think? Nigga please, I'm the one who pulled the trigger on that white bitch, not you. At least you can break me off and let me get the fuck out of dodge, D$Boy," said Secret with an attitude.
"That's what you want, Secret? Is that what the fuck you want?" D$Boy asked her.
"Yes, that's what the fuck I want, to get away, but I want you to go with me," she said gently rubbing the side of his face.
"Here's what I'll do...you can fly out the country to wherever and I'll come...," as D$Boy was cut off by the tapping on the backdoor window by Smack. He unlocked the door and Smack got in on the passenger side in the back. "What up, D$Boy and how are you doing, Ms. Secret? What's going on, Dave?" Smack asked him.
"That bitch, Precious is dead and so is Fila," said D$Boy.
"I know, it was on the breaking news. I guess its worldwide now. I told you I saw it," said Smack.
"Are you for real, Smack," D$Boy asked him again.

"Yeah, they showed both of them, on the news. They also showed the Meadows of Catalpa in Meadowdale. I didn't know that Fila was posted over there. I thought he was still in Huber Heights," said Smack.

"Yea, he was over there," said D$Boy and he continued. "We confronted Precious and the truth came out. She knew about the hit on the RENU sergeant in the Nati, I did with Bo-Gotti, because Fila was pillow talking with that bitch telling her our business," D$Boy told him with a sultry look even though he couldn't really see Smack's face.

"So that's why you killed Fila?" Smack asked D$Boy.

"Killed Fila, I didn't kill Fila, Precious did. He wasn't buying that she was the Jakes and went crazy. He was in love with the Bunny. He rushed her and she put two in his chest. Then...then...," he looked over at Secret and she gave him a look that would kill and D$Boy put his head down and Secret came out with it herself. "I killed Precious. I heard the shots and came into the bedroom to see Precious in a standoff with D$Boy and Fila were on the floor shot. I did what I was taught to do, shoot first and ask questions later. I shot the bitch in the head, because she had my man at gun point, there it is," said Secret and she puffed even harder on her Di'Jorum.

"Damn it, I wanted to dump her in Lake Erie, D$Boy," said Smack.

"Well it's a change in plans, Boss man. That nigga Fila was the one who told on Benzino. Precious let that cat out the bag," said D$Boy.

"Did anyone see you all leave from his place?" Smack asked them.

"I don't think so, but I switched cars anyway," said D$Boy.

"It's your call D$Boy, what do you want to do?" asked Smack.

"We want to leave the country, that's what we want to do. A matter of fact, tonight would be nice," as Secret took it upon herself to answer for D$Boy.

"Is that what you want to do D$Boy, leave the country?" Smack asked him.

"I was going to send Secret first and then meet up with her later," said D$Boy.

"Later?" Secret blurted out with an attitude looking over at D$Boy.

"Yes Secret, later. I'll give you enough money to leave on your own for a while until I get there. I need to see Larro and make sure I'm around when the cops start asking questions. I don't want to be obvious, you know," said D$Boy.

"Whatever, get me on a plane," as she let out a sigh and starred out the window at the rain attacking the glass.

"Well listen here, you both will check into the hotel and you can put her on a plane tomorrow. I'll give you fifty racks so she can go shopping in the morning and board a plane in the afternoon," said Smack.

"I can do that myself, Smack. I got eighty racks in the trunk. we'll spend the night at the hotel and I'll put her on a plane tomorrow," said D$Boy.

"Make sure you stay out of view of anything moving faster than you...meaning flashes," said Smack.

"I got you, big brah," D$Boy told him.

"Call me after she boards the plane. Only you should know where she is going and keep it to yourself," said Smack. Secret was eyeballing D$Boy the whole time while they were making arrangements for her departure. She wasn't feeling the vibe because she wanted D$Boy to go with her. "I will, Smack, and what time does Larro go to court tomorrow?" D$Boy asked him.

"At around nine, my girl is going to call me as soon as they come out of court and I'll let you know," said Smack.

"Alright, let me get her out of this pouring rain and into a warm bed," said D$Boy.

"Okay, one," said Smack getting out of the Mazda 3 going back to Delight's Infiniti truck. Secret rolled her eyes at D$Boy and didn't say a word to Smack. She was mad and wasn't feeling the sudden plans of being alone trying to escape the country. She didn't know D$Boy had eighty thousand dollars in the trunk. Her mind was now racing with new ideas and her heart was pumping with never ending adrenaline. Greed tempted her mind and she thought about it over and over again. The reasonable doubt not having a care in the world being a fugitive and leaving no witnesses to identify her. She was now a woman with no bounds.

Secret knew that her secret wouldn't be silent if things crashed like the stock market. It would get out that she was a cop killer. She was raised by hustlers and pimps and knew the code of the street.

Secret sat in the passenger seat watching D$Boy check them into the hotel. She rocked back and forth trying to gain thoughts of her next move talking to herself. She watched D$Boy give the clerk an extra two hundred dollars because he put the room in his alias name not using any identification. When he came out of the hotel lobby and got back in the car it was total silence. The windshield wipers were still going and Maxwell's 'Pretty Wings' was playing through the Bose speakers. He pulled around to the room in the back of the hotel. He parked and let out a huge sigh looking over at Secret.

"Well babe, let's go inside and try to get some sleep. Are you hungry? It's a Steak & Shake that's still open close by," said D$Boy.

"I'm fine, just a little exhausted," she said as she exerted herself to get out the car.

They were heading to the room and D$Boy shielded her with a jacket after he retrieved the black bag out of the trunk. Secret glanced at the bag and knew it contained the money. She got excited on the inside as she clutched her purse and wrapped her other arm around his waist and they walked up to the room door.

****

Smack walked in the door from the garage and he noticed that there were lights on that were off when he left. When he got close to the kitchen, he heard a voice that echoed. He turned the corner to see Rainell on her cell phone. He looked at her and she told the person on the phone, "I have to get off the phone, my dad's back home."

She looked up at Smack and he said, "Rainell, you're okay...just don't let your mom catch you and make sure those dishes are out of the sink before you go to bed."

She smiled at him giving him the thumbs up. She continued her conversation and headed upstairs to her bedroom. He walked in to find Delight knocked out. He didn't bother to wake her up, he just went and took a shower. His mind was vigor knowing he had to use his mental energy. This was becoming a heavy weight fight. He had to contact Antwan, check on Bodean and Larro and then make sure that Secret exits the country safely. His meditation ran deep as the water ran over his head. He returned to the bed and Delight awoke knowing that Smack was in her presence. "Babe, you're just now getting back?" She asked him. "I've been home for a while now, you were sleep when I came in," said Smack.

"So, what did D$Boy say?" She asked him.

"What I'm about to tell you stays here, Delight. Okay? This conversation shouldn't go any further and it will be the last time we talk about it," said Smack.

"I know, Simmion, but if it's that bad I don't think I want to know," said Delight.

"It's cool, Precious killed Fila and Secret killed Precious," said Smack.

"Are you serious, Smack?" Delight had to sit up in the bed.

"Yes, I'm serious and Secret is leaving the country tomorrow. They are at one of the hotels up by the Plaza," said Smack.

"It's getting real crazy, Simmion, you'll have to call it quits, baby. We are financially stable right now and don't need anything. It's over baby. You had your run in this life style to much shit is going on around you," said Delight.

"I know baby, I know," as he kissed her.

****

Meanwhile back in the hotel room, D$Boy had talked to Chill, Bo-Gotti, and Freaky D. Secret had taken a shower and put on one of D$Boy's t-shirt he had in the duffle bag along with the eighty racks she saw herself.

They laid across the bed watching Tyler Perry's House of Pain on TBS. Suddenly, D$Boy passed out. He was snoring and she knew he was exhausted as well. It was probably the Patron he was drinking that contributed also. She lit another Di'Jorum and walked over to the glass window pulling the curtains apart to look out. She stared out the window watching the rain hit up against the glass. Her mind was cold, but thirsty for an answer.

Her heart was like Yttrium with no feelings. She rubbed herself trying to get the chills off her as she glanced over at D$Boy and then back out the window. A voice came from within her, it was her alter ego. She was a Gemini and had a split personality. She came to her rescue. *"Damn Secret, or should I say, soft ass Sheena Price? You are not this weak; you are a strong black woman I thought with potential who makes her own decisions. This nigga got us fucked up like we stupid or something. He got eighty thousand sitting over there in that black bag with our name on it. He owes us, we killed that cop lady for him and the only witness is him. We aren't trying to go back to jail for this nigga, are we? So, you better be the bitch I know you are and kill this nigga and take the money. We can buy us some new dick when we get to where we are going,"* as tears began to form in her stained eyes. "No Sue, I can't. I love D$Boy, I love him, Sue," said Secret to herself. Secret was now staring at D$Boy. *"Bitch please, how you gone love someone when you know that nigga's only want some ass out in these streets. He don't love you like that, you're a stripper a bitch who sucks and fuck for the dough. Girl get that free money for all the times we did parties for his friends for free. Bitch, kill this nigga so we can get ghost,"* said Sue.

Secret looked around for the voice talking to her, "Stop it Sue. No, don't say that. I'm not like you. That life is behind me, get out of my head," said Secret. She held herself tight by grabbing each arm hugging herself.

She wiped away the tears that were streaming down her face with the palm of her hand.

"Secret, go and get the 3-80 out of your purse, he'll understand later. Be strong Boo, I got your back, us girls must stick together shit those nigga's do. Look he's worried about everyone else's well-being except ours. Let's get the fuck out of here. St. Thomas is waiting on two bad bitches like us with a lot of money and we can have all the dick we want," said Sue.

Secret rubbed her self even harder. "You're right Sue, he don't love me putting me on the back burner for everyone else. Fuck him girl, I deserve that money and a new life," as she was reaching insider her purse. She then stepped towards the bed standing over D$Boy while he was fast asleep in a dream that wouldn't wake him till morning.

"*Do it Secret, pull the trigger bitch, he won't feel a thing, go ahead,*" *as the voice of Sue commanded her to do so.*

"No Sue, I can't do it, I can't," said Secret as more tears began to flow.

"*Bitch don't punk out on me now, we've come to far, shit give me the gun and I'll do it,*" *said Sue.*

"No, Sue, I can't. I love him too much, bitch get out of my head...the devil is a liar," said Secret as more and more tears trampled down her face. "D$Boy, I'm sorry baby, I love you," as she took her aim off him pointing the gun to the floor.

She didn't even know how much she really loved him until now, but she knew she had to get out of the country.

CHAPTER EIGHTEEN
LACK OF EVIDENCE

Heather came to where Larro and the other inmates were being held before going to their designated courtroom. She was coming to escort him to Judge Phil Helmet's courtroom on the 3rd floor of the Court House. She had on her work uniform and her deputy badge was shining. Her nails and hair were done beautifully. She opened the holding tank and called his name. "Larro Boyd for Judge Phil Helmet's courtroom, can you step to the front, please," said Heather.

He looked up and saw it was Heather and he smiled. He came out the tank and she locked the door. "Sir, can you turn around for me please," she asked him and he did what she asked of him.

"Do you have anything on you besides your legal papers?" Heather asked him doing her job before frisking him.

"No, ma'am," said Larro.

"Put your hands behind your back, please," as she cuffed him and then searched him thoroughly grabbing his manhood. Then she whispered in his ear, "I'm getting some of that dick today when you get out Mr. You see I got my shit done just for you. I talked to Delight and she told me you should get out today," said Heather.

"We'll see," said Larro.

"You're right...we'll see. Sir, please step up to the red line and go up the hall to the elevators," said Heather. He did as he was told and when they got off the elevator to a small room with lockers that held weapons for the deputy Sheriff's, Heather retrieved her 9mm Glock. She led Larro into the courtroom from the back entrance and he saw the likes of Allen Taylor and Will Edmond in suits. His mom and pregnant girlfriend were also there. His lawyer wasn't present yet and Heather sat him down in the jury box. He could see the anger on the RENU agents face. Larro hadn't watched the news from last night and he didn't know that Precious and Fila was dead.

******

"Simmion, I'm glad you could join me this morning. It is fairly nice out today. So what is troubling you, my good friend?" Antwan asked him.

"A lot of unnecessary bullshit is happening Antwan. After this shipment, I'm out. It's getting too risky in my circle and my circle is in deep waters," said Smack.

"I'm sure we can handle the heat, Simmion. We are on schedule to make history, my friend. You can't pull out now," said Antwan.

"I have to, Antwan. This federal agent is asking questions about us and the drug. A female put him on to one of my comrades, but they already knew our names from Elliot Thrasher and now they have one of my comrades in custody," said Smack.

"Who is this female? We need to get rid of her and will your foot soldier talk?" He asked Smack.

"I've already dealt with the female situation and I doubt it if Bodean talks. My comrades only know of me and not you. But we have a bigger problem, my cousin who's downtown," Smack said to Antwan cut in. "Yes, the one that Jasmine is going to let go today," said Antwan.

"Yes, that's him. Some of his partners are mixed up with a cop killing that happened last night in Dayton. His friend got killed and a female undercover cop that he was dating. It's crazy, Antwan, real crazy," said Smack.

"Simmion, you tell me exactly what you need for me to do?" As Antwan stopped exercising on his Bo Flex machine he had in his office at Jillian's. He took a sip of his Labrot & Graham Woodford Reserve Bourbon.

"I mean, I can rid you any worries, Simmion, just tell me and it's done. My buddy Wally is in town," said Antwan with a grin.

"I'm just trying to be careful, Antwan. Look, I'll help you move this new shipment and then I'm calling it quits. I'm chilling out for a while. I'll probably plan this wedding and let this shit die down so they can get my name out of their mouths," said Smack.

"Simmion, when there's heat, we act like an infernal and turn the heat up on our end. I have artillery to cause havoc in this city to send a message," said Antwan.

"Let's stop a minute and think this through Antwan. I have a better solution give me a few days and I'll let you know," said Smack.

"Alright, Simmion," he answered and wiped the sweat from his forehead. Then a news flash came across the bottom of the television with breaking news. Smack looked closely at the hotel that stood behind the news reporter. Tylersville Road in West Chester came across the bottom of the screen. The news reporter stated. *"A man is in critical condition after suffering two gunshot wounds to the chest area. Apparently, it was attempt on his life. We are yet to identify the victim. Hold on wait. Okay, we just got word he's a black male in his twenties from Montgomery County. His name is David Baxter; he's a known drug dealer from that area out of Dayton, Ohio. He's a member of Diamond Cut. He was also wanted for questioning in the alleged shooting of Sergeant Davis back in May of this year in downtown Cincinnati. We will have more coverage on this shooting at twelve noon,"* said the reporter.

"Damn it, damn it. I just left them at around one this morning. He's one of my cousin's partners. His girl is the one who killed the cop last night in Dayton. He was supposed to put her on a plane today. She is real fucked up now," said Smack pointing to the TV.

"Do you think that she shot him, Simmion?" Antwan asked him.

"If she's nowhere to be found, yes, I would suspect she did. But I wonder why would she betray him?" Smack said looking at Antwan. At the same time, they said.

"MONEY."

"Simmion, did he have any money with him?" Antwan asked him.

"He said that he had around eighty thousand with him last night," said Smack.

"Do you want to try the Greater Cincinnati Airport to see if she's trying to board a flight by herself?" Antwan asked him.

"We can try to see if she's still around, Antwan, or even if she went in that direction. Let's go now," said Smack and then he mumbled to himself. "Larro is going to flip out, one of his partners is dead and the other one is in critical condition," said Smack.

He watched Antwan grab his car keys. "We are taking my red BMW," said Antwan.

Delight walked in the courtroom in a crème colored Liz Claiborne two-piece skirt suit. She had her purse on her shoulder, a piece of paper in one hand and her briefcase in the other. She smiled at the RENU agents as she walked pass them. She handed Jasmine the piece of paper which was a motion for dismissal. She looked over the courtroom and saw Heather, Larro, his mom and pregnant girlfriend, Jenny. Delight figured the older woman was Larro's mom because she resembled him and Smack.

"Ms. Finch, can we get this over with?" Delight asked her.

"Sure, as soon as Judge Helmet comes out of his chambers," said Jasmine.

Then the judge's clerk came out of his chambers. "Excuse me, Jas, the judge would like to see you, Ms. Heath, Will and Allen in his chambers," said the blonde female clerk.

Delight looked at Jasmine wondering why the Judge wanted to see them in his chambers. Apparently, something was wrong. The two RENU agents stood up and followed the two ladies into the Judge's chambers. He was looking over some papers of his own when they walked in.

"Judge Helmet, what is going on? We are wasting tax payer's money. This case in not worth trying to prosecute because the lack of evidence," said Jasmine.

"Ms. Finch, did you watch the news last night?" the Judge asked her.

"No, I didn't, Judge. Why do you ask?" Jasmine asked him.

Delight knew what he was speaking about, because she saw the news and got it from Smack.

"A female RENU agent was killed by a member of the Diamond Cut last night. She was dating one of the members which he was also killed last night, both of their bodies were found at his place. The police are suspecting foul play," said the Judge.

"What does that have to do with this case, your Honor?" Delight asked him.

"She contacted the RENU department before she was murdered and left these two gentlemen a message. She found out that a

David Baxter a.k.a. D-Boy was behind their sergeant getting shot and Larro Boyd was with him," said the Judge.

"On what grounds, your Honor? Because my client has been incarcerated almost a month now," said Delight.

"Mrs. Scott, this happened back at the end of May of this year," said Officer Allen Taylor.

"I beg your pardon, its Heath, sir," said Delight.

"I'm sorry, Ms. Heath, I didn't mean any disrespect," said Allen Taylor.

"So are you all going to try to charge him, because to prosecute him, you'll need a lot of witnesses and it seems like your key witness is dead," said Delight.

"Why you Bit-," Will Edmond blurted out and Delight immediately cut him short.

"I wish you would verbally assault me, you'll regret you ever had a pair of lips, so go ahead super cop," said Delight.

"There's no need for all of that Mrs. Scott, I mean Heath," as Judge Helmet spoke up adding, "They are going to charge him with felonious assault on an officer, Ms. Heath," as Judge Helmet was looking up at her.

"That's bullshit, Judge and you know it. Don't display an urgency of guilt and revenge because one of theirs is a victim," said Delight. She was steaming hot with anger.

"Ms. Heath, it was an ongoing investigation. It was just a matter of time so if he's not guilty he'll walk. Other than that, we must bring him and David Baxter to justice," said Allen Taylor fixing his tie.

"This judicial system is unbelievable and the upper courts are allowing this district to get away with a lot of injustice," said Delight.

"And what does that mean, Ms. Heath?" Judge Helmet asked her.

"It means that you all fix your own laws and don't uphold the law that I studied and took the bar exam under, but I'll fight this case until the end you can believe that," said Delight.

"I hope you will, Ms. Heath. Jasmine will you be trying the trafficking case on Mr. Boyd this morning?" Judge Helmet asked her.

"No, I'm not, your Honor," said Jasmine.

"Well let's close this out and get on to other business," said Judge Helmet.

Delight stood there with her hands on her hips in much disbelief. She knew that the RENU unit had no real evidence on charging Larro, but the information they obtained from Precious. No concrete proof at all or they would've been charged him long ago. Only thing she was hoping for is that he was strong and had patience to sit. She knew that whatever the bond set by the Judge would be outrageous if he even received one. She turned around and walked out of the Judges chamber. Heather and Larro looked at her as she shook her head walking towards them. She reached the Jury box and looked at Larro and shed a small tear.

"Larro, I'm sorry," she said.

"For what, what's going on, Delight?" Larro asked her.

"A whole lot of bullshit, but I'm going to represent you till the end," said Delight.

"They are going to pursue the case anyway?" He asked her.

"No, they are dropping those charges, but now these RENU bastards want to charge you with felonious assault on an officer," said Delight.

"What, are you serious?" as his voice carried throughout the courtroom.

"They claim that you were with David Baxter a.k.a. D-Boy when their sergeant from RENU was supposedly shot," said Delight.

"Are you serious?" Larro asked her again.

"Yes, but here's the worse news that Smack wanted to tell you today thinking you would be out. Fila was killed last night by Precious and she was killed, but I'll let Smack fill in those blanks for you," said Delight.

"What happened?" He asked her with a whisper. You could see the pain on his face.

"I don't want to talk about it here, but I'll be over to see you soon as they take you back across the street," said Delight.

"Make sure you tell Smack to come and see me today ASAP. Can you tell my mom and girlfriend what's going on and not to worry and that Smack is coming to see me today so they'll have to come tomorrow," said Larro?

"I will honey, I will. Is that your mom and girlfriend sitting over there?" Delight turned a little and pointed in their direction of the courtroom. She smiled at them and they waved to her.

"Yes, that's them, So what now?" Larro asked her.

"We wait until they arraign you and see what the bond is set at, or if they even give you a bond. So, don't trip if they don't but I'll take care of everything," said Delight.

Larro just nodded his head and Delight could see that her sister Heather was taking everything in and she even shed a tear for Larro. Delight stepped over to her and whispered in her ear and said, "Why are you crying, Heather?"

"Because I thought my young dick was getting out today," said Heather. Delight looked at her big sister and replied, "Girl, you are crazy!"

Delight placed her hand on Larro's shoulder and walked off back to where her briefcase was and grabbed another piece of paper handed it to Jasmine.

"Excuse me, deputy; you can take Mr. Boyd back.   He is not needed for this procedure," said Delight to her sister. Heather stood Larro up and escorted him back out the door that they entered. The RENU officers watched them closely whispering to each other. Heather told Larro, "I'll be to get you out of your cell today for a detail, okay?" Larro didn't respond, he just looked at her.

Delight went and spoke with Larro's mom and pregnant girlfriend. She introduced herself to Smack's aunt as his fiancée and her son's attorney. She explained to them what was going on and what happened last night in Dayton which his mom already knew. They both started crying for Larro and Fila.

****

Antwan merged onto I-75 south off 12th street in Covington, Kentucky. He was doing 80 miles per hour in the Beemer. Smack was holding on for his dear life.

"What's wrong Simmion, you don't like fast cars...only the fast life?" said Antwan.

"No, I like them, but do you always drive like this when something is wrong?" Smack asked him.

"Yeah, I'm used to it, because something is always wrong in the lane, I'm in. They drive like this on the Autobahn in Germany. There is no speed limit there, just fast and faster," said Antwan. Antwan was playing Jay-Z '99 Problems' as he was making good sense through the traffic at a high speed in the Z-4M. They got to the airport in no time being they were close by. It was packed on a Wednesday morning. Smack thought he saw the Mazda-3 and told Antwan, "That looks like the car they were in last night," So Antwan pulled right beside it. They got out and Smack checked the tags that had Montgomery County plates.

"This is the car or it's a hell of coincidence," said Smack.

"Well let's go, Simmion; you know what she looks like, right?" Antwan asked.

"Yes!" said Smack. They began to slow jog towards the entrance of the airport. They entered the airport and stood in the center watching every possible tunnel boarding a flight out of the country. Then Smack spotted Secret and she was heading towards a flight that read Hawaii. He tapped Antwan and they ran towards her even though she was way ahead of them. They got close to the entrance and security stopped them.

"Excuse me, I'll need to see tickets to board the plane," said the security guard.

"We don't have tickets. We are trying to catch someone," said Smack to the security guard pointing at Secret. He yelled, "Yo, Secret."

She ignored Smack calling her name and kept going.

"I'm sorry, sir, I can't let you beyond this point without any passes to board the plane," said the security guard.

Smack really didn't pay any attention to where the flight was actually going so he asked the security guard. "Damn it!" he said with much anger, "Excuse me sir, where is that flight going?" Smack asked him

"Honolulu," the security guard replied.

Secret smiled to herself and kept on going to board the plane down the walk way. She was going to Honolulu, Hawaii.

****

It was very early in a popular community in Cincinnati. The sun light came through the small opening of the curtains bright and strong. A dampness and tangy smell absorbed a portion of the room. It was a mixture of sounds bouncing off the walls and sweats and sex fluids. Her nails clawed the sheets as he penetrated her in the doggy style position ramming her vagina walls. The aroma was pleasant, not an awful fishy smell as her juices ran wild. Her moans met every pump justifying how powerful the friction was. She had one orgasm after another as she demanded him inside her. "Fuck me, fuck me, Worm, this is your pussy, I swear this is yours," said Miesha uttering out every word to him. She was having the time of her life at Worm's crib. She never knew she would be falling in love with a hard penis that she mainly played for a sport. The magnitude was greatly appreciated and with all due respect she knew she could conquer the world with her 42" ass. That's what she thought, as more verbal utters came from up under her breath.

"Oh, my goodness, Worm, I'm about to cum again, baby, oh shit, I'm cumming," as she was shaking grabbing the sheets and everything else in her reach. He pulled out and removed his condom and ejaculated wads of semen on her 42" ass. The sweat dripped from his forehead, "Miesha, you're going to make me put a baby in you," said Worm.

"I do want to have your baby, Worm; this is officially your poohnani, Boo. I promised you that I will never fool around on you and will fight for that dick," said Miesha now looking him in the eyes seriously.

"But Miesha, you know I have a girl?" said Worm.

"Who, Breyon? Please she ain't shit but a gaming ass bitch trying to get over on nigga's constantly. She is trying to talk to every nigga that's balling," said Miesha.

"But I think I'm in love with her," said Worm.

"Worm, you couldn't be, giving me all that dick. I'll make sure you forget about her real quick," said Miesha.

"Miesha, but em...," Worm couldn't get it out because she was now sucking his tribal piece and he was frozen to where he just melted.

****

Smack's cell phone was ringing as him and Antwan watched Secret board the plane. He saw it was his wife-to-be calling him 911.

"Hold on, Antwan, this is Delight calling," as he flipped open his cell phone to answer her call. Jasmine was calling Antwan at the same time. Jasmine called to let him know her step-brother, Will Edmond, wanted to speak with him privately.

Smack was unconsciously unaware of what was behind his fiancée's phone call.

"Hey Delight, what's the deal with Larro?" Smack asked her.

"It's all bad baby. They dismissed the drug charges, but they are trying to charge him with felonious assault on an officer. I went ahead and told him about Fila and Precious, but he wants to see you," said Delight.

"Assault on an officer?" Smack wanted to be sure he heard her correctly.

"Yes, David Baxter, which is D-boy and Larro supposedly, did the shooting back in May. I told him I was going to represent him, but I think it has something to do with the ole girl getting killed and they are retaliating this way because he is in D-Cut," said Delight.

"Well he's going to be even more pissed off when I go and see him," said Smack.

"Why honey, what's wrong?" Delight asked him.

"Because D$Boy was shot this morning and he's in critical condition," said Smack.

"How can that be, because you spoke with him this morning, right?" Delight asked him.

"No, I didn't speak with him, because it had to happen earlier this morning and Secret had to do it. I'm at the airport now and she's boarding a plane heading to Honolulu. I tried to catch her, but I couldn't. I saw it on the news when I was meeting with Antwan this morning," said Smack.

"I told you, Simmion that shit is falling apart around you. So now what?" Delight asked him with much concern.

"I've already discussed with Antwan that I'm getting out, but I have to get Larro out of his jam first, someway, somehow," said Smack.

"Baby, I'm here for you and your peeps 'til the end. I met your aunt today, also," said Delight.

"That's good to know. I'll call you back when I get to my car. I left it at Jillian's and I am riding with Antwan. I'll go see Larro while I'm in the city," said Smack.

****

(This was the conversation that took place with Antwan and Jasmine while Smack was talking to Delight.)

"Yes, Jasmine," as Antwan answered his phone.

"Antwan, I did what you asked of me in the courtroom," said Jasmine.

"Well what happened? Is the Herr out?" He asked her.

"He's free of my charges, but he's not out. My step-brother and his department have linked him with the assault on an officer, a sergeant was shot. It's out of my hands darling, they are holding him for that," said Jasmine.

"Okay, Jas, I'll let Simmion know. He's with me now," said Antwan.

"Oh, my step-brother would like to speak with you about some business. I think he wants in on the business," said Jasmine.

"I'll meet with him later at the restaurant. Bring him by there at around two in the afternoon," said Antwan.

"Okay darling, bye, my Chocolate Dream," Jasmine whispered through the receiver and Antwan closed his cell phone.

****

They gradually looked at one another in the eyes and both of them tried to speak at the same time. "Simmion," as he heard Smack say, "Antwan."

"You go first, Antwan," said Smack.

"It's okay, you go ahead first because you look puzzled," said Antwan.

"I just found out they let my cousin go on the drug charges, but they are holding him for an assault on an officer. what were you going to say, Antwan?" Smack asked him.

"Nothing Simmion, never mind, let's get out of here buddy. We can sort things out here and there and then take a flight to Honolulu in a couple of weeks to find our little secret. Or I can just send Wally after her, all I need is a picture of her," said Antwan.

"I think Delight has pictures of them from the cook-out," Smack told him looking in the air.

"Good, let's go. Let's get out of here," said Antwan looking around like he was being watched.

They left the airport and Smack was feeling a little soporific. He knew the streets would have to be his friend right now at this moment. It was a multiple magnitude of instant instinct to hold court in the streets. It was now time to clean up any avenues that would lead the law enforcement back to anyone in his circle. Cash rules everything around, get the dollar bill with no hassle. They stood outside of the red Z-4M BMW looking at the airplane that Secret boarded fly over them controlling the friendly skies.

****

"Smack must be fooling trying to stop me from doing me. By the time he tries to catch up with me. I'll be a totally different person. He won't even recognize me. Honolulu, here I come," said Secret to herself.

Secret sat in first class on the airplane with her shades on to cover her eyes. She had tossed her gun in the Ohio River on her way to the airport. She was eighty thousand to the good and she had no worries. She didn't even care about the bodies she left behind, because her mind was set on a new life among the waves and sunny weather in Hawaii. She was going to hide out on the beaches of Hawaii and start over. Her heart went out to D$Boy and his family only momentarily, as she shed a tear knowing he was dead. She wiped her eyes carefully with the heel of her palm and put her shades back on her face. She notices a guy sitting by himself and she decided to have a conversation with him. He was in a business suit and appeared to be important, "Hello," said Secret.

The guy looked at her and spoke. "Hello, Ms. Lady, you're on vacation all by yourself?"

He asked Secret with a small grin.

"No, I'm not on vacation, I'm moving to Hawaii," said Secret with a smile of her own.

"All alone?" he asked her.

"Yep, I just got up and left my city in search of a new life," said Secret.

"With no significant other and no kids, huh?" he asked her.

"Just me, all of me trying to find a significant other and have kids to be a family," Secret told him.

"Do you know where you are going to live?" the guy asked her.

"I won't know until I get there and look around. I might live in a hotel for a few months. I have nowhere to go and no family there," said Secret.

"what's your name, if you don't mind me asking?" the guy asked.

"It's Sue, and yours?" She removed her shades and looked gloomy eyed knowing she was lying to him. He saw a wounded female that looked confused.

"My name in Nya," he replied.

"Do you live in Hawaii, Nya?" she asked him.

"Yeah, I live in Honolulu," Nya told her.

"Are you from Hawaii, because you look rather Mexican?" Secret asked him.

"I am Mexican Sue, but my job had relocated me to Hawaii. I'm from San Diego, California," said Nya.

"And what type of work do you do, Nya?" Secret was fishing to see if she had one on the hook.

"I'm a Sales Representative for a demo-graph web designer called Nutron Boex. I was doing a seminar in Cincinnati and now I'm on my way home," said Nya.

"Home to the wife and kids?" Secret asked him.

"I'm a bachelor, I'm like you all alone," Nya gave her a smile.

"Oh, I see. Is Honolulu a nice place to live, Nya?" she asked him.

"It is beautiful. I fell in love with it when I first moved there. You will love it there. The people on the island would treat you like a queen," said Nya.

She blushed while adding, "I hope I like it."

"You will, Sue, and if I can be of any help, you can stay at my place until you find your own," said Nya and that made Secret smile even harder.

She wanted to shout to the top of her lungs, *"sucker,"* but she *stayed with the script.*

"Are you serious, Nya? I could be a murderer or something," said Secret.

"A beautiful flower like you wouldn't hurt a fly, and if you are a murderer then kill me dead," as he gave a soft smile behind his Spanish accent.

She smiled back at him knowing he would be in for a big surprise to find out that Sue was a killer and Secret was the one who cared.

They landed in the capital of Hawaii situated on the southeast coast of the island of Oahu; it is the seat of Honolulu County. The population was rapidly growing from 1982 of 781.899 until 2008. Honolulu is the business and financial hub for the Pacific and is Hawaii's primary city and port.

Secret would have no problem adapting to this new city, being Honolulu is the most popular U.S. vacation resort and she would probably run into a familiar face. Its natural assets which include Waikiki Beach, the Koolau Mountains rising dramatically beyond the hotels and extinct volcanic craters such as Diamond Head attract more that 2.5 million visitors annually. The city is known for its ethnic variety. About 30% of the population is Caucasian, 30% is of Japanese heritage and the rest are Hawaiians.

The Hawaiians are probably from Chinese and Filipino descendent. Honolulu is the center of study for Pacific culture. Nya and Secret got off the plane and she could tell they were below sea level in this new environment, because of the less humidity. All she had was her same clothes from the night before, loose clothing of D$Boy and the cash minus the deduction for the plane ticket.

"Sue, you don't have any luggage?" Nya asked her.

"No, Nya, just my little black bag, but I need to go shopping like right now. I need new of everything, from hygiene, panties and bra's, shoes, clothes, hair accessories and you know," said Secret batting her eyelashes.

"No problem, we can stop at the small boutique by my house and grab you a few items, like panties and bras and other personal hygiene items to clean yourself up a little. Then we can go to the mall in downtown Honolulu tomorrow. Do you have any money?" Nya asked her.

"Umm," as she tried to tell him yes, but he didn't let her get it out.

"Don't worry, I'll support you and when you find a job, you can pay me back," said Nya.

She smiled and he gave a smile back. It was just that easy she found a new piece of action. She knew she had to change her appearance and the first change would be her hair. It had to go from reddish brown to straight black with a short hair style. she had to cover up any noticeable tattoos. She also knew she had to get Nya's nose open and she knew just how, by giving him some of her bomb ass sex. That meant an around the world, from a good head clinic to fucking him real good. She had a real live sucker fish on her hand, she thought.

****

Delight had just left from seeing Larro in the Justice Center using her lawyers pass to get her in. She was now outside standing near the food stand on Sycamore and Court Streets. She saw Smack coming across the street in her direction and she could see the pain on his face. Her eyes met his and she got all glossy eyed, her fear and concern for him and no matter what she forced a powerful feeling to be there for him. He reached her and she immediately embraced him and her firm body brushed against his.

"I'm sorry baby," said Delight.

"Delight, it's not your fault, I must deal with this situation. I can only pick up the pieces and try to fix the puzzle," said Smack.

A tear magically ran down her cheek. She loved him and was willing to stand by her man, even though he wasn't in any serious trouble yet, but it felt as if he were.

"Smack, your cousin is waiting on you baby, he told me no matter what, he will remain silent about the operation and I didn't ask, he voluntarily just told me," said Delight.

"Are you finished down here for today?" He asked her.

"Yes honey, I'm finished for today, why?" Delight looked into his eyes.

"Good, because after I'm finished down here, I'll be home and we can start planning for our wedding. I want to be married before the middle of September," said Smack.

Delight felt a rush go through her body and she got excited.
"Are you sure baby, and why so soon?" She questioned him.
"Yes, I'm sure. I want for us to be married when our child comes into this world," said Smack.
"What about the leakage in the other areas around you, Simmion?" Delight asked him with a concern look on her face.
"I'm not going to worry about that, I'm just going to move ahead and gradually rid myself out the picture. Antwan and the others will have to conquer their own destiny of chaos by themselves without me," said Smack.
"Come here, Simmion," as Delight kissed him hard and long. She released him and said, "Go ahead, Larro is waiting on you. I'll see you when you get home."
Smack whispered to her, "I love you." Delight read his lips and absorbed his words watching him walk off heading onto the Justice Center doors. Heather was on her lunch break and saw them as she looked out the doors of the North building of the Justice Center.

****

Miesha was getting dressed in her sexy tummy tuck panties which had a deodorized and moisture wick to keep her fresh and dry all day. It was almost twelve noon when she was putting on a sassy sky-blue summer dress over her white panties and bra. After she was dressed in her attire and splashing herself with a touch of White Diamond perfume, she entered the living room where Worm was at burning the DVD of her having sex with Judge Phil Helmet. It was like a work of art watching herself perform on video. Worm was even amazed even though he just had her hours ago.
Her grace and style were luminous and she began to crave another orgasm watching herself on the video. It was a fruitful scenario and Worm just so happened to look behind him to see her standing there.
"Hey Miesha, I didn't know you were standing there. I'm just burning a DVD. I think Smack and P-Diddy are going to pay the Judge a visit in the next day or two. Meanwhile we can go to the boat in Indiana for a couple of days," said Worm.

"That sounds like fun, but I still haven't talked to Kyle yet," said Miesha.

"He knows what's going on and he's not mad at you. He's out of town hitting a million-dollar jewelry heist. Don't worry everything is going to be alright," said Worm.

"I feel so safe and secure around you, Worm," as she eased up on him rubbing his shoulders and back gently.

"Well I have to go out for a little while and when I get back, we can head to Indiana. They want me to keep you out of sight," said Worm.

She kissed him on the side of his face with her soft supple lips that were moist and firm.

****

Smack was sitting in front of the glass window waiting for Larro to come. It was a Mexican female visiting a guy on his left talking Spanish and a white female visiting a black guy on his right as he sat in the middle booth.

Larro came up the steps with a look of much concern on his face. His eyes were stained with redness like he'd been crying. His body language was sluggish as he came to the glass window sitting down and grabbing the receiver.

He looked Smack dead in his eyes and said, "Give it to me straight, big cuss."

Smack cleared his throat and spoke directly to Larro. "Lil cuss, I know Delight already told you about Fila and Precious, but its more bad news in the air. D$Boy was shot this morning and I think Secret did it and now she has fled to Hawaii. I just came from the airport watching her board a plane while trying to stop her."

"What do you mean Secret shot D$Boy?" Larro asked him.

Smack took a deep breath and continued. "She had to have been the one who shot him, Larro. I had just left them last night. They were supposed to get a room and he was putting her on a plane this morning. Well it was all over the news that David Baxter was shot in a hotel room and is in critical condition," said Smack.

"Why, that scandalous bitch! This shit is getting real crazy. Now I'm caught up in the bullshit that D$Boy and Bo-Gotti did. I had nothing to do with that hit," said Larro.

"I told them to leave that shit alone about that sergeant harassing me. I'm surprised they haven't come knocking on my door on account of the shit they did," said Smack.

"Big cuss, I told D$Boy not to do it, but he's always going to the limit trying to prove a point. what really went on with Fila?" Larro asked him.

"D$Boy and Fila confronted Precious about her being the Jakes and Fila didn't want to believe it and when he tried to grab Precious, she shot him and Secret did her."

Smack carefully looked at him and then looked at the phone letting him know that they were probably listening to their conversation.

"I got you, big cuss," said Larro.

"Well, I'm going to take care of everything. You just sit still and keep quiet. My good friend is going to go and talk to the Judge on your case and once I get you out, I'm getting out," said Smack.

"What about us cuss? The little goldfish in the pond still needs to eat," said Larro.

"I suffocated you with the game long enough. I gave you everything you needed and now you must leave the nest," said Smack.

"I don't have the connections or the man power now that two of my henchmen are gone. Especially dealing with this new stuff, the ratio turnover is like ten times greater than that white girl. In the next quarterly event, I could retire to. I know your numbers would be greater than mine, so why stop now?" Larro asked him.

"My future will not rely on this bullshit anymore, I'm planning a future, involving a wife and kids and a legal business. I have enough assets and money to get out. Yo know before a Judge hits his/her gavel giving me twenty to life for my involvement in an elite operation of illegal business," said Smack.

"Will the streets still love you if you get out now?" Larro asked him.

"I don't know Larro, and I don't worry about that," said Smack.

"Well big cuss, promise me this...if I do go down smoking in the third, you'll look out for my family. Can you at least do that for me?" Larro looked him in the eyes.

"It's a given Larro, you know I will, but you'll be able to do that yourself. You need to start thinking about another way of life besides the streets," said Smack.

"Big cuss, I never thought I would hear you say that. I don't know shit else, but the hustle. Like Jay-Z said, 'You can't knock the hustle' and that's what I'm doing until I die," said Larro.

They continued to talk for a little while longer before Smack left. He was going to meet P-Diddy at the store so they could put their plan into motion. It was of pure thinking and strategically under sensible measure. Smack was smart and a thinking man, regardless where he came from, he learned how to adapt within his means. He learned how to deal with society on their level; you know the ones in suits who tell lavishing lies.

****

Jasmine and her step-brother, Will entered the restaurant in the lunch crowd. They were greeted by the hostess, who didn't waste any time taking them to Antwan's study. The hostess knew Jasmine and she was aware that Antwan was expecting them. They went behind the isolated doors and entered his study.

He was on the phone sitting at his Oakwood desk sipping on bubbly. Antwan told the person on the other end of his phone conversation he would call them back. After hanging up the phone he stood up to greet Will Edmond, his girlfriend's step-brother.

"Hello, Herr, you must be Jas's step-brother, Will that I've heard so much about," as he extended his hand to confirm his greeting. Will was very surprised to see that Antwan was rooted to be a Blackman. All Will knew is that he was coming to meet a German guy. He couldn't and wouldn't question the fact that he was. All he knew was that Antwan had to be very wealthy and important for his step-sister to be involved with him.

"Hello Antwan. Yes, I'm Will and I've also heard a lot about you, too. Good things that is," said Will.

"what brings you in my direction, Will?" Antwan asked.

"Your name is ringing like chimes in the streets; you and Simmion Boyd and this Black Ice, the new drug that everybody is wanting. I hear ya'll are making a fortune and I'm not going to lie, I like money...as a matter of fact, a lot of money," said Will.

"Okay, and who doesn't, Will?" Antwan looked at him carefully. "I'm just saying Antwan, I want in plus the circle that Simmion surrounds himself with is in deep waters with the law. They killed one of our top undercover RENU agents last night and took a shot at one of our sergeants. It's just a matter of time before we bust their operation and I know Simmion will talk to save his lawyer girlfriend and I wonder who's name he will bring up," said Will with confidence.

"what are you getting at, Will?" Antwan asked him.

"You cut me in at twenty percent, give us Simmion and I will make sure you'll clear some millions in this area in no time. I will keep our guys out of your business completely," said Will.

Antwan was leery because of his deal that went sour with Elliott Thrasher, but he managed to answer him, "Can you guarantee that the police won't interfere with my business?" Antwan didn't move a muscle asking him this question.

"I can guarantee you anything as long as I receive my twenty percent off of your activities," said Will.

"I need Simmion for a few more months and after that you can bust him; he will no longer be of any use to me. So, you'll act when I tell you to Will.   do we have a deal?" Antwan asked him.

"Yeah, we have a deal," said Will.

Antwan went in his drawer at his desk and put ten thousand on top of the Oakwood desk in large crispy bills. "Here's ten grand to assure you and seal our deal. More will come your way, because I have a shipment coming in and I need for Simmion and his people to move it with no hassle. Can you make sure this happens, Will?" Antwan asked him.

"I will let every transaction take place, Antwan," said Will.

"Good, I'll give you another ten grand when the shipment arrives and after everything is handled, I'll then give you another twenty grand," said Antwan.

"What's already understood doesn't need to be explained, Antwan. You have a nice day and I'll be in touch," said Will putting the money in the inside of his blazer.

Jasmine and Antwan watched Will leave out the study and Antwan gazed over to Jasmine. "See Jas, your step-brother's greed will be his downfall. Americans are so selfish and greedy," said Antwan.

She baffled her eyes and said, "Do you think he will help your plans or hinder them?"

"It's not that Jas, he has a partner that he's not willing to share his fortune with, he's a bigger fool than I thought," said Antwan laughing out loud like a sick individual.

"And what did Simmion say darling?" Jasmine asked him.

"He has beautiful news, he's going to take care of the Judge and continue to move the drug through his people, but he's thinking about quitting the business," said Antwan.

"What you mean he's quitting the business?" Jasmine asked him in a frantic voice.

"He's going to stop dealing, but he'll be in for a big surprise before he gets out," said Antwan with a dark look in his eyes.

"I love you Antwan, you're always thinking ahead," said Jasmine giving him a kiss on the lips.

****

BACK AT THE GOODIE BAG, the Belvy Boyz and Smack were putting together a plan to free Bodean and get Larro a reasonable bond. Worm wasn't present because he and Miesha were heading to Indiana. They sat in the store while Kobe closed the store putting the "Closed" sign in the window.

"everything is in order P-Diddy?" Smack asked him.

"Yeah, Worm burned the copies this morning and I had my girl type out the message to the Judge," said P-Diddy.

"Good, where is Worm and Miesha now?" Smack asked him.

"Nice try cuss, like I'm going to tell you, he didn't even tell us," said P-Diddy.

"Okay, that's good everybody is on the same page. This is how it's going down...Delight's sister, Heather, will deliver the package to the Judge's chamber and then," as you could hear him whisper and it got quiet while he further discussed the plans with them.

****

THAT NIGHT, Delight and Smack were lying in bed talking about their wedding plans. She had a David's Bridal magazine flipping through the pages.

"Baby, what colors are we wearing?" Delight asked him.

"It's your wedding, Delight. If, we exchange vows, I'll be at the alter asshole naked," said Smack.

"Boy, you're silly, but it's your wedding too. So, what about purple and white as the main colors?" She asked him.

"That's cool. You know my friend, Lady Ray, whose daughter's softball team I sponsor? Well she works at David's Bridal in Tri-County. She can get us a huge discount on your gowns for you and the Bridesmaids also," said Smack.

"That's fine and I hope she's not one of your ex-flings Smack, because I'm not with being smiled at and then laughed at behind my back, negro," said Delight.

"Now you're silly. Biggie and I are just friends. I did date her friend, Bernadette a few times, but we never slept together. You know Kyle's cousin, Miesha, wants to be in our wedding," said Smack not looking at Delight.

"Who! I know that big booty heifer doesn't want to be in my wedding. I wonder whose idea was that?" Delight was now looking at him wide-eyed with an attitude.

"It wasn't my idea, it was hers. I'm not going to lie; she made a pass at me before, but I handled it like a man who's in love is supposed to. I told her that you were the only woman for me and we were getting married. She respected that and asked when it takes place, can she be in the wedding. I'm asking you, it's your decision," said Smack.

"I'll see. If my friend, Kalisha, can't make it from New York, I'll give Ms. Miesha that slot as one of my bridesmaids," said Delight getting up to go use the bathroom in their room. She had on a yummy tummy criss cross tank and some French cut panties.

"who's your Maid of Honor?" Smack asked her. She turned around and said, "Who's your best man?"

CHAPTER NINETEEN
TIME TO RECONCILE

That Friday at around 10:25am, Delight and Smack was sitting in the waiting area of the Mercy Hospital in Fairfield on Mack Road. She had a pre-natal appointment. They were talking more about the wedding and how many guests would be attending the special ceremony taking place in the middle of September.

"who's going to be your Best Man, Smack?" Delight asked him.

"It will most likely be Larro, if he's out, but if not, I'm going to ask P-Diddy...and your Maid of Honor is...?" He counters.

"I told you probably my friend, Elicia, if not then Heather," said Delight.

"I'm thinking about Word of Deliverance in Forest Park, letting Bishop Donny Milton marry us and then having our reception at the Torque in Fairfield on Route 4," said Smack.

Then Keisha Myles walked in, but Delight didn't see her at the desk checking in. Smack saw her and nudged Delight. "Look," as he pointed to Keisha.

"I wonder what this heifer is doing up here?" Delight asked and he shrugged his shoulders.

Keisha had on a pair of white khaki shorts, a pink Polo shirt with no collar and some lace-up pink and white sandals. Her hair was pulled back in a tight ponytail and even though she was in plain and simple attire she looked good. She turned around and was staring in the eyes of Delight and Smack. She rolled her eyes at them and went to sit down on a four seated chair in the far corner opposite of them. She crossed her legs and grabbed a magazine from the small table in the waiting area. Delight just burst out in a taunting fake laugh and said, "No she didn't."

Smack grabbed her hand letting her know to chill out and he kissed her. When he released from her, he said, "Be a lady, Delight, we are bigger than that."

She froze looking at him eye to eye. "You're right baby, you're definitely right."

They continued to cuddle and chit-chat waiting on them to be called for Delight's appointment. Keisha kept glancing over at them and she couldn't help but to notice the ring on Delight's finger. It was huge and Kendall was right, Smack did propose to her. It was eating Keisha up because Smack was with Delight at her appointment and Kendall wasn't there with her. She didn't want to fight with Delight about what transpired months ago, instead she wanted to be friends with her and live for today while not having to worry about tomorrow since she was pregnant by her ex-husband.

Keisha knew she had to be the bigger woman even though it may have seemed she broke up a family. She had to do what was right and let what was troubling her come to pass and reconcile with Delight.

Keisha stood and placed the magazine back on the table shaking her clinging shorts from her skin. She left her little Prada purse in her seat and then walked over to Delight and Smack.

"Excuse me Delight and Smack, but I need to talk to Delight so I can clear the air," said Keisha standing over them with her new baby bump.

"Keisha, we have nothing to talk about." Delight replied giving her the ghetto neck movement.

"Delight, please, I feel like I've caused all of this chaos between you and Kendall," said Keisha.

"You didn't and I don't blame you totally. It takes two to make a thing go around and round. He wanted you and apparently you wanted him. I'm happy and I sure in hell hope that you both are as well," said Delight.

"I understand that but I would like for us to be friends, Delight," said Keisha.

"Oh yeah, really?" Delight folded her arms looking at her.

"Yes, I'm trying to reconcile with you, "said Keisha.

"Keisha, this is not that movie, 'One Night Stand' where we go out as couples forgetting what happens being the best of friends. I'm over him. I've moved on. I'm about to get married next month and our child is due in the spring," said Delight.

"Well congratulations to you and Simmion. Kendall and I are expecting, too," said Keisha.

"Keisha, I know you don't call yourself rubbing that in my face, because I don't care. That's none of my business. I'm happy for you and Kendall," said Delight.

"Delight, it's not like that. I admire you and I've always wanted to follow in your footsteps," said Keisha with a sincere look on her face.

"Yeah, by fucking Kendall, but like I said, I don't blame you, because if it wasn't you, it would have been someone else. what's done is done," said Delight.

Smack was just looking and then his phone rang and both women looked at him while he answered it. "Vegas never sleeps and neither does I," said Smack.

He just listened before answering the person on the other end. *"I'm at Delight's doctor's appointment right now. We should be finished by one o'clock," he said looking over at her. The two women were still looking at him as he continued to talk.*

"I drove her, but as soon as she is finished, I'll be down that way, okay," said Smack.

He closed his phone and Delight asked him, "Who was that baby?"

"It was Antwan, he's ready for me," said Smack.

"Go ahead, I'll catch a cab home or I'll call you when I'm ready," said Delight.

"No honey that can wait. My family is first priority," said Smack.

"Delight, we can have lunch on me and I can take you home after your appointment. This way we can finish talking woman to woman," said Keisha.

Delight looked at Smack and he nodded his head telling her it was okay.

"I don't know about that, Keisha," said Delight.

"Please, Delight, Smack doesn't mind," said Keisha begging Delight.

****

Judge Phil Helmet was opening a legal envelope containing a DVD and letter that had instructions for him. It read:

Judge Helmet, read and read well. You tell Steve O'Hara to release Jamal Irvin immediately; also, when Larro Boyd goes in front of you or whomever for his bond hearing, give him a reasonable bond. If you don't cooperate, your days of being a Judge in Hamilton County will be over. Enclosed is a DVD that I think you may enjoy, but wouldn't want the public eye to see.

Copies of this DVD will be sent to all the news channels and to your friends you golf with at the Country Club. TMZ and Inside Edition will also receive copies...among others."

He urgently removed the DVD and placed it in the player. It was fuzzy at first and then his face appeared in a sexual act with Miesha Jones, his lover and mistress. He was eating her out, getting spanked and everything else that would embarrass him and get him off the bench. His face turned beet red.

"Why that little bitch, she's helping them blackmail me," he said. He started dialing Steve O'Hara's number and his blood pressure was sky high.

"Steve, let that Jamal Irvin guy go right now," said Judge Helmet yelling through the receiver.

"But why, Judge? What's wrong?" O'Hara asked.

"They have me, Steve, my career could be ruined if this DVD is released to the public," said Judge Helmet.

"What DVD, Judge?" O'Hara asked.

"I can't explain now, just release Jamal Irvin for me and let me get back with you later. We have to find Miesha Jones and get rid of her," said Judge Helmet.

"If you say so, I'll call over to Boone County and let them know to release him ASAP," said O'Hara.

"Thanks." Judge Helmet told him before hanging up the phone.

****

Smack walked in the restaurant to see Antwan, Wally and two other guys sitting enjoying lunch. Even though the restaurant was empty it seemed live in spirit.

"Simmion, come join us and have a drink on the house," said Antwan.

He walked over to the table and Antwan poured him a shot of Remy.

"Well sit down, Herr, I want you to meet my little cousin, Fat Daddy and his associate Weevee," said Antwan.

"What up?" Smack spoke and Fat Daddy and Weevee just nodded to him.

"They are going to drive the drug to wherever you want them to. Do you have the picture of the female, because Wally and those two are flying out to Hawaii tonight? They will fetch the girl and bring her back to us," said Antwan.

"Yeah, I got them with me, here," as Smack handed him around four different photos of Secret. "As you can see, Antwan, she has a Panther tail coming from her vagina down her thigh with paw prints on each side. They need to notice this just in case she changes her appearance," said Smack pointing to her tattoos.

"She has a unique tattoo. I guess she's saying her sex is of a kitty cat," said Antwan admiring the pictures of Secret.

"Well they can follow me down to the store on McMicken with the shipment," said Smack.

"Whenever you're ready, Simmion, it's your call," Antwan told him.

"Antwan, how much is it?" Smack asked him.

"You have exactly five thousand bottles and I have another five thousand on hold. I went on ahead and sent for ten thousand bottles, you don't mind, do you?" Antwan told him.

"I guess that's more than enough, that should take us into October, Antwan," said Smack.

"Don't worry my friend, after this shipment we can take our show on the road, LA, Miami, New York...I love New York. These places are waiting on us. In the meantime, Wally and those two will take care of our little Secret in Hawaii," said Antwan with a grin. He put his glass up to toast with Smack on their upcoming success.

****

"Keisha, girl, you are crazy. The waitress is going to quit her job the way you keep running her around," said Delight laughing.

"Delight, I like my food just right. She better hope I leave her tired ass a tip," as they both laughed out loud.

They were sitting in IHOP across from Cincinnati Mills Mall on Winton Road.

"Keisha, are you all planning on getting married?" Delight asked her.

"I don't know Delight; I can't foretell the future with him. He's still stuck on stupid about you being involved with Simmion. I don't think he's over you. He had a sucker attack after you both left divorce court," said Keisha.

"Are you serious, Keisha?" Delight asked her, but was kind of happy to hear that.

"Yes, girl, I had to check Kendall about that shit. He was bugging out girl, drinking Hennessy and shit right out the bottle like a mad man. Oh, I forgot to tell you, I did move in," said Keisha. Delight held her fork in her hand looking at Keisha for a long moment and then she continued to eat her food. "That was nice of him to let you move into the place we once shared," said Delight trying not to let it show she was not agreeing with it.

"I'm trying to get him to buy this house in Fairfield. I didn't change anything, everything is just like you left it," said Keisha.

"Girl, you don't have to do that, because I'll never be living there again. Don't be stupid, that house is paid for. You need to take charge and make the house suitable for you and yours, especially if you plan on being with Kendall on that other level," said Delight.

"I'll think about it. I admire your strength and passion as a black woman and to have a man like Simmion in your corner is a plus," said Keisha.

"Why do you say that, Keisha, do you know Simmion?" Delight asked her.

"Not all like that, Delight, I've seen him around and have heard good things about him in the streets. But Kendall hates him with a passion. You didn't hear that from me," said Keisha as she slapped Delight's hand laughing.

"Okay girl, I hear you," said Delight.

The waitress brought Keisha's food back out to her. "Here you go, Ms., and I hope it's hot enough for you. Can I get you ladies anything else?" The waitress asked them standing there with her hands on her hips.'

"Yes, you can get us the manager, this shit is still lukewarm," said Keisha and Delight looked at her and said, "Come on Keisha, it's not her fault the food is not hot,"

"I know, I'm going to complain about the cook in the back. If he was out here, I would throw this shit in his face," said Keisha.

"I must apologize for my friend...she's pregnant." Delight told the waitress.

****

It was a venue, a strange approach declared upon sources of evil with intent to reach the top. A sure race to Witch Mountain or any type of mountain and the strip on McMicken was calm and richly in its rare form with streetwalkers parading up and down the streets. They were jumping in and out of cars selling their sex to known customers and new. It was a money day on a Friday and the day was just beginning to grow. The store was a resort to rescue those in need of a fix, a cold drink, condoms, smokes and some hardy grub.

Smack had Fat Daddy and Weevee park down the street from the store as he got out of the Q45 Infiniti and entered the store. It was like a small gathering, a party going on and despite that a grill was outside cooking various grades of meat, on the inside it was laughter and a sign of relief.

Bodean was back amongst his family and they were drinking rounds of Belvy. Smack saw him and greeted him. "What up, Bodean? It's good to have you back," as Smack shook his hand.

"I'm glad to be back, now where is that bitch, Miesha, she needs to be dealt with?" Bodean asked him.

"She's safe and she's put up," said Smack.

"Why haven't ya'll gotten rid of her? She told the feds about us?" Bodean asked.

"My friend, calm down, she didn't tell on everybody, just you, but she's the reason why you are out. They didn't tell you? She helped in a very big way, so calm down, big fella," said Smack.

"No one has told me anything, Smack. All I know is that Kekou told me how I got jammed up and that Miesha couldn't go through with the rest of it...that's all that was told to me," said Bodean.

"Well, Miesha had the Judge, who's associated with the Federal agent who grabbed you, on video tape fucking her.   we submitted to the Judge for you and Larro a release, we are sort of blackmailing him," said Smack with a grin.

"Are you serious, Smack?" Bodean asked.

"Yes, I'm serious. She's the real reason behind you getting out. do me a favor when you come across her, leave that issue alone, okay, because we have bigger fish to fry? I have five thousand bottles ready to go out to the locals for sell," said Smack.

"It's in like that?" Bodean got excited.

"Yes, it's in cuss! Yo, P-Diddy, Dante and Kobe we have to shut this down for a little while. I know ya'll are glad to see the big fella, but I just came back from the Grippo store and the chips are in," said Smack.

They looked over to where Smack and Bodean were standing and he gave them that look and they knew what time it was. The product was in, the shipment that everyone has been waiting for. They told the females and other guest they had in the store to follow Meeka over to her apartment on Vine Street for a while until they handled some business. Antwan had put the bottles of Black Ice in Grippo Potato Chip boxes. They emptied the store and started unloading the truck with the drugs in the potato chip boxes.

Each Belvy boy received a hundred bottles of the Black Ice to distribute to the locals. After that P-Diddy and Smack took the rest of the Black Ice to a stash house in Avondale on Greenwood before you get to Washington Street

He would wait for Larro's release before dealing with any of the remaining D-Cut. He did manage to call Mucho and K.G. to come down and get a supply of what they needed. Kobe called Gutter, Ron Don and Lil G in Atlanta to come up and get them what they would need. After the samples they received it was a demand for the drug in the strip clubs in Atlanta.

Everything was in motion; the numbers after this shipment would appreciate the value. There was no room for carelessness, because the day was a good day in the Tri-State area. A revelation with promising and well-deserve results.

Later, that night everyone met up at Game Works on the Levee in Newport and Smack treated everyone to drinks and food. Mucho and K.G. came down and stayed for the occasion and even Heather came out to join them for the night. She got reacquainted with K.G. even though she was now obsessed with Larro.

All the Belvy Boyz was there with their female friends and Miesha came out with Worm for a hot second. Delight was up under her man and she knew why Smack called this gathering, it was to announce their upcoming wedding and his retirement from the game.

****

Earlier that day when Smack was finished handling his affairs in the inner city, he returned home to see an unfamiliar car sitting in the drive-way. It was a 2007 Saturn Aura XR all gold, but he didn't panic because he eased out his 9mm Glock from the secret compartment of the Infiniti Q45. He had just spoken to Delight about twenty minutes ago and nothing appeared to be wrong. The dogs were lying cozy on the lawn and there were no forces of entry form the look of the front door. The dogs had on their collars for the invincible fence. The gold Saturn was parked behind the QX56 and his Cadillac truck. He eased the garage door up to go underneath it and dogs didn't pay him any attention and kept lying there. When he reached the door to allow him entrance into the house it was slightly open. He had his Glock out ready for any surprises or threats. When he entered the house, he heard two female voices coming from the kitchen area laughing and talking. He then placed his gun in the small cabinet along the wall unit in the hallway before getting to the kitchen. When he reached the kitchen, he saw his wife to be and Keisha Myles sharing warmth of venue, drinking beverages with color added.

"Oh, Simmion, I didn't hear you come in, baby," said Delight looking up at him.

"I just got home and I didn't know you had company," said Smack.

"Keisha and I had lunch and upon her dropping me off, I invited her into our lovely home so she could see the lions," said Delight.

"Well we are having dinner at Game Works tonight so I can tell everyone about the wedding and the other business we discussed," said Smack.

"That's fine baby, I'm going to finish talking to Keisha and then I'm all yours so I can tell you what the doctor said about the baby," said Delight.

"Simmion, your home is lovely and the lions are beautiful. Delight has her hands full," said Keisha.

"Thank you Pep-," as he caught himself from calling her by her stage name. "I mean Ms. Keisha," said Smack.

"And yes honey, I gave her a tour of the house," said Delight.
"That's cool, I'm downstairs if you need me," said Smack walking
off and he was wondering if Keisha told her about the time, they
ran a train on her at Suave's after hour. Keisha asked Delight,
"Do you think he's okay with me being here, Delight?"
"He's not that type of person, Keisha. He's okay with it, trust me.
Anyway, our colors are white and purple and he said something
about some church in Forest Park call the Word of something,
who knows? I'm excited though, a new man, a new baby and a
new life," said Delight.
"You go girl, to the both of us, starting over fresh with the new,"
as Keisha put her fruity drink in the air to toast with Delight.
The two women made a heave acquaintance before Keisha went
on her way. About a half hour later, Delight joined Smack in the
basement. He was watching the World News with Peter and found
out the shell casing they found on the scene at Fila's condo didn't
come from Precious's gun. It was a shell casing from 3-80 hand
gun; the same gun that David Baxter was shot with. They ran a
worldwide finger print on the shell casing and found out the prints
belonged to a convicted female felon by the name of Sheena Price
out of Dayton, Ohio.
It was Secret when they showed her mug shot on the news. Now
he knew the police was looking for her also to question her about
the shootings. They would probably put her profile on 'America's
Most Wanted' to help them locate her whereabouts.
Delight sat next to him on the sofa couch and she rubbed his face
gently knowing something was bothering him. "Hey babe, what's
wrong, what's going on?" she asked him.
"They just showed Secret's mug shot on the World News linking
her finger prints to the shell casings found at the scene when
Precious and Fila were killed and to the same bullets that shot
D$Boy. Her real name is Sheena Price," said Smack.
"what now, Smack?" Delight asked him.
"They are looking for her right now," said Smack.
"I thought you said she went to Hawaii?" Delight asked him.
"She did, but that's still a part of the U.S. She's still wanted by
the law. I hope that Wally finds her first," as he mumbled the last
few words.

"You hope who finds her first?" Delight asked.

"No one, Delight, I was talking to myself.   what did the doctor say?" He asked her.

She knew he was hiding something from her, but she still answered him.

"She said the baby is fine and growing and for me to eat healthy, also to get as much exercise as I can if you know what I mean. She also told me to stay stress free and wrote me a prescription for iron pills. I'm due in late April, but all this stuff going on in your little world it may be sooner," said Delight looking at him carefully.

"Don't say that Boo, I'm getting out soon. So, Keisha was there for the same reason?" he asked her.

"Yes, her and Kendall are expecting a child too. It's crazy...she's a nice person after all and her breath doesn't stink anymore," Delight told him with a grin. She added, "I hope you didn't mind her seeing our home?"

"This is your home too, Delight. So how do you feel about her and Kendall having a baby?" He asked her.

"That's none of my business. This family here is my only concern. Oh, I also told her they are invited to our wedding," she told him looking down away from his eyes.

"I don't care, you can invite the whole world if you like," he said with a little sarcasm.

"I'm just saying, Smack, I didn't want for you to be uncomfortable if Kendall came, which I know he won't. I was just trying to be polite," said Delight.

"Okay, you need to go and get dressed. We are leaving for Game Works in about an hour. Call Heather and see if she wants to come with us because K.G. is coming down and he'll be there," Smack told her.

He was going to tell the Belvy Boyz he was calling it quits after the shipment was gone and he was going to let them deal with Antwan without him being involved.

****

They were laughing and talking having a good time on Waikiki Beach. Nya was enjoying his new friend and lover and Secret liked her new surroundings. She cut her hair and dyed it jet black. She covered up a few tattoos on her arm and back and even her lower leg, but she didn't cover up the tattoo between her thighs. It was pure satisfaction, more than pretty wings more than the ruffles of dreamt affection under a love ballet. Her worries were never a problem, her courage was a headache and her knowledge itself was a stream of pleasure. Hawaii was now her home, her reason to be and she wasn't leaving any time soon. She wasn't aware of the news back home that displayed her mug shot across the country, but her mug shot was now far from her new appearance. Who would know it was her? She was safe and sound in the arms and comfort of her new lover and friend Nya.

****

Game Works was crowded on this Friday night while they played games and ate gracefully. Smack told the Belvy Boyz that he was getting out the game. His move was glorified with the thought of his new beginning with his wife to be. She was a solid gift of moral passion for prime-time clarity. He was ruthless, but sociable in regards of making a life with a beautiful seed that was well bred in so many ways, an older woman for him to grow old with.

He was making closure with no grief and relief with no pressure, he was making the most aggressive decision he ever made in his life. He was stepping away from something he loved; to be with someone he was in love with.

They left Game Works and took their party of twenty plus over in Covington to Jillian's nightclub. They took on the third level of the club with their party.

Chantell was the barmaid behind the bar and it was packed, the music was loud and everyone was interacting. Smack told Chantell to bring him a case of Moet, a case of Laurent-Perrier and a case of Dom Ruinart. Then Antwan and Jasmine just so happen to show up and Antwan told Smack and his party to follow him through some double green doors. It was a private ducked off area from the rest of the club, like a smaller club where celebrities would hang out. You could still hear the music from the speakers that surrounded the room. It had its own dance floor and bar with a large seating section. It had to be VIP because he had called downstairs and had them to bring up food trays. One food tray had caviar from the Caspian Sea that was banned by the U.S. More guest of the Belvy Boyz showed up because Vino had made a phone call to his friend, Te'Anna and her friends which were Breyon, Fe-Fe, Ebbie and Beth. Dante was pissed off at Vino because Beth showed up and he was with Joan not wanting to cause any confusion amongst the party. The only thing that could really bring more drama to the party if his baby mom Eva showed up, because she and Joan had words in the past and Dante swore to Eva that he was breaking up with Joan soon.

Antwan, Smack, P-Diddy and Dante were having a small conversation of their own sipping Laurent-Perrier. "So Simmion, you're calling it quits Herr?" Antwan asked him.

"Yeah, I'm getting out, I'm getting married and after the shipment is gone, I'm out," said Smack.

"What about your team, these guys of greatness you deal with?" Antwan asked Smack.

"That's what I wanted to talk to you about; this is P-Diddy and Dante. I would like for you to continue to deal with them concerning the Black Ice," said Smack.

"Are they willing to step away from Cincinnati and do business?" asked Antwan.

"Yes, we are willing to do whatever it takes to get this money," P-Diddy answered Antwan. Then Antwan gave him a smirk and said, "I'm talking about major trips to LA, Miami, New York, China and France, my friend?" Antwan told them.

"It's whatever, with the Belvy Boyz, we are about the business show us that way and we'll follow, ask Smack," said Dante.

"I've heard great things about your organization and if Simmion wants to pass the torch to the Belvy Boyz, then I'm all for it," said Antwan. You could hear Cameron's 'Get it in O-HIO' in the background.

"If you know like I know, you should lay low killa I used to get it in O-hio"

****

OUT IN MASON Kendall and Keisha were sharing a candle light dinner in their home. Keisha had prepared a meal of perfection for her man which was the Tour of Italy. She even bought him a bottle of Hennessey 1800. They were eating their dinner and managed to spark of a delightful conversation.

"Kendall, the doctor said I'm doing fine and the baby is too. Guess who I saw at the hospital today?" said Keisha.

"Who"? Kendall asked.

"Delight and Simmion," said Keisha with a smile.

"Was Rainell with them?" Kendall asked her.

"No, Delight had a pre-natal appointment also," said Keisha.

"she's going to have his child after all?" Kendall was upset.

"That's not all Kendall, they are getting married next month and she invited us," said Keisha.

"What do you mean, she invited us?" He asked her.

"Delight invited us to her wedding. She and I had lunch today after our appointments and a gang of conversation. I even went to their house in West Chester. They have a nice home. Simmion has pet lions and a big iguana lizard looking thing. Delight and I decided to be friends and not enemies," said Keisha.

"What a fucking slap in the face, Keisha, you're kicking fast times and having laughs with my ex. I hope you enjoyed yourself," said Kendall with much anger in his voice.

"Kendall, let's be adults about this. I felt bad because I honestly thought I caused you two to get a divorce, so I wanted to make amends with her," said Keisha.

"Next time, let me in on it before you do, okay?" as he threw his fork down in his plate and removed himself from the table. Keisha dropped her fork saying, "Damn it, Keisha."

She picked up his glass of Hennessey and downed it.

******

Delight and Smack were off in a corner of the VIP room watching everyone enjoy themselves. She nibbled on his ear while everyone else was still getting their party on.

The others were also getting their thoughts together thinking about who they would end up in bed with tonight. Miesha was still eyeing Smack wanting to be in Delight's shoes even though Worm was now sexing her real good. Delight didn't pick up on Miesha's vibe, because she had a vibe of her own.

"So, Smack, which one of these little hoochie's you done been with and don't lie?" Delight asked him.

"I've only been with Fox, the one over there standing by Worm's sister, Yvette," as he pointed to Fox.

"How many times, Smack?" Delight asked him.

"Delight, that's my past, anyway I think she's messing with Dante from what I hear," said Smack.

"Who Packman? I've heard a few females talking about ole boy tonight, he's nasty from what I hear," as she gave Smack that look adding, "Anyway, and at least Fox is cute,"

"Oh, you are choosing females now?" Smack playfully asked her.

"Na'll, I'm just saying if ya'll fooled around at least you were messing with someone who was cute and not ugly. You know how some of you guys do and don't have a conscious about where ya'll stick yo dick at. But she's not cuter than me," as Delight smiled at him.

"Well I hope it doesn't bother you that she's around us," said Smack.

"Why would it?" Delight showcased her ring letting him know the she was the catch and was wearing his ring and not her.

****

Outside the Koko Head looms behind Hanauma bay, Secret laid on one of the most beautiful beaches she ever saw. Waikiki beach lined up with hotel and Condominiums buildings and the crescent shaped beaches that stretched from the Ala Way Canal to the peak of Diamond Head. Nearly five million tourists visit Hawaii annually and Waikiki is still their primary destination. The beach was fairly crowded as Secret lay in the sun in a yellow bikini thong set wearing designer shades to hide her eyes. Her short haircut and new looks sparked energy throughout her body, mind and soul. She was lying on her back and you could see the paw prints and tail with a slight glance of the eye. Her skin was perfectly oiled and all the natives were admiring this woman who was built like a stallion. She even got questioned about her identity.

"Excuse me, Ms. Lady; are you by any chance the famous actress who played Jordan in the 'Best Man'" the native asked Secret.

"No, I'm not her. I'm not Nia Long, but thanks for the compliment," said Secret.

"Well you should be a superstar, because you sure do look like one. You are gorgeous, sorry to bother you; can I buy you a drink?" The native asked her.

"I must decline, I'm with someone and I'd rather be left alone, please," said Secret. The native took one more look at her and then walked away.

"Damn, everyone thinks a black woman lying on the beach is a movie star. Is it because of my swag? Or does every woman of color look the same?" Secret questioned herself.

The day grew and she wasn't in any denial that the sun was making her hormones start to boil over in need of the touch of a man.

Secret rose up on her elbows as she looked over the beach. She happened to see two black guys walking along the beach looking like they were out of place. She zeroed in on them and caught one of them talking exposing his gold teeth. She thought the two were from somewhere back home, maybe Miami, Texas, New York, New Orleans or Cincinnati. This must be the vacation spot for the ballers to come. She was thinking about a threesome, hoping they had some exotic marijuana in their possession or ex-pills.

Nya had gone to work leaving her alone on the beach. She was alone, hot and horny and willing to participate in the group thang if needed. Her eyes locked in on the two husky guys approaching her at a slow rate. She could see them somewhat arguing as the bigger guy in the wife beater with noticeable tattoo's was pointing his finger at the other guy. He was also the one with the gold teeth.

"Fuck that Fat Daddy, all this fresh poohnani on this beach and I'm supposed to just ignore it. The hell with you and your cousin, I'm fucking something before leaving Hawaii. Just look at the thick ass bitch over there," said Weevee pointing to some Hawaiian female in a bikini going towards the water.

"Look Weevee, we are down here on business, to find that girl Secret, and feed her to the fishes, nothing else," said Fat Daddy.

"Man, if opportunity comes knocking before, we find ole girl, I'm handling my business with one of these tribal bitches. I put that on the E-Etown Ezock," said Weevee.

"Weevee, just watch out for ole girl," said Fat Daddy.

"Fuck that nigga, it's a thousand bitches on this beach just waiting to get with the Weester and I'm going to make that happen," said Weevee.

"Man, just look out for ole girl on the picture," said Fat Daddy. They kept walking in Secret's direction and now she was standing up wrapped in a silk piece of material to cover up her bikini bottom and part of her leg that exposed her tattoo, but you could see her curves. Secret thought of the many lines she would try on these two fellas. She cleared her throat, checked her nails and toenails and then looked them straight in the face.

Fat Daddy saw the beauty of the week staring at them as they got closer to her. He saw her blush a little and he picked up his pace towards her. Weevee caught an eyeful also and got excited.

'When a gift for a charitable purpose is excessive for accomplishment of the stated project or purpose or excess funds remains after the purpose of the gift has been accomplished.'

This time Secret was the gift, but they wasn't aware of it. They reached her and Fat Daddy spoke first. "Hey, Ms. Lady, what's up with you?"

"You tell me, I'm listening," said Secret smacking her lips.

"My friend and I are just out trying to relax away from the city life," said Fat Daddy.

"I see, ya'll don't have any pussy tagging along with ya'll?" Secret asked them.

"Na'll, just us, no female company. We came to Hawaii to get away from Cincinnati for a while," said Fat Daddy.

Weevee just looked at him like, *"I know he's not fronting; he was just getting on me about chasing skirts while we are here on business."*

Secret put her hands on her hips. "Oh, some Nasty Nati boys, ooh I know ya'll got some Kush, Purple Haze or Dro with ya'll, some ex-pills or something? I'm trying to party and its whatever if you know what I mean," said Secret.

Weevee tapped Fat Daddy and said," Business dog, business first remember?" he whispered to Fat Daddy.

Fat Daddy waved Weevee off and replied to Secret, "Oh yeah, party though, Ms. Lady.

Well we might have what you're looking for back at our hotel room. We go Cush and some pills better than ex," said Fat Daddy.

"Good, what are ya'll names?" Secret asked them.

"I'm Fat Daddy and this is Weevee," said Fat Daddy.

"Well my name is Sue, I live here with my dude, but I'm free for the cause, let's go," said Secret.

"Sue, do you have a friend for my friend?" Fat Daddy asked her.

"The only friend I trust and have is between my legs, Ms. hot to death, so let's go and get our smoke and fuck on. I know you two niggas can handle little ole me," as she smiled at them. She grabbed her towel and small bag so she could follow them to their hotel room.

CHAPTER TWENTY
THE WEDDING

"What type of pill is that again, Fat Daddy?" Secret asked him.
"I's called Black Ice, but I call it pink passion, it's heavy where I'm from back in Ohio," said Fat Daddy.
"I'll pass on the pill, but you can smoke another blunt with me," as she placed Fat Daddy's manhood in her mouth and started sucking him off again.
Weevee came back into the hotel room shouting, "I found some rubbers!"
He saw her giving Fat Daddy a head job and said, "Oh shit, it's on and popping,"
Her ass was in the air on the bed and Weevee got behind her moving her thong to the side. He put on a condom and entered her from that position. She was so with it that she eased off Fat Daddy and pulled Weevee from insider her passage to come out of her bikini set to be naked. Neither one of them paid any attention to her paw prints or the tail that was tattooed in the area by her vagina. She got back to business with Fat Daddy and Weevee.

****

The next morning after the outing with the Belvy Boys and friends, Delight awoke to breakfast in bed. Smacks had cooked for her and placed a single rose on her tray. She smiled at him as he fluffed her pillow so she could rest on it for support while she ate in bed. Her eyes began to water as a single tear dropped down her cheek.
"What's wrong, Delight, is something going on with the baby?" Smack asked her caressing her hand gently.
"No, Smack, everything is fine. I'm just overwhelmed wondering do I really deserve this. You do everything a woman needs from time to time, all the year Kendall and I spent together he never once thought about giving me breakfast in bed. This means so much to me, I'm at a loss for words," as she put her head down and started crying.
"Baby, it's okay; you deserve this, because I appreciate you to the fullest. Plus, my mother always told me that a kind heart will

never go wrong, it's my duty to serve and protect the woman I love," said Smack.

"Thank you and thanks for being so modest, I love you, Simmion," as she lifted to kiss him gently.

"Well I'm going out to look at some Tuxedo's and Heather is coming to get you so ya'll can go and see what Lady Ray has to offer at David's Bridal today. I already talked to her," said Smack.

"Okay, Mr. Wedding planner. Simmion can I ask you a question?" Delight asked him.

"Sure, go ahead," said Smack.

"How much money do you have put away?" Delight looked him in the eyes.

"In cash alone, probably close to two million," said Smack.

"Then why are you still trying to win in the game? Isn't that more than enough, baby?" Delight was rubbing his arm.

"It's never more than enough, but when I make my exit, I wanted to be ten million clean that was my goal, but I understand it's over. I've won and I know that I must get out now before the doors come crashing down," said Smack.

"Two million at twenty-eight years old from dealing, your passion for the hustle is phenomenal, Smack. It is time to move on, like that rapper say, *"Move rhymes like weight, we gone push something else like weight like a legal business,"* said Delight.

"Right baby, you're definitely right," as he left her to eat while he went to maintain other chores around the house.

Delight did indeed appreciate her new found love. After eating breakfast, she showered and got dressed. She put on a pair of cropped pleated black pants by Bebe, a slinky tank top by AZEN, a collection out of Saks Fifth Avenue that was white and some edgy heels by Report Signature. She sprayed herself with a little LOLA by Marco Jacobs, a new fragrance for women. When she was ready to go, she found Smack out by the pool cleaning it.

"Hey honey, can we take the Benz?" she asked him while holding him.

"I don't care, is Heather here already?" He asked her.

"She should be pulling up with Rainell in a few minutes," said Delight.

"Rainell is going with ya'll?" he asked her.

"Yes, she's going with us."

"Damn baby, you smell good. What's that perfume you're wearing?" he asked her.

"It's LOLA, by Marco Jacobs," as she kissed him.

"Okay," said Smack as his phone rang.

It was Kyle as he answered. "Are you outside?" he closed his phone after answering.

"Delight, can you let Kyle in on your way out for me and tell him I'm out by the pool?" said Smack.

"Yes honey, I will see you later," said Delight walking off back into the house. She grabbed her purse and shades and went to the garage. She climbed into the Benz and remotely opened the garage door. She saw Kyle and Miesha standing there and she had on a fierce Apricot skirt with a small split and a white vee shirt with some designer Fendi shoes. Delight slowly pulled out of the garage and Miesha waved her hand. Delight rolled down the window and told them, "He's out by the pool." She kind of rolled her eyes at Miesha and kept going down the drive-way. Heather and Rainell were pulling in the drive-way. Delight pulled closer to them and told them, "Park on the street and jump in...you are rolling with me."

****

Meanwhile out by the pool, Smack was finishing up when Miesha and Kyle came through the sliding doors. Nevada and Goliath were in their fenced in area as well as Bruce. He saw Miesha's thickness in the little skirt and was wondering why she came with Kyle.

"What up, Kyle, why is Miesha out knowing those cops are still looking for her?" Smack asked him.

"She got into a fight with Worm's girlfriend last night after the party ya'll were at. So, I went and got her earlier this morning when I got back from Detroit so Worm could sort things out on his end," said Kyle.

"You know we are going to get fitted for Tuxes in a few?" said Smack.

"I know I was thinking maybe she could stay here until we get finished with that," said Kyle.

"I guess that would be cool," said Smack looking over at Miesha.

"Oh, I need to make a run real quick before we leave, up on Smith Road and meet these two cats name Buck and Pete from downtown so they can buy some of this jewelry. I'll be back in twenty," said Kyle.

"Hurry back nigga, and don't be all day. I have a lot of shit to do like go to the Bengal's and Philly pre-season game tonight," said Smack.

Miesha was looking at Smack like he was a piece of meat and she was aiming for another shot being she would now be alone with him.

****

Secret's naked body lay across the bed in the hotel room while Fat Daddy and Weeve were asleep. She got up from being sexed and high to go and rinse the sex from between her legs. She felt one of them cumming inside her from the rubber breaking and knew she had to make sure she took one of her day after pills. She showered and wrapped herself in a big towel sitting at the edge of the bed. Then she noticed some loose pictures over by the TV on the dresser and a small portion of the blunt they were smoking. She went to grab the blunt and looked at the pictures to see her at the cook-out. Instantly, she knew they were looking for her, but she didn't panic. She started snooping around going through their belongings. She found a Sig Sauer in one of the duffle bags. She quickly put back on her bikini set and the silk wrap material and her sandals. When Secret was stealing the rest of the Kush from off the dresser in a plastic baggy, the hotel room door opened. She came from around the corner to see a huge Russian looking guy and she had the gun pointed at him.

"Who are you? I think you have the wrong room, sir," said Secret pointing her gun at his chest area.

It was Wally, he glanced down at her thick figure and over at the bed to see Fat Daddy and Weevee asleep. The silk garment had managed to fall from her waist and Wally's eyes traveled to her body and he saw the paw prints. He smirked at her and paused. He continued and said," I've been looking all over for you my little Secret."

His accent was vague, but she knew he was a foreigner. "What did you call me?" Secret asked him.

"Aren't you Secret a.k.a. Sheena Price? Your picture is all over the news, a cop killer, as a matter of fact you're wanted for multiple shooting back in Ohio," said Wally.

"I don't know what you are talking about, but my name is Sue," said Secret trying to figure out who these guys were, because she hadn't seen them before around Smack. Fat Daddy and Weevee began to wake up from the conversation, because Secret got a little loud. "Yo Wally, what's up man? Why are you bothering our company?" Fat Daddy asked him rubbing his eyes.

"Why you pathetic fools, that's Secret right there," as Wally pointed at her.

"Na'll Wally, man her name is Sue, we met her down on the beach today," said Weevee.

"Look you idiot," as Wally pointed to the paw prints. "The paw prints fools," said Wally.

"Well, I'll be damned.   It is her right in our fucking faces," said Fat Daddy.

"You two up here having whoopee with her and are supposed to be taking care of business. I told Antwan to let me come alone," said Wally.

"We were taking care of business, but not that kind of business," said Fat Daddy.

"Yeah, we let our guns bust," said Weevee with a little laugh.

"Shut up, fool," said Wally.

"Listen here, I don't know who ya'll are or what ya'll want with me, but I'm walking out that door so don't try to stop me," said Secret still pointing the gun.

Wally started to come towards her. "Stop, or I'll shoot," said Secret.

He stopped and said, "You won't shoot me!"

"The hell, I won't," said Secret and Wally continued towards her and she took the gun off safety and fired three shots dropping Wally in his tracks. Then she pointed the gun at Weevee and Fat Daddy. "Do ya'll want to be next?" She asked them.

"Na'll slim, we're good. Go ahead about your business," said Fat Daddy and Weevee was just shaking his head. The shots were heard by the other guests in the hotel and someone called hotel security.

****

Miesha desperately wanted Smack's attention, despite him shooting her down. That made him a challenge for her. It was eating her up to try one more time before he said "I do" to Delight.

They were downstairs in the basement just lounging while waiting on Kyle to return. The skirt she had on was turning Smack on and no matter how good she looked or how much he wanted her sex; he wasn't going to fall victim to a suicide mission. She got up to get herself a bottle of water out of the refrigerator behind the bar and she had to walk pass him to do so. She purposely bent over in front of him so he could see the G-string she was wearing along with her muffin. He instantly got aroused, but continued to watch TV. When she came back, she stood in front of him sipping her water blocking his view of the TV so he could see all of her. She put her water down on the side of the sofa and then she pulled him up to her covering his mouth with an intense kiss. He pulled away from her.

"Miesha, what are you doing?" said Smack, because he was caught off guard. She didn't answer him and she pulled him over by the pool table and he didn't resist. She sat on the edge of the table and wrapped her legs around his waist. That melted him and he ran his hands up her thighs all the way to her breasts before placing them back around her hips and then cupping her ass. He picked her up taking her back over to the sofa. He lay her down pinning her arms above her head as his tongue explored her neck and her lips. She writhed beneath his teasing flicks as his tongue embraced her skin. She gripped him between her knees, moaning at the incredible sensation of him touching her body.

"You're like cotton, Miesha, so soft," he whispered in her ear.

"Make me cum then, Smack, take what you want, fuck me," Miesha panted and Smack released his hold taking off his shirt and then pulling off her shirt and helping her remove her skirt. He was still positioned between her legs. Miesha touched him all over and her nails were digging into his brown skinned complexion, but not leaving a mark.

His eyes were on hers and he lowered his head and teased the base of her nipples with his tongue. "Smack, do you have a condom?" Miesha asked him gasping for a breath.

"No," he said with a strong and hard made lust.

Lying down on top of her he pushed her legs apart looking into the depths of her eyes, he buried himself inside her. Not really caring about the consequences, if any. Miesha moaned softly and wrapped her arms around his neck as he drove into her holding her close to his chest. She lifted her hips so he could slide back and forth over her wet spot. Over and over Smack pumped until his groans met her cries until ecstasy explored between them both and Miesha shook as the intensity struck her.

"Oh my God, Smack, that was the best quickie I ever had that actually made me cum," said Miesha.

"Miesha, we shouldn't have done this," said Smack trying to catch his breath.

"Yes, we should have, we both wanted it to happen, but my mouth is shut, it's our little secret. I don't kiss and tell. We both were curious and now it's done," said Miesha wiping the small beads of sweat from her forehead.

"I'm just saying, Miesha, I think I came inside you," said Smack.

"Don't worry boy, I can't get pregnant...I don't think and I just got tested for STD's, so everything should be okay. I need to go and freshen up so, excuse me," as she got up and headed towards the bathroom in the basement. Miesha knew what she was doing because she was ovulating and she wanted a baby badly. Worm would always use a condom when they had sex. Smack sat there for a spell looking stupid, because he knew he just did something fowl and was mad at himself for going against his morals and being weak. He climbed the steps to go and shower and change clothes. He punched the door going into their bedroom.

"You are stupid, Smack, just all out dumb," he said to himself.

****

Kyle stood outside the garage door of Smack's house waiting on him to answer his cell phone so he could be let in. Smack didn't answer so he called Miesha.

"Hey Miesha, come and let me in. Smack is not answering his phone," said Kyle.

"Okay, her I come," said Miesha as she hung up to go let him in. After Kyle got in the house, they headed back down to the basement.

"Yo Miesha, where is Smack?" Kyle asked her.

"I don't know, he left me in the basement," as they both went down the steps.

Soon as they reached the bottom step, Kyle could smell the sex in the air and he looked Miesha. She looked with an attitude and asked him, "What, Kyle?"

"Damn, it smells like sex down here. I know you and Smack haven't been down here fucking, Miesha," Kyle was holding his mouth and nose.

"Kyle, you're tripping. It doesn't stink down here," said Miesha.

"It smells like someone has been fucking," said Kyle.

"You're tripping hard, Kyle," Miesha was looking at him.

"I'm not stupid, Delight is going to kill you and him if she finds out you both have been fooling around. He needs to spray something, that shit is loud as fuck...it stinks," said Kyle.

"I guess he will eventually spray something, but in the meantime, you be quiet, Kyle. I told him I wouldn't say anything and he didn't exactly want to; I kind of forced myself onto him. So please don't say anything to him about this, Kyle," said Miesha with puppy eyes.

"I won't say anything, but you need to quilt acting like one of these nigga's, Miesha and start acting like a lady," said Kyle and he was serious.

****

Delight, Heather and Rainell walked into David's Bridal and it was semi-crowded with customers and employees. Delight didn't know who Lady Ray was so she asked another employee. "Excuse me, Miss, is Lady Ray in today?"

The pale white woman looked up and said, "She's over there by the Prom dresses," as she pointed in the direction, she was in.

Delight looked to see that Lady Ray was a plus sized woman.

"Thank you, Miss," said Delight. She, Heather, and Rainell walked over to the section where Lady Ray stood. Even though Lady Ray was a plus sized woman, she had a jazzy swagger about herself. She had her hair done nice, a cute stylish outfit with heels and some expensive eye wear.

"Excuse me, Lady Ray," said Delight.

The plus sized woman turned around and replied with a smile. "Yes?"

"I'm Smack's fiancée, Delight. He told me to come and see you concerning a wedding package," said Delight.

"Hey, girlfriend, I've been waiting on you. This must be your daughter he told me about," said Lady Ray.

"Yes, and this is my sister, Heather," said Delight.

"Hey," said Lady Ray to Heather showing her a pretty smile.

"Hey," Heather replied with the wave of her hand. Rainell waved her hand as well.

"Well, we have a lot of packages to choose from especially if your Bridesmaids and Maid of Honor are getting their dresses from here as well," said Lady Ray.

"Okay," said Delight.

"What type of price range are you looking for?' Lady Ray asked her.

"He told me don't worry about the prices and to just get the dresses fitted and ordered within two weeks," said Delight.

"Oh, I forgot whose fiancée you were," said Lady Ray with a laugh gently placing her hand on Delight's shoulder.

****

Boom-Boom-Boom! "Open up, someone called about shot's being fired in this room," as hotel security was knocking on the door.

"Shhh," Secret put her finger to her mouth telling them to be quiet still pointing the gun at them. "You better go and stall them if you want to live," said Secret in a whisper.

"What to tell them?" said Weevee still eyeing the gun.

"I don't know, make something up," said Secret.

Weevee walked to the door and put his head down. *Boom-Boom-Boom!* They knocked.

"Open up or we will break the door down," said security.

"What's the problem, sir?" Weevee asked on the other side of the door.

"We got a call about gun shot's coming from this room," said security.

"Can we see for ourselves, can you please open the door, sir?" the security guard asked him.

"Umm-umm hold on, we have to put on some clothes," as Weevee turned to Secret and Fat Daddy. Secret pointed to Wally and for them to put him in the bathroom. "Take him in the bathroom and put him in the tub and close the curtain and turn the water on," said Secret.

They quickly did what she said and they put down some loose clothing to cover up the blood stains on the carpet. Secret sat on the sofa chair with her small bag hiding the gun and Fat Daddy sat beside her. "Fat Daddy, you better be still when he opens that door," said Secret putting the gun up against him so he could feel it.

Weevee calmly opened the door slowly to see two security guards standing before him. Weevee stepped to the side so they could come into the room. When they came in, they saw Secret snug up under Fat Daddy on the small sofa chair holding him at gun point with the gun out of sight. They heard the shower going and asked, "Who's in the bathroom?" One of the security guards asked.

Secret was on her P's & Q's and answered him. "Oh, that's my girl, Trina taking a shower."

The other security guard looked at Weevee and he dropped his head In the direction of one of the shell casings what was visible. He looked over at the shell casing and his eyes met back up with Weevee. Then Weevee glanced over at Secret and the security guard's eyes followed his once more. He then notices how awkward Fat Daddy was sitting next to Secret.

"Excuse me Miss, do you live around here?" the security guard asked Secret, but she ignored him and sat there in complete silence.

"Ms. I'm talking to you; do you live around here?" the same security guard shouted his last words.

Secret replied, "Yes, I live around here," she was now agitated.

"Well, you need to grab your things and go home," said the security guard.

Even though it was her ticket out of there, how could she get around them without showing the gun? She was quick on her toes. "My girl and I are spending time with our friends and I'm not ready to leave yet," said Secret.

"Well we are about to terminate your friends stay at the hotel and refund them their money, so you'll need to leave now," said the other security guard.

She shifted her body slightly and the security guard managed to see the gun. He immediately drew his gun. "Ms. I'm going to only ask you once to put your weapon down," said the security guard who was suspicious of her standing by Weevee. She grabbed Fat Daddy and stood him up with her exposing the gun to everyone.

"I'm taking him with me and I'm walking out that door. I will shoot anyone who tries to stop me," said Secret. Weevee said out loud, "She will shoot a mother-fucker."

"Shut up fat boy," said Secret.

"Please don't let her kill me; she's a killer, a real loose cannon. She's already killed our friend and put him in the bathroom," said Fat Daddy about to cry.

"Shut up, you little bitch. Everyone remain calm and still while we make our exit and everything will be fine. You two fake cops step over there with fat boy," said Secret waving the gun for them to move out the way. They did and Secret and Fat Daddy started to back out of the hotel room she bumped into another security guard and the Honolulu police. The other security guard grabbed her arm and secured the gun and she screamed in pain as he bent her arm back. "Ouch, you're hurting me," said Secret.

Fat Daddy turned around and punched Secret in the face. "That's for calling me a little bitch, you crazy bitch."

Blood appeared at the corner of Secret's mouth and she replied, "You hit like a bitch, too."

Weevee looked out the door and saw Fat Daddy pissed his pants and started to laugh at him. "Fuck you nigga, you were scared too," said Fat Daddy.

****

"Lady Ray, this is nice, I like this dress," said Delight looking at a gown suitable to her liking.

"That can be altered in at least two weeks," said Lady Ray.

Then a plus size woman came into the store fussing to herself with two kids, a little girl and a little boy in a stroller. She was light skinned complexioned with a large bottom and huge breasts. Dante a.k.a. Packman was helping her in the door with the kids. Delight saw him and she told Heather, "Yo sis, there go Dante a.k.a. Packman," Delight said as she pointed to him.

"Delight, you know my brother Dante?" Lady Ray asked her.

"Yes, he and his peeps are friends with Smack. I've seen him numerous times with different females, but I've never seen her before," said Delight.

"That's my friend Toya. They are seeing each other, I assume. She lives in West Chester," said Lady Ray.

"I think he's in our wedding with a few of his Belvy Boyz friends, but I thought he was messing with some young girl named Joan?" Delight questioned.

"Girl, he's a mess. You never know who he's bringing to an event," said Lady Ray giving Delight a wink and a smile.

Dante looked up and saw them and he waved. He kissed the plus sized female and the kids and left back out the door. They watched him get into a gold Toyota Sequoia and the plus sized female walked over to where they were trying on gowns still fussing.

She spoke to all four ladies. "Hello, how is everyone doing?"

"Girl, we are fine, but what's up with you and him?" Lady Ray asked her and Delight, Heather and Rainell waved their hands to her.

"Girl, Dante's lying ass, talking about he's in some wedding and they are going to be fitted for tuxedo's today across from the Tri-County Mall. Someone dropped him off at my house last night and he smelled like some other bitch. He thinks I'm stupid, but if I find out he's lying, I'm going to kill his ass, girl," she exclaimed to them because Rainell was listening.

"Toya, I don't know about him being with another woman last night, but I do know he's not lying about the wedding, because he's in her wedding. This is Smack's fiancée," said Lady Ray and Delight added. "Yes, girlfriend, they should be getting fitted for tuxedo's in about fifteen minutes or so," as Delight was looking at her watch.

"Oh, I'm sorry Toya, this is Delight, the bride. This is her sister Heather and her daughter Rainell," said Lady Ray introducing them.

"It's nice to meet everyone. he's in your wedding?" Toya asked making sure, but wasn't looking for an answer. "Lady Ray, I still think he's sleeping with someone else, because he can never keep it up now or he has E.D." Toya explained to her.

Delight, Heather and Rainell was all ears. "Ooh," as Delight covered her mouth trying not to laugh.

"Toya, you're crazy girl," said Lady Ray playfully slapping her shoulder.

"I'm serious, girl," said Toya.

"He must be doing something right in the bedroom for you to let him drive your truck and you're not on the passenger side," said Lady Ray.

"I mean he does that one thing real good, I am not one to even front, but I be wanting to feel that one thing inside me and I'm tired of using my toys," said Toya seriously. The other three women were laughing and said, "I know that's right, girl."

Rainell didn't have a clue as to what she was talking about.

Delight told Rainell, "Go look at the dresses over there and take her kids with you."

"Oh, that's Aden and Jocelyn," said Toya to Rainell.

Rainell gave her mother a look, but didn't contest her ruling. She grabbed the handle on the stroller and Jocelyn's hand and walked off from the adult conversation.

"Speaking of Smack, this is him calling me now," said Delight.

****

Smack, Kyle and Miesha stood outside the house by the Cadillac truck while Smack called Delight. He was now feeling a little uncomfortable around Miesha. She was eyeballing him the whole time he was on the phone. Kyle just shook his head in disbelief.

"Hello Delight, I was calling to tell you that I was leaving Miesha at the house until we got finished at the Tuxedo store," said Smack.

"Yeah right, you better drop her ass off somewhere," said Delight.

"We are already late babe, Dante and P-Diddy are waiting on me," said Smack.

"Don't leave that heifer in my house, a matter of fact drop her ass off up here so she can get fitted for a dress, too. I have to keep my eyes on her; I see how she looks at you and shit. Plus, she might be like Stefani, trying to sniff a bitch panties and shit," said Delight.

"what are you saying, Delight?" Smack sounded defensive.

"I'm just playing boy, quit tripping, but I don't trust her around my man," said Delight.

"So, you're letting her be in the wedding?" He asked Delight and Miesha eyes lit up hearing him ask her that question.

"Yes, I'll just have an extra bridesmaid and you'll have to get an extra groomsman," said Delight.

"Alright, I'm on my way, baby," said Smack hanging up his phone and Miesha smiled from ear to ear.

"Miesha, I'm dropping you off at David's Bridal with Delight and the rest to get fitted for a dress," said Smack.

"That's what's up. I'm in your wedding," said Miesha hugging Smack. "Thank you," she said. He looked at her and replied, "Don't thank me, thank Delight."

Kyle just looked at them both in disgust and when Smack hit the alarm on the truck, Miesha and Kyle walked around to the passenger side together saying to her, "Cuss, you are on some bullshit, you're crazy for real." said Kyle.

She smiled at him and said, "No, I'm not, I'm just doing me," "Yeah, and all my boys, too," said Kyle opening the back door for her so she could get in the truck.

****

BACK IN HAWAII Fat Daddy and Weevee left the police station from being questioned. They were holding Secret for a felony warrant back in Ohio. They didn't even charge her with Wally's death because they felt like she did them a favor. He was wanted in Hawaii for a few murders and organized crimes.

When they got back to their hotel room on Waikiki Beach, Fat Daddy called Antwan. He knew he would be mad for the news he had to tell him, not because of Secrets capture, but for Wally's death. Antwan didn't know how much Secret knew or what she knew and he couldn't take that chance. He knew now that he would have to sink Smack sooner and not later. He really didn't want to take him down, because he was taking a liking to him, but it was about survival with Antwan. He was gritty and grimy and didn't show any love when it came to his business and survival.

Smack, Kyle and Miesha pulled up in front of David's Bridal's next to Wal-Mart and to Smack's surprise, Kyle was rolling a blunt.
"Yo, Kyle, don't leave none of that Bobby Brown in my truck, nigga," said Smack.
"Bobby Brown, yeah right nigga, this is your shit, Kush," said Kyle.
"Where did you get some Kush?" Smack asked him.
"When I met Buck and Pete, they are selling the shit heavy downtown like hot cakes. Thirty a gram or sometimes twenty-five with fat ass buds look," said Kyle showing Smack a bud.
"Why didn't you sprinkle them niggas with the Black Ice?" Smack asked him.
"I tried, but it's not their style, they fuck with straight exotic weed and heroin. That other shit won't fly with those cats," said Kyle.
"Yeah, okay, but still don't spill shit in my ride, nigga," said Smack. Kyle opened the passenger door and got out to brush the dust that fell into his lap off his clothes. Miesha touched Smack's ear and the back of this head before getting out the truck.
"Smack, thank you for everything, especially for sampling this pussy and showing me that I can get everything by opening my legs all the time," said Miesha.
"We're good. I just want to forget this day," said Smack.
"And neither will I," as she got out the truck.
"Come on Kyle, we are already late as it is," said Smack. Smack wanted to pull off before Delight came running out the store. Kyle climbed back in and they pulled off. Kyle lit the blunt and Smack looked at him long, but briefly. Smack was wondering why suddenly Kyle's swag had changed. He never brought any real exotic weed before, hell he hardly ever smoked. Smack knew something was wrong. Something was in the air. He had to know what was on Kyle's mind. Smack turned the music down and

asked, "What's up, Kyle, what's going on? You're buying Kush and smoking it...something's not right," said Smack.

"There's nothing wrong, I'm just doing me," said Kyle.

"No, that's definitely not you, that's me, so what's going on?" asked Smack.

"You tell me what's going on? Why did you fuck Miesha back at your house, Smack? You are tripping man; she ain't shit, even though she's my cousin. Why would you jeopardize your shit with Delight over someone who doesn't give a fuck about you? She only cares about herself and money. She's my family true enough, but she will destroy your happiness if given a chance," said Kyle.

"Kyle, you are tripping, I haven't touched Miesha," said Smack trying to tread water.

"Smack, you're a lying mother-fucker. I smelled the sex in the air when I came back from meeting Buck and Pete. Miesha was looking all simple and shit like she always does when she has done something that she wasn't supposed to do. She didn't bluntly say that you both had sex, but her not saying anything told another story. Plus, it was a stain left behind on the sofa couch in the basement. All I'm saying is she's not worth losing Delight for," said Kyle.

Smack knew he was right and didn't say a word in his defense.

"Let me hit that," said Smack.

"Hell, to the no! You probably kissed her and she be eating nigga's up like crazy," said Kyle laughing.

"Fuck you, nigga," said Smack.

They finally made it to Mr. Tuxedo's on Kemper across from the Tri-County Mall. He pulled next to P-Diddy's Dodge Charger. P-Diddy, Worm and Dante were standing outside the car waiting on him.

CHAPTER TWENTY-ONE
BETTER DAYS

The following week Larro was released from the Justice Center on an O.R. bond. The RENU agents were upset at Judge Phil Helmet. Everyone was in the store on McMicken who were grooms and the best man getting ready to go out to Forest Part for rehearsal. They were meeting Delight and the females out at the Word of Deliverance church.

Things were shaping up in the city and life of a go-getter was about to come to an end. The Feds were still looking for Miesha Jones. It was about to be a rumble in the streets of Cincinnati and Antwan was about to make a decision that would destroy the life and times of a scholar in the game. The race was about to begin, but who would finish the race?

Everyone was now in the church located on Fresno off Southland in Forest Park. The premature justice of reality taking it's stand for the most part of it and over Baseball, Smack chose to cook it raw, take it and dig. But now he was taking steps towards a future of legitimate measures and a promising new beginning. Smack, P-Diddy, Larro, Worm, Dante, Kyle, Kekou, Denise, Heather, Elicia, Lanetric, Miesha, Star and Delight all stood inside the church. The Quatrum elite forces escaped under a smooth and stainless surface. They laughed and challenged themselves to a well-rehearsed performance. Delight asked Tyree's mom, Denise to be one of her bridesmaids. Denise was in a world of new being around these outgoing drug dealers and career women who had a greater concept of doing their business. She didn't have a clue only her assumptions could make her believe they were drug dealers, but she liked the crowd.

****

Antwan sat in his study with Will Edmond discussing their new plans and for some strange reason, Antwan didn't like his company. Under his relentless witty ways, he knew he had to deal with this individual so he could continue his reign.

" Antwan, when can I take Simmion down?" Will asked him. Antwan carefully looked into Will's eyes and answered him. "The perfect time would be on his wedding day in a couple of weeks."

"Are you sure you can manage to place the drugs on him?" Will asked him.

"I will call you and give you the exact locations you can make the bust. Do not, make an attempt before that, William. I also know a sly fox who may have something for us in the meantime," said Antwan rubbing his goatee.

"I want," said Will carefully looking over his shoulder at his step-sister walking into the study.

"Hello Jas, I was just finishing up with your step-brother, I will be ready to leave in a few," said Antwan.

"Take your time darling. Hello William," said Jasmine.

"Hello Jasmine," said Will watching her sit down on one of the handmade chairs.

"Oh, Will, the person behind killing Patricia Simms was caught in Honolulu," said Antwan.

Will looked at him, because Antwan should not know this information yet as they had just received it at the station.

"I know our department was notified and we already sent personnel to Hawaii to bring Ms. Sheena Price back to face justice," said Will.

"She might be able to give you some information on Simmion and his involvement with the Black Ice, if you know what I mean," said Antwan winking his eye at Will.

****

"Delight, we are about to go to BW3#'s in Forest Park and watch the pre-season game," said Smack.

"Who's playing?" Delight asked him.

"I think the Bengal's and Indy," said Smack.

"We want to go, don't we ladies?" Delight invited the females who were at their rehearsal.

"Sure, Delight," as Elicia answered for everyone.

All the wedding participants went to BW3's. They had an entire section of the sports bar. Smack and P-Diddy ordered wings and drinks for everyone. Even Denise's boyfriend Doug came out to join them. Everyone was enjoying themselves with laughter and conversation while watching the football game, but Dante was up to his old tricks. He was trying to spark something with Delight's friend Elicia and Delight wasn't having it knowing his history.

Delight pulled up on the two with a problem. "Dante, I know you're not trying to talk to my friend?" said Delight.
"Delight, Elicia is a grown woman. I am sure that she can take care of herself," said Dante.
"Yes, Delight, I'm a big girl...I can handle him," said Elicia.
"Girl, he's not the problem, let me see," as Delight paused for a second and continued.
"What about Joan, Toya, Beth, Fox or his baby's mother, Eva...should I go on?"
Dante shook his head and Elicia was just looking at him waiting for him to respond and he didn't. instead he walked off not saying a word.
"Damn, Delight, he's a whore, huh?" said Elicia.
"Girl, he's cool peep, but he's nasty with a lot of action from what I hear. The females I've met of his are crazy about the Negro. I don't know what he does to them, but they love his ass and they call the Negro Packman, so watch out," said Delight giving her friend the look to be careful if she does go down that road.
"Why do they call him Packman, Delight?" Elicia asked now curious.
Delight looked at her and said, "Girl, you don't want to know."
The rest of the Belvy Boyz had showed up with their female friends at BW3's. Weezy was meeting Day-Day and Dre-Cole from the West Side to give them a few bottles of the pills. When he was finished handling his transaction in the restroom, Smack and Kyle was coming in. Smack and Kyle was using the urinals and afterwards they were at the sink washing their hands and Kyle dropped science on Smack in a major way.
"Yo Smack, have you picked out Delights' ring yet?" Kyle asked him.
"I found the perfect ring at Kay's that I'm going to pick up Monday, but why do you ask, Kyle?" asked Smack.
"Smack, you're my guy, hands down, and I admire your style and you're always looking out for me no matter what the circumstances may be. I have mad love for you and for you to quit the game lets me know that you are serious about Delight. So, from me to you, this is my wedding gift to the both of ya'll. Make her happy, my guy," said Kyle giving him a ring.

The ring sparkled and it almost blinded him. It was set in platinum and had to be more than three karats. "Kyle, what is this?" Smack asked him.

"Smack, I want for you to wed your new wife with this ring that I lifted from those clowns in Detroit, it's worth over forty thousand," said Kyle.

"Kyle, I can't take this," ask Smack tried to give it back to him.

"You would make me happy by accepting it and I would be very much appreciative if you did so," said Kyle.

"But Kyle, this ring is too much, look at it, I can tell it's worth a pretty penny. I can't accept this Kyle, get your money, my guy," said Smack.

"I have other pieces that's worth more than this. I can get my money. I lifted over a million dollars' worth of jewelry in the D, I'm good so please accept the ring. It's a token of our friendship, so make me proud and take it," said Kyle.

Smack shed a tear and embraced him and then he places the ring in his pocket.

"Smack don't get all mushy on me," said Kyle.

"I'm not," said Smack wiping the one tear that he had shed. He knew the clarity of the ring had to come from a blood diamond mine in Africa.

"Come on Smack, let's go and finish watching the game and I want to holla at Delight's friend, Elicia, she's hot," said Kyle.

"Alright Kyle and man, I love you and I mean that," said Smack. Kyle patted him on the back and they walked out of the restroom to join everyone else.

****

Kendall, Keisha, Bryant and his friend Keva, walked into BW3's that same night to watch the football game. They saw a crowd of people, but didn't notice off hand who was in the crowd in a noisy section of the sports bar.

They got a table close to the crowd of people enjoying the game. They must have been huge Bengal fans.

Keisha observed Kyle having a conversation with a red bone female which was Elicia, and she knew that Kyle wasn't the in-crowd type of guy and that Smack was probably close by like always. She carefully looked over the small party and bingo, she saw Delight and Smack to her surprise. She tapped Kendall on the shoulder and pointed to the small party locating Delight and Smack. Kendall was vexed and instantly became uneasy and tried to hide his emotions from Keisha vaguely. Kendall exploded like a volcano.

"Let's get out of here, Keisha," he said standing up and she grabbed his arm pulling him back down to his seat.

"Fuck that, Kendall, we came here to eat and enjoy ourselves and watch the game. What are you going to do every time you see them out somewhere, you're going to leave?" said Keisha. She looked him in the eyes and continued, "You need to get over whatever is bothering you, because it is what it is, she's happy and pregnant and is never coming back to you, Kendall," said Keisha.

He looked at Keisha and she could tell he was very angry, but he knew she was telling the truth. The fury was in his eyes and a clout held in his throat to where he couldn't say a word.

"You know Kendall, to get over the problem, you need to speak to them to let them know that you've moved on with your life as well. I'm going to go over and say hello. Are you coming with me?" Keisha asked him. He looked at her and said, "What do you think?"

"Well, just sit there with your stubborn ass and I'll be back. Can you order me a Dr. Pepper and twenty-four spicy garlic wings, please?" said Keisha and then she asked Keva, "Will you go over here with me, Keva?"

Keva got up from the table and her and Keisha walked over to where Delight was sitting so she could speak to her.

****

Later, that night, Delight was in the basement filling out invitations while Smack was up in their room relaxing. Rainell and her friend Daysha, were in her room listening to music and texting on their cell phones. It was a school night and Delight let Daysha stay all night anyway, because she was taking them to school in the morning.

Delight sat back on the sofa couch to take a break from sealing up envelopes and she held her stomach. "Boy, I think I ate too much," she said out loud. Then she happened to look to her left and saw a small stain on the couch. She got up to go get the disinfecting cleaner and stain remover and before she sprayed the spot, she smelled it to see if it was a grease stain and it smelled like a female's scent. It was strong, but not an awful fishy smell. The first thing she thought was that Daysha and Rainell had some boys over while they were out. She got a little angry and then reminded herself that Rainell was now on birth control and thought back to the days when her and Heather used to sneak boys over.

She just smiled to herself and looked in the air. "My baby is doing the nasty," she said to herself. Smack came down the steps in his silk pajamas and slippers. Unaware he walked up on Delight and asked her, "What are you doing babe?"

"I was filling out our wedding invitations and then I noticed this stain on the couch. I think the girls had company while we were at BW3's tonight. Someone has been having sex on this couch recently because it smells like a female's vagina," said Delight. He just looked at her and didn't say a word because he knew where the stain came from.

"Well, it's getting late, let's go to bed," said Smack.

"Okay baby, but we are going to have to throw this thing out, because don't nobody want to be sitting in sex fluids," said Delight smiling at him.

His eyes angle expression brought a deeper thought to mind. *"YOU ARE MY ROCK AND MY FORTESS THEREFORE FOR YOUR NAME'S SAKE LEAD ME AND GUIDE ME," said Smack silently speaking to God, as he and Delight went up the steps.*

****

Keisha was lying in the bed while Kendall was showering. She was having mixed emotions and was confused about where they stood in their relationship. Even though she was upset with him because of his actions that night, she wanted his manly embrace. He came out the bathroom drying off and sat on the bed putting the towel next to him. Keisha got up still on the bed and grabbed the towel to dry off his back. "Thank you, Keisha," he said.

She turned him around to look him in the face and said, "Baby, he caught you good and gave you a shiner," as Keisha caressed his face where the bruise was.

"It was a lucky punch, but it's not over," said Kendall putting on his boxer briefs.

"Kendall, leave it alone, you were in the wrong and it's not even worth it," said Keisha.

"Fuck that, little drug dealing ass punk, we'll cross paths again and you or Delight won't be able to come in between us," said Kendall standing up.

"If you say so, boo, but there's no need for you to be putting those things on because I want some before, we go to bed," said Keisha tugging on his boxer briefs.

Keisha knew deep down inside Kendall didn't want any parts of Smack and was just being a real dick head about the situation.

****

Earlier, while they were at BW3's, Delight and Keisha were holding a conversation and Kendall came to get her. He pulled up and snarled at Delight and gave Smack a mean mug from left field. "Yo, Keisha, we are over here and your food is getting cold," said Kendall.

"In a minute, baby. Here I come," said Keisha. She and Keva were standing there talking to Delight about the wedding. Kendall looked at her and got angry because she didn't move. He couldn't take it anymore. "Now, Keisha! We have company of our own to attend to," his voice rose with aggression.

"Damn it, Kendall, she'll be over there when we are finished talking," said Delight.

"You need to mind your own business as this doesn't concern you," said Kendall.

"What did you say?" Delight asked him dropping her bottom lip.

"I said this doesn't fucking concern you," he said with force behind it.

Smack heard him speaking to Delight this way and wasn't having it at all. He came over closer by them and said, "Hold on, home boy, and slow your roll. You can choose a better tone when addressing a lady, especially this one," said Smack.

"You don't tell me what the fuck to do, partner, this is my...," as Kendall couldn't get his words out, because Smack cut him off.

"This is your what, baby mama? Regardless of that fact, you will respect her as my woman," said Smack.

"Or what, little punk?" said Kendall as he pushed Smack.
Smack's first reaction was punching Kendall, which he did right in the face and Kendall stumbled backwards. Delight and Keisha stood in between the two.
"Stop it, Simmion!" said Delight.
"Kendall!" Keisha yelled putting her hand out.
"Why, I'm going to kill you little boy," said Kendall.
"I'm right here. I'm not going anywhere," said Smack.
"Move Keisha," as Kendall moved her out the way. P-Diddy and Dante was now in front of him. "Hold on playboy, what's the problem?" said P-Diddy.
Kendall looked at the 6'5" P-Diddy and backed off. "Simmion, this ain't over," said Kendall grabbing Keisha and they walked off. Kendall through a few bills on the table and they left.
****
The next morning Delight was getting ready for work and to take Rainell and Daysha to school. She went and woke the girls up at 6:30am. Rainell asked her mom still half sleep, "Mama can you plug up the curlers, please?"
"Girl, you are lazy and get up, Ms. Daysha," as Delight left the room.
She went to the bathroom down the hall and plugged up the curlers. Delight just so happen to look in the trash can to see a tampon rolled in toilet paper and a mini-pad. She knew Rainell used the pad and not the tampon and she didn't know that she was on her cycle. Because to Delight's knowledge, she thought that maybe her daughter had experienced with sex last night from the stain on the sofa couch in the basement. She went back into her daughter's room to ask a few questions. The girls were up and moving around at this time as Delight stood in the doorway with her arms crossed watching them move ever so slowly. Then she cleared her throat to get their attention. They turned around and Rainell said, "Mama, we are up."
"I know, Rainell, I was just wondering when you started using tampons?" asked Delight.
"I don't, Daysha does. Why?" asked Rainell.
"I just saw one in the bathroom trash can. So Rainell, you just came on your period?" Delight asked her.

"I came on Saturday, Daysha and I came on at the same time, but I'm off now," said Rainell.

"Oh, I see," said Delight thinking hard.

"Why, what wrong, mom?" Rainell asked her.

"Nothing, you girls go ahead and get dressed...it's 6:50," as Delight left the room wondering where did the stain come from...more than that, *who* did it come from? She knew her and Smack didn't have sex in the basement and to top it off, the stain wasn't there last Friday before they went out to Game Works and Jillian's. it wasn't there when she showed Keisha the house either.

The only other female besides herself and the girls who was at her house was Miesha that Saturday when they were getting fitted for dresses.

"Was it her scent? She thought about it and then told herself, "I know Smack wouldn't betray me like that."

****

Delight was dropping Rainell and Daysha off at school on Chester Road in Sharonville at Princeton High School.

"Call me when you get to your aunt Heather's house, okay?" said Delight.

"Yes ma'am. Can I still go to the football game and dance tonight, remember?" said Rainell.

"Oh, shoot, I almost forgot ya'll play Colerain tonight, Tyree's mom asked me to go to the game with her. Okay, do you have any money?" Delight asked her.

"No ma'am," said Rainell.

"Here," as Delight went inside her purse and counted out three hundred dollars.

"Here is three hundred dollars, tell your aunt to take you to the mall and buy you a new outfit and shoes. Take Daysha with you and buy her an outfit, too," said Delight.

"Okay mama," said Rainell as her and Daysha got out the 750 BMW.

"You both be good, I love you and bye," said Delight.

"Thank you, Ms. Delight," said Daysha.

"Bye mom," said Rainell.

****

Roughly the storm was coming and the informative pleasure was changing positions. The infamous team of players was collecting the most recent numbers from dealing. The Black Ice was doing numbers in the streets, serious numbers far from dealing a hundred kilos of cocaine or a thousand pounds of marijuana.
Its projected gross was 7 million and five hundred thousand from five thousand bottle sold at fifteen hundred a piece. They would split the money off the bottles equally down the middle. They knew it would be more greedily consumed at this price and it was plentiful to market the drug at this same price.
Smack blessed the boys from D-Cut as promised with the drug. He told Larro that Antwan would be dealing with the Belvy Boyz, but they would cut them in. smack had put a few bottles over Fox's crib in the Four Towers to let her hustle the drug to. She was selling the pills at work where she was a barmaid at the Golden Nugget on Queen City. She also worked at the after-hour spot on Central Avenue down from Queen Ann's bar called the Candy Shop. She served drinks and cooked. She went straight to the Candy Shop when the bar closed.
D$Boy was recovering from his gunshot wound, but was still in a coma. Larro and the guys would visit him frequently and his room was filled with flowers and balloons. everything was getting back on track as the days counted down for the big wedding.
****
Larro stood in the hospital room of D$Boy with his mom, and the mother of his child, Timberland. They were right by his side making sure he was cared for. Larro was mad; he couldn't stand to see him hooked up to all the machines. He shed a tear for his partner and looked at his family. "Yo, Timberland, whatever you and the baby need, we got you...you too, Ms. Stephanie. Timberland, take this money and go buy a new car or something flashy with rims to let them know D$Boy is still alive and is getting it."
He handed her a small black bag with thirty thousand dollars in it.
"Thank you, Larro," said Timberland.
"Timberland, make sure you buy something foreign. He's going to pull through, he deserves to live," said Larro.

"I hope so, we need him. I don't know what we would do without him," said Timberland beginning to cry. He grabbed her and gave her a hug and a kiss on the forehead. He walked out the room. He knew that D$Boy would do the same for him if he was in the same situation. Jenny had his son and he was going to her house to see his son.

CHAPTER TWENTY-TWO
THE END OF THE ROAD

That following week, Antwan and the Belvy Boyz gave Smack a bachelor party at Jillian's. it was packed and more like a strip party if anything. Antwan flew in a variety of women to take off their clothes; he had Chinese, India, Kriol, Mexican, White, and Black, Haitian, Hawaiian and Puerto Rican women stripping for Smack.

It was more women in the club than men. You would've thought Jay-Z had sold out the Garden's this night. The club was surrounded by ballers and the Ritz wasn't doing numbers this night. They dedicated this night to Fila and D$Boy as well. Even Miesha showed up with Worm. The crowd was so thick no one paid any attention to Will Edmond and Allen Taylor. Jasmine was also at the party with Antwan. Miesha got sick and had to make an early exit with Worm. P-Diddy and Kekou were popping bottles spraying the crowd with champagne. D.J. Rob G. was in the building on the ones and twos. Jeremiah was playing and the crowd was chanting the words, *"Flashy lights, tell me where we are."* The strippers were getting loose and personal where they could have filmed "The Nasty Nati 4". There were condom wrappers everywhere and it was sex going on in the club for real, Usher nor Young Jeezy wasn't even involved. Smack was getting a lap dance from one of the strippers and Weezy had one of them bent over hitting her from the back. It was going down like Young Joc would say. It was going down in Jillian's this night. Smack knew this would be his last night at having fun without his wifey to be around, but he only went as far to getting a lap dance. He could have had his way with any of the strippers or any female in the club, but he respects his mind as well as his partner for life. He also knew someone was recording this party and was going to put it on YouTube.

****

MEANWHILE all the ladies were out at Rhino's in Sharonville on Chester Road giving Delight a Bachelorette party with an all-male review that showcased Hurricane Tony, The Storm, Wesley Pipes, and Bam.

It was a crowd of females the ones who were in the wedding along with many others. It was about thirty other women who were friends of someone else at the party. These women were just as wild as the men were at the strip club. Meco and Rachelle had sex with two of the male strippers in front of everyone. They were drunk and horny partying like "Rock Stars". Then China got crunk with it by showing all the ladies how she could deep throat a man's tribal piece, she use to be with Worm now creeping with Kobe.

The night had ended for the ladies at around three in the morning, but Smacks party didn't end until seven in the morning. Everyone leaving Delight's party ended up at IHOP or the Waffle House on Sharon Road. Delight and Elicia was giving out a few invitations to the wedding reception.

At Jillian's, D.J. Rob announced Smack's wedding reception was open to the public out at the Torque in Fairfield on Route 4. The big wedding would we two weeks from that night at the Word of Deliverance church.

When Smack came in the house at around 8:15 that morning, Delight, Heather and Elicia were in their nightgowns sitting in the kitchen having breakfast. Smack stood in the entrance staring at them while they were acting silly. He was indeed exhausted. He had strands of fake hair in his head from the stripper who gave him a lap dance. Delight just so happen to look up in his direction and said, "Hey baby, I see you finally made it home to me. Come here and let me smell your dick," said Delight smiling at him.

Elicia hit her arm and said, "Girl, no you didn't...you're crazy." Smack looked at Delight like she was crazy, because that caught him off guard.

"Na'll Elicia, because I know how wild those parties can get. I watch Jerry Springer and Maury. Hell, look what happened at my party last night. I just want to see if he's going to blame him cheating on the Alcohol, see if he took the opportunity to get it in before he say, 'I do'," said Delight.

"Delight, quit playing. I'm tired as hell. I'm about to take a shower and go to bed," said Smack.

"Are you hungry?" Delight asked him.

"I'm good," he said turning to walk off and he stopped and turned back around.

"Oh, hi Elicia and Heather," said Smack turning back around and leaving from their sight.

Delight yelled, "I'm still checking your underwear nigga,"

Elicia and Heather laughed. Heather added, "That young boy is going to drive you crazy, Delight."

"No, he's not, not before I drive him nuts," said Delight with a small chuckle.

While Smack slept most of the day, Delight, Heather and Elicia sat with the wedding planner finishing up the plans for the wedding.

****

P-Diddy and Dante were at Lenhardt's discussing plans with Antwan having lunch in a private section of the restaurant.

"P-Diddy and Dante, the quantity will come larger next month, I'm thinking about thirty thousand bottles, will ya'll be able to handle that much at one time?" Antwan asked them.

"It's whatever with the Belvy Boyz, we'll get the job done no matter what the shipment may consist of we will handle the business," said P-Diddy.

"I'll give ya'll the same exact deal I'm giving Simmion, we split the profit down the middle. Market the bottles between fifteen and two grand and the numbers will be great," said Antwan.

"No, problem, Antwan," said Dante.

P-Diddy knew that they were making a mill ticket from the drugs from this last shipment that came in and he quickly did the math and knew the Belvy Boyz would be millionaires. Even Dante was doing the math after the numbers Antwan told.

"How much of the shipment if is left I gave Simmion?" Antwan asked them.

"It's like eight to six hundred bottles left, if that. They should be gone in the next couple of days," said Dante.

"Well I have like five thousand more bottles left and after we are finished eating, I'll take you two where I have them stored," said Antwan.

"What about the money we have of Smacks?" said P-Diddy.

"Please, finish doing business with Simmion and off these five thousand bottles you should make three million and seven hundred dollars after we split the gross total which would be seven million and five hundred thousand and that's selling the pills at fifteen hundred a bottle," said Antwan.

Dante looked at P-Diddy and they both knew that Smack was making a fortune off their hustle. "We are with that, Antwan," said Dante.

"When Smack gives it to us, we usually whole sell it as two to three grand, why so cheap now Antwan?" said P-Diddy.

"We are not trying to keep the drug around; we are trying to get rid of it quick as possible. Then it's around eight of ya'll to divide three million between. You do the math after splitting three between eight," said Antwan.

P-Diddy thought about the numbers and said, "That's three hundred and seventy-five thousand to be divided between us,"

"Exactly," said Antwan giving him a grin.

"Damn, now that's what's up, I'll be able to move Eva and my daughter out of Evanston for good," said Dante.

"Ya'll just keep the love with the streets and everybody make some money and success will be ours. Simmion is already three to four million to the good. Who do you know is a billionaire from just drug money alone in the U.S. without investing?" Antwan asked them and P-Diddy stared in the air searching for an answer, but couldn't find one.

Then Antwan said, "You can think all you want but you'll never think of anyone. No American Gangster, none. If ya'll ride with me and stick to the script, we will make history and be the first, trust me my friends," said Antwan looking at Dante and P-Diddy. They were feeling him at every angle. "I'm bigger than life and I have all kinds of connections around the world. I even have an army in another country, so war is nothing to me, if we must go there. I say screw the government officials to a new beginning of getting rich," said Antwan raising his glass in the air so they could toast. America was about to feel the wrath of a new kind of terror. P-Diddy and Dante couldn't wait to give the news to the rest of the Belvy Boyz.

When they left Antwan after receiving five thousand more of the bottles of Black Ice, Dante was on the passenger side thinking about his future out loud.

"Marry Eva, quit Joan and Beth, buy a house in the suburbs, fuck with Shots and the Base Boys with that music and live like a boss," said Dante.

P-Diddy looked over at him and said, "Joan is going to kill you along with Beth and that big girl, Toya out in West Chester and if you play with Eva's heart this time, she probably will kill your punk ass too."

"Nigga, fuck you, I run shit with my bitches, they don't run Packman," said Dante.

"Yeah, whatever nigga, we'll see," said P-Diddy.

"We will," said Dante.

****

Antwan had watched P-Diddy and Dante pull off from the Colerain storage facility where he had the Black Ice. His phone rang and he answered it. "Hello Jas, what's going on darling?" said Antwan.

"I'm waiting on you, Chocolate Dream," said Jasmine.

"I'll be there in twenty minutes. I just gave the Belvy Boyz the rest of the shipment that I had. They are not quitters like your boy, Simmion; they are indeed go-getters, Jas. My plan will follow through dealing with these guys. I like them a lot and too bad for Simmion. We could've made a great team, but shit happens," said Antwan.

"Okay darling, I'm waiting on you. I'm absolutely naked lying in bed," said Jasmine.

"Did you get your dress for the wedding?" He asked her.

"No, not yet darling," said Jasmine.

"I bought you something of pure elegance to wear. It comes from France. It cost me around ten thousand American dollars," said Antwan.

"I'm sure it is stunning and beautiful. I can't wait to wear it for you," said Jasmine.

"I can't wait to see you in it either," said Antwan.

"Well don't keep me waiting. I'll see you soon," said Jasmine.

Antwan didn't even say bye, he just hung up his phone and then he received another call.

It was an unfamiliar number, but one that he recently stored in his phone book. It was Fox; she managed to get next to him the night they all were at Jillian's after attending Game Works.

"Hello," Antwan answered pulling off in his 500 GT Shelby Mustang.

"Antwan, this is Fox, are you busy?" She asked him.

"No, not really and I see you finally decided to call me," said Antwan.

"Yeah, I'm kind of bored, so what's up with you?" Fox asked him.

"Not much, why?" asked Antwan.

"Because I would like to see you now...to see what the Chocolate Dream is all about," said Fox.

"Where are you, Fox?" he asked her.

"I'm at home. I live in Western Hills in the Four Towers off Ferguson Road. My address in 2009 apartment number 7." She paused briefly and said, "Oh, can you bring some of those pink pills? Smack has some over here but he has told me not to touch them. I need to get high and you can do whatever to me, I mean whatever filling up every hole if you know what I mean," said Fox licking her lips seductively, but he couldn't see her.

"I'm on my way, I just punched your address into my GPS," said Antwan.

****

P-Diddy and Dante walked in the store and all the Belvy Boyz were present; Vino, Bodean, Worm, Weezy, Kobe and Kekou. A few groupie females were also in the store and some kids playing video games. The traffic came and went so they shut down the store to have a private moment to discuss their business.

"Listen, we are about to be real major getting unbelievable dough. This Antwan cat just cut us in that one way. Did ya'll know off five thousand bottles at fifteen hundred a bottle Smack and Antwan was clearing seven million clean?" said P-Diddy.

"That's loochie cuss" said Bodean.

"Yeah, you're telling me," said Dante.

"Instead of selling the shit at $2,500 a bottle like you suggested Vino, we would be up that one way, but $600,500 to split between us was good money. This guy Antwan, is trying to make us billionaires behind this new move," said P-Diddy.

"Look how quick the shit went like hot cakes, what we got like eight hundred bottles left?" Vino was making his point.

"You're right, but listen here he just gave us another five thousand bottles to move with same deal he gave Smack. We drop the price to fifteen hundred like Smack wanted off the shit and we walk away with three million to divide between us instead of six hundred thousand," said Dante.

"Yeah leaving us with four hundred racks and some change a piece putting everyone close to a half million and it don't stop there, because next month we are getting like twenty to thirty thousand bottles. whoever's not with it take your earnings and leave now, we family and we are going to do this the right way," said P-Diddy. He stood up and put his hand out waiting on everyone else to join him in the circle and everyone else followed his lead. "All is one and one is all, we must protect the house," said Vino and everyone else repeated him. "We must protect the house," said everyone.

"Oh yeah, I forgot to tell ya'll do not deal with the cat named Fred a.k.a. Remy a.k.a Lo who be over in Millville, he's working with the Feds. My dude Dre-Cole said he set him up," said Weezy.

****

You could hear screams coming through the wall from Fox's apartment. Antwan was ripping away inside her anal. She gave him every hole as promised with much pleasure. The Black Ice had her numb, but not that numb where she couldn't feel his tribal piece digging inside her backside. She was loving him as her eyes rolled in the back of her head several times and she even squirted a few times having uncontrollable orgasms.

He was getting it with much force and her sex was good, so good he forgot that Jasmine was waiting on him. Fox couldn't take it anymore; she couldn't hold her mud as she begged him to stop.

"Please stop, Antwan, I can't take it anymore. Please take it out, Antwan, I'm about to," as she couldn't get it out. Instead she had a bowl movement on Antwan's rod releasing contaminated waste on his manhood.

"Oh, Fox, that's messed up, you shitted on my me, how gross," said Antwan as he pulled out of her anal and she was still defecating. He went directly to her bathroom to clean himself up. Fox was too exhausted and numb to move so she just collapsed. Antwan got dressed and placed a few more pills on her dresser and made an exit from her place. When he left Fox was still lying in the mist of her own waste.

A few hours had gone by and Dante showed up at Fox's apartment. He was paying her a visit also. She was cleaning up the accident she had in her bedroom removing the sheets and rest of her lined to be washed. She had showered and was in her bath robe. The smell was still in the air, because she hadn't sprayed any air freshener yet and only lit a few scented candles. "Damn Fox, it smells like badussy in here, ass and pussy. What have you been doing in here? It smells like shit," said Dante.

"I was babysitting my neighbor's dog and she used the bathroom everywhere even in my bed. I'm cleaning it up now. Here, spray this," as she handed Dante some air-freshener in a can. He sprayed it and she looked at him shrugging her shoulders.

"Dante, I want to try something new, I want you to fuck me in my ass," said Fox. He looked at her crazy, because every time he tried to put his fingers in her anal, she wouldn't allow him to and now she wants it in her anal, he was confused. Just that quick, she was turned out on getting pounded in her anus.

****

Miesha was wondering why her menstrual cycle hadn't come yet as scheduled. She was confused, because she knew her and Worm always used protection. Then she thought about her stressful situation hiding from the Feds. She sat there and then her inner senses of her thoughts surfaced; the day she sexed Smack at his house in the basement. Maybe she was pregnant? Ain't no way after all the mishandled sexual encounters she had leading her up to her adulthood and now and she never conceived. She figured she couldn't get pregnant and her eyes dimed to the slim possibility. She would give her period a few more days to show before getting checked out and doing a pregnancy test.

CHAPTER TWENTY-THREE
"I DO"

Limos were lined up outside of the Word of Deliverance church in Forest Park. It was a super stretched Hummer, a Chrysler 300 and STS Cadillac. The church was packed to capacity. It was like it was a sold-out concert.

The colors of purple and white decorated the church as the director signaled the pianist to start the ceremony. Smack stood at the alter awaiting his bride.

His mom, Larro's mom and Jenny were present as well as other family members. Delight's family was also there. Heather three daughters had flown in for the wedding and Delight's uncle Melvin was giving her away since her dad was deceased. Antwan and Jasmine showed up as well and Jasmine's dress looked like she was in a royal wedding herself.

****

Earlier before everyone was piling inside the church, Antwan and Smack were in the restroom of the church exchanging mere conversation. Smack had removed his tux jacket and went into one of the stalls and Antwan managed to slip a bag of pills inside Smack's jacket pocket.

"Simmion, we are going to miss your presence in the game, but life is awaiting your true destiny," said Antwan.

"Antwan, just because I'm getting out of the game doesn't mean we have to stop being friends. We can still hang out and travel to various countries, plus when I move out of this country, you can visit me." Smack said flushing the toilet. He came out of the stall going to the sink to wash his hands.

"Herr, Simmion, that would be fabulous to remain close as the best of friends," said Antwan with a grin.

"No problem, Antwan," as Smack finished washing his hand and drying them off.

"Well I guess this is it buddy, the end of the road for you. Go and marry that beautiful lawyer, my friend," said Antwan as he embraced Smack. Smack grabbed his tuxedo jacket and put it back on unaware of the pills he now possessed. They walked out of the restroom heading for the main entrance of the church.

****

Smack stood firmly strong at the altar; he was a handsome young man waiting on his Princess to arrive in his arms. Elicia walked down the aisle with the best man, Larro. Delight's maid of honor was looking pretty as ever. Then P-Diddy and Heather followed them and Dante and Denise, Worm and Miesha, Kyle and Lanetric and Kekou and Star brought up the rear. They all stood across from one another smiling and cheesing with expression looking over at Smack to see how nervous he was.

Then the Belvy Boyz lady friend Te'Anna accompanied her friend Ebbie to sing a ballet to announce Delight's entrance with her uncle Melvin. Ebbie's voice carried throughout the church as she sung the perfect song by Keisha Cole. "Sent from Heaven". Ebbie was sexy with large full-size lips. Her mild mint brown skin complexion was smooth with glittered lotion across the surface of her cleavage and arms which were exposed. Te'Anna was shimmering with make-up that set her skin tone to magnificent heights. Both ladies could sing.

Delight's entrance through the open doors was breath taking as everyone stood. Her gown was light purple and lengthy. There were certain individuals who started shedding tears as she made advances towards the altar. When she reached the altar with her uncle, he gave his niece to Smack. There were camera's flashing liking crazy as Ebbie sung her last words and then the Bishop Donny Milton hand motioned for everyone to be seated.

"We are gathered here today to witness the union of two who want to be joined together in the name of the Lord, Amen," said the Bishop. "Who is giving this fine young lady away?" The Bishop asked and Delight's Uncle Melvin stood and said, "I am."

****

"Ruthy, I'm about to leave out the house now. I have to pick up Carmen first and then you," said Fox.
"We are going to be late Fox, the wedding starts in twenty minutes," said Ruthy.
"We'll be about ten minutes late, so what," said Fox as she was taking one of the pink pills.
"Well c'mon, I'm waiting on you and I'll be sitting on the porch," said Ruthy.
"Alright, bye girl," said Fox hanging up the phone.
She grabbed her purse and car keys and was heading for the front door and the door was busted open by a battle ram. Boom!
"Awe," Fox screamed.
Then detectives came through the space with guns and their badges around their necks.
"Get down, get down on the floor now," as one of the RENU agents demanded her.
"What's going on?" Fox cried out.
"You know what's going on Ms. Sanya McKinney. Your involvement with Simmion Boyd and the Black Ice," said a detective.
She started crying as a group of detectives searched her apartment. One of the agents came from the bedroom saying,
"We got it, and it's like ten bottles, enough to give Ms. McKinney ten years in Marysville," said the RENU agent.
Another agent said, "Ms. McKinney, do yourself a favor and help yourself, we know this is not yours. Just give us a written statement to who it belongs to and you'll walk."
She looked up at him and shook her head "yes" drowning herself in her own tears.

****

At the same time when the RENU agents were kicking in Fox's door, D$Boy's eyes opened for the first time bringing him out of his coma. Timberland was right there with him.

"It's okay baby just be calm. I'm here," said Timberland with tears in her eyes. He tried to move, but was too weak.
Timberland started crying and said, "Thank you, Jesus, thank you."
She then text Larro saying, "D$Boy just came out of his coma."

Will Edmond texted Antwan and it read, "We just caught Fox and she's willing to write a statement on Simmion."
Antwan texted him back saying, "Good, now you can raid the wedding reception tonight at the Torque. I placed the pills inside his jacket pocket,"
"Okay, Antwan, I'll talk to you later buddy, and tell Jasmine I said hello."
"I will, Will, see you later on tonight." Antwan texted him last.

****

Smack and Delight exchanged vows that they wrote to each other with Delight going first.
"Simmion, you're everything and the moment I met you I knew you were the one for me. You were the man I heard so much about growing up as a little girl. The man my father told me to look for and I found my rock, my perfect love, my reason to be happy. I want to love you until the end of time and even after; I want to grow old with you to quiet my storm, raising our family fruitful in every way possible. I'm yours Simmion, yours to be." said Delight.
Her eyes never left his while telling him her vows. It was silent as Simmion's turn came to tell her his vows.
"Delight Heath, I couldn't sleep last night trying to think of what I was going to say to you," as he paused. *"I couldn't figure it out, so I asked God for guidance and a little voice inside me told me to tell you how I feel completely about you."* He stopped for a breath before continuing.
"Delight, I love. I'm endlessly in love with you. My eyes light up when you enter a room, my heart skips many beats thinking about you, whenever you are, I want to be there, to share and to hold you and love you completely. No matter how long it takes for me to develop the gift, I will do it. I only want you by my side to love and cherish, to build and grow, to seek happiness forever.

Thank you for allowing me to go to that next level with you," said *Smack.*

Elicia and Denise shed a few tears knowing Smack's words were beautiful and meant the world to a woman who was listening. Delight got glossy eyed and a few women in the audience even began to cry. A tear dropped from Delight's emotion and Kyle even shed a tear and Elicia saw it, as he wiped it away. That turned Elicia on tremendously seeing him all emotional.

Then the Bishop said, "The ring, please."

Larro went into his suit jacket and gave Smack the ring wrapped in a cloth.

"You may place the ring on her finger, Simmion," said the Bishop.

Smack removed the cloth and the ring was glistening. Everyone was frozen seeing it. All the bride's maid's mouth was stuck open. The ring stood out so perfect, so raw and even Lady Ray saw from her seat and was like, "Damn!"

Delight was even shaking looking at the ring she knew cost a fortune. It made her previous ring look a little shabby. The ring slid on her finger just right.

"I pronounce you husband and wife, you may kiss your bride," said the Bishop.

Smack kissed his new wife passionately and long.

Everyone stood up and watched them walk back down the aisle. In the main lobby, they took professional pictures with the groom's men and bride's maids. Then Smack and Delight got in a carriage awaiting them being pulled by Clydesdales and escorted by police. It was now almost eight o'clock and the reception would begin in forty-five minutes. They rode around up by the Tri-County Mall and the carriage would take them to the Torque on Route 4 in Fairfield. Everyone else left the church heading to the Torque and D.J. Rob G. was already set up.

When P-Diddy and the Belvy Boyz pulled up in one of the stretch limos the bride's maids was in another one with Lady Ray and their family was in the third one. The caterers were already there and Ms. Pauline and Sheila from Queen Ann's bar was set up at the bar serving drinks. There was unlimited liquor and champagne to be served as well as juice, pop and water for the kids and non-alcoholic guest.

It was a table set up for the wedding party by the dance floor and when the bride and groom arrived the DJ played Vanessa Williams 'Save the best for last'. After Delight and Smack danced to the song, they took their seats and P-Diddy stood up with his glass of champagne hitting the side of the glass with his fork getting everyone's attention. Someone had signaled the DJ to turn the music down a little.

"I would like to make a toast, to the bride and groom. It was a pleasure to make ya'll acquaintance and I wish the both of you a promising and bright future together, congratulations, I love ya'll," said P-Diddy.

"We love you too, P-Diddy," as Delight shouted back to him.

Then Larro stood up. "Wait a minute now I have something to say. I would like to tell everyone that D$Boy has come out of his coma," said Larro.

"That's what's up?" said Dante.

"Hell yeah, I knew my boy would pull through," said Bo-Gotti. Smack lifted his glass to Larro. "So today is a good day, but Delight at first I thought you were taking my cousin away from me and I was wrong. You brought us closer together and thanks. I wish ya'll the best and I can't wait until it's my turn. I love ya'll," said Larro as he threw them a kiss with the wave of his hand from his lips.

Delight kissed her hand and sent one back to him. Smack held his glass to him and nodded his head. Larro and Smack's mom held each other hand and shed a tear. When Larro sat back down next to Jenny she nudged him and said, "Yeah right, you can't wait until it's your turn though?" she managed to sit by him.

"Yeah, I'm going to ask you to marry me some day," said Larro in a low whisper.

"Yeah right, we'll see about that," said Jenny and leaned over and gave him a kiss.

Heather looked at him in disgust, because she was hoping after the reception, she was going to get her groove on with Larro.

K.G. didn't make the wedding as he was attending a relative's funeral.

Everyone was drinking and laughing at the table having a good time. Dante saw that Joan had come to the reception and he was looking for Eva to show up hoping she wouldn't, because he wanted this night to be drama free.

Ruthy and Carmen finally showed up without Fox and they were looking for her, but no one had seen her. She didn't make the wedding either from the information they received from Puff and Yvette.

Dante had excused himself from the table to speak with Joan and then he separated from her to go and get her a drink. While he was at the bar Ruthy had pulled up on him.

"Hey Dante, have you seen Fox?" asked Ruthy.

"Ruthy, I haven't seen her, but she's probably somewhere in here she doesn't miss any events," said Dante.

"She didn't pick me or Carmen up like she was supposed to and she hasn't been answering her phone. She made us miss the wedding," said Ruthy.

"You know her, but I'm sure she's in here," said Dante and out of nowhere Toya showed up. "Busted, Dante, who is this?" as Toya was pointing her finger in Ruthy's face.

He was caught off guard. "That's Ruthy, my dude CHP's sister and my friend. What are you doing here? I thought you were in Flint, Michigan?" said Dante.

"Surprised to see me, huh? I lied so I could bust your trifling ass with one of these bitches. You're probably fucking ole girl you walked down the aisle with," said Toya.

"Girl, you are tripping hard, ain't nobody with no one in here especially not Denise," said Dante.

Ruthy looked at him and smiled. "Dante, I'll talk to you later and if you see Fox before I do, tell her I'm looking for her please," said Ruthy.

"Okay, Ruthy, I will," said Dante.

D.J. Rob G. was mixing Prince's 'Erotic City' with Puffy's 'Last Night'.

Toya looked at him holding the two drinks. "Where are we sitting, Dante?" Toya asked him.

"What do you mean? I'm sitting with the wedding party," he told her pointing in that direction.

"Who's the daiquiri for?" she asked him.

"It's for umm-umm," as she cut him off. "Quit stuttering, because you are about to tell a lie," said Toya. Then Joan came out of nowhere and grabbed one of the drinks, the daiquiri.

"Thanks, baby," said Joan and she kissed him. She looked at Toya and said, "Dante, who is this, your sister?" Joan asked him.

"His sister," said Toya with her hands on her hips rolling her eyes.

"Check that, I'm his girlfriend, Toya," said Toya with an attitude.

"Yeah right boo, quit fooling yourself, this is my man boo," said Joan turning around to show her the tattoo of his street nickname on her back because she had on a dress with the back out. 'Packman's Property' big as day on Joan's back.

"I knew it, I knew it. I suspect you were fucking around on me, Dante," said Toya mugging him in the face.

Joan wasn't having it and she aggressively pushed Toya. "You got me fucked up. Don't you ever put your hands on my man, bitch," said Joan.

"Fuck you bitch," Toya responded.

"Fuck you, fat bitch," said Joan throwing her drink on her.

"I'm going to kill you, move Dante," said Toya trying to get to Joan, but he held her back.

Then some other guys helped to keep the two women separated. Lady Ray came over to get her friend because she saw the commotion. "Dante, what did you do to Toya?" Lady Ray questioned him.

"His bitch right there threw her drink on me. Take me home, Lady Ray, and I'm fucking you up Dante. Girlfriend, this is hardly over," said Toya. She was mad and her stained outfit told it all. Lady Ray grabbed her and they started to walk off.

"Girl, bye," said Joan giving her the middle finger. Joan looked at Dante and said, "Dante, have you been fucking that fat bitch?"

"I used to mess with her way before you. She's obsessed with me," said Dante.

"You must have eaten her pussy real good then and who pussy you haven't ate around here?" Joan asked him.

"Now, you're tripping real hard," said Dante and he saw Eva making her way towards them.

"You think? Na'll you are, I'm not on fighting these bitches, because you sucking their guts out and shit," said Joan.

"Just worry about you and come on," as he grabbed her arm and she yanked away from him, because she saw the mother of his children coming too.

"Now I wonder what this heifer wants," Joan said loudly.

Eva pulled up and stared Joan down. Joan put her hands on her hips. "What?" asked Joan.

"Don't even go there little girl. Dante, we need to talk, now," said Eva.

"Little girl, you must have forgotten who I am, Eva," said Joan.

"Nothing to me, nor him. Didn't he dismiss you on your eighteenth birthday? He helped saved you and you're still sweating him. We are getting back together Joan, so don't even sweat it," said Eva.

"Is this true, Dante?" Joan asked him.

He looked at her and she looked back at Eva. "It doesn't matter because I have his name tattooed on my back," said Joan.

"Yeah dumb little girl, you'll just be scarred for life because I'll have his last name and my name is tattooed on his ring finger," said Eva.

Joan looked at him again with a surprised look on her face.

"Dante, is this so?" Joan asked him. He didn't answer her and she looked at his finger which had a ring.

"Remove the ring, Dante," said Joan.

"Yeah, Bootie, remove the ring and show this little girl," said Eva. He did and Joan saw that Eva's name was tattooed on his finger. She started crying and hit Dante in his chest. "I hate you, Dante, I hate you," said Joan running off.

"Don't run little girl, I also have his baby," said Eva giving a fake laugh.

"Now to you, Negro, when are we moving in together like you promised me. You know the house in the suburb? Khalani and I already picked out a house in West Chester," said Eva

"Soon, Eva," said Dante.

"And you need to get your shit together, because I'm not on it once we move in together and get married again. The bitches get them out of your system," said Eva.

"Okay, Eva, I hear you and I'll be over to your place after this is over," said Dante.

"Where are you going now? Khalani and I have a table over there and DaSheila is with us. you might as well come on over there so we can be a happy family," said Eva.

"You know I'm with the wedding party, Eva," said Dante.

"Fuck them, you were in the wedding and now it's over. Your daughter's ad I would like to spend some time with you, hell you're always up under them," said Eva with a sincere look on her face.

"But um, um," said Dante lost for words. Eva cut in. "But um nothing you need to respect me and your daughters and be a little more responsible, you've already been out of their lives long enough so come on and be the father I know you can be," said Eva taking him by the hand. He looked up at the wedding party and P-Diddy pointed at him and Dante shrugged his shoulders walking off with Eva.

Keisha and her friend Keva went over to the wedding party to say hello to Delight and everyone else. Her friend Keva was a plus sized woman with a redbone complexion and light freckles. She was cute and she caught P-Diddy's eye, but he already knew her from her friend Keyana that he used to be involved with. They laughed and celebrated with the friendly faces that surrounded them.

****

Antwan and Jasmine was on the dance floor dancing to 'Planet Rock' being mixed with Mariah Carey's 'Touch My Body' and they were hugged up with each other. Antwan received a text from Will Edmond so he looked at his BlackBerry.

The text read, "We are about to come in." Antwan thought he had secured his cellphone after reading the text, but he accidentally dropped it. He whispered in Jasmine's ear. "The police are coming; the police are coming." She smiled at him not saying a word. She really didn't like the idea of him setting Smack out to dry with the police. Then suddenly it was a lot of commotion at the entrance way of the facility. RENU agent's and Sheriffs rushed the reception. They immediately told the D.J. to shut the music off. Will Edmond stood in the middle of the floor and the other police pushed the crowd back a little. He stared up at the wedding party looking for Smack.

"Sorry folks, but we came here to arrest one person amongst you that has an outstanding warrant," said Will Edmond.

Everyone who was associated with any illegal activity was on the edge knowing their number could be called.

"Oh, by the way, congratulations to you, Simmion and your lovely new wife, Delight, but I'm sorry that you, my friend, are under arrest for the sell, distribution and shipment of an unknown narcotic we believe to be Black Ice in Hamilton County," said Edmond.

"What? You are some low down dirty mother fuckers," said Delight standing up. She was in an outrage knowing the cops were on some bullshit.

"Sheriff, can you please place Mr. Simmion Boyd under arrest and don't forget to read him his rights because his lawyer is present. He's going downtown, D.J. can you play us some traveling music?" said Will Edmond with a smirk.

Smack just had a warm expression on his face and he downed his glass of Remy along with the champagne he had in front of him.

Everyone else who probably had warrants was at ease, but was wondering what was really going on.

Two Sheriff's grabbed him up from his seat and obtained the tuxedo jacket on the back of his chair. They searched him thoroughly along with the jacket. They found the small bag of pills in his inside pocket. The Sheriff who searched the jacket held the pills up to Will.

"Here it is," said the Sheriff. "Take him down, Bob," said Will Edmond.

Smack turned to the Sheriff while the other one was cuffing him and said, "That's not mine, someone is trying to set me up."

Delight began to cry. "This can't be happening, not on my wedding day," she said.

She tried to touch him, but the Sheriff's yanked him away from her touch.

"Smack?" she said breaking down in more tears. Her sister Heather and Elicia came to comfort her. "It's going to be alright, Delight," said Heather rubbing her back.

"Yes, Delight, he'll get out," said Elicia.

"We'll be right behind you cuss," Larro shouted out.

Delight looked up at Larro and said, "There's no need for us to go down there, because he won't have a bond because today is Saturday."

Smack's mom and aunt was in disbelief knowing that one day his lifestyle would lead to this, but no one wanted it to be on his wedding day.

Delight's wedding was becoming a nightmare, a day she would want gone now that her husband was being charged for his involvement. She told him to get out the game. They were set to go to Aruba, but it would be post-pone until further notice. Rainell started crying and even Miesha shed a tear that she quickly erased from her cheek.

****

The reception ended moments after Smack's arrest. Everyone left in bunches going home or to The Garage, Rhino's, Jellies and other known clubs in the area that was still open. P-Diddy, Worm, Kyle and Weezy stayed back to help Delight gather all their wedding gifts and to escort her home. It was plenty of food and drinks left that they hauled in the stretch Hummer to Delight and Smack's house. Elicia and Heather went to so they could keep her company. Miesha had to go because Worm went also. Before they left the Torque, one of the cleanup guys found a BlackBerry phone and gave it to Delight. She put it away thinking it belonged to one of the guests and they would come looking for the expensive phone that was lost.

It was complete silence in the house and Delight went straight to their bedroom lying across the bed in her gown crying. Heather was right by her side. "Delight it's going to be okay, don't be down like this and think about the baby you're carrying. You don't need the extra stress," said Heather.

"Heather, my wedding day though, my man is in the county jail. We are supposed to be flying to Aruba in the morning. I should be fucking him right now, not lying here by myself all alone it's not right, it's just not right," said Delight.

"Delight, you know and I know this might have happened because of his involvement in the streets," said Heather.

"Heather, you're right, but he quit the streets so he could have a life with me and his unborn child," said Delight trying to muzzle her hurt.

"So, what now, Delight?" Heather asked her.

"Something isn't right, Heather, I can feel it. He was set up. I know he was, because he wouldn't be carrying anything on him, he's not that careless he don't even bring anything here. He keeps that shit out there. Someone planted whatever the police found, but whom? I'm downtown first thing in the morning," said Delight taking off her wedding gown.

"I'm going with you. My brother-in-law is down there," said Heather.

"What about your job, Heather?" Delight asked her.

"Fuck that job. I'm tired of Simon Says anyway," said Heather. That comment brought a smile to Delight even though she was upset.

****

Dante and Eva took Ruthy and Carmen over to Fox's apartment at the Four Towers. He escorted the two ladies to Fox's front door and they could see where someone damaged the door and tried to fix it. Ruthy knocked on the door. Fox came to the door all sluggish and answered the knock by saying. "Who is it?" It was in a low tone.

"Girl, it's me and Carmen. Open the door," said Ruthy. The knob slightly turned and the cracking from the broken door hinges made a loud noise. It finally opened and the slender Sanya McKinney a.k.a. fox stood before them.

She had on a red spaghetti nightgown that was very revealing to the eye, a scarf and her eyes were blood shot red with stain.

"Girl, what happened to you? I've been trying to call you all night and we missed the wedding," said Ruthy.

"I know, someone broke in and robbed me when I was about to leave out the door, they kicked it in and took the stuff I was holding for Smack. They said they were going to kill me if I didn't cooperate," said Fox.

"Did they hurt you? Are you alright? Did you call the police?" Carmen asked being concerned.

"No, I didn't call the police and no they didn't hurt me, Carmen. They just shook me up a little. Now if you all will excuse me, I'm tired and just would like to go to sleep," said Fox standing there trying not to fall over.

"Hold up, Fox, did you see what they looked like?" Dante asked her.

"No, because they had on masks and waving big guns," said Fox rolling her eyes at him.

"Well the police got Smack at his wedding reception about an hour ago and shit is all fucked up," said Dante.

Her eyes moved in a milli-second and formed salty tears of hurt and pain. One tear followed another as she turned and ran to her bedroom leaving them standing at the door.

Carmen and Ruthy ran after her. "Fox!" They both called her name.

Dante was clueless all he could think was that she was still sleeping with Smack.

"Damn is she still fucking Smack, too?" he asked himself.

****

In Mt. Adams looking over Cincinnati, Jasmine occupied a condo close by where Judge Phil Helmet lived. She and Antwan were lying in the bed. Antwan was resting his eyes and Jasmine was wide awake. He opened his eyes and ran his fingers down her cheek.

"After all the excitement today, I thought you'd be exhausted as well," said Antwan.

He smiled at her and his face boyish from sleep. "I'm just thinking about the day and how it turned out," Jasmine confessed a weary smile on her lips. He released her face and said, "I think Will had a blast, especially seeing the look on Simmion's face," He studied her.

"Is there something wrong Jas, you seem so quiet?" said Antwan. She shrugged her shoulders and replied, "I'm fine, I wish today could go on forever."

"True romance doesn't last forever and I think I know that better than most," he snorted.

"And that's why you have to make the best of what you have. The RENU agents seized the day," said Antwan with a fake laugh a more undesirable laugh.

"I think we did that today, Antwan, without a doubt and we seized the night as well," said Jasmine. He smiled and nipped at her breast and aggressively sucked one nipple coming up for air.

"I think we did, too, but it's hard to make everybody happy. Do you think we can do without Simmion, Jas? I mean I'm not that stupid, I know you like the Herr, you've had those eyes on him all the time we were in China," said Antwan.

"That's not true, Antwan, my heart goes out to Delight. Her world is now crushed. She feels the same way that I would if something drastic would happen to you, my love," said Jasmine.

"There's no room for sympathy, Jas. It is what it is, we must remain focused. I know life isn't fair at all," said Antwan.

She released a bitter sweet laugh. "So, you want more, Antwan?" she asked him.

"Jasmine, I always want more," said Antwan growling rolling over on top of her pining her beneath him. She looked up at him with lust in her eyes. Then he kissed her stroking her with a passionate kiss. She knew it was for him to set Simmion up with the police, but how could she go against him? Only a fool would contest the sick mind of Antwan Klein. She settled for his touch instead. "Antwan make love to me," she said sexy in his ear. He gently nudged her legs apart so he could enter her passage.

****

Keisha and Kendall were sitting in the living room of their home and she was trying to explain to him what took place at the wedding reception. Kendall was getting the best news ever, better than when Keisha first told him she was pregnant.

"Kendall, it was crazy they just busted up in the Torque and grabbed Simmion. Delight was delirium and I feel so bad for her," said Keisha.

"For what? That's what she wanted a drug dealing little punk. She got him and that's what she deserves...she'll be alright. It couldn't have happened to some better people," said Kendall.

"Kendall, that's messed up to say and on her wedding day, too? And you don't have any sympathy for her at all?" said Keisha.

"Yes, I do, just not for them," said Kendall smiling.

"That's messed up, Kendall, I wonder what you'll do if I were in the same boat after having your child and I need your help after we broke up. You would treat me cold and be distant huh?" said Keisha.

"It depends," he said and she cut him off. "Depends on what, Kendall?"

"What we broke up for," he said.

"Kendall, you never amaze me with the shit you say out of your mouth. I'm going to bed," said Keisha getting up from the sofa. She was very upset at him and she knew he was being selfish, not only to the mother of his oldest child, but to her as well.

"Can we have sex, Keisha?" he yelled out to her.

"I have a headache; do what you do best jack-off Negro," she yelled back to him going up the stairs.

CHAPTER TWENTY-FOUR
EVERYTHING COMES TO THE LIGHT

The next day, Larro, Bo-Gotti, Chill, and Freaky D were in the hospital visiting D$Boy. D$Boy baby mom Timberland and his mom was there as usual. D$Boy couldn't talk; he just looked around at his partners. His memory was not perfect, but he could identify who they were. He knew whatever the case was he was being loved by many.

****

Delight had on a dazzling Armani skirt and suit jacket which was dark blue and some two-tone blue and white Cole Haan shoes. Her hair was stylish and cute like the day before. Heather had on her work uniform as they walked into the Justice Center to see Smack.

There was no visiting on Sundays to the public, but she could have a special visit being she was his lawyer. He was located on the 2nd floor and was still in his street clothes to await court Monday morning for arraignment.

He came from one of the pods looking tired. He saw Delight and she gave him a soft smile. He walked up on her and they hugged and then kissed momentarily. They both sat down at one of the tables and Heather stood guard by them.

"Smack, what are they saying, baby?" Delight asked him.

"Someone planted the drug on me and the RENU bastards are talking about I'm the one behind this new drug movement, the master mind. They say that they have a star witness to take me down, but who?" asked Smack.

"It's probably one of those Belvy Boyz, they are grimy as fuck. All of them want to be on your status, nigga," said Heather while snapping her fingers.

"She's right baby, you can't rule anyone out, from the Belvy Boyz to your cousin and his click, Kyle, Miesha even guys from your past," said Delight.

"Bitches too, they be hating," said Heather.

"I know ya'll, I know," said Smack putting his head down.

It was funny, because none of them even thought about Antwan, why? Was it because he was the one who was behind the Black Ice for real?

Why would he set Smack up knowing Smack could flip it on him easily?

"Well tomorrow is court, hopefully they'll give you a bond, but don't count on it. I'll handle everything so don't worry and it will come to the light, baby. Are you hungry?" said Delight.

"A little," said Smack.

"Okay, because Heather's friend is working and they will get you whatever you want to eat," said Delight.

"That's cool, you be careful. I want you to put the money in that one spot in the other one, because I know they'll probably hit the house. The house is paid for and the cars are secured where they can't seize anything," said Smack.

"Okay, honey," said Delight touching his hand gently.

"Brother-in-law, I'm right here for you also. I'll bring you a cell phone tomorrow just in case they don't give you a bond, that way you can keep in contact with us while you're down here keeping them out of your business," said Heather looking around to see if anyone was coming.

"Heather, I can't have you losing your job on account of me," said Smack.

"Brother-in-law fuck this job; I'll do anything to help my sister get her man back. Her happiness is worth it and plus she's all I got. If you are in here that means I'll have to hear her whining and shit and I don't want to hear it, been there done that," said Heather with a fake laugh of her own.

"Well honey, I'm about to go and play detective and see who knows what, so I can get you out of here," said Delight looking him in his eyes.

They stared at each other for a long moment and Heather saw that her sister had the same lustful look she would have when she was horny for a man. She stepped away from them to tell her friend, Robyn, who was on duty that her sister and new brother-in-law was going to the back room and handle a little business. Robyn and Heather came back around to where Delight and Smack were sitting and they were still holding hands.

"Look you two, ya'll go ahead to the back and handle whatever business is needed. I guess the honeymoon will be in the Justice Center instead of Aruba," said Heather.

"Ya'll need to hurry up because the Sgt. is making rounds in about an hour," said Robyn.

****

Elicia and Kyle were back at Delight and Smack's house having an intimate moment in the mini-theater. A desire that a woman wants for her partner to convict the heart. A title of devotion in a flexible cradle of love and Elicia panted as Kyle caressed her breast. Her nipples were reddish brown from her light skin complexion and they stood erect directing all her nerves to that area. He manifested hunger as he lapped his tongue over and over her nipples. It was a pleasure principle deriving within her.

"Wait Kyle, not in my friend's home." Elicia begged him to stop, knowing this is what she wanted.

"No one will find out Elicia, they are downtown and Rainell is at her friend's house," said Kyle.

"Kyle, let's just wait, I don't think I'm ready," as she gently pushed him away from her.

"Okay Elicia, you're right let's wait because I don't just want you for the moment, I want you forever," said Kyle and it melted her. She placed her hand on one side of his face. "Kyle, that's so sweet, come here baby."

She kissed him and her eyes began to water. She put her bra and shirt back on and they returned upstairs and to their surprise Delight was home in the kitchen eating a piece of chicken. She looked at Elicia and smiled at her shaking her head.

Heather had gone home to entertain her daughters who were in town.

Elicia put her hands on her hips and tilted her head a little and said, "What?"

"Nothing girl, you want some chicken?" Delight asked her.

"No thanks, so what did he say?" Elicia asked her.

"We don't know much at this point, but someone set him up. They put the drugs in his tuxedo jacket," said Delight licking her lips.

"That's fucked up, but who would do such a thing?" Kyle asked.

"We don't know Kyle, that's what we are trying to figure out," said Delight.

"No clue, no suspects?" Elicia asked her childhood friend.

"In Smack's eyes everyone is a suspect, including me," said Delight and she saw the look on Elicia and Kyle's face. They were wondering now why would Smack suspect his wife would set him up? Kyle was now wondering if Smack thought he had a motive behind it.

"Are you serious, Delight?" Elicia asked her to be sure.

"Yes, I'm serious Elicia, but that's okay. I know I didn't have anything to do with it."

Delight looked up at them still eating her chicken. She wiped her hands and caught Kyle getting a little uneasy. His body language changed and Delight noticed it.

"Kyle, are you okay honey?" Delight asked him.

"Yeah, I'm cool. Well, I need to go and change clothes...you know, freshen up a bit. Also, I need to get out in the streets and see what I can find out," said Kyle.

"Okay, Kyle, if you find something out be sure to let me know," said Delight.

"I will, Delight, and Elicia, can I see you later?" Kyle looked Elicica in her eyes.

"Sure Kyle, I'll be here with Delight," Elicia told him and then she kissed Kyle on the lips. Delight was in shock and held her drumstick in her hand with her mouth open. She was still looking at Elicia when Kyle made his exit. Elicia looked at her and didn't say a word. Delight came back to reality and asked her friend, "Ms. Thang, I know you didn't give him any that quick. You been fucking in my house, heifer? You're a bad girl, Elicia. You need a spanking," said Delight shaking her head and giving her a grin.

"Delight, no I haven't. We just talked and kissed a little, nothing more and nothing less.   Kyle is a sweetheart," said Elicia.

"You better watch that nigga, he might steal your heart, because he's a good thief...be careful," said Delight with a laugh.

"I will Delight," said Elicia thinking about the warmth she shared with Kyle. She added, "But are you serious about Smack thinking you might have set him up?"

"I just put that out there for Kyle to go run and tell everyone else, but he's not ruling any of them out," said Delight.

"That's messed up for someone to do him like that especially that he was getting out the game," said Elicia.

"I know Elicia, but whoever's behind this didn't want him to get out the game. They are some haters...straight haters," said Delight.

"Who would want that, for a black man to not get out the game?" Elicia asked her.

"That's a good question, Elicia," said Delight.

****

"Listen up, I just got off the phone with Kyle. Smack was set up and he's not ruling anyone out; not even his wife and I know any of us wasn't behind this right. We need to find out, because dude was good to us, so let's return the favor," said P-Diddy to the Belvy Boyz.

****

The next morning, Delight, Elicia and Kyle was at Smack's arraignment downtown inside the Justice Center. Delight was representing her husband.

"Your Honor, we are requesting a reasonable bond and my client can be placed on a monitoring box," said Delight.

"I'm looking over Simmion Boyd's record and you have two felony convictions and these six pending felony charges, bond denied, no bond, bailiff," said the sitting Judge

"But Judge," as Delight tried to plead her case, but he cut her off, "Next case please."

The Judge called out to the court. Smack went with the bailiff. Delight yelled out to him.

"I'll be to see you in a few."

Elicia, Kyle and Delight walked out of the courtroom and Delight was agitated. Her hormones were raging badly. She was now faced with reality that her husband may never get out. She would have to raise a newborn child all alone. Is life fair? Who could she turn to for peace, God? She knew she had to get on her knees and call on the Lord.

****

That Wednesday the Belvy Boyz, Diamond Cut, Heather, Miesha, Elicia and Kyle were at Delight's place along with her daughter and her friend, Daysha.

Elicia had been there since the wedding and they were trying to solve the unsolved mystery that loomed over them. Who was behind the plot? Delight had prayed and prayed for an answer and today she would get an answer.

P-Diddy was trying to call Antwan to see if he heard anything, but as usual for the last three days he received no answer. He would have to leave him a message. The BlackBerry was vibrating on the kitchen counter where it had been for three days. Rainell and Daysha was in the kitchen eating while everyone else was in the basement trying to brainstorm about the situation at hand.

Daysha kept hearing the phone buzzing and asked Rainell, "What's that noise, Rainell?"

"That phone on the counter, it's been vibrating for three days now," said Rainell.

"Whose phone is it?" Daysha asked her.

"I don't know, it's probably one of theirs downstairs," said Rainell.

"They probably don't know it's up here and someone is calling them, it may be important Rainell," said Daysha.

"You're right, Daysha, I'll take it downstairs," said Rainell.
She grabbed the cell phone off the counter and it took it down the steps. The phone was still vibrating in her hand. She reached the basement to see lonely and confused faces. Delight saw her first and said, "What's wrong, Rainell? I told you that we grown people are talking in privacy," said Delight.
Rainell put her hands on her hips and replied, "I know mama, but someone left their phone in the kitchen and it keeps going off. Mama, I know what's going on...I'm not a baby anymore," said Rainell. She looked at her daughter and said, "Give me the phone."
Rainell handed her the phone and Delight held it in the air. "Is anyone missing a phone?"
Everyone checked for their phone and no one was missing one. P-Diddy was still trying to call Antwan's phone. The phone started vibrating in Delight's hand and then she remembered that one of the guys on the cleaning crew found the phone and gave it to her at the reception.
"Oh, this is the phone that was found at the reception and given to me. Someone is trying to call it now," said Delight.
"Well answer it. It may be the person to whom it belongs to," said P-Diddy while holding his phone to his ear hoping Antwan would pick up. She answered it. "Hello." Her voice echoed and another voice came through the receiver. "Hello, hello."
"Yes, who are you looking for?" Delight asked the person on the other end.
P-Diddy was just looking at her because the question she asked was in his ear.
He closed his phone and said, "Delight, that's Antwan's phone." She closed the BlackBerry, but before doing so she saw that he had several missed calls.
"He must have lost it at the reception and he has about thirty missed calls and text messages," said Delight.
"Check his text messages, girl," said Heather always being nosy.
"I'm not going through his phone Heather, you're nosy as hell," said Delight.
"hand it here and I'll do it," said Heather taking the phone from her sister.

Heather hit a few buttons on the phone and read a few incoming messages out loud.

"Dis P-Diddy, give me a call ASAP."

The next one she read said, "Everything went as planned, Antwan."

Then Heather scrolled through his previous messages. She couldn't believe her eyes.

"Ooh wee, ya'll ain't gonna believe this shit here, Delight look girl."

Delight grabbed the phone and read the message out loud.

"We just caught Fox and she's writing a statement on Simmion."

"So what Heather, what does that mean?" said Delight.

"Simmion, Delight? Go to the next text that Antwan sent out," said Heather.

She went to the outgoing messages and clicked it and it read.

"Good, now you can raid the wedding reception tonight. I managed to place the drugs inside his tuxedo pocket," Delight close the phone and said, "Thank you, Jesus, thank you." She shed a tear and added, "Why that double-crossing low life M.F. I don't believe this shit, Smack is going to flip out when I tell him this," said Delight.

Only Heather knew what she had read, because she didn't read it out loud.

"What, Delight?" P-Diddy asked her.

"It was Antwan's punk ass, he set my husband up. He put the drugs in his pocket. who's the Fox? The person that texted him said they caught a Fox and she wrote a statement on Simmion," said Delight.

"Antwan must be dealt with by the way of the streets," said Dante.

"Right, that mother-fucker has to die no other way," said Larro.

"But who's this star witness that wrote the statement?" Heather asked out loud and all eyes turned to Miesha.

She immediately came to her own defense. "Don't start looking at me, it wasn't me! I did that stupid thing once and I have made up for it," said Miesha.

"Wait a minute; you said they mentioned they caught a fox? When I dropped Ruthy and Carmen off at Fox's apartment to check on her after the reception and her door was fucked up like someone used a force of entry. She told me she was home invaded like I told ya'll, but she wasn't all hysterical and shit like someone whose had their space invaded," said Dante.

"what are you saying, Dante?" P-Diddy asked him.

"I'm saying she didn't act like someone had her at gun point fearing for her life. She didn't look like she'd been crying and when I told her that the police got Smack, the bitch took off to her room crying," said Dante.

"you think she's the one who's the star witness, Dante?" Delight asked him.

"It's a strong possibility, Delight," said Dante.

"Well you, Worm and Vino go and holla at her while me, P-Diddy, Larro, Bo-Gotti, Chill and Weezy go pay Mr. Antwan a visit. Kobe, Bodean, Kyle and Freaky D, ya'll stay here until you hear from one of us," said Kekou directing traffic.

"Ya'll be careful out there and I'll tell Smack what's going on when he calls me on the cell phone that Heather gave him," said Delight rubbing her arms.

Delight was with whatever they planned for Antwan and she didn't care if they ended his life. Hell, he tried to end hers by setting up her husband. Everyone went to their assigned destination and Delight was crying tears of joy rocking back and forth on the sofa in the living room waiting on Smack to call her. The women sat in the living room. Heather, Elicia and Miesha helped her ease her pain by cracking jokes.

"Girl, you gonna get your young dick back, quit crying," said Elicia.

"Yeah, Delight, he's going to be back in between those thighs real soon," Miesha added.

"See bitch, that's why I don't be bothered with that lovey dovey shit, I fuck nigga's like a sport, dick on call from a variety of sources. But he'll be back so man up bitch," said Heather.

Delight couldn't do nothing, but laugh at their comments. They cheered her up for the most part.

Miesha didn't come on her menstrual cycle yet and she was kind of feeling uneasy around Delight, but she didn't let it show. She would find out Friday at her doctor's appointment whether she was pregnant or not.

****

Dante, Worm and Vino were standing outside of apartment number seven waiting for Fox to answer the door. It took her a long time before she opened the door. They could tell the door was still messed up from it cracking. She had on a nightgown and had sleep in her eyes, her hair was messy and she looked a hot mess.

"What up ya'll? I'm glad to see you Dante, I know you got something good for the Fox, I'll fuck all three of ya'll for some of those pink pills or some blow," said Fox.

Dante was mad just from looking at her. "Get yo ass in the house, girl look at you and this house, it has never looked like this and it stinks, hell you stink," as they stepped in her apartment. Dante saw a glass instrument in her ashtray and that meant one thing, she was getting high off of crack cocaine.

"You're smoking that shit now, Fox?" Dante asked her and he was hot under the collar. He was furious and he slapped her in the face.

"Fuck you, Dante, I'm grown and I can do whatever I want to. Come here Vino, I'll suck your dick better than my cousin Trice, if you give me some of those pills," said Fox trying to pull on him. He just looked at her and said, "I'm good Fox, why are you letting yourself go like this?"

"Shit is fucked up and a bitch ain't got shit to live for anymore," as she broke down and started crying.

"Oh shit, Fox, you got that green monkey? You got that man down disease?" Worm asked her with much concern.

She couldn't take it anymore. She had to tell them what she did to Smack.

"No Worm, I don't have AIDS, but I did some bullshit. Imagine a bitch that's thorough like me going out like a sucker. The police kicked the door in and they knew Smack had some shit over here. They threatened to take my son away from me and I love my son and I love Smack, too. I wrote a statement on him. They were talking about ten years in Marysville and I can't do that much time not now, so go ahead and kill me, I deserve to die," as she cried even more tears.

"Ain't nobody gonna kill your ass, Puff and Yvette will never forgive us," said Worm.

"Yeah, I'm not going to let anyone do nothing to you, but you'll have to disappear until Smack's case is over, but where?" Dante asked.

"My aunt lives in Dallas, Texas," as you could hear her sniffling.

"Okay," as Dante grabbed her face and said, "Sanya, I care about you and love you, but if you surface and testify against Smack, I won't be able to protect you from them. Do you understand me?" Dante looked her in the eyes and she shook her head "yes" and was frightened. She knew he wasn't lying about the words he spoke from his mouth. Her tears were huge as they ran down her cheek. "Now go in there and clean yourself up and this house. I'll be back to see you later," said Dante.

MEANWHILE up in Clifton, P-Diddy, Kekou, Weezy, Larro, Bo-Gotti and Chill were at the restaurant. Antwan's 500 Mustang and BMW Z-4 were in the parking lot. They all were carrying automatic weapons, because P-Diddy had already told them that Antwan was a dangerous man. To their surprise Jasmine greeted them at the entrance.

"Hello gentleman, what can I do for you today," Jasmine asked them with a smile.

"Jasmine, where's Antwan?" P-Diddy asked her.

"He's out of the country at the moment in China getting everything prepared for you, I suppose. He should be back next week. Why? Is something wrong?" she asked him.

"Nothing is wrong, we just have a small problem, but we can handle it," said Kekou.

"Have ya'll heard anything with Simmion?" she asked them.

"Yeah, your man's a snitch," said Larro under his breath where she couldn't really hear him.

"Excuse me, I couldn't quite hear what you said," said Jasmine.

"We haven't heard anything, but you work down there and I'm sure you can find out something for us," said P-Diddy looking her dead in her eyes. Jasmine got aroused by his strong voice and stare, she began to get moist.

"My eyes and ears will be open and I'll keep in touch. Would ya'll like lunch, it's on the house?" said Jasmine trying to calm herself down.

"No thanks, Jasmine, just tell Antwan we stopped by and I've been trying to call him," said P-Diddy.

"P-Diddy, he lost his phone so give me your number and I'll pass it on to him," said Jasmine in a seductive voice.

****

Everyone reported back to the house with nothing that would satisfy Delight. She hoped that Antwan would be dead. She blurted out.

"Next week, he'll be back next week? Fuck that my skies are falling down in my face and I'm sure his is too."

"Delight, be patient," said Miesha.

"Fuck that, Miesha, when I see him, I'll pull the trigger myself," said Delight wanted her own justice.

"Delight, I might have a better idea. Tomorrow, we will take a ride and give Mr. Antwan a taste of his own medicine," said Miesha.

"What do you have in mind, Miesha?" Delight asked her. She came over to where Delight was sitting and whispered in her ear and everyone else was just looking at her. Miesha thought it was the least she could do after sleeping with her man in her house.

The next day Delight and Miesha stood in front of the person who would make her life easier and give her justice in the streets. She didn't care she was going against the Belvy Boyz and Diamond Cut's wishes. Smack wouldn't approve of her actions either, but she did it anyway.

"Delight, are you sure you want to do this?" The person asked her and she stood firm and strong. "Yes, I'm positive Steve O'Hara. Here's a picture of us in China and at our house. Antwan is the bald head one with the goatee. He's the one behind the Black Ice and bringing it to the U.S., Simmion's involvement is minor."

Delight didn't feel indispensable at all and explained that they were not indiscrete at all.

Steve O'Hara knew that Will Edmond and Allen Taylor were crooked cops and were investigating the RENU unit in Cincinnati. It would be triumphant to bring down the RENU unit and Antwan Klein.

Delight had told him everything she knew that Smack told her. She told him all about Antwan's private study at the restaurant and his office in Jillian's. She also told him how the Black Ice was getting into the U.S. which she didn't actually and made it up, but it sounded good to her.

"So Miesha, you've been hiding real good, the Judge has been worried sick about you," said O'Hara.

"No, he hasn't and he probably wants me dead," said Miesha.

O'Hara raised an eyebrow and said. "Just stay out of sight. I don't know what he's up to, but I haven't seen you," he winked at her.

"Steve, when will you take Antwan down?" Delight asked him rubbing her arm.

"You said he was in China now, right. So as soon as he returns, we will raid his premises, okay," said O'Hara.

"Okay, well you have a nice day and if anything comes to mind, I'll give you a call," said Delight.

"You ladies do the same and Delight that was very brave of you and a wise decision you made," said O'Hara.

They looked passed the agreement and was relying on the pre-ignition of the situation and Antwan was about to feel the raft.

****

Worm, Dante and Big Tom picked up Fox to take her to the airport so she could board a one-way flight to Dallas, Texas. She was going to visit her aunt for a long time. She let her mom, Ms. Delores a.k.a. thirty-eight special care for her son while she would be away. Big Tom was a close friend of the Belvy Boyz from back in the day when they were just hustling on Hewitt Avenue out their grandfather's house. When they use to do unlimited things in the streets, they would call on Big Tom to do the dirty work. They use to call him the "Rock Man" on Burnett Avenue in Avondale.

They were riding in Worm's truck with tinted windows. Dante was driving while Worm and Big Tom sat in the back. Big Tom sat behind the passenger seat and Worm was behind the driver's seat. Fox got in the truck after Dante secured her luggage in the back of the truck. "What up, Worm and how are you doing?" Fox spoke to Worm and Big Tom. She never saw Big Tom before and was now wondering what he was doing with them. It spooked her out. "What up Fox, I see you are looking like your old self. You good?" asked Worm.

"I'm good now that I'm not thinking about ya'll killing me anymore," said Fox laughing a little.

"Fox, you are silly as hell. You know Dante isn't having that shit," said Worm.

"Yeah, you are tripping. You know I won't let anything happen to my Foxy Lady," said Dante pulling off from the Four Towers. They were going down Queen City going back towards the highway and Fox was still wondering who Big Tom was.

"Dante, who is your friend? I've never seen him before," said Fox pointing to the back seat.

"Who, him? Oh, that's Big Tom, he's flying down there with you to make sure you get there safe," said Dante.

"I'll be fine flying by myself, Dante," said Fox.

"Are you sure, Fox?" Dante asked her.

"Yes, I'm positive," said Fox as they were merging up under the bridge that would take them to the I-75 southbound. Big Tom reached around Fox's neck with a skinny rope and started strangling her. She was kicking and gasping for air while pulling at the rope and looking over at Dante asking for help. Dante almost wrecked. "Help me, help me," said Fox in panic. Dante pulled over on the highway and said, "You big dummy, why didn't you wait until we reached the airport, as planned? You had to do it in front of me, Big Tom?" asked Dante.

"It was the perfect time," said Big Tom with a husky voice.

"You almost killed us idiot...are you ignorant?" Dante asked him. Worm had burst out laughing at Big Tom from Dante calling him ignorant.

"Shut up fat boy or you can be next," said Big Tom.

"I'll shoot your ass dead, old D-Bo looking ass nigga," said Worm.

"Both of ya'll quit tripping," said Dante looking over at Fox's lifeless body. "That was my girl; she had some bomb ass head on her. Big Tom, where did you get that idea?" Dante asked him.

"I saw that shit on the Last Don, when dude strangled the bitch in the limo for Cross," said Big Tom.

"Fuck it, it's done. That's all that matters, now let's dump the body," said Dante.

****

That Friday, Miesha found out that she was indeed pregnant and her mind was filled with extreme thoughts of having the baby. Her first child and she knew it was Smack's child. Her warm smile adjusted to a fumigated frown knowing that Smack wouldn't accept them, especially after saying "I do" two weeks ago.

She was disturbed and willing to sacrifice everything just to have this baby. She liked Delight and she knew the news would crush her world even more, not because she was pregnant, but who the father was. Miesha didn't care, she would tell Smack whether he accepted it or not. She was having this baby and abortion was not an option.

CHAPTER TWENTY-FIVE
THE BIG STING

Antwan had returned from China and Steve O'Hara and his agent got word he was back in the country. They had set up a sting to capture him and bring him down. It would be a commercial balance, but a brilliant plan to unarm him to a ripple. The music was loud in Jillian's and Pat Benatar, *"Love is a Battlefield"* was playing in his office.

The Feds had two groups of men set up, one at the restaurant in Clifton and the other over at Jillian's. Steve O'Hara was with the group over at Jillian's in Kentucky.

Steve O'Hara made the call for the group to raid the restaurant. Antwan was in his office at Jillian's smoking a blunt looking over some paper work for the establishment.

Steve O'Hara had the Covington police department to assist with the raid. When they hit the doors of the club, there was instant gun play. One of the security guards turned fire on the agents shooting one in the leg. He didn't have a chance as three 40 caliber bullets ripped through his large frame. Antwan just so happened to look up at his monitors to see the forces coming into his establishment.

He was high, but managed to grab his Heckler & Koch and two extra clips out of his desk. The Alphabet Boys were on alternate angles and from the adrenaline Antwan felt like he had angina pectoris. He had moved codify off the door and headed for the trap door. He made it shooting several police on the way. He knew the terror was coming for him, elite of thirsty individuals. It was only after the fact that one thought about it, after that it would've been a closer call. No matter how common sense it was or now impersonal Antwan believed one only gets so many chances and death will be cheated only so many times. He was not a fatalist thinking lives were ruled by statistics, so he just pretended that life was a roller-coaster ride full of excitement. He made his way through the adjustable double doors that led him to a hidden garage and he ran into Chantell.

"What's going on, Antwan? Why are we being raided?" she asked him.

"I don't know, but I need to get out of here, now," said Antwan.
"Go and I'll hold them off," said Chantell.
"That's a good girl," as he kissed her long and hard. He released
her and you could see the tears forming in the corner of her eyes.
"I love you, Antwan," she confessed holding a MP-5 and Antwan
looked at her one more time and kept it moving. He then heard
massive shots coming from her MP-5 and then he heard return
gunfire and her utters of being hit. He knew that she was dead,
because he didn't hear her gun anymore. He balled his fist tight
for the pain and the love he felt for her. He didn't get emotionally
confused still trying to get to his 500 GT Shelby Mustang.
****

A DAY BEFORE THE STING, Steve O'Hara was discussing the
plans with his commandeering chief of operations.
"Yes Steve, what do you have?" the elderly well-groomed white
man asked him.
"Sir, two women came to the office with valuable information that
was helpful. One of the women tended towards certain superiority
over both me and her friend. But it's a harder job for a woman
and that balance between authority and approachability can be
difficult to find. The interview didn't take long and it was a case of
good leads," said Steve O'Hara.
"what are we waiting for, O'Hara, Christmas?" the chief of
operations asked him.
"No sir, we are on it. We are setting up teams now to bring this
Antwan Klein guy to justice. She also told me that he was behind
the Mayor of Cincinnati, Elliott Thrasher's death," said O'Hara.
****

BEFORE DELIGHT AND MIESHA saw Steve O'Hara that day to give
him the information on Antwan, they paid Smack a visit. They
didn't have time to dwell on it and Delight had to ask him
questions and he gave her exact answers. She told him about
Antwan setting him up and he couldn't believe it.
"Why that mother-fucker, so he's behind all this bullshit," said
Smack in anger.
"Uh huh baby, but don't worry, we are handling things out here
for you. P-Diddy and Larro are going to take care of Antwan, if
you know what I mean. That girl, Fox, you know the one you

used to mess with, yeah her, she's the one who wrote the statement on you. They kicked her door in and found the drugs and she told them they belonged to you," said Delight smacking her lips.

"Unbelievable, well kick my ass," said Smack in frustration.

"I should, but not right now, I have to get you out of here first. where does Antwan keep the drugs?" Delight asked him.

"I don't actually know Delight; I think in a storage facility or probably the restaurant or the club. I know he has weapons in the restaurant though," said Smack.

"Is there anything you might be involved in on his account that you're not aware of?" Delight drilled him for more information.

"I know he killed Elliot Thrasher and that teenage girl and he has a warehouse in China and that's where the drug is being made up at and some way, he is shipping it back over here in Grippo potato chip boxes. Don't ask me how, because I don't know," said Smack.

"Okay honey, I have to go. Miesha is waiting on me downstairs," said Delight.

"Why did you ask me all those questions, Delight?" Smack asked her.

"Baby, I'm your lawyer and I need to know to fight your case properly," said Delight, but she had a hidden agenda.

"Delight?" as he looked at her knowing she was up to something.

"What?" as she gave him the big-eyed look.

"You're not telling me everything and why is Miesha with you?" he asked her in defense.

"Business, baby, strictly business, so give me a kiss and I'll talk to you later. I love you and Heather is bringing you some food that I made for you," said Delight. She got up and walked off and he watched his wife leave from the sally port of the 3rd floor in the south building of the Justice Center.

The Mustang started up and roared heavily through the garage and Steve O'Hara heard the car and knew it was probably the person they were after.

"He's in the car, let's go," said O'Hara. When they made it outside of the club a white 500 Shelby Mustang came leaping from the garage doing an enormous speed. They were in high pursuit after who they suspected to be Antwan Klein as the car turned the corner. You could hear the tires screeching and sirens as the chase began. The white Mustang was going down 12th Street flying across the bridge as its suspensions lifted off the ground for a split second. O'Hara knew this had to be Antwan, because his body wasn't found at the club by the other law enforcement doing the search.

The Mustang turned onto Madison heading towards Latonia and when the person driving the Mustang looked in his rearview mirror, he saw the flashing lights in a good distance, but he knew they were for him. He looked back again to check where they were and when he turned back around in front of him it was too late. He crashed into a train, because he drove through the yielding signs and he couldn't stop. The person in the car who was suspected to be Antwan Klein died on the spot from the impact. The Shelby Mustang blew up into flames from the crash. When O'Hara and the rest of the police who was chasing the Mustang arrived on the scene all they could do was watch the burning car. There was debris that blew everywhere as a gust of wind made the smoke rise high above the street.

Two other federal agents stood outside their car with O'Hara watching the blaze.

"I guess I'll make the report and have an interview with the news cast that's coming," said Steve O'Hara.

****

Later, that evening Jasmine and her step-brother, Will Edmond, were at her condo watching the latest news. She had been drinking and took two pills of the Black Ice trying to calm her nerves. She was grieving and the ivory in her eyes were stained red from crying. They carefully listened to the news reporter.

"*Today, the Federal agents raided two local businesses; one in Covington, Kentucky, Jillian's nightclub and Lenhardt's restaurant in Clifton. They had warrants to arrest this man,*" as they showed a picture of Antwan.

"*Antwan Klein, as known to the government officials s the Chocolate Dream a known terrorist and arms dealer from Germany who's wanted in other countries to face trial for some of the serious crimes he has committed. He was allegedly behind* the marketing of this new drug known on the streets as Black Ice, a pink pill used like a narcotic. The federal agents chased him from Jillian's down Madison to where the suspect crashed into a moving train and was pronounced dead on the scene. The Feds confiscated weapons and drugs from both establishments and more arrest are being made dealing with this matter. This is Karen Allen reporting live at Jillian's nightclub," said the reporter. "That was Karen Allen reporting live from Jillian's nightclub in Covington, Kentucky covering breaking news from channel 12 where we get the news first. We will have full coverage on this story on the 11 O'clock news."

Jasmine turned the TV off with the remote and then slamming it down on the sofa.

"William, what am I going to do, now that Antwan is dead?" asked Jasmine.

"You, what the fuck am I going to do if they link me to him?" Will asked her in a more aggressive tone.

"That's all you ever think about is yourself, no one else really matters, you selfish bastard," as she pointed her slender finger at him and her words were slurred.

"You should be worried about them asking you questions too. You're his girlfriend and a prosecutor as a matter of fact the head prosecutor for Hamilton County," said Will.

"I'm clean as the board of health. They can't link me to any of his dealings," said Jasmine.

"I know Simmion can linked you to him by association and the little trip you all took together, so be careful. I know you have money of his stashed away so you need to leave the country for a little while," said Will.

"I'm not going anywhere; I'm going to find out who's responsible for Antwan's death. I was informed about the operation hours after it happened and even though he's dead, those federal agents will pay. Antwan darling, I'll seek your revenge, I promise you," said Jasmine drinking the rest of her liquor in one big gulp.

****

P-Diddy and the rest of the Belvy Boyz were thinking ahead and instead of dumping Fox's body in the Tri-State, they had Big Tom and their cousin, Ike take her body to Dallas anyway. They told them to find a streetwalker and let her get a room at a Motel. They were to kill the streetwalker and put Fox's body with hers making it look like a double homicide and they were prostituting and they ran across a serial killer. It would probably throw the authorities off a little being she was a long way from home and she was the states star witness.

Now that the star witness was dead, Delight would have to work her magic in the courtroom. Antwan was dead and the Feds were going to give testimony on Smack's behalf that Antwan Klein was behind the operation and Smack's role was minor and was just an ordinary dealer.

RENU agents even searched the premises of Smack and Delight's home, but they came up empty handed. They did try to give them a fine for the lions.

They couldn't give them a fine because he had a permit, they weren't within city limits. Delight felt like she had done the right thing by telling O'Hara the information to bust Antwan, but she didn't really want Antwan to die. Instead she wanted him to face justice like her husband was about to. Smack's trial date was set for December 12th 2008 in Judge Phil Helmet's courtroom and Jasmine Finch was the prosecutor on the case.

****

A few days went by and Fox's body was found in Dallas, Texas with some strange woman from that area. Worm's two sisters, Yvette and Puff walked into the store all sad and teary eyed from mourning Fox's death. They were angry and under a lot of stress. Puff knew that her own family was probably behind her death, but she couldn't prove it, especially that she was found in Texas. Puff gave it a shot to see if they knew anything or would confess without knowing. She accused them without giving it a second thought.

"Why did ya'll kill her?" Puff screamed with much emotion.

"Killed who, Puff, what are you talking about?" Worm asked his little sister.

"So ya'll want to play stupid? Haven't you all seen the news? Fox is dead, she was found in Dallas in a Motel with some white woman and Fox didn't fuck around like that, she was strictly dickey," said Yvette.

Dante started acting like he was upset throwing punches at the air and making faces like he was about to cry.

"Sis, we didn't know and we surely didn't have anything to do with it," said Worm.

"No, not my Fox, oh God, no," said Dante out loud.

"She told me everything, about ya'll sending her to Dallas to visit her aunt until Smack's case was over, but she thought ya'll were going to kill her. I don't believe you, Packman, you let them do it and she was two months pregnant with your baby. She was going to tell you once she got settled in down there," as more tears ran down Puffs red cheekbone.

"Puff, I gave her the money to catch a plane down to her aunts and I wasn't going to let anyone harm her in this circle that's why I suggested she leave until Smack's trial was over. She's not dead, she can't' be," as Dante broke down and started crying even more playing his part.

"I hope not and if I find out that ya'll had anything to do with her death, I will never speak to ya'll again," said Puff. You could still hear Dante crying.

"Me neither, c'mon Puff, let's go," said Yvette grabbing her little sister and they walked out of the store. Everyone else just looked at Dante and burst out laughing.

"You're a damn fool. You are crazy, Packman," said Kekou clapping his hands.

"They killed my Fox," said Dante loud and then he started laughing.

****

In the beginning of November, Larro, Kyle, Miesha and P-Diddy paid Smack a visit down in the county jail. He was happy to see them all and he spoke with Kyle and P-Diddy first and then Larro.

"Big cuss, you know D$Boy is doing good trying to walk and get his memory back completely," said Larro.

"That's good news...real good news, Larro," said Smack.

"But I think they are still trying to charge him with the assault on the officer. I go back to court in February. Delight pushed my court date back until your case is over and hopefully D$Boy will be able to testify on my behalf," said Larro.

"Well hopefully he will be able to. I need you out there when I go to jail," said Smack.

"Cuss, don't say that, Delight is going to beat the case anyway I believe she will. She's good at what she does," said Larro.

"I think they have Sheena Price down here," said Smack.

"Who?" Larro asked him.

"Secret, nigga, they brought her back from Hawaii and I think that Jasmine is using her as a witness for the State since Fox is no longer with us. You know their scheme, help us and we'll help you bullshit, but she killed one of theirs and ain't no helping her," said Smack.

"Her word ain't shit, she's a cop killer. Delight will eat her up on the stand. Don't worry cuss she got this. Do you need anything down here?" Larro asked him.

"No, I'm good. I have everything I need. I even get pussy on a regular from wifey. So, I'm really good!" said Smack.

"That's what's up. Oh yeah, Miesha went to holla at the Judge before we came down here and he's not going to Judge you on account of this chaos, well we hope so. She gave him all the DVD's of them in return of him giving you a fair trial," said Larro.

****

A few hours earlier, Kyle, P-Diddy and Larro waited on Miesha to come out of Judge Phil Helmet's house in Mt. Adams. She was making things right between them hoping things would be settled and Smack would benefit from it.

"Judge, like I told you, I'm here to call a truce, no more blackmail or anything of the kind. Your cousin's death was revenged and the person who killed Elliot Thrasher is dead. The person who's really behind the drug coming to this area is dead. I know you talked to Steve and all I'm asking is for you to make the right decision in the case of Simmion Boyd next month. He's not guilty of conspiracy or anything dealing with the Black Ice. Here's the DVD's and you don't have to worry about other copies surfacing and all I'm asking of you is to give him a fair trial," said Miesha.

"And what is he to you, Miesha?" the Judge asked her.

"Just a very good friend, Judge, an honest person with a good heart like you," said Miesha.

"What about you and I, Miesha?" He asked her.

"There is no more you and I. We are too different people living in different worlds. I've moved on with my life by living within my means," said Miesha and she thought about Smack's baby she was carrying.

"Are you sure, because this is still available to you," said Judge Helmet showing her his place in the wave of his hand.

"I'm positive, Judge," said Miesha.

"Can I at least enjoy your company for the last time, Miesha?" He asked her with a pathetic look on his face.

She reached up and kissed him on the cheek and said, "Watch the DVD."

She walked out the door letting him see her 42" booty for the last time. He wanted her, but Miesha had another agenda.

****

Larro and Smack was still on the visiting phone talking.

"So, Miesha did that for me Larro?"

"Yeah cuss, she did that for you. She wants a word with you so take care and I'll see you soon, one," said Larro.

"One Lil cuss," said Smack looking pass him at Miesha.

Larro turned and said, "Here, Miesha," as the phone was dangling from his hand waiting on her grab it. She walked up to the glass window looking good as ever as she sat down. She was staring into the pits of his eyes the whole time.

"Hello Smack, how are you doing?" she asked him.

"I'm good, Miesha, and yourself? Larro told me what you did today with the Judge," said Smack.

"It was nothing, but I need to tell you something of much important," said Miesha.

"And what's that, Miesha?" Smack asked her.

"Smack, I like you a lot and I know you are married now and will never leave Delight for a bitch like me. I'm not mad about that and I'm not trying to come in between none of that," as a tear slowly dropped for her eye.

"Smack, I'm pregnant and it's your baby," said Miesha with much emotion.

"Quit playing Miesha, that's not funny," as he tried to laugh it off. But she didn't laugh back at him as she was serious with a concerned look in her eyes.

"I'm serious Smack, and it had to happen that one time at your house in the basement. I don't want to spoil your world, but I want this baby, not to ruin your life, but making mine more pleasant," said Miesha.

"What about Worm, Miesha? You can't count him out," said Smack.

"He has never fucked me raw, Smack, only you," said Miesha still dropping tears.

"You can't have this baby, you must get rid of it," said Smack.

"Fuck that," as she screamed through the receiver getting Kyle, Larro and P-Diddy's attention. "I'm not getting rid of shit; I don't want shit from you and I'm not going to destroy your life with your wife. No one has to know, meaning Delight. I'm sorry, but I'm having this baby, I love you Smack, and I'm sorry," as she dropped the receiver walking away from the glass window.

Larro, Kyle and P-Diddy mouths were open from the news she just broadcasted. Smack just stared at her getting on the elevator leaving her cousin, Larro and P-Diddy in suspense wondering what was going on between them.

****

Later, in the month, P-Diddy was in a twist of terrific company, because he spent Thanksgiving in a spacious place away from family and friends.

He sat on the Italian leather sofa looking in the fireplace while lounging in his boxer briefs. A well-shaped woman straddled him, kissing him completely. She gently spoke in his ear, "Why don't you come back to bed, you'll have to leave in a little while to be with your family," the feminine voice told him. He couldn't resist her nakedness touching his skin. Her touch was vibrant, but delicate.

"Okay, Jasmine," he said downing his glass of Belvedere vodka mixed with cranberry juice. "So Jasmine, you took it upon yourself to use my number?" He asked her.

"I'd figured it would be of good use and now that Antwan's dead, it will be of a greater use. I need for you to fill up these holes that get lonely at night," as she slid between his legs pulling his tribal piece out from the slit of his boxers. She firmly gripped it and

327

then started giving him pleasure orally. P-Diddy just put his head
back and enjoyed her thunderous head clinic.

CHAPTER TWENTY-SIX
SMACK'S TRIAL

Delight was putting the finishing touches on her hair. She was now five months pregnant and seemed to be nine months. She was in the mirror and gave herself a quick look over and sighed. Then she rubbed her stomach and said, "Well little man, let's go and try to free daddy."

She walked out the bedroom heading down the stairs to see the likes of Larro and B-Gotti who were escorting her to the courthouse. They were driving Smack's 750 BMW downtown.

They parked on Court Street in the payee parking lot and walked over to the courthouse. Delight had on an all-black maternity skirt and a white ruffled blouse by Vera Wang and some Gucci heels and a lengthy fall jacket. Larro helped her by carrying her Coach briefcase.

When they reached the courtroom, it was like it was a celebrity on trial. There were news reporters and the courtroom was packed. Larro opened the door for her and she saw a crowd of familiar and unfamiliar faces. The jury wasn't present yet, even though they picked them weeks ago.

Delight had her game face on and she was ready to win her case and free her husband. Jasmine had on a two pieced grey Donna Karan pant suit. She was ready to prosecute and add another win to her record. She liked Smack, but she was still mourning the death of Antwan and she wanted revenge at any cost.

Miesha, Kyle, Lady Ray, Elicia, Mucho, K.G., Diamond Cut, the Belvy Boys, Smack's mother and aunt along with many others were there to show their support for him. Heather was working and had escorted Smack to the courtroom.

Even Kendall and David Jennings form Slogin & Cummons were in the courtroom listening in on the case. Smack was already sitting at the table waiting on Delight.

Delight took her jacket off and placed it on the back of her chair. She was seated and she glanced over at Jasmine and gave her a half smile. Jasmine gave her a snarl in return. She then spoke to Smack and told him she loved him and he had to read her lips.

The jurors entered the courtroom and took their seats in the jury box.

Then the bailiff said, "All rise. The Honorable Judge Phil Helmet residing."

Everyone stood while Judge Helmet came out of his chambers and took his seat.

"You may all be seated," said the bailiff.

"This is case number B0678-99, the State of Ohio vs. Simmion Boyd, being charged with conspiracy, distribution and drug trafficking. Is the defense ready?" he asked Delight and she nodded her head. "Is this prosecution ready?" he asked Jasmine and she answered. "Yes"

"Then you may proceed by calling your first witness." The judge told Jasmine.

Jasmine stood up and said, "Thank you, your Honor. The State would like to call its first witness, Ms. Sheena Price, please."

Everyone looked around for her and Smack just sat there in his jailhouse attire. He didn't wear a suit or any street clothes. Two other bailiffs escorted Secret into the courtroom in shackles. They sat her down in the box next to the Judge and un-cuffed her hands so she could be sworn in. "Please place your left hand on the Bible and raise you right hand. Do you swear to tell the truth, the whole truth and nothing but the truth, so help you God?" the bailiff asked her. She looked him in the eyes and said, "I do."

Then the judge said, "The prosecution may proceed on direct."

Then Jasmine Finch approached Secret slowly looking at her with vigorous eyes.

"Can you state your name for the record," said Jasmine. Secret cleared her throat and said, "Sheena LaShayna Price," as she looked over at Smack.

"Ms. Price, can you tell the court how you came to know the defendant, Simmion Boyd?" Jasmine asked her.

Secret smiled a grimace and then replied. "Who doesn't know Smack, I mean Simmion Boyd, and he's a known drug dealer."

Delight spoke out. "Objection, your Honor."

"Sustained." Judge Helmet said.

"Ms. Price, can you just keep it simple and tell the court how you came in contact with the defendant?" Jasmine asked her.

She adjusted herself in her seat and looked Smack dead in the eyes and said, "Well, my ex-boyfriend David Baxter, is associated with Simmion's cousin, Larro Boyd which they are a part of an organization called the Diamond Cut in Dayton, Ohio. I met Simmion through them which David Baxter gained access to kilos of cocaine from Simmion Boyd that I witness several times."

"Objection, your Honor," Delight once again objected to her statement.

"Overruled, please continue, Ms. Price," said Judge Helmet.

"Since I was a stripper and all, I would perform for the Diamond Cut and sometimes I would sleep with a few of them for entertainment and cash and Simmion joined in a few times, said Secret.

"you are telling the court that you were intimate with Simmion before?" Jasmine asked her.

"What do you think? Yes, I fucked Simmion Boyd several times," said Secret bluntly.

The audience in the courtroom made a sound of "Awe" and Judge Helmet asked for order in the courtroom. "Order, order in the courtroom. Ms. Price, I'm going to warn you once and please choose a better word selection."

She nodded her head. "Yes, sir," said Secret.

"So that's the extent of your relationship with the defendant?" Jasmine asked her.

"I guess so other than receiving these pink pills from him," said Secret.

"What pink pills, Ms. Price?" Jasmine asked her walking close to her.

"A new drug he introduced to the Diamond Cut and he also introduced it to me. It's called Black Ice," said Secret.

Jasmine walked over to where she was sitting and grabbed a small bag of pills. She held them up and said, "Are these the same pills that defendant Simmion Boyd introduced you to?"

"Yes, those are it," said Secret.

"Your Honor, I would like to enter this as exhibit A. Ms. Sheena Price, how many times did the defendant give you these pills?" Jasmine asked her.

"Twice at his house during a cook-out and once when David and I met him at a gas station on the outskirts of Cincinnati," said Secret batting her eyes at Jasmine looking over at Delight and Smack.

"I have no more questions, your Honor. Thank you, Ms. Price," as Jasmine walked back to her seat looking at Delight with a fierce look of destination.

Then Judge Phil Helmet said, "Would the defense like to cross examine the witness?"

Delight got up from her chair holding her stomach only momentarily. She was ready to poke holes in the States witness. Secret looked at her as Delight slowly approached the bench holding her belly. "So, Ms. Sheena Price, you're a known stripper?" Delight asked her.

"Yes, I am," said Secret with a serious look.

"So, Simmion Boyd had countless sexual encounters with you?" Delight asked her.

"He's a man, isn't he? Of course, he did," said Secret with an attitude.

"your boyfriend, David Baxter, was okay with you prostituting your body?" Delight asked.

"Objection, your Honor, this has nothing to do with the case," said Jasmine.

"Sustained, counselor, get to the point," said Judge Helmet.

"I was just trying to see how Ms. Price had sex with the defendant and her ex-boyfriend is a jealous and abusive man. Isn't that right, Ms. Price? Why I say this is because of the statement she made in her report that he beat her for just looking at another man. Isn't that right Secret, I mean, Ms. Price? I would like to enter this report as exhibit B as evidence of the defense where Ms. Sheena Price had filed a TPO on David Baxter and he was charged for Domestic Violence," said Delight and Secret head just dropped followed by tears.

"Please answer the question, Ms. Price, was he abusive and jealous towards you," said the Judge.

She looked up at Delight and said, "Yes, he was very abusive and he didn't like my line of work."

"members of the Jury, how could my client have been sexually involved with the States witness when her abusive boyfriend wouldn't allow her out of his sight. She doesn't know the defendant and only encountered him through David Baxter and she's awaiting murder charges for Patricia Simms, a RENU agent," said Delight.

"Objection, your Honor," Jasmine stoop up in rage. "Sustained," said Judge Helmet.

The audience got loud again and the Judge had to get order. When they settled down Delight continued. "Well with that I have no further questions," as Delight walked back to her seat next to her husband.

"The prosecution can call their next witness," said Judge Helmet to Jasmine.

Jasmine stood and said, "The State of Ohio would like to call RENU agent, Allen Taylor to the stand."

Allen Taylor stood up and fixed his tie and walked up to the stand passing Delight and Smack. When he sat down the bailiff swore him in and carefully did so.

"Can you state your name and occupation for the record, sir," asked Jasmine Finch.

"My name is Allen Taylor; I'm a special agent for RENU in the drug task unit. I've been on the force for seven years now," said Allen Taylor.

"So, Mr. Taylor, can you tell us a little about this new drug called Black Ice?" Jasmine asked him turning to the jury.

"Well from our investigation and research it's a pill heavily used in Europe and it is made from a mixture of cocaine, heroin, and hash," said Taylor.

"Is the drug harmful for those who come in contact with it?" Jasmine asked him.

"Come on, what do you think? It's a narcotic; of course, it is harmful to anyone who uses it. You can ask Simmion Boyd, he used it to off his ex-girlfriend, Stefani Blake," said Allen Taylor.

"Objection, your Honor, my client isn't on trial for murder," Delight blurted out.

"Sustained, I will not have any personal opinions deriving in my courtroom," said Judge Helmet.

"Sorry, your Honor, I apologize, but there were known deaths as a result of this drug. I say it is very harmful and if it is misused, it can be deadly," said Taylor.

"Officer Taylor, can you identify the defendant?" Jasmine asked him.

"Yes, he's Simmion Boyd, a well-known person throughout the Ohio Valley," said Taylor.

"How is that, is he known for giving out charity?" Jasmine asked him.

"Are you serious, Ms. Finch? He's quote on quote a drug dealer," said Taylor.

"Objection, your Honor, he's making my client appear to be guilty under his own speculations," said Delight.

"Sustained, Officer Taylor, please do not put any labels on the defendant," said Judge Helmet.

"Yes sir, your Honor. We confiscated a large supply of the drug from Sanya McKinney's apartment who wrote a statement on Simmion Boyd claiming the drug belonged to him and he stashed it at her place," said Taylor.

"For the record, Ms. Sanya McKinney cannot testify today because she was mysteriously murdered two months ago," said Jasmine walking back over to the table where she had her paper trail. "Is this the written statement, Mr. Taylor?" Jasmine asked him handing him the paper and she also gave a copy to the jury.

"Yes," Taylor told her fixing his collar.

"I would like to enter this evidence as exhibit C for the prosecution. Thank you, Officer Taylor, I have no further questions," said Jasmine walking over to her seat smiling at Delight and Smack.

Delight got up and approached Taylor. She didn't waste any time cross examining him. "Officer Taylor, you said that this new drug is very harmful?"

"That is correct," Taylor replied.

"Then tell the jury what drug is not harmful. I'll wait if you can find one," said Delight.

"Umm-umm," as he thought about it and Delight cut him off.

"Exactly, Officer Taylor, none. All drugs are very harmful and if any of them are misused they can be deadly. Even over the counter drugs can be harmful if they are misused, am I right?" Delight asked him.

Delight gradually walked closer to him to hear his answer. "Yes, that is correct," said Taylor.

"And to this statement that the late Sanya McKinney allegedly wrote, was she promised anything?" Delight asked him looking him in the face.

"Objection, your Honor, counsel wasn't present when the statement was written," said Jasmine.

"Sustained, Mrs. Boyd, please use a better selection," said Judge Helmet.

"Yes sir, your Honor. Officer Taylor, do you have any concrete connection between Simmion Boyd and Sanya McKinney besides her telling you she knew him?" Delight asked him.

"No, not actually, but we did find an old phone bill of his with her address on it, 2009 Four Towers apartment number seven," said Allen Taylor and Delight was unaware of this piece of evidence. She was caught off guard.

"Your Honor, when was this submitted to the court for evidence?" Delight asked the Judge.

"I submitted it at the Suppression hearing, Mrs. Boyd, with all the other evidence. You weren't aware of this?" Jasmine told her.

"It must have slipped by me, no further questions," said Delight.

"Officer Taylor, you may step down. We will continue this case tomorrow at 9 a.m. sharp. This court is now adjourned." Judge Helmet hit his gavel.

Delight knew Jasmine didn't mention or even add the evidence about the phone bill at the suppression hearing. The State was withholding evidence and then out of nowhere submitting it. Judge Helmet was allowing it to happen in his courtroom. She knew the cards were stacked against them. Heather escorted Smack back to the Justice Center and news reporters tried to get a comment from Delight, but she ignored the reporters and kept going pass them.

Jasmine, on the other hand stopped for an interview to give the public what they were looking for. "Today was a successful day for the prosecution. We will see what tomorrow brings and hopefully that will be justice for the tax payers in this country," said Jasmine.

"Ms. Finch, do you think that Simmion Boyd is guilty?" a reporter asked.

"It's too early to say," as she looked over at P-Diddy leaving out of the courtroom.

"Can you at least give the public some type of certainty?" the reporter asked her.

"I'm sorry, I can't do that. No more questions, please. I must go," said Jasmine walking off trying to catch up with P-Diddy.

Kendall knew she was losing the case by a small default. Delight needed a big lift tomorrow and he knew with his input she could fight a better battle.

Later, that night, Kendall and Keisha were lying in the bed and Keisha was eating a hot pickle. She wanted to know what happened in court today involving Smack's case.

"Kendall, what happen at Simmion's trial, because I know you were there?"

"Why you say that Keisha?" he asked her.

"Because you weren't in the office when I called you and then when I tried your cell phone, it was turned off. what happened in court?" she looked at him.

"Nothing, just a few testimonies, nothing major, that's all," said Kendall.

"Do you think Delight will win the case?" Keisha asked him.

"It's hard to determine at this point, but if it was based on what went on today, she would probably lose. If she had my input, I could probably help a lot," said Kendall.

"So why don't you help her, Kendall?" Keisha asked him looking him in the eyes.

"It's not my case; she is a grown woman and a professional. Simmion is her husband now, and not me," said Kendall.

"Kendall, she is pregnant and the mother of your oldest child so have a little dignity and compassion for once. Don't let the past stop you from getting blessings and helping her. All I'm saying is do the right thing," said Keisha giving a short pause. "She needs you and regardless of her new life, you should be there for her. If she is unhappy, it will affect Rainell, I've been through the same thing when I was younger dealing with my parent's separation. You loved her once, so have some gratitude and negritude about yourself," said Keisha.

The negritude hit home and he realized then that Delight didn't do anything wrong in their relationship he did. She was always there for him no matter what the cost was. Delight had put up with a lot of his bullshit during the course of their relationship. He thought about it hard and long.

****

P-Diddy sat in the Cadillac Ranch café in downtown Cincinnati with Jasmine having a drink. It was around ten that evening after the first day of trial. Her eyes were gloomy and moist, but intoxicated with lust. A formal introduction wasn't needed, because the affair they were having was already stamped. P-Diddy was cheating with her on his baby's mother and girlfriend, Asia, for what reason? Who knows, but P-Diddy was sleeping with the enemy behind enemy lines. No one knew it was his and her little secret. He was sleeping with the woman who was trying to put his business associate and friend away for a long time. She couldn't hide the fact that she wanted him inside her sweet hole of seduction. She had recently come off her cycle and hadn't been with a man since Thanksgiving, which was him. Her hormones were throbbing inside her and her thoughts of him inside her rushed through her body and then disappeared and came again.

"P-Diddy, let's get out of here and go back to my place, for perhaps a well-deserved fuck," said Jasmine biting down on her bottom lip.

"That's good idea, but you still haven't answered my question," said P-Diddy.

She stroked her glass of Patron and glared at him and said, "I just can't' throw the case away like that. It has brought too much public and national attention. These Republican hard ankles want convictions, P-Diddy. Delight will have to be the lawyer I know she can be for Simmion to walk away free. I didn't like the fact what Antwan did to him either, but that's life and it's my job to prosecute those who break the law. It's nothing personal darling, hell, I like Simmion myself so don't think I'm fully against him. Outside the courtroom I think the world of him," Jasmine caught herself from shedding a tear.

"I think I understand, Jas, but after tonight I don't think it would be best for us to see each other until the case is over, it's nothing personal, I just don't want others to get suspicious of my acts," said P-Diddy.

"That's not fair, I yearn for you and I've falling in love with you," said Jasmine.

"Jasmine, we only saw each other twice, so how can you possibly be in love with me?" P-Diddy asked her.

"It's your massive structure and gently presence that took my breath away. Your spirit is of greatness and everything about you is like a romance, a true romance and I'm eager to seek more with you. I want to see what life has to offer with P-Diddy. I want to love you and it doesn't matter if you love me or not. I'm willing to love you and share with Asia. I have lots of money that Antwan left behind, I mean millions and I would like to share with you so you make the decision," said Jasmine.

His memory of Shakespeare "Macbeth" came to mind and he knew that she was a fatal attraction. How could she be in love so quickly, so suddenly and so soon?

He knew after he sexed her tonight, he would have to get rid of her and excuse himself from any other intimacy with Jasmine Finch.

"Let's just get out of here, Jasmine, and we'll further this conversation at your place," said P-Diddy downing his drink. He put a tip on the bar for the barmaid and they left.

****

Delight was in her bedroom talking to Smack on the phone and she was upset. She believed she couldn't win the case and her doubts came with loneliness and depression with less clarity.

"Baby, it's going to be alright whether we win or lose. I know you did your best," said Smack.

"Simmion, I'm scared and I just want you home with us. I just don't know if I can beat this case or not and I don't want to let you down," said Delight sniffling.

"Quit crying Delight, everything is going to be okay. I put this in God's hand he knows how much I can handle and I believe in you. That's all that matters so keep your head up and things will get better, Mrs. Delight Heath-Boyd," said Smack.

"I hope so baby, I love you, Simmion and I don't want to lose you to the system for a long time," said Delight.

"You won't lose me. I have to go now; a deputy is coming. I love you and I'll see you tomorrow in court. Kisses and more kisses, bye," said Smack.

"Bye honey and I love you, too, kisses," said Delight hanging up the phone. She pushed out more tears crying herself to sleep.

The next morning it was the same atmosphere as yesterday and the stage was set. Delight walked into the courtroom wearing a Mahogany pant suit and some suede brown stiletto heels. She was looking sexy as usual and Rainell didn't attend school this morning instead she was in a different classroom; a class of real life dealing with reality. Kendall and David Jennings were present again in the courtroom and Rainell sat with her biological father. The same familiar and unfamiliar faces were back in the courtroom. Jasmine walked in the courtroom wearing an astonishing eggshell white bell bottom pants and matching blouse that was short sleeve and tie up. She had on some black pumps about a quarter inch. Her pants were so tight you could see her panty line. Jasmine smiled at P-Diddy and snarled at Delight. She took her seat and couldn't do nothing but notice the way Delight's wedding ring sparkled from the lighting in the courtroom. Jasmine wanted her life, a life of being married with a child. The thought came and went, because she had business to attend to and that was winning this case. Once again, the bailiff did the honors of announcing the Judge and this time the defense called their first witness which was Steve O'Hara. The bailiff swore him in and Delight approached him understanding that he would be the key to setting Smack free. She knew her performance would have to be of Oscar performance.

The sexy pregnant lawyer was ready to claim her fame in the courtroom. Her words were sweet and loud as she began to examine the Federal agent.

"Can you please state your name and title to the court for the record please," said Delight.

"My name is agent Steve O'Hara and I'm a federal agent, I've been an agent for thirteen years," said O'Hara.

"Mr. O'Hara, you follow this type of cases all the time, right?" Delight asked him.

"Yes, I do quite often," he answered.

"In a case like this, how do government officials track a guy like Simmion Boyd, and alleged drug dealer?" Delight asked him.

"Guys like Simmion Boyd must be on our hot list for us to conduct an investigation," said Steve O'Hara.

"Has his name been mentioned or even put on the Feds hot list in the recent year leading up to now?" Delight asked him.

"No, I haven't heard anything about Simmion Boyd until now," he said.

"do you believe he's able to flood this city by bringing illegal drugs to this country from across sea's?" she asked him.

"It's possible Mrs. Boyd, but he's only been out the country once, so his movement is unlikely to provoke an epidemic," said O'Hara.

"How do you know this, Mr. O'Hara?" Delight asked him.

"We keep track on the movement in and out of the country of people who are not a part of major corporations or businesses, especially since 9/11," he told her.

"I see, so what does the Feds know about this new drug known as Black Ice?" Delight asked him.

"We know that it's a new drug that is not well-known in the U.S., but has surfaced here from Europe in this area," he said.

"Do you know who's behind this new drug coming to the U.S.?" she asked him.

"We had a good notion that a known arms dealer was bringing it through customs and he was smart by targeting Ohio first instead of LA, Miami, or New York. He made a major move faking out government officials, but we got wind of it," said O'Hara.

"Who was this evil person the person who dealt arms; this mad man who made a major move on American soil?" Delight asked him being sarcastic.

"It was a known terrorist and arms dealer by the name of Antwan Klein known as the Chocolate Dream the American Nightmare," said O'Hara.

Delight walked over to where she was sitting and grabbed a photo. She walked back over to O'Hara and said, "Is this him in the photo?" She held the picture for him to see. He looked at the picture and responded. "Yes, that is him. The dark-complexioned bald-headed guy is Antwan Klein."

"Can you identify anyone else in the photo?" Delight asked him.

"Sure, that's you, Simmion and Ms. Finch," said O'Hara. The courtroom was shocked to hear him acknowledge them all together. Delight handed him a picture of them in China.

"You're absolutely right, associates of ours while we were on vacation inside the dragon in China for the summer Olympics. We met Antwan Klein and his lover and girlfriend, Jasmine Finch on our vacation," said Delight.

"Awe, oh," as the courtroom got loud from the confession of Delight.

"Objection, Your Honor," as Jasmine stood up pointing her pen.

"Objection over ruled, settle down people. Counsel please continue with your witness," said Judge Helmet.

"It is not a surprise that Ms. Finch is probably connected with this operation, correct me if I'm wrong, Mr. O'Hara?" Delight asked him.

"Unfortunately, Ms. Finch checked out to be clean and was just a person in a relationship who was not aware of his activities. We seized this new drug and the weapons from two of Antwan Klein's establishments in this area. We couldn't put Antwan Klein and Simmion Boyd together as a team of any operation. If Mr. Boyd was associated with Mr. Klein, he was just a dealer more like a peon and not manufacture shipping the drug for sell," said O'Hara.

"Thank you, Mr. O'Hara, I have no further questions," said Delight receiving the picture back from the jury.

"Ms. Finch, your witness," said Judge Helmet looking over the brim of his glasses at her. Jasmine stood up and shook her clinging clothes from her dampened skin from perspiring because of the picture raising her blood pressure a little.

She approached the bench and asked O'Hara. "Mr. O'Hara how did government officials find out about Antwan Klein's involvement?" Jasmine asked him.

"We got a well-deserved tip," he said.

"So, you all never did a full investigation before raiding Mr. Klein's businesses?" she asked him.

"No, we just went on the tip and it was helpful," said O'Hara.

"you really don't know for sure if Simmion Boyd is or were associated with him far as being the leader of an elite operation? And you didn't follow procedure at all and you say you've been and agent for thirteen years, come on, Mr. O'Hara you're not that illusive, are you?" Jasmine asked him full of energy.

"My supervisor made the call, not me," said O'Hara.

"you're not sure if Simmion Boyd is behind the drug or not?" she asked him.

"My educated guess tells me that he's not the mastermind," said O'Hara.

"We are not dealing with educated guesses; we are dealing with facts. Did you get any drugs off of Mr. Klein, yes or no? Jasmine asked him raising her voice.

"No, we didn't, but we did obtain them from the club and restaurant he owned," said O'Hara.

"Well, Mr. O'Hara, RENU agents seized the drug off of Simmion Boyd person. He possessed the drug in his possession when he was arrested and those are the cold hard facts. With that I have no more questions," said Jasmine as she walked back to her seat switching her hips. She snapped her head back before sitting down telling Delight in so many words to top that.

"We will take a twenty-minute recess and continue this matter afterwards," said Judge Helmet.

It was small chit chatter in the courtroom and Delight went out in the hallway to get some air. Kendall was standing in the hallway with their daughter. He looked at the woman he was once married to and loved. She was pregnant and had re-married. Rainell walked over to her mom and said, "Mommy, I don't know that entire lawyer talk, but my daddy said you're not being the lawyer you were born to be in there."

"Oh, yeah, he did? What does he know about being a lawyer who I really am and he don't know who he is," said Delight?

"Mama, he's really concerned about you winning this case," said Rainell and Kendall was easing over to where they were standing.

"Rainell, he's only concerned about himself," said Delight.

"That's not true Delight, and I admit that I wasn't with you being involved with Simmion at first, but I'm over it. I was indeed selfish. I should've been supportive towards your happiness and I can accept it now, so I'm here to support you. You are a better lawyer than the person I'm seeing in that courtroom," said Kendall.

"I don't know what is wrong with me," said Delight.

"Just relax and no matter what stay in the legal field and don't let your emotions get involved in the case. You have to get the facts out of your head that you are representing your husband and the father of your unborn child," said Kendall.

"But she's winning in there, Kendall," said Delight.

"Delight, you can bounce back and convinced one of the jurors to vote in your favor. That's all it takes, is one," said Kendall.

"You're absolutely right, Kendall, and thanks, I needed that," said Delight.

"No problem, I'll do anything for the mother of my child. If you're happy then my daughter is happy," said Kendall embracing her with a hug.

"Now, go in there and handle your business and win this case for your husband," Kendall told Delight with a smile. Rainell was cheesing at her parent's.

****

Delight walked back into the courtroom feeling a little more confident about herself and winning the case. She knew she had to take charge and be that aggressive lawyer that she's grown to be. She sat down next to her husband and gave him a kiss. She smiled at him and said, "I love you, Simmion."

"I love you too, Delight. Are you okay, is something bothering you?" He asked her.

She rubbed his hand gently and replied, "I'm okay, let's take charge and win this trial baby. The State only has one more witness and that's Will Edmond."

The Judge came out of his chambers. "All rise," said the bailiff. Everything started back up and the jurors were ready. Jasmine and Delight were ready staring each other down like they were in a heated debate.

"Everyone may be seated." The bailiff said.

"Ms. Finch, who's your next witness," said Judge Helmet.

"Your honor, I would like to call Will Edmond to the stand as my next witness for the State," said Jasmine looking over at her step-brother.

Will Edmond stood up dressed in his cheap J.C. Penny's suit and approached the stand.

The bailiff swore him in and he sat down and then Jasmine took flight.

"Sir, will you state your name and title for the record, please," said Jasmine.

"My name is William Edmond, I'm a RENU agent and I've been with the force for nine years," said Will.

"Officer Edmond, do you recognize the defendant?" Jasmine asked him.

"Yes, he's Simmion Boyd a.k.a. Smack, an alleged drug dealer from Dayton, Ohio," said Will.

"How did you know the defendant?" Jasmine asked him.

"From a drug bust, we busted him on his wedding day," said Will.

"How did you know he had the drugs on him this day?" Jasmine questioned him.

"Our staff and department had been investigating Mr. Boyd and Diamond Cut for quite some time now. The late Elliot Thrasher gave us a tip on Mr. Boyd through his associate, Antwan Klein. Mr. Thrasher was part of a sting buying weapons from Antwan Klein and then the two men introduced the drug known as Black Ice to Mr. Thrasher. We were about to make our bust and Mr. Thrasher was found dead, so we had to back off," said Will.

"What else is there about the defendant?" Jasmine asked him.

"Then we go another tip form our C.I. the late Sanya McKinney which she told us about the defendant stashing the drug at her apartment and their relationship," said Will.

"How did you know it was a drug you confiscated from Mr. Boyd the day of his arrest?" Jasmine walked closer to him asking him the question.

"I conducted a test on the spot and then sent it to the lab for more testing," said Edmond with confidence.

Jasmine walked back to her seat and grabbed a piece of paper walking back towards him.

"Is this the lab report, Officer Edmond?" She showed him the piece of paper.

"Yes, that's the lab report," said Edmond quickly looking it over.

"Tell the jurors what it says for me please," said Jasmine.

"It says that fifteen pills unknown were submitted for lab testing. The weight consists of three grams. The pill was broken down into three components of known control substance; #1 cocaine, #2 heroin, #3 hash," said Edmond.

"Objection, your Honor, under rule 702 the witness is testifying as an expert and it hasn't been established that the witness is qualified as an expert by specialized knowledge, skill, experience, training and education regarding the subject matter of the testimony as it pertain to this lab report," said Kendall standing up coming to Delight's rescue. He looked over at her and she was in shock, even others in the courtroom were in shock because he came out of nowhere.

"And who are you, may I ask?" said Judge Helmet.

"I'm Kendall A. Scott and this is David Jennings, we are co-counsel with Mrs. Delight Boyd, your Honor. We are attorneys of law at Slogin & Cummons," said Kendall. He and David Jennings went and took seats next to Delight and Smack. Delight received a wave of energy knowing she had help from two brilliant lawyers.

"And further more your Honor we object to this piece of evidence, due to its deficiency, this particular report never fails to fully inform my client that this report would be used for prima-fascia evidence against my client. Pursuant under 2925.51-C this lab report only advises my client of the minimum under 2925.51-D, State vs. Smith. Which to sum it up, your Honor, a lab report that fails to fully inform an individual of the consequences for failing to demand the testimony of the lab technician renders the lab report

deficient on its face and therefore should be excluded from the State's evidence,"
 said Kendall.

Everyone was in awe of Kendall speech. Smack was extremely surprised by Kendall's actions to help him. Kendall stuck his hand out to Smack and they shook hands. Delight couldn't believe it and she dropped a tear. Then Jasmine quickly rebutted the objection by the defense. "Your Honor, the States witness is not testifying as an expert witness, pursuant to evidence rule 701. The RENU officer Mr. Edmond's testimony is only being offered to help get a clear understanding and determination of the facts in the issue. Furthermore, your Honor, the State would like to be granted a short recess at this time so the State can further research the lab report if the court would allow it," Jasmine carefully looked at the Judge hoping he would grant her a recess. Judge Helmet looked at her and said, "We will take a fifteen-minute recess."

They all had a meeting in the Judge's chamber and he heard the State's rebuttal to the second objection. He didn't go into any details about his ruling and whatever he said in his chambers was off the record.

The Judge as well as the counsel and prosecutor returned to the courtroom. Judge Helmet rendered his ruling of the first objection by the defense not allowing it into evidence and allowing the second objection to be over ruled.

Jasmine continued to question her step-brother, Will. "So, Officer Edmond, do you feel that the RENU department has done its job by taking Mr. Boyd off the streets?" Yes, I think we've done a hell of a job bringing Mr. Boyd to justice. We know that a large percentage of America would be damaged by this drug if it would've spread to bigger cities," said Will.

 "do you think the war on drugs is over?" Jasmine asked him. "Not by far, but if Simmion Boyd is convicted today, it would be a plus to the war on our side receiving justice getting a major dealer off the streets," said Will.

"Thank you, Officer Edmond, I have no further questions," said Jasmine walking back to her seat rolling her eyes at the defense.

"Counselors, your witness," said Judge Helmet letting the defense know they could cross examine Will Edmond. Delight stood up and Kendall grabbed her arm pulling her back down to her seat. She looked at him, like what are you doing? "Delight, let David cross examine him first," Kendall whispered to her. She nodded her head as if to say okay. David Jennings was an Afro-American male in his early thirties. He stood at 5'8" in height with a medium built. He had a clean face and was bald head with a thin mustache. He had on an Armani suit which was off gray with a light blue tie. He got up and approached the stand looking Will Edmond directly in the eyes.

"Mr. Edmond or can I call you Will?" David asked him.

Will replied. "I don't mind, counselor."

"Well, Will, did you present a search warrant to the defendant before entering the premises where he was arrested?" David asked him.

"We didn't need a search warrant for a public place," said Will.

"From my understanding the Torque is privately owned, so did you clear it with the owner before raiding the premises or went on good faith?" asked David Jennings.

"No, we didn't clear it with the owner," said Will wondering what he was getting at.

"So, you went on good faith," said David.

"We got a tip," said Will.

"So rightfully Mr. Boyd was violated of his Fourth Amendment. He rented the facility and was pretty much leasing the facility and you didn't clear it with the owner nor did you present a search warrant to my client, because you think you are above the law instead of upholding the law. You broke the law, Officer Edmond," said David walking over by the jurors.

"Objection, your Honor," said Jasmine as she stood with anger in her voice.

"Over ruled. Sit down, Ms. Finch. Please continue counselor," said Judge Helmet.

"I'm going to pass it to a team member; I have no further questions for the witness. Mrs. Boyd, your witness," said David Jennings walking back over to the defense and sat down.

Kendall helped Delight get up and then when he sat back down, he asked David, "How did you know they didn't have a search warrant?"

"A good friend of mine owns the Torque and he called me seeing if he could sue the Hamilton County police department for entering his establishment the way they did during Simmion and Delight's reception. They have a law suit that I submitted on my good friend's behalf," said David.

Delight slowly moved towards Will Edmond and the fact that David exposed the witness for the State his expression gave her much confidence and energy to close out.

"Officer Edmond, didn't you have an equal relentless relationship with your sister's boyfriend Antwan Klein?" she asked him.

"What are you talking about?" he countered.

"You're step-sister, Jasmine Finch right over there. She dated Antwan Klein or am I wrong?" Delight was determined.

"I barely knew him and my step-sister's personal life is none of my business," said Will.

"So, I see you have never hung out with Antwan Klein before, at his club or the restaurant before?" Delight asked him.

"Never, like I said, I barely knew the guy, I only heard about him through, Jasmine," said Will.

"Are you sure, Officer Edmond?" she asked him again walking back towards the table grabbing a folder. She opened the folder and looked over some notes. "Yes, I'm sure," said Will.

"So, for the record, Officer Edmond, what's your cell phone number?" she asked him.

"Why? My cell phone number has nothing to do with this case," said Will.

"It certainly does, Officer Edmond," said Delight.

"Answer the question, Officer Edmond," said Judge Helmet.

In a low voice, Will Edmond rushed the number. "344-9194."

"Excuse me, can you speak up for us, Officer Edmond, the rest of the court would like to hear you," said Delight.

"It's 344-9194," he said it loud and clear.

"So, are these text messages coming from your cell phone going to Antwan Klein's cell phone and his going to yours look familiar?" Delight asked him.

"Objection, your Honor, she never submitted those into evidence," said Jasmine standing up in a rage.

"Over ruled, please continue counselor," said Judge Helmet.

"So, I would say you two were the best of friends being that Antwan Klein is now deceased, according to these phone records. Where would you like for me to start, Officer Edmond?" said Delight opening the folder she had in her hand.

"You texted Antwan stating you caught a Fox and she's willing to write a statement on Simmion Boyd or when he texted you and said he planted the drug on Simmion's person and you can raid the wedding reception. It gets even better when this message came from your phone, quote, 'you can distribute the Black Ice. My guys will be out the way and I'll pick up the rest of my money from the restaurant tomorrow'. That text very much tells me that you were helping Antwan Klein with his operation, so were you Officer Edmond?" Delight asked him.

A steam of hot air floated to the top of Will Edmond head and you could see his face turning red. He was mad, mad enough to choke her if he could get his hands around her neck. He didn't want to answer her question, but he did. "No, that's a lie. Someone must have directed their messages to my cell phone," said Will in anger.

"You were getting paid to help put the drugs into the community. You should be the one on trial and not Simmion Boyd. He's innocent and should be set free today. He should not be convicted of conspiracy or any other charges in this courtroom. Its cops like you that give a black eye to the American justice system," said Delight handing the text messages to members of the jury for them to view it.

"Officer Edmond, you were actually helping a known terrorist, helping him bring drugs and weapons into our country. The sting went from you trying to catch a crook to you becoming a crook, huh, Officer Edmond?" Delight was getting personal.

"Objection, your Honor," screamed Jasmine and stood up again.

"Over ruled," said Judge Helmet.

"your Honor, I would like to enter this evidence in as exhibit D for the defense and now the defense rests. I have no further questions," as she walked away going back to her seat giving the team a thumbs up.

"Counselor, I will allow this evidence to be submitted at this time. Ms. Finch, do you have any closing statements?" Judge Helmet asked her.

"Yes, I do, your Honor," said Jasmine getting up to approach the jury's box. Will Edmond had already returned to his seat. Jasmine guided her hand across the wooden railing of the jury box before stopping in the middle. She lifted her head and stared every juror in the eyes.

"We have a case of deception and simple unjust here, but for whom, Simmion Boyd? We know that Simmion Boyd and Antwan Klein had prior dealings from the photo that was taken in China and I dispute that fact whether Mr. Boyd's involvement was minor or major, he was involved.   let's not forget that and if you let him walk away free today our streets once again will be polluted with narcotics which destroy lives across America. He is still a known drug dealer and with that the prosecution rests. Thank you," said Jasmine slowly walking back to her seat. She picked up her glass of water and took a well-deserved sip. Then she started twirling her pen in her fingertips.

"The defense may have their closing statements, now," said Judge Helmet.

Delight stood up once again and the baby started kicking, but she ignored the kicks and powerfully walked towards the jury box holding her head high. She shared a slight smile before giving her closing remarks.

"It's been a long day of testimonies on both sides, but one particular testimony stood out and took the court by surprise and that was the testimony of Officer Will Edmond. A man of law, who was getting money for an innocent man, Mr. Simmion Boyd, to take the fall by framing him. How much weight should Simmion Boyd take in this matter?

Why should he be punished and other should go free? Let's look at the evidence on hand and have a little common sense in the matter. It's like pointing the finger at someone, but at the same time they are doing wrong. I leave the decision in your hands today the jurors to make the right decision in the case of

Simmion Boyd vs. the State of Ohio and with that, the defense rests."

Delight walked back to her seat and they all huddled and David Jennings and her ex-husband gave her praises. Smack was satisfied with his wife's performance.

The jury left the courtroom to deliberate and Judge Helmet went into his chambers. It only took the Jury thirty minutes to deliberate on the case and come back with a verdict. When court was back in session it was quiet as everyone waited on the verdict.

"The Jury do you have a verdict?" Judge Helmet asked them.

Then one of the jurors stood up and said, "Yes, your Honor, we have a verdict."

The older black woman held a piece of paper in her hand.

"Can you tell the court your decision, please?" Judge Helmet asked.

"Yes, your Honor," said the black woman clearing her throat and she read the verdict.

"We, the Jury, find the defendant, Simmion Boyd, not guilty of conspiracy, but guilty on drug trafficking."

Smack's head dropped in disbelief. Everyone in the courtroom was disappointed even Jasmine was, because she knew they would sure win from the text messages. The courtroom got extremely loud. "Order, order in the courtroom. Mr. Boyd, I will sentence you on the eighteenth of December. This court is adjourned," said Judge Helmet.

Lady Ray, Miesha, Rainell, Smack's mother and Delight started crying for him.

This day was like a powerful person had died. Delight had to be rushed to the hospital from passing out she was so hurt by the decision.

****

SIXTEEN MONTHS LATER Delight was visiting Smack at London Correctional Institution in London, Ohio. She was patiently waiting on him to come out into the visiting room where he would normally come out since her last past twelve months of visiting him.

He walked out the door to see his wife looking good as ever. She had on a tight t-shirt and some Capri pants and some small heels. Smack had on his normal blue prisoner khaki set that was standard prisoner apparel. She stood up to greet him still wearing her huge ring giving him a huge smile. She kissed him long and hard.

"Hey baby, I miss you," said Delight.

"I miss ya'll too, come her Simmion," said Smack taking his son out her arms.

He kissed his little boy and they sat down. It was now the year April 10, 2010. Delight had Simmion Jr. on April 5, 2009 and he was now one years old.

"Boy, you are getting big fella, Delight what are you feeding him?" Smack asked her.

"Nothing, but his normal formula. He's just greedy like you when you were a baby, that's what your mother told me," said Delight.

"How is Rainell doing?" Smack asked her.

"She's fine and she misses her step-dad. She told me to tell you she loves you."

"How is the law firm doing?" Smack asked her.

"Everything is going swell, Kendall and David are handling their business," said Delight with a slight pause. "They said hello and Simmion Jr. and Kendall Jr. are having their birthday party together at Chuck E. Cheese's in Tri-County this weekend. We are moving our office downtown in the Nathaniel Ropes building next month. I have to go and visit this lady named Bonita Maples in a Federal Prison in West Virginia next month. She wants to hire us for her appeal," said Delight.

"Ya'll are doing the damn thing, huh?" Smack asked her.

"Yes, especially after your trial it seemed like everyone wanted our legal advice. Even though we lost, they really know you won and we've gotten a lot of calls from Atlanta, Texas, and California. I'm glad we teamed up and we all can practice law all over the country," said Delight.

"That's wonderful and you are doing what you love to do and you've made a name for yourself," said Smack.

"No, what's wonderful is that you are coming home in two months and I can do you. I can't wait and I am going to lock the doors and send the kids off to your mom's house. I've been wearing this birth control ring inside me to keep me from coming on my period so the calendar will be correct when you get out," said Delight.

I can't wait either and Judge Helmet did look out for me by only giving me twenty months," said Smack.

"He sure did, because I just knew he was going to give you anywhere between five to seven years being you were facing three to ten. God is good," said Delight.

"He most definitely is good. I love you Delight," said Smack.

"I love you too baby. Oh, I forgot to tell you that Shatarah had three cubs last week and I had to give Cerberus to the Cincinnati Zoo he was getting out of control. Nevada and Goliath are doing okay and Nevada is pregnant again. I think we should get Goliath fixed," said Delight.

"That's fine, you can do that. What about Bruce?" Smack asked her.

"I didn't want to tell you, but Bruce is gone. It was an accident baby, I didn't mean to," as she tried to explain and he cut her off. "Delight, you killed Bruce?" He asked her.

"Like I said, baby, it was an accident. Shit, I have to care for the animals and our children.   It's a lot to do when you're not there to help me. Buy another dragon when you come home," said Delight.

"It's okay, I was just saying, but we cool though. Are you coming to get me when I get out?" He asked her.

"No," said Delight bluntly.

"What do you mean, no?" He countered

"Because P-Diddy and Dante are coming to get you when you get out in June," said Delight.

"I don't want a coming home party either," said Smack.

"Well, it's too late. It has already been planned at our house so act surprised. Oh, and you need to talk to your little brother Dmitri when you do come home. He dropped out of college, you didn't hear it from me and your mom didn't want to tell you," said Delight taking their son from his arms. He put his head down and then looked up at her.

"Are you serious, Delight?" he asked her.

"Yes, I'm serious."
"Why would he throw his life away like that? He has a full scholarship to UCLA, a 4.0 GPA and his basketball skills, he's tripping hard. It's probably those females he's chasing," said Smack.
"You didn't hear this from me, but I think he's been hanging out with Larro," said Delight.
Somehow Smack knew life sometimes repeated itself and he didn't want for his little brother to follow in his footsteps. June couldn't come any sooner for Smack.

PREVIEWS FROM DELIGHT PART II
DELIGHT PART II (A MILLION DOLLAR LOVE)

P-Diddy and Dante picked Smack up from London Correctional Institute as scheduled in June.
P-Diddy was now driving a 2010 all black Lexus SC430 drop top with peanut butter leather interior with 20" Asanti rims.

Smack walked out of the facility to see them and was surprised and stunned.

"Damn P-Diddy, you just copped this joint?" Smack asked him getting in the car.

"Yeah, I got it last week, my guy," said P-Diddy.

"What are ya'll doing out here now?" Smack asked him.

"We're eating, everyone is eating that one way, you'll see, big brah," said Dante.

"I'm through with the game, I told ya'll before I went in," said Smack.

"We know, just sit back and smoke on the Kush blunt Dante rolled up, because I know you haven't quit smoking. relax and enjoy the ride to the house," said P-Diddy.

They drove down state route 56 to I-71 going south. When they reached his house, Smack saw a lot of new flashy cars in front of his house and driveway.

His Cadillac truck and her Infiniti truck were sitting at the front of the driveway. Nevada and Goliath were relaxing on the front lawn as usual. When they stepped out of the Lexus, Smack called his dogs and they came running to their master. They remembered him. After petting them, he told them. "Gehen sie zu spielen."

He told them to go and play in German. Then Smack was curious about the new cars he was seeing and he started pointing and asking questions. It was 2009 BMW M-5, he pointed at first.

"That's Larro's new car," said P-Diddy.

He pointed again at a black Bentley Continental GTC on 22" Asanti rims.

"That's Worm's new car," Dante told him. He pointed to a gray Range Rover Sport.

"That's Bodean," said P-Diddy. Then Smack pointed over to a dark blue Lotus Evora on 20" Asanti rims. "That's Weezy's new car he like them fast," said Dante with again.

"Wow what the fuck ya'll into out here P-Diddy?" Smack asked him.

"Money Smack, lots of it that's all," said P-Diddy.

Then whose Mercedes Benz SLR Roadster is that?" Smack asked pointing to it.

"That's Vino new car and the red Porsche Cayenne truck is Kyle's new whip. The green Gran Turism is Kobe and the black Quattro Porte executive GT Maserati is Bo-Gotti. We all have new Bentleys too. You see the all-white drop top Lamborghini Gallardo Snyder over there is Jasmines, " said P-Diddy and Smack gave a frown.
"Jasmine, what is Jasmine doing here?" Smack asked him.
"It's cool, Smack, she's not the prosecutor anymore. Delight didn't tell you anything I see," said P-Diddy.
"Delight, ain't told me shit," said Smack turning his nose up.
"Well come on my guy it's a lot more going on, we are made brothers now and even though you are out the game we didn't forget about you. How could we, you made us who we are," said P-Diddy.
Smack looked at him and Dante wondering what was really going on. The cars they now possessed weren't some cheap off the lot cars for a few grand, they were showroom material. He looked at Dante and said, "Then Packman what type of car you own now?"
"That's my new gray Mercedes Benz SL 63 drop over there," said Dante.
"Ya'll got to be out here robbing banks and shit," said Smack.
"Na'll man we halfway legit out here, come on so we can celebrate you coming home," said Dante.
They walked towards the garage and Smack hit the code to open the garages and it was still the same. He couldn't believe his eyes when he walked into the garage. His 750 BMW or the hard-top Benz wasn't in the garage. Delight had replaced them with new vehicles. He was now staring at a 2009 Bentley Brockland all gold on 24" Asanti rims. She even replaced his bike with 2009 Ducati 1098S.
"What happened to my cars?" Smack asked them.
"Man, Delight wanted to upgrade like everyone else did," said P-Diddy.
"I know that Jag cost about ninety thousand fully loaded and that Bentley cost about a hundred racks. Damn she got me a Ducati bike, a fucking Ducati. I hope she hasn't spent all my money on things like this," said Smack rubbing his head.
"Money is not a problem, Smack, we eating that one way," said P-Diddy. Delight and Jasmine walked over to them. Jasmine

looked every bit pregnant from Smack's view. She smiled at Smack when she walked up. "Hello Simmion," as Jasmine kissed him on the cheek. "We are glad to have you back amongst us. Things wouldn't be right without you."

Smack was in shock more puzzled and confused if anything. Her words flew right over his head. He looked at Delight and she smiled at him.

"Baby, I'm about to go and wake up Simmion Jr., he's been asleep for a while now. P-Diddy will tell you everything. Jas, will you come with me?" said Delight.

"Sure Delight," said Jasmine smiling at Smack and they walked off and Jasmine was still smiling at him. P-Diddy was now standing in front of him and he immediately started to question him.

"Be straight up with me and tell me the truth no beating around the bush. Tell me what's going on and why is she at my mother-fucking house?" Smack looked at P-Diddy squared in the eyes.

"Alright, Smack, when you went to jail, we still had five thousand bottles of the pills that Antwan had given us. He had thirty more thousand bottles already over here in a storage binge in Colerain Township. Jasmine has taken over the operation. She now owns the restaurant. We own the clothing stores in every mall in the city also stores in Dayton. Jasmine has control over the warehouse you visited in China, I've been there also. She's my girl now, and we are expecting our child in November. Hold up, yo Kyle, Kobe, Dante, Worm, Vino, Weezy, Bodean, Larro and everyone else affiliated with us come over here," said P-Diddy. Everyone he called left their female company to see what he wanted. All the women were there, too along with D$Boy and his baby's mother, Timberland. Smack notice something different about all the females, because they were dressed a certain way and had on unfamiliar jewelry.

All the fella's surrounded them. "Yo Worm, where is that bag?" P-Diddy asked him.

"Right here Diddy," said Worm handing it to him. DJ Rob G was plying 'Put it in the bag' by Fabulous.

"Smack, this is yours, it's for your trip to Aruba." said P-Diddy handing him the bag. Smack unzipped the bag to see crispy bills stacked up in rubber bands.

"How much is this, P-Diddy?" Smack asked him.

"That's a hundred and fifty thousand right there and Delight put up the three million, plus the revenues we bring in from our businesses. We have the hottest stores in the city and we now own the hottest clubs in the city.

"I can't accept this, I didn't put in the work to get it," said Smack.

"It's already done Smack, even though you are out of the game we still doing us. The Black Ice is so wanted across the States we are like Executive Millionaires raising the bar in the game. You should be thinking about a bigger house like us. You use to have the bad house inside the circle now we all live in gated communities," said P-Diddy.

" this is the big secret Delight was keeping from me?" said Smack.

"Yes, we guess so and here," as Dante gave him an engraved Coat of Arms signet ring.

"What's this?" Smack asked him.

"It's our family ring and like the Mason's we have one also. It's a Coeur De Lion and if you get pulled over or into any trouble just show the ring. Even all our women have them in their special designs. We made nigga's, Smack," said Weezy.

He thought about the ring Delight was wearing when she came to visit him, but he really didn't pay it any attention.

"I never really paid the ring that Delight was wearing any attention," Smack said real low.

He saw everyone else ring design in crushed diamonds like his.

"Plus, we have the best law firm backing us in Boyd, Scott and Jennings Law firm. We living the life kid handling things and we even have our own private jet," said Vino.

Smack embraces everything that was going on and noticed Miesha sitting at a table with a little girl. He was now wondering if it was the mistake, he made with her.

"Is that Miesha over there, Kyle?" He asked him.

"Yep, with her daughter Simone," said Kyle looking at him with a glow in his eyes.

Then Heather yelled out. "The food is ready, come and get it." Everyone scattered towards the food leaving Smack standing there by himself. Miesha saw them leave and she made her way over to where Smack was standing. She had her daughter in her arms when she approached Smack. Her daughter was cute and to Smack eyes she looked like Simmion, Jr. Miesha smiled at him giving him a small twinkle and then spoke. "Hello Smack, I see you're still looking good as ever and I'm glad you are home," said Miesha not losing eye contact with him.

"Thanks, and the same to you. You're looking good yourself. How are you doing and what's the little lady's name?" He asked her and her daughter was trying to get out of her arms and into Smack's arms. "I'm fine and her name is Simone Iesha," said Miesha.

"She's cute, how old is she?" Smack asked her fishing for answers.

"She'll be eleven months in two weeks," said Miesha.

"Is that?" he started to ask her and she cut him off. "Yes, this is your daughter, Smack, if that's what you wanted to know," said Miesha.

"Um..do...," as she cut him off again. "I don't know if Delight suspects that you are the father or not, but her and Simmion, Jr. plays together with Keisha's son. I think everyone else knows and Worm knows that she is not his, but he takes good care of her," said Miesha with a tear forming in the corner of her eye.

"Hey Miesha, I'm sorry," said Smack with sympathy.

"Don't be sorry Smack, be a father to your daughter the door is open whenever you decide to step up," said Miesha as her daughter was still trying to get to Smack.

"Do you want to hold her?" Miesha asked him.

"Sure." He reached out to the baby and she came right to him.

"Hey lil mama," said Smack and Simone was laughing and smiling unaware that her biological father was now holding her.

Then Jasmine and Delight walked out of the house and she had Simmion Jr. in her arms. Delight saw them standing there talking and she walked up on them.

"Hey Miesha, hey Simone her go your buddy Simmion," said Delight smiling at the little girl.

Miesha began to feel uncomfortable and panic. "Smack give me my baby so I can feed her." Miesha held out her hands to receive her child. Smack gave her Simone and she looked at him and then at Delight. "Delight, I'll talk to you later," said Miesha and she walked off with her daughter.

"Delight, I'll be over there too, I'm hungry and so is the baby. I have to get some of Heather's cooking," said Jasmine walking off leaving them standing there with their son. He looked at Delight and she said, "So, did P-Diddy tell you what's going on, because I see you have a ring," said Delight.

"Yes, he told me and you are with this?" he asked her showing her the ring.

"I'm just a lawyer and it is you they were being loyal to, not me. They love you, not me and I'm just playing my position like a bitch is supposed to do. It's your call baby," said Delight.   He saw that his wife's attitude had changed completely. Her lingo and swagger were up a notch. He could see straight through the madness.

"So where is Shatarah, I don't see her?" Smack asked Delight.

"I gave her ass to the Zoo also, the bitch started tripping I guess she needed some dick like me, but I kept two of the cubs a girl and a boy and I sent the other one with her ass. I named them Mark Anthony and Cleopatra. They are over there in the little fake den," said Delight.

"I see the puppies in the kennel and where's Rainell?" he asked her.

"She's in the house, she's not feeling well," said Delight.

"Oh, I see and what other changes have you made around here?" he asked her.

"I re-did the basement and threw away the sofa couch you fucked Miesha on. It smelled like wolf pussy," said Delight and it caught Smack off guard. He looked at her all crazy. "Don't look at me like that, I'm not stupid I know because the proof is in the pudding. Look at Simone, she looks just like Simmion, Jr. and that's why I keep him around his sister. I'm just waiting on ya'll to come clean and you take a blood test to see for sure. I'm not mad and I'm not going anywhere. I love you that much to accept the bullshit and it had to happen before you said, 'I do'," said

Delight. She didn't take her eyes off him trying to see his facial expression but he gave none.

"Plus, you are mine until death do us part, but any other bullshit will not be tolerated. I hope you got all that other shit out of your system while you were in jail, I'm playing for keeps Negro. Oh yeah, and Kyle told Elicia that Simone was your baby as if she wasn't going to tell me. So ya'll need to handle that situation soon because we have a lot on our plate honey," said Delight giving him a smile.

Smack's head was now spinning and he needed a drink in the worst way. Then Rainell came out of the sliding doors and Smack saw her and smiled. She smiled back at her step-dad as she got closer to them Smack's smile turned upside down to a look of concern. He saw that Rainell was fat in the front. She was pregnant and he looked at Delight. "Oh yea, I forgot to tell you that your daughter is pregnant and you need to talk to her," said Delight. He closed his eyes as if he was in a bad dream.

....

Keith Andre Albright

In Loving Memory of
KEITH ANDRE ALBRIGHT.
Sunrise 9-17-68   Sunset 10-15-2015

It's an honor to have met a guy like Keith. If it wasn't for Mr. Christopher Martin Sr. bringing our paths together, Keith and I never would have met. Keith was a visionary with a lot of energy. His vision was about change, not only in the community, but to change other people lives.
He saw things in people that they didn't see in themselves. I would like to thank him for letting ME be a part of his vision pushing me in the right direction towards my dream.
No one really knew your reasoning for your actions, but we knew your vision, Ozie, Chris and I. Suicide is now the cause of many young lives today. A serious matter we must recognize and deal with as a whole community.
If you know anyone in a need for help or is crying out for help, who's discussing harming themselves or others, please contact the Suicide Hotline.
1 (800) 273-8255
They will help you and anyone else who needs help.
KEITH, we love you and your vision is now our vision.
KAPPA ALPHA PSI
ΚΔΨ

This Book is dedicated to the memory of my cousin Sekou A. Lewis Sunrise 03-16-72 Sunset 08-18-2007

My nephew Vince E. Turnage Jr. Sunrise 2-6-94 and Sunset 11-17-2013

RIP Dondi Anderson Sr.

www.ingramcontent.com/pod-product-compliance
Lightning Source LLC
Chambersburg PA
CBHW032228010726
47494CB00002B/404